About the author

Gibson Dickie is a Scottish writer who mainly spends his time between Mandurah in Western Australia and Hua Hin in Thailand. Having achieved a life's ambition when *Count to Ten* was published, he has continued to write, finding it a welcome distraction during the lifestyle restrictions imposed by the 2020 pandemic. He is often frustrated by having ideas for his novels while walking or cycling, then forgetting them when he reaches home, a common affliction for someone turning sixty. He has developed an unnatural affinity for Amy (Jessica), the character he created, justifying her murderous intent and lack of remorse along with her unusual sexual behaviour. She is not based on anybody he knows, unlike some of the other characters. He recently swam with whale sharks, but ran away from a spider. A continuation of *Then Start Again* is in process.

Find Gibson on Twitter @DickieGibson and on his website https://www.gibsondickie.com.

THEN START AGAIN

Gibson Dickie

THEN START AGAIN

Vanguard Press

VANGUARD PAPERBACK

© Copyright 2021
Gibson Dickie

The right of David Gibson Dickie to be identified as author of this work has been asserted by him in accordance with the Copyright, Designs and Patents Act 1988.

All Rights Reserved

No reproduction, copy or transmission of this publication may be made without written permission.
No paragraph of this publication may be reproduced, copied or transmitted save with the written permission of the publisher, or in accordance with the provisions
of the Copyright Act 1956 (as amended).

Any person who commits any unauthorised act in relation to this publication may be liable to criminal prosecution and civil claims for damages.

A CIP catalogue record for this title is available from the British Library.

ISBN 978-1-80016-135-1

*Vanguard Press is an imprint of
Pegasus Elliot MacKenzie Publishers Ltd.*
www.pegasuspublishers.com

First Published in 2021

**Vanguard Press
Sheraton House Castle Park
Cambridge England**

Printed & Bound in Great Britain

Dedication

For Caroline, for being my wife, my lover, the mother of our children, the Lola of our grandchildren, for following me around the world, for trying to keep me sensible, and for being my best friend.

                Love, David

Acknowledgements

To everybody who purchased and/or read *Count to Ten*, thanks for your faith and support. To my family and friends who offer endless encouragement, I appreciate what you do for me. To my test reader and reviewer, Sabrina Rasid, thank you for your constructive feedback and for rescuing this story.

This is a work of fiction. Names, characters, businesses, places, events and incidents are either the products of the author's imagination or are used in a fictitious manner. Any resemblance to actual persons, living or dead, or actual events is purely coincidental.

One
Monday, 11th February

"What the fuck?"

Detective Sergeant Terry Holmes was not a happy man. Sharing rank with his supposed colleague, Barry Chappell, he had been dispatched to this winter crime scene while Barry strutted like a prize rooster with the Wrexham DCI. No doubt sharing tea and biscuits within the centrally heated station, while Terry froze his nuts off in the winter drizzle.

February in North Wales. Perpetually cold, perennially damp. The grey sky populated by heavy dark clouds offered little prospect of relief. He kept his hands in the warmth of his pockets, reluctant to suffer exposure to the elements, knowing his fingers would become painful, sore as hell.

Through the partially open garage door he could see the deceased man, maybe in his forties, lying in a crumpled heap on the floor, impervious to the ambient temperature. Unmoving, lifeless, deceased, absolutely dead as fuck.

A black Three Series Beamer provided an alternative centrepiece to the garage interior, dominating the area through its prestige marque and physical dimensions. The driver's door was ajar while the remaining doors were closed, the rear passenger door distorted by the presence of a green garden hose taped into and through the window. The hose leading from the window to an exhaust, attached to the metallic pipe by an abundance of silver fabric tape, generously applied to provide a textured funnel, ensuring an efficient flow of gas.

Extracting his black elasticated notebook from an interior pocket, locating a suitable pen from his jacket, Terry began to describe the scene before him. Meticulous in garnering detail, unblessed with fantastic memory, he found taking notes necessary and efficient. Observing the vehicle, the tool bench in the background, the partially damp concrete floor, the victim. The deceased ungraciously abandoned or unceremoniously dumped, his skin a pallid grey colour consistent with somebody who hadn't drawn breath for a while. His greying hair closely matching the pallor of his skin, incongruously spiked with an impressively long-lasting gel.

Terry was conflicted. His delight at being awarded the opportunity to lead a serious case for the first time tempered by that award coming from acting DI arrogant wanker Barry Chappell and the sheer mess of the environment before his eyes. Train-wreck was insufficient to accurately reflect what would be a defence lawyer's wettest dream, any evidence discovered likely to be compromised by weather and inadequate scene isolation.

Resigned to his situation, he entered the house via the internal door, acknowledging a shivering constable as he went. Once inside, circulation commenced a slow return to his extremities, briefly raising his mood. The improvement stalled as he observed a forensics investigator sitting with a uniformed sergeant and a female constable in the living room, consuming steaming cups of something warm, accompanied by an elderly woman in an apron. Their actions compromising any likelihood they had of finding DNA or other helpful evidence within the living room of the deceased's home. Worst of all, no bastard had made any attempt to offer a comforting warm beverage to him. Without addressing anyone specifically, he barked, "Coffee, white, two sugars, leap to it." Formerly a WPC, now simply a constable, the female officer rose with her cup in hand, making her way to the kitchen.

"Okay, guys, can you bring me up to speed?" His tone was conciliatory, but his expression revealed his true feelings. As he waited for a response, his coffee arrived in a black oversized mug sporting white print professing 'World's Best Shag'. Sipping the acceptable brew, he inclined his head towards the sergeant, indicating that he should begin.

"Right, oh." He spoke with a pronounced Welsh accent. "Sergeant Clive Owen from the Rossett station. We received a call this morning from a member of the public, stating that a body had been found at this address." Pointing at the apparent cleaner, he continued, "This lady found the body when she came to work this morning. She cleans this house. Upon doing so, she opened the garage door and ran into the street.

She found a passer-by, and that person called the station. I grabbed a constable and came across immediately. The constable is in the garage, looking after the situation. Shall I bring him in?"

As the female constable returned to her seat, Terry looked at her, inviting her to explain her presence. "Constable Janice Owen, no relation. I walk the beat down the road. I saw the commotion here and came up for a look-see." No relation, but identical accent.

Returning his attention to the sergeant, three stripes prominently displayed on his arms. "Clive. When you got here, what did you do?"

"I called for the SOCOs — you know, forensics — I have them in my contacts list. Once they agreed to send someone over and mobilise the civilians, I called CID and appraised them of the situation. Which resulted in you arriving here, apparently."

Terry had a strong urge to remind the sergeant that he should have called CID first, leaving responsibility for forensics to the senior investigating officer. Seeing the expression on the sergeant's face, he knew he knew, and any reminder would be superfluous.

"Okay. Here's what we do. Janice, you remain here with me while we interview this lady. The rest of you get into the garage and secure that scene properly, protect what we have, get what you can. Clive? Can you call the Pathology Centre and arrange to get someone over here? Until he or she arrives, do not touch that body. Meanwhile, nobody comes back into the house until I say so. We will chat again later, yes?"

Having dispersed the team from the living room, Terry turned his attention to his key witness, the elderly woman, retaining Janice as a second pair of ears and a potential comfort to the witness should she require support.

Using his interpersonal training allied to his investigative technique, DS Holmes extracted some pertinent information. Her name was Liz Lloyd and she lived nearby. She cleaned for three local gentlemen, her word, all of whom were single with a requirement for somebody to control the mess in their homes. She had arrived as usual at eight fifteen, gaining entry to the house with her key issued by the owner. Arriving to a relatively tidy house, she had heard the car running in the garage, but thought little of it, assuming her employer was preparing to leave for work. It was a few minutes later when she went to the garage, as she could still hear the car running. When she opened the door from the hall to the garage, she smelled the exhaust fumes right away.

"What did you do next?"

"I reached in and pressed the button. The manual release for the garage door is just inside the garage on the left. Then I closed the house door, to keep the smoke out."

"Could you see anything within the garage?"

"Not at first because the smoke was swirling. I waited a while in here, with the door closed, to let the smoke out of the garage."

"And then what did you do?"

"Well, I opened the door from the hallway to the garage again, and it was a bit better. I could see Mister Mark sitting in his car with the engine on, not moving; him, I mean, but the car as well, you know. So, I go in and open the driver's door. Mark is not moving, the car interior is full of smoke, and I drag him out of the car onto the garage floor. He falls out a bit floppy, then rolls over on the floor. That's when I notice he has his lad out." She folded her arms, her expression reinforcing her obvious disapproval.

Terry and Janice exchanged glances, certain of what they had heard, but requiring confirmation. "His lad?"

Mrs Lloyd nodded her head in confirmation. "Yes. His lad. His willy. Sticking out of his trousers, zip not done up. Terrible thing it is." As an afterthought, she added, "It was."

Further questioning revealed that she had turned off the car engine, replaced "his lad" and zipped the trousers. She had acknowledged that her employer was dead, running into the street to find assistance and asking a stranger to call the police, before returning to the garage to disperse the smoky exhaust fumes from the car. She had opened every door in the car except the one with the hose then closed them again before the police arrived. Whilst waiting, she had vacuum cleaned the living room, and washed the dishes in the kitchen sink.

Shaking his head in disbelief at her actions, DS Holmes attempted to extract personal information about the victim. He learned the deceased was Mark Forrest, resident at this address. His cleaner had worked there twice a week for almost six months. He was separated from his wife and daughter, drank quite a lot, was liable to use crude language and had a liking for those Asian women. Said with distaste, before business cards for a Thai massage parlour in Wrexham were extracted from their storage position within the cutlery drawer. He always paid on time, always in cash. Liz Lloyd emphasised that she declared everything she earned to the Inland Revenue.

Receiving permission from the DS, Constable Owen asked a few questions. Pertinent, relevant, her calm voice seemed to have a soothing effect on the witness. The cleaner was unaware of Mark having any current girlfriend or other relationship. She had no knowledge of any friends, but knew his employer was located somewhere down near Birmingham. She had seen a lady walking on this street the previous evening, Asian looking, wearing a cream-coloured long coat with her hair up. Mark's type, she had suspected, but could not be sure that the woman had even been to this house. She could not remember what time she had seen the woman.

Terry listened, vaguely. His distraction being the state of the garage, the moved body, the rain ingress, the car tampered with, the cleaned house. Everything designed to make his investigation more difficult. Sipping his lukewarm coffee, he resisted the urge to smash the cup against a wall. Gathering his thoughts, inhaling a deep breath, noting the cleaner's full contact details, he advised the constable to remain with her for now.

Excusing himself from the lounge, he returned to the garage, seeking a progress report. The scene-of-crime technician had become two, belatedly donning their paper suits and overshoes while partially closing the garage door to restrict the rain access. They had opened the ceiling light and were in the process of dusting the vehicle exterior for prints. A black sheet had been tossed over the body, effectively if untidily. A moderate improvement, still far from ideal.

Sergeant Owen caught his attention. "Is there anything I can do for you, while we wait for the scientists to do their stuff?" He indicated the paper-clad investigators as he spoke.

Standing adjacent to the open driver door, about to reply, Terry saw a dust-covered white stain on the internal armrest within the door. "For fuck's sake, guys!" Seeing the panic on Owen's face, he continued, "Not you, Clive." Addressing the forensics investigators, their attention gained. "Since when do we put fingerprint powder on a DNA sample? On what looks suspiciously like semen." He pointed into the car, aware that neither of them could see where he pointed, their positions making that impossible.

His voice muffled by the hood, one of the forensics investigators objected. "How do you know it's semen? Are you qualified to make that assumption?"

"Hm. Let me think about that. It's white. It looks sticky. The deceased had his cock out. Do the fucking maths. And I am qualified enough to know that you bastards have a never-ending list of materials from which you cannot take fingerprints, and I am very fucking certain semen is one of those materials."

Bemused, frustrated, disbelieving, he turned to Owen, remembering his offer. "Can you do a quick door-to-door, just this street, ask if anyone saw anything, heard anything? Any sightings of an Asian-looking lady in a cream coat yesterday evening. Get back to me if you find anything interesting. Thank you."

Taking his cue, Sergeant Owen departed from the garage.

Two
Monday, 11th February

The time was approaching one o'clock in the middle of the night. The truck and trailer sat silently in a countryside layby alongside the A494, on the left as you headed away from Ellesmere Port towards Shotton. The recessed area sat back from the road by a sufficient distance, providing an ideal location for those who wished to express their physical love in the back seat of their vehicle. The cab carried minimal markings, suggestive of a freelance or independent haulier, while the white refrigerated trailer was marked with an unconventional Morrison's logo. The situation indicative of a truck driver taking a break, catching some zeds, before delivering his load on schedule when the supermarket opened early in the morning.

The tranquillity was interrupted by the arrival of a gold Volvo XC90, its diesel engine emitting an unpleasant gurgle while discharging invisible carcinogens into the night sky. The car parked behind the trailer, leaving adequate space to open the twin rear doors, adjacent but not too adjacent. The front seat passenger exited the car, strolling nonchalantly to the cab, then climbing the step below the door to attract the trucker's attention. Following a brief exchange of hand signals, the truck driver alighted, joining the car passenger as they approached the rear of the trailer. The SUV driver sacrificed the comfort of his warm car to join them, shaking hands with the trucker as the trio gathered.

The truck driver climbed onto his vehicle, supporting himself on the rear bumper. He produced a key to unlock the three-inch elongated padlock, releasing the horizontal bar from the swivel hooks, allowing the vertical locking bar to be turned via the perpendicular release lever arm. Returning to ground level, he applied pressure gradually, breaking the seal around the door, pulling the right door ajar to its fullest extent. The left door remained untouched. Stepping back, the denim-clad trucker invited the SUV occupants to access the trailer.

Dai, the Volvo driver, entered first, disappearing into the gloom, using the torch on his mobile phone to penetrate the darkness, identifying the remaining contents of the trailer. Five women of Asian appearance sitting against the wall, hands shielding their eyes from the sudden invasion of light. Uniformly petite, ages difficult to assess, they remained on the floor, seemingly awaiting instruction from the white man standing before them.

"Welcome to Wales." His brief statement, possibly not understood, nevertheless initiated the women rising to their feet, instinct overpowering comprehension. "Come with me. Yeah?" He indicated the open door of the trailer, moving towards the exit, inviting them to follow. They did. He jumped to the ground, turning to offer his hand as assistance to the ladies, aiding their laboured efforts to exit the vehicle, to join the men in the fresh, cold night air.

The trucker handed over an untidy sheet of paper. Dai inspected the supposed document, providing Nesbo, his assistant, an opportunity to assess and inspect the ladies. The trucker offered his assistance. "Okay, bucko," his accent regional southern England, possibly Suffolk, "these two," pointing at the youngest-looking pair, standing together dressed in jeans, "they go to this address in Prestatyn." Pointing at three addresses listed lower in the document. "The older one," indicating the only lady wearing a dress, "she goes to this address in Wrexham." He again referred to the addresses. "While the final two are going to the Chester address." The remaining ladies, dressed in some form of randomly patterned loose-fitting trousers, were placid, accepting of their situation.

"So, who are they, and what's going on?" Dai, displaying his limited intelligence, asked curiously.

"Come on, bucko. You know better than that. Just load them in your car and drop them where you've been told." Recognising the harshness of his own voice, aware of being in an unfamiliar location and outnumbered by the locals, he offered a softener. "Asian ladies for the massage parlours. Probably hookers. Hard job to get a work permit for. Though I am surprised by the older one; she looks past her best."

Nesbo snorted his agreement. "Yeah, looks like she's been around a bit. It would be like shagging my mum, if my mum was Chinese, which she's not."

Dai offered a conspiratorial grin without speaking, unwilling to reveal that the older lady was the one he found most attractive. Her features were softer than the others, her hair carrying more shine, more evidence of style. She seemed less fearful of the current predicament, while her younger colleagues visibly betrayed their nervousness.

"Are we done? I need to get back on the road. This was my final discharge."

"Yeah, mate. We're done. You can take off. We'll get these to their new homes, then call it a night."

Awkward handshakes complete, the trucker returned to his cab. Bringing the powerful vehicle to life, he executed a perfect turn towards the M56 and the ease of the motorway network.

Returning to the Volvo, they herded their flock into the seven-seat configuration. Two ladies in the rear row, two further ladies in the traditional back seat, alongside Nesbo. Dai took his place behind the wheel, the elder Asian lady taking the shotgun position. "Is everybody ready? Shall we go?"

He asked the question to break the silence, not expecting a response, allowing that his colleague, the idiot, might reply. Surprised, he heard the lady beside him murmur gently, "Yes. We should go."

He looked at her in surprise. "You speak English?"

Holding his gaze, she replied, "Of course. Otherwise, why should I come to the United Kingdom." She turned, breaking their eye contact.

Unaware of the exchange beyond the words he had heard, Joseph Nesbitt picked his nose, attempting to shield his activity from the other passengers. Putting the automatic gearbox into "D", Dai drove the Volvo with its seven occupants away from the recessed layby, heading to Prestatyn, the one address where he had delivered before. Within minutes, he had accessed the North Wales Expressway, facing twenty-four miles of night-time dual carriageway driving, the road as quiet as his passengers.

Mostly concentrating on his driving, Dai sneaked an occasional glance at the front-seat passenger. Beginning lower, he identified slim, acceptable legs, her green dress sitting attractively above her knee. Coming higher, he observed her lithe body, indicating flexibility, suggesting physical strength, curving into a moderately proportioned chest stretching the fabric in that area. On closer inspection, her face seemed younger than his first impression. Rounder than the others, unblemished by wrinkles, the first suggestions of laughter lines, her small nose barely capable of supporting sunglasses. More attractive than his first impression, drawing his undisclosed attention.

Arriving at their first destination, he parked on double-yellow lines, unconcerned about the possible presence of traffic wardens at this hour. The girls in jeans from the middle seats alighted from the car, looking around their surroundings as they did so. Assessing them, Dai judged them to be younger than the front-seat green-dress lady, in one case very much younger; *not my place to comment*, his opinion uttered under his breath. Knocking three times on the nondescript door, he waited. The door was opened by an overly made-up local girl, pasty white with uneven mascara, hair scraped behind her head, assessing Dai and the girls before waving them inside. "Thanks for bringing them over. They look better than the last lot; hopefully they'll do all right." Her friendly words contrasting with her earlier demeanour. "I'm Gwyneth. This is my shop."

"Hi, Gwyneth," introducing himself, "Dai. How's business?"

"Oh, you know, pretty good. There are always plenty of dirty old bastards looking for a good time. They pay for an hour, get a half hour of genuine massage before the girls offer them a happy ending. Not many resist the temptation and the bigger money changes hands."

"I wondered how it worked." Unsure how to continue, he stumbled, "Thanks for that."

"You should come around some time. Avail of the staff discount. Choose your favourite. I'll sort you out. Don't wait too long, though, as this young one might be worn out pretty quickly."

"Thanks. Best be off, then. Anything else you need?"

"All done. Drive safely. Bye now." The final words faint as she closed the door. Returning to the car, he noticed that the remaining girls had moved forward, beside his colleague. Green Dress remained in the front.

Pulling away from the kerb, he advised everyone that their next stop would be Chester.

"Ho, Dai. We should drop this old one in Wrexham, take the turn-off at Mold, go straight down, then go on to Chester. Easier that way, and we are almost home when we drop the final lot off."

"Nah, mate. It's quicker to go straight down the fifty-five to Chester. Drop these two off. I can drop you as well if you like. Then take this one to Wrexham. Makes it quite easy for me to get home."

Too exhausted to argue, Nesbo dropped his challenge. He would be home quicker this way. He suspected Dai wanted to get into the old bird, wondering at his colleague's severe lack of taste.

The twenty-nine miles to Chester passed comfortably, three of the occupants dozing, their chins on their chests; only Dai and the young girl sitting centrally remaining alert. A token attempt at conversation failed miserably, Dai deciding that her English was non-existent, the woman unable to translate through his overpowering accent. Arriving at the nominated address, he repeated his process, knocking on the door three times, a brief exchange with the woman inside, before handing over the two Asians. Not invited to return this time, relieved to complete the transaction promptly, he headed to Hoole to deposit the idiot at home. Within a quarter of an hour, he was alone with the Asian lady in the green dress, on their way to Wrexham.

Travelling steadily along the A483, he spotted a deserted layby, pulling over, bringing the vehicle to rest. The woman's eyes remained closed, asleep or feigning sleep. Dai assessed her soft features. He had never found Asian women especially stimulating, but this one, the first one he had seen so closely, was eliciting responses from his body.

Her breathing remained unchanged, despite the car coming to rest, suggesting perhaps genuine sleep. Emboldened, he placed a hand on her leg, above the knee, his thumb slipping beneath the hem of her dress. Receiving no reaction, he moved his hand higher, sliding up her leg, relishing her smooth, supple skin, his entire hand beneath the fabric. Preparing to go higher, he heard "Stop now." Her words sharp, her tone authoritative. Her eyes now open, addressing him with an uninviting expression.

Compromising, he kept his hand where it was. He matched her gaze, initiating his best smile, seeking to disarm her. Remembering her capable

English skills, he attempted charm. "You are beautiful." His voice low, his manner engaging, his desire probably evident. "Very sexy."

"I know." Her response surprising him. "Beautiful. Sexy. But not for you."

Despite the stalemate, he tried again to move his hand higher on her leg, closer to his destination. She countered his motion, using both of her hands to block his, applying pressure to coax his hand back down her leg.

"Final warning. Not for you." Her tone remained level, her voice low. Failing to appreciate her intensity and confidence, he mustered his energy. Raising his other hand, reaching across the car, he roughly grabbed her breast, simultaneously launching a further attack below her clothing, fingers reaching her underwear, attempting entry. Aware of her resistance, he continued pulling at her pants, seeking access, denied by her twisting body, legs crossing, thighs coming together.

Followed by pain. His right cheek pierced by sharp fingernails, three of them breaking his skin. Curling like talons, gripping his face as they dragged downwards, tearing flesh as they went, drawing blood, stinging. Attempts to access her privates forgotten, he recalled his hands to defensive duties, snatching at her wrist, wanting to pull her fingers from his face, his disjointed movements increasing the agony. A second hand, her right, clamped onto his forehead, nails scraping across his flesh, inflicting a further field of agony, the diversion failing to deflect the pain in his cheek. His own hands now at his face, seeking to block her from inflicting further damage. His ears heard his cries, his brain failing to register the sound, shattered epidermis sending electrical impulses of severe distress to his nervous system.

Fighting the pain, fighting her, he heard a seatbelt unbuckle. He became aware of the temperature drop as a door opened, his faculties unable to comprehend her actions, combating torment his only priority. Realisation came to him. He was no longer being attacked. The Asian woman had vacated the car. His face ached, blood caking his shirt collar, the engine running, his eyes unfocused, unsure where she had gone. The salt content from his tears providing a new source of agony to his damaged face, counter-productive to sensible reasoning. Closing his eyes, he held his breath as he mentally assessed his situation, the consequences he could face, prioritising his next actions, considering his options.

Squinting, inspecting the familiar car, he located a packet of baby wet wipes. Extracting a tissue, mopping his face, pressing firmly to staunch any continuing flow of blood, the stinging of the chemical infinitely preferable to the earlier pain. Gradually returning to full vision, he surveyed his surroundings, noting the open passenger door, the absence of the woman passenger or her clutch bag. He saw the cradle for his mobile phone, empty. He scanned the footwell of the car on both sides, unable to see his phone. Assuming she had taken it, he was confident she would be unable to access it, nevertheless accepting that the deprivation of his device had changed the situation. Looking outside, he sought her presence, wondering if she had remained close by, suspecting she would have run, her direction unknown. The road and fields around their location offering too many possibilities for her to take cover, to evade him.

Continuing to hold a wipe against the damaged cheek, he left his seat, standing on the door edge to increase his height, seeking his quarry but failing to sight her. A glance at his watch showing beyond two thirty, a time when everyone should be asleep. Following an instinct, Dai began to walk forwards along the edge of the road in the direction he had been following. Picking up speed, he was soon a hundred yards from the car. Hearing a sound behind him, turning, he saw her getting into the Volvo, taking the driver seat, her expression suggesting victory, her attention distracted as she sought something in the vehicle. Understanding, Dai raked in his pocket, producing the vehicle key, holding it aloft, shaking it. Emphasising his possession of the car's most vital component, he walked steadily towards her.

Failing to find a key within the car, she looked up to assess his position. His flaunting of the car key, her escape route now blocked, her predicament worsening. Maintaining her logic, she pressed buttons on the driver door console, successfully operating the central-locking system, seeking to deny him entry to the vehicle, to her.

Click. The doors unlocked, the mechanism operating as he pulled the car door ajar, reaching into the vehicle and grabbing her by her dress, dragging her from the vehicle into the road, her moan revealing discomfort as her knees raked across the asphalt. Evading her extended arms, he took a firmer grip of her dress, the bodice area tightly grasped, dragging her from the car towards the grass area alongside the angled road surface. She fought, twisting her body, changing direction, arms flailing at him, attempting to gain purchase on the grass as she was pulled across it. Her nails achieving some contact with his trousers but unable to inflict further damage. His expression cold. His intent no longer ambiguous. Her situation deteriorating.

Having achieved a position partially unseen from the road, he used his hold on her dress to throw her backwards onto the grass verge. Fabric tore as she fell, her neck and cleavage becoming visible. She understood her vulnerability, suspected his intentions, prepared to defend herself, to fight.

No words had been exchanged, none were necessary, the perceived language barrier no longer an obstacle. Both suffering pain and indignity. Both apprehensive, cautious, aware. She made a conscious effort to stand, surprised as he permitted her to do so. Separated by an arm's length, she curled her fingers, intimating her next attack, her fingers relaxing as his punch struck her nose, shaking her brain within her skull. Consciousness impaired, aware she was falling, unable to brace, her head striking the sparsely grassed earth prior to her torso, the impact solid, her remaining conscious capabilities draining from her.

Coherent thought evaded Dai. The woman who he perceived to have attacked him was down, unable to hurt him. He should end the matter here, load her into the car and take her to the nominated destination. These rational thoughts were barely considered. Obsessed by a need to avenge his pain, to slate his thirst, he focused on her figure lying on the ground, her dress torn, her chest revealed to an extent, the lower part of her dress dirty, stained, ridden high on her legs. His earlier predatory motives rekindled, he kneeled before her, pushing the dress higher, his fingers curled into her panties, lowering them while overcoming the obstacle of her prone figure, revealing her intimacy, arousing him. Unbuckling his trousers, disengaging himself from his underwear, hard, desire overcoming residual pain, he lowered himself onto her body, pushing through her dryness, plunging into her, his breathing loud and rapid as sweat formed on his brow.

His invasion of her body awakened her. Preservation instinctively aroused, she felt him inside her, opening her eyes to confirm her situation, his assault at once repulsing her and rekindling her energy. Delicately, she raised her hands, approaching his head from beyond his peripheral vision, again attacking his face with her hands configured like claws, scratching, pulling his face towards her, baring her teeth. She sensed his arousal reducing, his presence within her compromised, his yell confirming her achievement. Empowered, she continued to seek ways to hurt him, to defend herself. Her tactical naivety betraying her as her undefended throat was encircled by his splayed fingers applying immediate pressure, gripping harder, inhibiting her ability to breathe.

She abandoned her assault on him, shifting her focus to removing his hands from her neck. His grip strong, her breathing already impacted, her situation dire.

Having repelled her counterattack, his focus became singular. No more pain. To ensure his revised objective, he tightened his grip on her throat, the erection having deserted him, that recent pleasure already cast into memory. He felt her weakening attempts to dislodge his hands. He responded by increasing the pressure, applying his entire weight advantage to the task. Her resistance reducing, he maintained his position. Her resistance subsided, he maintained his position, drool dripping from his mouth, landing on her chin, eliciting no reaction from her.

Releasing her throat, he sat back. Observing what he had done. Her body motionless and unresponsive. Her partial nakedness exposed by her disturbed and dishevelled clothing. He held a finger below her nose, feeling no breath. He felt for a pulse in her neck, finding none. He placed his ear against her lips, hearing and feeling nothing. The natural motion from inhalation and exhalation, absent from her chest. No signs of life. His exertions had strained his anatomy, a complicated mix of pain and exhaustion dominating his physique. Looking at what remained of her, the admirable spirit snuffed out, unable to rationalise the consequences of his actions, he found his erection strangely returning. Without cohesive thought, he encouraged the arousal, using one hand as he admired her neatly trimmed intimate area, at once his inspiration and temptation. Adjusting their relative positions, he acquiesced to the urges from his stimulated appendage, his internal response accelerating, grunting as he finished.

Thought processes in turmoil, uncertain of his next action, he saw his mobile phone discarded where she had dropped it, close to the tarmac. Locating the device bringing him a disproportionate degree of satisfaction.

Three
Monday, 11th February

Amy was satisfied. Several bottles of supermarket-brand mineral water had cooled the portable barbeque, allowing her to return it to the trunk of her car. The charred contents had been ceremonially dumped in a public litter bin at a random location, further complicating any possible trail leading to her.

Dressed in tight jeans and a loose woollen jumper to combat the winter chill, she had burned her clothes from the previous evening. Saying goodbye to the cream coat and long tee-shirt had barely registered with her. Losing the thigh-high grey socks had been more regrettable, the leg-flattering accessories deserving of a repeat wearing. Her panties had originated in a chain store multi-pack, her residual DNA now destroyed by fire and water, along with the spunk-stained gloves.

The smashed carcasses of the craft beer she had shared with Beamer boy were in a field, thrown from the perimeter fence to disappear into the long grass.

Her knife had been returned to the pocket in her handbag, the wet wipes to her kitchen, the condoms to her bathroom vanity. The dishcloth had endured two cycles of the washing machine. The remaining Valium tablets were stored at the rear of her medicine cupboard, obscured by a carton of low-dose aspirin.

"Zero." Audible but quiet, she confirmed the reset of her count, repeating the numeral for emphasis. Relieved and ready to resume her normal life, Amy steered her red Clio towards Asda, requiring supplies to restock her fridge, which was low on almost everything. She figured she had adequate time to grocery shop before her hairdresser appointment. Glancing at her reflection in the rear-view mirror, she remained indifferent to the mess her hair had become, making no comparison with the long, dark, natural wave she had groomed and cultivated over the last year. Accepting she had taken a prudent course of action, which would be partially redeemed today, she offered a pout to her reflection.

Concentration drifting on the quiet road, she wondered if Mark's corpse had been discovered. Gently suffocated, she had been very humane in the manner of his demise. He had deserved a violent end, something brutal. Instead, he had drifted into unconsciousness under the influence of Valium and carbon monoxide. She imagined the discovery of his death with his little cock exposed, the image bringing a smile to her face, releasing her inherent attractiveness. She laughed aloud as she recalled him raising his hips, jerking almost uncontrollably, excited yet inwardly disappointed as he ejaculated into and onto his precious car. His fluid making no direct contact with her beyond some dribble on her gloves. *Too fucking predictable!*

Curious how his death would be perceived by the North Wales Constabulary, she wondered if they could or would make any connection to her. Amy remained confident they could not, as the relationship between Mark and her was almost non-existent and her precautions had been meticulous.

If the police were able to connect me to both deaths, would I be a serial killer? A spree killer? A run-of-the-mill multiple killer? The options circulated in her mind, the terminology alien to her.

She had taken care of Jed when he tried to molest her inappropriately. Jed had physically attacked her, making her fear for her safety. Her actions had been in self-defence. Justified!

Killing Mark had been more premeditated. He had insulted her repeatedly, he was a prick, he was disrespectful. She had concerns that his intrusion into her life would increase. Justified! In both cases, she had reached her count of ten, restricting her choices, directing her actions.

Arriving at the grocery superstore, she found a convenient space in the enormous parking area. Gathering a handful of fabric bags, she walked briskly to minimise the effect of the chill, her eyes lowered and unaware of movements around her. Inside, the temperature was uncomfortably warm, in sharp contrast to that outside. She began to regret coming here, persevering only because she had already placed the pound coin in the trolley mechanism while understanding that she had little nourishment at home.

Her reverie was broken by a young man crashing his trolley into hers, the jolt surprisingly solid. Facing one another from behind their wheeled devices, he spoke. "Oops. Sorry about that." Appraising her, continuing, "Well, hello." The final word containing an element of innuendo, informing her that he was appreciating what he saw.

Completely disinterested, she restricted herself to a simple "Okay."

Undeterred, he spoke again. "Must be my lucky day."

Amy managed to bring her trolley around, allowing her to stand close to the stranger. Leaning towards him, offering false encouragement, she whispered, "Never going to happen."

Thirty-five minutes later, she was safely ensconced in her car. The shopping bags were nicely snuggled beside the kettle barbeque, pride of place reserved for a three-litre plastic bottle of Olde English cider, a beverage she had not enjoyed since her student days. After a misfire, her engine caught, and she steered carefully between the cramped vehicle columns.

Checking the time, she chose not to travel home, instead heading into Chester city. Her revised plan was to park in the shopping centre and walk to her hairdresser appointment. She was excited to finally fix this mess on her head, although it had not been a deterrent to the clumsy bloke in Asda. Her mother would have described her hair as "a midden". She reckoned her groceries were unlikely to spoil in these cold conditions.

Taking a seat within the shopping mall, she tried calling Puss-Puss. Her friend picked up on the third ring. "Hey, Amy, what's new?"

"Hey, Holly. On my way to the hair doctor. Killing time. Are you still coming over on Wednesday?"

"Yeah, that's the plan. Providing you still want me to come around."

"Of course, I do. Is there a problem?" She detected stress in Holly's voice and words.

Hearing her friend lower her voice, Amy instinctively listened with greater attention. "You know those photos we exchanged. The naughty ones."

Curious, concerned, she muttered a brief "Uh huh," allowing Holly to expand.

"Terry says we have to delete them. Completely. From all media. Right away. He was very insistent." The extended pause suggesting

Holly had finished speaking, Amy, unprepared to offer a response, remained silent. "Are you still there?"

"I assume that he has seen them, then. Was he searching your phone? That's not respectful, is it? What's his issue?"

"He says that the photo contradicts your statement at the police station. The date and time proving you misled them about when you dyed your hair. He says we have to get rid of the evidence."

Taking time to consider this development. Terry, a Detective Sergeant, had noticed the inconsistency in her story, had seen the photographic proof, yet was advising them to delete the incriminating photo. Strange. Unexpected.

"He also suspects the alibi I gave you is false."

Fuck! Shit!

"Do you still want me to come to your place on Wednesday?"

Without hesitation. "Absolutely. Please come. Sounds like we have something to talk about. And I have cider, so you have to come."

The relief in Holly's voice was palpable. "That's good. I'll come after work; should be there not long after five. I hope you're not too upset. Sorry, huh."

"Hey, relax. I'm looking forward to seeing you." Noticeably, their conversation contained none of the nuances of their recent dialogue, no delicate flirting or ambiguity, an absence of phrases capable of misinterpretation.

Claiming work pressure, Holly ended the call. Amy sat, replaying the conversation in her head. An unexpected development for sure, worthy of further analysis. Walking to the salon, allowing her smile to return as she prepared for the reinvention of her hairstyle.

Four
Monday, 11th February

Lowering himself into the black leather-effect poly-something plastic swivel chair, DC Grahame Beecham searched for the telephone number of the Asda superstore at the Greyhound Retail Park. The chair protested with a squeak as the physically imposing policeman settled into a comfortable position. His impressive diaphragm was augmented by muscular arms and legs, a recent exercise regime having reduced his waistline without affecting his overall intimidating presence. Locating the 01244-prefixed number, he made a call. Identifying himself as a police officer, he demanded to speak to a store manager, his patience tested as he suffered two misplaced redirections. His efforts were rewarded when connected to a well-spoken lady who was only too delighted to assist. Having explained his intentions, she suggested he come to the store, where she would ensure everything was prepared for him, including a facility to make CCTV copies if he required. She would also provide warming coffee and cakes.

DC Beecham had questioned Ruth McGarvey in her holding cell. As their primary suspect, she had been remanded and would appear in court today to be charged with the murder of Jeremy Campbell-Foulkes. In their conversation, she had again denied the insinuation that she had been in Saltney on the suggested Saturday morning. "I was in Asda, definitely Asda."

Doris was concerned. Caught up in the momentum and excitement of the interviews, he had acquiesced to the universal opinion attributing guilt to Mrs McGarvey. She was certainly no angel: her propensity to violence coupled with a penchant for illicit sex made her a good candidate. Unconvinced about her guilt, still harbouring an instinct for an alternative suspect, he had chosen to follow through on Ruth's story, keen to avoid an inaccurate charge and possible perversion of justice. If her story folded with the supermarket CCTV, he could relax and allow the system to follow its natural course. Should her denial be supported, his antenna maintained a preference for Amy Meadows as the suspect. To his mind, she was a more likely killer. Cold, manipulative, evasive. Armed with the essentials, he left the station.

"Where's Doris off to?" Barry Chappell asked the desk constable.

"No idea." Then, as an afterthought, recalling Chappell's acting promotion, "Sir."

"Give him a call, ask him where he's going, and what time he'll return. Tell him I am asking. And he better not be later than three thirty." Delegation complete, he returned to the incident room.

Coaxing his beloved Mazda through traffic, Doris was pleased to see the rain lifting. The improved light revealed grey roads bordered by darker grey pavements surrounded by brown fields and bald trees, with occasional splashes of green reducing in frequency as he approached the built-up areas.

The radio remained silent within the car. He had no tolerance of angry, unintelligible hip-hop, allied to an active dislike of talentless boy bands, while retaining an impulse to arrest any banality-rambling disc jockey on sight. Comfortable with his own thoughts for company, his journey concluded without incident.

The process to access the supermarket CCTV images was seamless. Announcing his arrival at a Customer Service desk, he was escorted to the Duty Manager's office, where introductions and appreciation were exchanged. From there he was led to a viewing room furnished with coffee flasks, assorted cookies and mineral water. A security guard had been allocated to assist him with operation of the system.

They commenced with footage from the camera located above the primary entrance, between the external and internal sliding doors, starting at nine o'clock on the required date. They watched the early birds arriving for their Saturday morning groceries, single men and women, couples, families with reluctant kids and the occasional suspicious-looking group of teenagers. Doris had placed A4 photos of Ruth McGarvey on the desk, allowing the security guard to compare her to the people seen on camera. The recording was played back at double speed, regularly paused as somebody of similar appearance was identified. Aloud, Doris had explained that their target was likely to be in a pale blouse and dark skirt, any coat most likely hanging open. At nine forty-two, he positively identified Ruth McGarvey arriving at the premises, the high quality of the image removing any ambiguity.

"Bingo. That's her entering the store." He made notes in his book, transcribing the time stamp from the paused video. "Can we switch to a camera focusing on customers leaving the store? Maybe beginning at ten?"

The recorded data was promptly updated, the new footage showing a view from above the sliding doors, on the inside of the store, facing directly towards the checkouts, where any misbehaviour was more likely to occur. Draining his coffee, nibbling a dark chocolate Hobnob, he renewed his focus. At eleven minutes past eleven in the morning, Saturday twenty-sixth January, he confirmed the departure of their prime suspect from the supermarket. "Oh, dearie me, this is going to upset a few people." Again, with the footage paused, he annotated the event in his notebook. "Is there a chance we could find footage of her in store, somewhere in the middle of this time frame? Ten thirty or thereabouts?"

"We have cameras over the bakery, the deli, and in random aisles. I could set these up in turn, do a check, ten twenty to ten forty. How does that sound?"

"That sounds bloody marvellous," he enthused. "A certain lady is going to love you." Pouring two fresh coffees from the large pot, adding milk and sugar as he had seen earlier, internally acknowledging, *but a certain acting Detective Inspector will probably hate you with a vengeance.*

Further analysis of the CCTV confirmed Mrs McGarvey in the store at ten twenty-nine, selecting cold cuts from the delicatessen counter. Requesting copies of the three relevant sets of footage, Doris internally joined the dots. *Entering at nine forty-two, confirmed in store at ten twenty-nine, departing at eleven after eleven. No way she could be the woman seen at Boundary Lane leaving the general area of the crime scene. We have a fuck-up. A monumental, balls and all, fuck-up.*

Returning to the lady manager's office, Doris expressed his gratitude for her assistance, her allocation of resource, and the quality of the CCTV system pictures. She explained the massive national annual losses to shoplifting, making quality monitoring services a relative bargain. He concurred that conviction should be simple with footage of this clarity. Receiving copies of the relevant pictures, backed by a portable USB, he took his leave.

During the return journey to Mold, he reflected on a pleasant experience, positive interaction with an organisation, unmitigated support from the manager, unwavering assistance from security. He wondered aloud, "Why can't it always be like this?"

Entering the station, his positive attitude began to wane. The higher ranks were going to literally shit a brick when he confirmed his findings. He expected Chappell to be difficult, making it essential that a third party be in the room, preferably DS Holmes or PC McGarry, both of whom had been involved in the case. Failing that, a senior ranking officer, perhaps the DCI from Wrexham. Raising this evidence on a one-to-one basis with Barry Chappell was not his preferred option.

Seeing PC McGarry in the corridor, he signalled she should follow him as he entered the incident room, noting the absence of Chappell, seeing papers and equipment in disarray, the case documents partially filed. Felicia McGarry entered the room, her growing dark hair restrained in a haphazard bun, anonymous looking despite her height and obvious curves.

"Hey, Flick. You need to see this." He took a seat at the monitor combo, slotting the Asda-provided USB drive. She sat beside him.

"Okay, Doris, I'm intrigued. But if this is another film of your butt, I am reporting you." She smiled, he reciprocated, allowing the footage to unfold.

"Greyhound Asda, Saturday twenty-sixth January, morning. At the time we identified Ruth McGarvey leaving Saltney with a sports bag. Watch this."

The content had been reduced to the relevant times only, a few minutes before and after each sighting. Words were unnecessary. Flick saw their suspect, as Doris had, clearly blowing away any possibility that she had been the woman seen leaving Jed's house. Blowing away any possibility of their charge leading to a safe conviction.

"We need to inform the CPS." Her words almost a gasp.

"And acting DI Chappell." His words suffused with reluctance and an undercurrent of smug disguised as concern. Raising his mobile, he dialled Chappell, waiting as the call connected on the fourth ring. "What's up, Doris? I've got my hands full."

"Some CCTV which might affect our case against Mrs McGarvey." Careful to add, "Sir."

"Go on."

"CCTV proves she was shopping at Asda at the time she was supposed to be leaving Jed's apartment. Time stamped, clear, unequivocal."

"On my way. Don't move!"

The connection terminated; Doris placed his phone on the table. Flick asked, "How did he take it?"

"He said we must not move. Even though I never said where we were. Wish I had called him from the store; that would have confused him. Get ready for some fireworks."

Waiting for the imminent tantrum, they booked the new evidence into the case file, following procedure strictly. The USB drive was tagged, the photos were annotated and filed, an email was sent to the involved officers confirming the existence of potentially conflicting evidence. A back-up of the USB drive was inserted into the machine, ready to run.

Ending the uncomfortable silence, the constable spoke. "So, where does this leave us? If Ruth didn't kill Jed, then who did? Why? When? How?" Recognising signs from the detective constable preparing his reply, she anticipated. "Don't tell me. It was Amy Meadows. Even though she has an alibi, too. Because you want it to be her, so much."

Doris considered his reply. "Amy Meadows' alibi is verbal only. Nothing to support it. I can break her story. I feel it in my bones, she did it. Now even more so. I can't see it being any of the others."

Further expansion of his theory was prevented by the arrival of the angry acting DI barging through the door, his face contorted with rage, his suit immaculate, his solid height and build dwarfed by his colleague. Attempting a DI Catt show of seniority, he barked, "Show me!" His attempted power trip failing, his physical and oral intimidation skills some way below those of the convalescing leader. Unfazed, he took a seat adjacent to Beecham, leaving the lady standing.

Watching the entire copy together, Barry waited until the end, his frustration indicated by clasped hands and tapping heels as he leaned forwards.

"DC Beecham. On whose authority did you decide to investigate the CCTV at Asda in Chester? Certainly not mine. What the hell have you done? You have just threatened to unravel our entire fucking case. Did you even consider that? Do you hate me so much that you had to jeopardise the entire bastard conviction? The case was closed yesterday; why are you still raking around in the debris? Have you got fuck-all to do, because I can sort that for you, I can give you plenty to keep your little fingers occupied? Jesus."

Almost disappointed, having expected something more aggressive, DC Beecham held his ground. Addressing his superior officer, in parallel with the constable, he replied in a controlled tone, "I felt the charge was unsafe, sir. I wanted to eliminate possible sources of contradiction likely to come from the defence. Just a few quick checks. Cross the T's, dot the I's." Waiting for a reaction, receiving none. "Just something her attorney would do. Better to be wrong now, than in front of a judge. It can't be her, sir; we have to drop it and start again." Folding his arms, his position defined.

Barry surveyed the room, the evidence boards, his colleagues, reluctantly accepting the inevitable. Ruth McGarvey fitted the bill, but her alibi was indestructible. He had no alternative.

"All right. I'll set the wheels in motion. You can go downstairs and prepare her for release. I am certain the DCI will want to thank you in person, Doris, for collapsing this case under your own initiative."

"I prefer DC Beecham, or Grahame, sir!"

'Get out of my sight, you turncoat bastard." Turning to Flick, choosing to share his ire with her. "You might as well piss off back to uniform; you're not needed up here anymore."

"Sir!" Beating a hasty retreat, avoiding any CID loyalty issues. Mindful of her fledgling career, she left the incident room.

Doris stood, imposing his full physical presence, calmly issuing prepared words. "You gambled, you cut corners, you followed your gut. You ignored our Guv'nor's instructions. You're getting what you deserve. You can blame me if you want, tell anyone who'll listen that I fucked this case. But you and I know that the troops know me and respect me and they will believe me before they believe you. Everyone knows I broke the DNA conundrum, not you. The fault, mate, is yours."

"I still outrank you, Constable. Do not forget that. You need to watch your tone when you speak to me."

"Yes, you do, sir. For now. Maybe not when the DCI hears about the charge being dropped. Could be I will outrank you. Keep that in mind."

Stand-off complete, nowhere to go, they left the incident room to pursue their newly identified obligations. DS Chappell was not a happy man.

Five
Monday, 11th February

Having achieved as much as he could at the scene, Terry decided to expand his investigation. Unable to identify a rational strategy, inhibited by a requirement to wait for forensic results, uncertain if a crime had even been committed, he mentally considered possible options. The Forensic Pathologist had arrived, distinctively sporting a ponytail, his ethnic Chinese appearance evoking comparisons with the villain in a Jackie Chan movie. He had promptly declared the body deceased, endorsing movement as necessary and suggesting his initial opinion: a "thrill wank gone wrong", subject to laboratory confirmation.

The scene-of-crime lads had committed to nothing of interest, their feathers ruffled by the attitude of the DS on his arrival. The cleaner had yielded little of further value, her elderly metabolism succumbing to shock. The uniforms demonstrated increasing levels of boredom.

Issuing a few final instructions, accompanied by his contact details, Terry acquired a confirmed recent photograph of Mark Forrest, the business card from the Thai massage parlour and a chocolate biscuit from the plate. Dodging the rain, he made his way to his parked vehicle, a trip to Wrexham beckoning.

Engine running, waiting on warmth, Terry put the address into his phone map app, trusting the directions provided. Commencing the journey, he replayed the scene, trying to make sense of what he had seen. The body position was irrelevant, having been moved by the cleaner, who had also replaced the exposed penis into the deceased's trousers. That exposure, combined with the semen stain, was suggestive of a sex game. Suicide? Maybe. Auto-erotic asphyxiation? Possibly. Murder? Unlikely. Inconsistency at the scene? Definitely.

Optimistic that he would learn something about his victim from the massage place, he found a suitable parking spot on a double-yellow line less than fifty metres from his destination. Tracing of the victim's former spouse had been delegated to a constable; he planned to follow that lead next.

Originally named, the Bangkok Massage front premises were similarly dimensioned to a standard shop, the low-key external décor bookended by a newsagent and an apparently vacant politician's clinic. Entering through the partially glassed doorway, DS Holmes instinctively accepted his presence in the foyer of a brothel. Hideous furniture, a background smell and low lighting with the primary function of hiding skin blemishes and cheap make-up while disguising the true age of the lady providing the service. A bell had rung as he entered, resulting in the arrival of a small Asian woman behind the reception desk.

"Hello, welcome." Heavily accented, though easily understood. "You want massage?"

Approaching the desk, he sought to impose his size advantage over the woman, despite only measuring five nine and possessing gentle features with a hint of mean. Reaching into his pocket, shaking his head, he presented the picture of the deceased man. "Hello, madam," attempting respectful, barely achieving polite, "can I ask if you know this person?" He turned the picture to an orientation allowing her a normal view.

"Are you a policeman?"

Reaching into his pockets again, he produced his identification, offering it to the woman. "Yes, I am a Detective Sergeant in the North Wales Police Force."

She took her time studying his ID, mouthing his name, committing it to memory. Taking a further glance at the photo, she addressed DS Holmes straight in the eye. "I have never seen him before. Ever. He is not a customer here, I am sure." She demonstrated solid English language skills, technically accurate, her accented delivery diminishing the impact.

Engaging with the woman, Terry persisted. "I understand you must see lots of men here, and maybe he is not a regular, but please take another look. It is quite important." Aiming for a friendly smile, receiving a scowl in return. "Maybe one of your masseuses might recognise him?"

"Anyone who comes here has to register with me first." Her accent sharper, harder, her emphatic words indicating irritation even in her second language. Seeking an engagement tool, assuming she was Thai, he asked the obvious question. "Which part of Thailand are you from?"

"Why would you want to know that? I haven't done anything wrong. Why are you asking so many questions? I told you that I do not know this person." Her position ratified, the lady from the land of smiles continued to avoid displaying one.

Trying to suppress his impatience, Terry repeated his earlier, unanswered question. "Maybe one of the other ladies might recognise this picture? Can I talk to them?"

She folded her arms. "Sure, you can ask the ladies working here. If you have a search warrant! I have already stated, I do not know this man!" After a pause, she continued, "We have a powerful friend in the police force. Commissioner Graham. He is your senior officer."

With his frustration increasing towards anger and any semblance of control dissipating, Terry leaned forward, seeking proximity intimidation per the training manual, his voice rising. "The man in this picture had a business card for this facility on his person. Can you explain that? And while you think about your answer, consider this. There is no Commissioner Graham, not in North Wales, not in Cheshire. Not in any police force. I think you are being conned by some dickhead looking for a free happy ending. I will get a warrant if I need one, and bring several policemen, and we will put on our lights, make a noise, frighten away customers. We can come every day if it suits us. So how about you offer some assistance, please?"

"We do not offer a happy ending here. This is a clean establishment. Massage only. Provided by a pretty lady, with soft hands, having trained for many years. Only massage." Her statement scripted, automatic, implying her experience in addressing these accusations.

Shrugging his shoulders, he surrendered. "Fine." Making a point of collecting and storing the photo safely, he grabbed a handful of business cards from the display case, deliberately dropping them to the floor. "Oops!" He was pleased to see her small nostrils flare, a point scored. He turned away, making for the door, raising his tone to impart a final message. "I will be back, with a warrant. Just wait and see."

"Goodbye, Detective Holmes."

Closing the door, arriving on the damp pavement, he saw a traffic warden looking closely at his windscreen. He suspected the warden was attempting to read the note on police letterhead placed on his dashboard, advising a CID detective on police business. The warden's first challenge being to decipher the notice through the damp windscreen, his second being whether to believe the notice, or issue a parking ticket anyway. Discretion triumphing over valour, the parking enforcer moved away in search of an easier target.

Six
Monday, 11th February

The shrill ring from his mobile dragged Joe Nesbitt, part-time bartender and hoodlum, from his extremely pleasant slumber. He had been dreaming of himself starring in a five-way with the younger Asian ladies from last night, while Dai and the old one filmed the revelry with an ancient camcorder. A five-way, where everybody had been satisfied. Partially awake, the chaotic dream receding, he reluctantly answered the call.

"Yo. Go for Nesbo."

The caller was in no mood for humour. "Where the fuck are you?" Bringing his awareness to an increased level, recognising the caller's voice, he added a note of respect to his own. "I'm home, just woke up. Is anything wrong?"

"Is Dai with you?"

"No. He's probably at home. I can give you his number if you need it."

"I have his number, you moron; he's not fucking answering. He's not at home, so I am asking you if you know where he might be."

Attempting to think quickly, never his strong point, he remained silent, attracting further ire from the caller. "Any fucking idea? Hello? Is there anybody in there?" The caller's Manchester accent exaggerated as his brusque tone amplified, his breath coming in shorter bursts. "Did you stay with him until the job was completed last night?"

"Almost." Responding to the latest question first. "He dropped me in Chester after the second delivery. He carried on to Wrexham with the old bird on his own." Defensively, "It was his idea."

"Forgetting the point that we insist on two people with every shipment until it is complete, as you fucking well know, have you any idea where he could be now? Because he never arrived at Wrexham, and neither did the woman. If he's had an accident, she could be in trouble as she has no valid documents. He is not picking up his phone, so we must assume something has gone wrong. What else can you tell me?"

Assessing the situation as serious, understanding he could be in trouble, he followed the obvious path and dumped on his colleague. "From what I saw, he had a bit of a thing for the old lady. You know, talking to her, looking at her. Fancied her, I reckon. Reckon that's why he dropped me, so he could be alone with her." Pausing to consider his next words. "We had a bit of banter with the truck driver, took the piss out of her, but Dai didn't join in, seemed a bit serious. He might be shagging her somewhere, slipped her a few quid maybe?"

Following a prolonged silence, both participants in the conversation thinking, the caller finally spoke. "You. You will call Dai on my behalf. He might respond to your number. You will keep calling him until he picks up. You can text him as well, ask him what's going on. You will think of places he likes to go, pubs he likes, addresses for his family, shit like that, and you will send it all to me. Get yourself in a fucking motor, drive the route you would most likely take from where you are now, to the address you were given in Wrexham. See if there is any sign of him or her, or of an accident. You find anything, you call me on this number. If you find Dai, I want to know immediately. Help me out here and you might survive with just a kicking, instead of losing some of your fingers. Get your arse in gear. I am waiting for your call."

Fear apparent by the shaking within his voice, Nesbo replied, "I don't have the address in Wrexham. Dai kept the paperwork; I just kept an eye on the ladies."

"Google Maps, you moron. Bangkok Massage, Wrexham. How hard can it be?" The caller hung up, leaving the barman to contemplate the situation he found himself in. *Fucking Dai. Fingers. Fuck.* Scrolling through his contacts, he found Dai's number, putting the device on loudspeaker, allowing him to hurriedly dress as the device attempted to connect. The number rang out. "Come on, you twat, where are you?"

Stymied. Uncertain about his next action, he waddled into the bathroom, relieving himself with a short burst of urine before brushing his teeth hastily. Neglecting to wash his hands, he grabbed his phone, composing a text message to his mate. 'Hi, it's me. Where are you man. Do you want to go for a beer at lunch time?' Rereading the text, pleased with the content, gently inquisitive without displaying any urgency or panic, no suggestion of fingers being removed. Hitting Send, he made his way to the kitchen, craving toast.

Refreshed from four slices of warm buttered toast and a pint of diluted orange cordial, he left his home. He had sacrificed a shower to save time and possibly fingers, masking his body odour with a liberal spray of Axe.

Steering his mature Volkswagen into traffic, he headed towards Wrexham, conscientiously scanning the roadside alternately left then right, looking for unexpected situations, listening hopefully for the sound of an incoming text message.

Forced to stop at a set of traffic signals, with four cars in front of him, he took the opportunity to compose a further brief message. 'Yes or no to a pint mate. Let me know.' As the message uploaded to the atmosphere, he heard a knock on his window, seeing a dark hat perched on a short haircut, suggesting he might like to lower the window. Complying while expecting the worst, he was confronted by a young-looking traffic cop, anticipating the words before he heard them. "Texting while driving, sir, is an offence. Kindly pull over to the kerb in a safe and orderly manner, when it is clear and appropriate to do so." The copper stepped behind his car, extending his arms to slow the approaching traffic, offering him a straightforward opportunity to move his vehicle to the roadside. Cautiously, he parked a suitable distance beyond the signals. Watching the uniformed policeman in his mirror, he mouthed a quick obscenity. *Wanker!*

Joseph Nesbitt grew increasingly frustrated. The policemen, his partner having joined the festivities, were taking their sweet time processing his offence. Having taken his details verbally, they demanded to see his licence, followed by his insurance. One then circled the car, scrutinising his road tax disc, before insisting on performing a breathalyser test. The other inspecting his tyres, measuring the tread with a coin. Every task accompanied by inane questions, time-consuming irrelevances he could do without. The quiet one had returned to his in-car computer, confirming details, while the talkative plod explained the seriousness of his offence. "Using a mobile phone while driving presents a danger to life which cannot be tolerated." Raising the fact of his vehicle being stationary while he texted had been shot down by the officer, so Nesbo maintained a sombre expression to complement his taciturn silence.

Catching the officer closing his ticket pad, assuming his ordeal was complete, he asked for a favour. "Being police and all, maybe you could help me. My friend is missing, with his vehicle. Everyone is worried in case he has had an accident. Is there a way you could check and see if anything has been reported?"

The expression of the talkative policeman revealed his disinterest, but the quiet one responded positively. "Give me the name and registration number, I'll take a look." Ignoring his colleague's intolerance, he entered the given details, "Dai Harris. Volvo XC90." He repeated the number plate, paused, scanned the screen, looked up, smiling. "Well, that's a piece of luck. Seems your XC90 was clocked doing ninety-four in a sixty limit after three in the morning. Speed camera, near Bersham. No reports of an accident, but he is looking at six points and a hefty fine. Just like you."

Murmuring his appreciation, keen to escape, he accepted his citation and returned to the car. Making sure the road was clear, he drove off, seeking a convenient place to stop and turn the car around. Pulling into the first layby, he switched off the engine and exited the vehicle, ensuring the bastards in blue had nothing on him if they followed him for their own sadistic pleasure. The Mancunian answered on the third ring.

"News?"

"Something. Just a hunch. But it seems Dai was clocked speeding last night on the A483, heading beyond Wrexham."

"How did you come to know this?"

Invisibly swaggering, asserting his self-importance, he continued, "I have my sources. Anyway, his mam lives down in Oswestry, so I guess he might be heading down there. He still hasn't returned my calls or messages."

"Not bad, little man. Address?"

"I don't have it. You could try Harris in the phone book."

"Don't get lippy with me, you little shit. Your fingers are still at risk. See if any of your mates know his mother's address, on the down low. Let me know." A click and he was gone.

Planning to try calling Dai again, he postponed that action, moving to the edge of the verge, where the longer grass grew around the fence posts. Glancing over his shoulder, observing no traffic, he unzipped, taking a more satisfying slash into the grass. Releasing a low growl of relief at the release of fluid, he scanned his surroundings. While shaking off the drips, his eyes widened as he saw something unexpected. Stepping forward to improve his view, he froze. "Oh, Dai, what the fuck have you done?"

Beyond the fence, on an area of shorter winter grass, lay the body of a woman, small in stature, her green dress covered in dirt. His next movement involuntary, his chest lurching, his upper body sniping forwards. He barely had time to open his mouth before vomit gushed from him, tears joining the exodus of fluids, retching followed by more vomit, his mouth invaded by acidic reflux, unhearing of a vehicle coming to rest behind him. Now doubled over, agony competing with horror, disgust enveloping both, lurching as he regurgitated his partially digested toast.

From the stationary traffic patrol vehicle, the passenger asked, "Are you sure he passed the breath test, because he looks totally fucked-up now." Not waiting for a response, he left the car while replacing his hat on his head, raising his voice. "You must be really stupid. We only did you ten minutes ago. Pissing and puking by the road, you'll be lucky to have a licence by tomorrow."

Becoming aware of the police presence, through the tears of horror and despair, spitting sour saliva, he managed to croak, "You guys need to take a look at this."

Unprepared for the image presented to him, the policeman turned immediately, signalling to his colleague. Making every attempt to avoid regurgitation, his face draining of any residual colour, he fumbled for his handset. Inhaling deeply, he prepared to make the call which would initiate the frantic process of death.

Seven
Monday, 11th February

Rumours swept through the station at Mold. The usually talkative chauffeurs were revealing nothing, having delivered the top brass via the rear entrance. The entire detective contingent corralled into the largest office within the building. Serious expressions, minimal conversation. An air of uncertainty dampening spirit. An assortment of media had gathered for an impromptu scheduled press conference. A scattering of solicitors. An abundance of public relations personnel. Somebody would be getting their arse kicked.

The internal meeting behind closed doors ended at three forty-two. Very senior officers huddled with their PR aides, urgently preparing for the imminent press conference. Detectives split into their social groups, dissecting the content of the internal meeting, reviewing their activity. Forensic investigators, separate, different, licking their wounds. Constables, uniformed and plain clothes, unsure how to act, keen to escape, but reluctant to try. Acting DI Barry Chappell standing alone in a corner, isolated but defiant, the scapegoat. Seconds slowly passing, the majority waiting for the highest ranks to attend their moment before the cameras, to deliver their politically motivated message, to sacrifice whoever or whatever they had to. Protecting the image of the North Wales Police Force their only concern.

The top brass departed, the closing door a catalyst for an outpouring of discussion. The volume increasing to a level normally associated with rock concerts. Multiple simultaneous conversations competing to be heard.

Senior forensic investigator Emyr Christopher extended his hand, the gesture reciprocated by Barry Chappell. "Well, mate, seems you and I are to blame for everything. Funny how shit never reaches the Supers." They exchanged a small smile, bonding against adversity. Barry summarised the situation.

"Yeah. I get to carry the can for this one, your department gets a slap, the DCI who endorsed the charge emerges unscathed, and the Crown fucking Prosecution Service remains the pillar of our society, as always. Are you planning to watch the press junket downstairs? See how they phrase our little *faux pas*?"

Emyr loosened his tie, sighing with pleasure, his outgoing smile returning below his uncombed brown hair, his rugby toned body responding to the removal of the restraining item. "I'll watch the highlights on the telly. Get the truth." His natural grin returning, his broad face banishing concern. "Sergeant Annie will be wetting her knickers at this. Should put her right in line for the promotion she has been actively seeking. Good luck to her, she is brilliant at office politics. And she's got nice tits. I know you're dating her, but she has. Only saying."

Nodding, Barry agreed. "She has, no argument there. Doris will be like a dog with two dicks. Junior officer on a fucked-up homicide case, and he gets a promotion. A fucking promotion? The world has gone mad." His attempted joviality failing to cover his inbuilt resentment.

DS Holmes and PC McGarry stood together, having personally survived the onslaught, but professionally tarnished by involvement in a high-profile case gone wrong. "You, okay?" Terry asked Flick.

Surprised by the question, she responded, "I'm fine. My rank is too low on the totem pole for these knobs to register. You guys bear the brunt of it." Taking a moment to recollect her thoughts. "We mostly did okay, didn't we? It was, is, a difficult case."

Touching her gently on her forearm, he conceded, "It is a tough case; you did really well, honestly. Barry cut some corners, Beecham and I should have blocked him, pushed him to interview more people. Lesson learned." They were joined by Doris. "Well, well. If it isn't Detective Sergeant Grahame Beecham. Or can we still call you Doris?"

The big man adjusted his physique, a hint of a smile challenging the low-key environment. "Serge. Sir. Grahame. Boss. DS Beecham. Pick one, or stick with Doris, I'm fine with that. I want you to stay on the case with me, Flick. Are you okay if I make the request?"

Flummoxed, Flick looked at each DS in turn, seeking guidance, clarity, confirmation. "Okay. If you're sure?"

Doris, turning to the shorter man, engaging. "What are you working on, Terry? Anything interesting?" Terry gave a synopsis of his case: dead guy in a Beamer, the uncertainty relating to murder, suicide or accident. Adding his frustration at the meeting, delaying his request for a warrant to search the massage facility in Wrexham. At the mention of Bangkok Massage, Doris assumed an increased interest. "A warrant? Why? All you'll find is a collection of Asian ladies with moderate to zero English skills. And zero Welsh. They give blokes a nice back rub, and make a few extra quid tossing off perverts. Thereby keeping those perverts satisfied, making our streets safer for women to walk in, without fear." Despite the grim atmosphere, Terry laughed, Flick smiled, their amusement heightened by the apparent serious expression on DS Beecham's face.

Hearing the laughter, seeing three members of his case team together, Barry strode across the room, confronting them. "Funny, is it? Funny that I get demoted back to DS, on a case where you all, every fucking one of you, agreed we should proceed to charge. Enjoy your moment. Oh, and congratulations, DS Beecham. Well-earned and richly deserved. Not." Offering no opportunity for response, he turned and left the room and the building, heading straight to his car.

"No further questions. Thank you for coming." Popping flashes, camera mechanisms whirring, the press conference at the Mold police station disintegrated. The shining reflective buttons on the senior officers' uniforms receding behind a screen, through a manned security door, returning to the relative warmth of the facility. "Well done, sir. That went well." The Superintendent's driver pandered to his superior's ego.

"Yes, I rather think it did." His proper language coupled with his public-school accent largely obscuring his Edinburgh upbringing. "Jones, I need a file, tomorrow. Meadows. I seem to recall a case in Fife, a domestic gone wrong. Beecham mentioned a possible new suspect. I'm curious if there may be a link."

Nilesh retreated to the carpark, collating his impressions of the police press conference, suspecting the Q&A had been effectively stage-managed. The entire event was recorded on his phone, for reference. Looking around, he watched the BBC reporter do her piece to camera, live, breaking news, sensational. The gusting breeze revealing the darker roots in her hair, less blonde and pristine in the flesh than she appeared on the broadcast. The jam-packed car park was beginning to empty, would empty quicker if drivers showed a modicum of patience. Ask anybody in this country about driving standards and they were universally adamant that Indians were the absolute worst. The scene before him cast doubt on that assertion.

A journalist at the *Leader* newspaper, part of the Wrexham-based NWN Media Group, Nilesh was unimpressed with what he had heard. Mentally preparing his submission, he circulated thoughts, trying to assimilate the key content of the situation. A man in his thirties had been murdered in Saltney. The body was found more than a week later. Why so long? The case was run by a pair of Detective Sergeants — no Detective Inspector was available. Why not? Budget restraints? Lack of qualified personnel? There were hints of cross-border jurisdiction issues such as an English pathologist reporting to Welsh police. A residual issue previously admitted yet remaining unimproved. They had charged a woman, held her in the cells, but prior to presenting her at court, another detective had found conflicting evidence, leading to charges being dropped. They claimed credit for the diligence of this other detective. What evidence had been identified so late that it could bring the police to drop the charge? Why was it not found earlier? Had they ever had compelling evidence? Why had the CPS representative declined questions? He had framed a question, hoping the cameras would pick him up. *Are you stating that a murderer remains free on the streets of Cheshire and Flint, yet you have no idea as to their identity?* Of course, they never took his question; they had planted their own questions with their preferred journos, the ones who would exchange integrity for the eventual cleansed inside story. His interest was piqued. Who was the victim? What is his story? Why was he killed? Why did they suspect a woman? What were the forensic misinterpretations? So much wrong here. Nilesh sensed a career-defining story. He decided to open a file, beginning the walk to his production office.

Ruth McGarvey exited the police station accompanied by her husband and their solicitor. The press, preoccupied with their deadlines, had failed to notice either their presence or their departure.

DS Terry Holmes lodged his request for a search warrant for the Bangkok Massage in Wrexham. DS Grahame Beecham took a seat before the case file computer, commencing his assigned task to undertake a thorough review of the entire case, preparing to renew the investigation tomorrow. DS Barry Chappell took comfort in the arms of Sergeant Annie Freeland, talking shop for a while, receiving sympathy for the removal of his promotion, consoling himself with her lovely face framed by blonde hair, and her fantastic body.

Amy Meadows watched the news at home. No mention of Beamer boy's death. The press conference relating to the release of the suspect in Jed's murder barely registered with her. Running fingers through her undyed, newly styled hair, count at zero, Amy was happy.

Eight
Tuesday, 12th February

Holly Dryburgh stretched, trying to expel the sleep from her body. Her extended left hand searched for Terry, her eyes remaining closed, reluctant to face the light. Her fingers encountering an empty bed, she surmised he was on a case, accepting there would be no morning glory today unless she provided her own stimulation. Risking one open eye, she confirmed she had time for a snooze, instantly warming as she pulled the duvet across her ample chest.

****

Having risen early, reluctantly resisting Holly's partially exposed curves, Terry showered quietly, before driving to the station. He planned to write the preliminary report from yesterday's suspicious death while he waited for his warrant to come through, then commence the tedious process of interacting with forensics, the pathologist and the local uniforms.

****

Rob, editor-in-chief at the *Leader*, considered today's published paper before him, pleasantly surprised with Nilesh's article accurately reflecting the police statement, while raising significant questions about the competency of the North Wales Police. It was infinitely better than the equivalent story in the *Express*, which overlooked the implications of the unsolved murder completely. Nilesh had expressed a desire to investigate further. Based on the copy in his hand, he was inclined to support his reporter. Finishing his already cold tea, he prepared to leave the office, planning a trip to Chester to buy trousers.

****

Barry Chappell, having had his morning nuptials request politely rebuffed by Annie, was not looking forward to the day ahead. Formally disciplined, demoted to his previous rank without a live case to concentrate on, he expected to be assigned to something shitty. His mood was not enhanced by the ringing of his mobile, the caller ID display showing Mold PS. Reluctantly picking up, he offered an impersonal, "DS Chappell."

"Good morning, sir. I have a message from DI Peter Jones at the new CID offices in Llay. You are to go straight there today, as quick as you can. You have been seconded to a case requiring an experienced Detective Sergeant. His words, sir. Can I inform him that you are on your way?"

"Thanks. I will be there." Checking the bedside alarm clock. "Within an hour. Cheers." His emotions mixed, positively that he had been assigned to a case, negatively that he would be at the fledgling new facility, working with an unfamiliar DI. Rising from the bed while scratching his balls, he plodded towards the shower, hoping for a tasteful glimpse of Annie.

****

Dai Harris had slept badly. Sitting upright, secured to a chair with packing tape across his mouth, his facial wounds unattended, his request for painkillers unforthcoming. His retrieval from Oswestry had been slick, efficient, polite, the understated menace clear to him yet blissfully missed by his mother. They had found him quicker than he had expected and brought him to the familiar warehouse near the border in Deeside. Under interrogation, he had consistently described the woman's attack against him, using his facial injuries to support his version of events. He explained that she had run from the vehicle, his search for her being in vain. He admitted his failure to follow established procedures.

****

The Superintendent relaxed over a frothy cappuccino; the press reporting of his statement had been fine, as good as he could reasonably expect. Within the force he had kicked some backsides, flexed his muscles, dictated guidelines for the future and generously drawn a line in the sand. Prone to cliché, detached from reality, he applied himself to thinking outside of the envelope.

****

Newly promoted DS Beecham prepared to formulate his team with a combination of familiarity, Flick, and some fresh perspective, yet to be selected. Having reviewed the case again, prior to going home at midnight, he remained suspicious of Amy Meadows, liked her for it. But he was committed to following due process, and the suggestions received from the Guv before his bad turn. The Guv was usually right. By following those principles, he would get a result at the end.

****

Amy assessed her reflection, revelling in the stunning transformation achieved by her hairdresser. The badly dyed, botched self-decimation had disappeared, replaced by her naturally dark brown hair, interspersed with black, lowlighted with restraint, the uniform length brushing her shoulders, the natural wave enhanced by some expensive salon product. The style complemented her features, her almond-shaped brown eyes somehow larger, her cheekbones more prominent, her lips untouched yet fuller. Her slim figure a brief diet away from skinny, her vaguely olive coloured skin enhancing her almost Asian appearance, she knew she looked good. "Yeah."

****

Recently transferred and promoted Forensic Pathologist, Seng Ten Tay, preferring Steven, pushed his ponytail behind his head as he carried out his ritual for starting the day by clearing emails. On only his second day since moving across from Cheshire, where he had trained under the well-respected Stephen Andrews, he was anticipating his first top priority post-mortem examination. A lady found beside the A483 yesterday, her death suspicious, declared by paramedics at the scene. He intended to be fastidious, beyond reproach. The promotion carried a significant salary increase, and his family back in Singapore were proud of his status. The body lay in the morgue, awaiting the arrival of the lead detectives to watch him perform. He planned to slice the BMW thrill-wank guy in the afternoon, time permitting.

****

Joe Nesbitt had endured a series of nightmares. The dead Asian lady, rising from the earth, asking why he had left her alone with Dai. Eyeless sockets staring at him, pleading. The police accusing him of murder, forcing him to touch the dead body, introducing his DNA to simplify their case. The Mancunian presenting him with a choice: kill Dai or die. The images unreal, nevertheless haunting him.

****

DS Chappell sat across the desk from DI Jones. His initial impression of the DI had been of a laconic paper-pusher with an overly tidy office and an unusual accent. Having returned from the post-mortem, his opinion was adapting, his new boss impressing him as thorough and organised, the office representative of his manner.

"What are you thinking, Barry?"

"There's a lot to consider, sir. The poor lady was strangled, beaten, raped, abandoned. We have a sicko on the streets."

DI Jones offered an earnest expression, his reply considered, delivered in a gentle Anglesey manner. "Horrible thing to happen, horrible. I am puzzled by her complete lack of identity. We should probably assume she has been robbed as well." Changing tack. "The new FP was good, I thought. His Asian background was quite helpful, identifying her as Thai. I have to be honest, most Asian people look the same to me."

"Tut-tut, sir, that's not a politically correct thing to say." Their mutual smiles defusing any inference in the words, a relaxed relationship already developing between them.

"The psychology interests me. I like your term, sicko. It keeps things simple. Yet it is complex. We know he has committed rape and we have a concern that it may have been after, or at least very close to, death. Yet, he attempted to replace her underwear. That was an unnecessary risk in a location where he could have been seen. Does he have modesty issues, respect for women issues. The replaced underwear being back to front, does this mean he is unfamiliar with the ladies? Or is it a signature, and are we about to see a series of similar killings? Complex. Concerning."

Barry offered no comment, absorbing the insights, further increasing his respect for the DI.

"Barry, I hear that you are a good field operator. I want you to do the legwork on this, run the physical side of the case. Leave me to do the reporting, the requests for resource, the boring stuff. What's your plan?"

Referring to a folded sheet of lined paper placed on the desk, he ticked the first item. "Get the semen tested for DNA identification, top priority." Tick. "CCTV footage for the road, time of death 3am, give or take. Any vehicles between midnight and six to be listed, perform a DVLC check on the owners, bring in anyone suspicious or with form." Tick. "Foot soldiers to the scene, fingertip search of the field and the layby, bag and tag everything, no matter how insignificant." Tick. "Interview the civilian who found the body, make some time to chat to the traffic lads involved as well."

"Good start. Get going. I'll set up resource for the case file, lean on the forensics for that semen, get the Roads Department to share their footage. Hopefully, there are not many cars at that time of the night. You can get a crime-scene team. Emyr's office is directly below this one. He'll help you out."

Barry found himself happy. Surprisingly. A high-profile new case. Working with a top DI who seemed appreciative of his skills. An excellent post-mortem report forthcoming. Expectations of top forensic support from a familiar face. Still smiling, having descended the stairs, he knocked on the office door, accepting the invitation to enter. "Hi, Emyr. Got a minute?"

"Of course. I'm surprised to see you down here, especially after yesterday's fiasco. Did you see it on the news?"

"Didn't bother. Reporters just make me angry. They usually get about a quarter of the detail correct, another quarter wrong, and take a wild guess at the rest. Anyway, I need a few of your lads for a fingertip search on the A483, overnight homicide."

"Oh, you're working with PJ, are you? He's a good bloke, really sound. How many do you need?"

"I'm thinking four. Not a huge area, but it's a nasty crime; we need to be thorough."

"Ordinarily," the word pronounced or-din-err-alley, "there wouldn't be an issue. But…" He allowed the word to hang between them, causing Barry concern. "We have new activity restraints, budget responsibilities with a new theme, imaginatively entitled one two three four. Some psycho bastard babble expert has convinced the bean counters that this theme will make us think more efficiently and consider our use or waste of resources."

Barry groaned. "Another fucking money-saving wombat programme?"

"Hey, I only have to deal with it till Friday, until I sit with the suits, get my demotion, and return to the real world."

"Friday?"

"Yeah. Morning, clean shirt, tie, the lot. Charlotte will go mental. She hates ironing midweek."

"So, what can I have?"

Emyr, surprisingly chirpy for a man facing demotion while operating under new fiscal limitations, made an offer. "One forensic investigator, two plods, three rolls of tape, four hours. But you need to supply the fish and chips if it goes past shift change."

"Come on, Emyr, this is a rape slash murder, you must be able to do better. Shall I get DI Jones to come down? Put you under pressure?"

"Makes no difference who it is. I've done the course. Now, if you had a couple of rolls of crime-scene tape in your car, and if we're honest, we all keep some just in case. Useful for small repairs at home. I could do one roll of tape, two investigators, three plods, four hours. Bit better, eh?"

Barry, seeing the system, proposed an alternative. "How about one tape, two hours, three investigators, four plods. That should do it. No need for fish and chips."

"Don't take the piss, DS Chappell. Bring your own tape, I'll sort the remainder. We should be on-site within an hour. I assume you will be there. Don't you dare say you won't be."

"Thanks, buddy, that works." Objective achieved, looking around, he casually asked, "Where does Sergeant Freeland sit?" Emyr offered his famous grin, replying without malice, "After Friday, right where I'm sitting now."

Returning to DI Jones' office, he updated his superior on the forthcoming site search. Jones informed him that the CCTV would be with them this evening, adding that the semen was away for analysis and cross-matching. Progress ongoing, he headed for his car, tossing the earplugs he had worn up his nose to combat the smell at the post-mortem into a litter bin.

Nine
Tuesday, 12th February

Shopping at the Grosvenor Mall, Amy felt fantastic, without a care in the world. Her count was at zero, her hair looked incredible, and her face was lightly enhanced by negligible make-up. She had dressed in butt-wrapping jeans with sensible heels and a pristine white blouse, her jacket over her arm. Stepping confidently, aware that she was attracting subtle glances of approval from the male population and the occasional appreciative female.

She was looking to buy a dress. She felt she needed a nice everyday dress, open to inspiration for an impulse buy should she find something impossible to resist. She had cleared her credit card balance as a precaution. Amy had enjoyed walking to her car this morning, the climate dry and mild, no sad prick in a BMW liable to pass and ruin her day, an enjoyable upside to her weekend activity.

About to enter Next, she felt somebody's eyes addressing her, not uncommon this morning, but the intensity higher than before. Glancing to her right, her gaze located the culprit. A tall guy with crazy hair, unfazed at being busted. Accepting the unusual situation, instincts suggesting no threat, she released a limited smile as she stepped towards him, asserting her confidence. "Can I help you?" Her voice stable, her tone neutral. Closing the distance between them, she reassessed his age: older than her first impression, thirties, recently shaven, scruffy, six feet tall or thereabouts.

Undaunted by her approach, her question, he made direct eye contact. "Hi." Seeing her, finding her impossibly more attractive as the distance reduced. "I just wanted to tell you that you look stunning." Delighted he had managed to produce the words under pressure, enjoying her reaction, her glance away before returning her eyes to him. Other shoppers around them, irrelevant and inconsequential. He anticipated her response, hoping for a positive reaction.

Her voice softer, she held his gaze. "Thank you. That's a nice thing to say." Standing at a natural personal space, she extended her hand. "Amy." Internally chastising herself for using her real name. "And you are?"

Taking her hand, small in his, her skin soft. "Rob. I am really pleased to meet you."

Reclaiming her hand, maintaining her position. "Do you often approach strangers with a compliment?"

He replied without hesitation. "Never. First time. I saw you from a distance, and as you came closer, I, eh, kind of, couldn't help myself."

Only marginally aware of his explanation, assessing him, his prompt reply intimating honesty, his manner comfortable, nice looking if unconventional, his hair needing the same levels of attention as hers had yesterday. "Well. Thank you, Rob. You have provided a lovely start to my day." Offering him an opening, discovering she hoped he would take the chance. Make an invitation of some sort.

"Would you have some time to join me for tea or coffee, Amy?"

Relieved, resisting her urge, make him wait, wait, wait. "Some tea would be nice. Thank you."

Ten
Tuesday, 12th February

"If a search is so inconvenient, I suggest you close the premises and stay away for the day. Okay? Have a good one. Bye."

Having entered the detective room through the already open door, Terry took his usual seat, unloading his rucksack. Hearing the conversation finish, he offered, "Good morning, DS Beecham."

Doris made a point of turning slowly, not having heard Terry arrive, distracted by his telephone call. "Morning, Terry. There's a warrant for you over in the in-tray."

"Thanks." Terry collected the document, duly annotated, dated for today, no latitude, no permission to force entry if required. Minimal, but suitable for his needs, allowing him to gain access to the massage parlour and show the victim's photo to the workers, hoping for some form of connection.

Too early to call the medical guys over at the Maelor Hospital, he began to assess the evidence and reports obtained so far.

"So, you landed a possible auto-erotic asphyxiation case." Phrased like a statement, spoken like a question. "Do you want to bounce a few ideas around? Then you can do the same for me, revisiting the Jed case, try to see what we missed."

Appreciating the logic, Terry agreed, moving across to the desk occupied by the experienced detective. "I'll start. Dead IC1 male, exhaust into the car, dick out, semen stain on the car door. No sign of violence, no apparent trace of another person. Crime scene a total mess, garage door open, allowing rain and wind ingress. Forensics sharing hot drinks with the woman who found the body. She had already pulled the body from the car, put his dick away, touched anything and everything. He has some petty form, cease-and-desist from his estranged wife, claims that he was threatening her and their child. Been locked up overnight after a fight in a bar, and nine points on his licence."

Doris absorbed the information, considering, formulating a question. "Does it look like a homicide to you? Anything that says this is a murder? Even if it is just a gut feeling. Start there."

Scratching his ear, Terry continued, "There is nothing really. Murder. Thrill sex. Accident. Suicide. Nothing sticks out. I really need the blood analysis to see if there were drugs in his system. I need the pathology report. I'm not too optimistic about the forensics — the dozy twats covered a potential spunk stain with fingerprint powder."

Unable to control himself, Doris laughed, aware his colleague seemed less than amused. "Come on, that's funny. The ultimate cross-contamination. Fingerprinted semen. I wonder who assumes responsibility for testing that. Tell me, did the deceased have a smile on his face?"

Terry groaned, his relative inexperience exposed by his failure to look at the victim, content to see the bundle on the ground. Seeking to cover himself, he stated, "Not especially."

Doris continued. "If he has a smile, he was probably wanking, you can call it an accident, walk away. Subject to the blood and other reports. If you can find a wound on him, most likely unlawful killing. If you find more spunk, then go with that auto-erotic bollocks. What's your next move?"

Inclining his head towards the warrant, Terry shrugged. "Question the tarts at the Wrexham massage place, while I wait on the results." Seeing curiosity on Beecham's face, he explained. "I found massage cards at his house, went around to ask about him, got a severe rebuff from the old bird at reception. My suspicions are aroused."

"Worth a look, I suppose. But don't expect much. These places are straightforward. They don't like questions, as they know they are breaking the law providing hand-jobs and blowjobs to the punters who come in with their sore backs, not exactly organised crime."

"Speaking from experience?" Instinctively asking, regretting immediately. The look on Doris's face confirming the end of that conversation. Seeking redemption, he asked, "What do you want to ask about the Jed case?"

"I plan to follow through on the Guv's suggestion and interview that extended list of about forty people. Do you think I should? And did any of the people we brought here tick your boxes? Amy Meadows? Jenny Coleman?"

"I think interviewing the longer list is the way to go. The time pressure is off, for now. Take the chance, be thorough, follow your nose. The suits will cut you some slack since you saved their bacon already. And if it comes back to those two, you'll at least have some justification. Having Flick with you will help; she's okay on the interpersonal assessments. Give her a chance to fly with you."

Simultaneously standing, they prepared to begin their next tasks. "We should do this more often. Share ideas. Can't do any harm?" Clutching his warrant, Terry headed downstairs to snag a pair of uniforms for the search, his embryonic case file held beneath the warrant.

Finding a pair of lazy constables enjoying a mid-morning tea break, he commandeered them, sending them to pick up search warrant kits and sequester a vehicle, warning them to be ready in ten minutes. Utilising his free time, he dialled the Forensics division in Llay, connecting to Senior Sergeant Christopher.

"Hello, DS Holmes. Must be my lucky day. First your mate Chappell, now you. What can I do for you?"

Replying. "I'm checking if you have anything to report from your scene techs from yesterday, the Rossett body?" Continuing, unnecessarily, "Not that I expect much; your guys left a mess at the scene. I'll take anything I can get."

The impatience in Emyr's voice was implied, the annoyance in his words was unmistakable. "Mess, was it? In your expert opinion?" Sarcasm compounding the other emotions. "Blame my technicians since you can't tell if you have a murder or a suicide. Didn't take you long, did it?"

Recognising his error, seeking an escape, Terry tried to build a bridge. "Nobody is covered in glory at this one. Even me."

"You might be aware, Detective Sergeant Holmes, of the new management initiative we are all being encouraged to adopt. One two three four. I'm sure you received the memo. Anyway, with regard to your request for information about your case, I can inform you as follows. One. You and I are equivalent rank; if anything, I have a slight seniority. Try to respect the hierarchy. Two. It has been less than twenty-four hours since we attended the situation; exercise some patience. Three. Your assessment of my team is misinformed. They were at the scene an hour before you arrived, had already swept the area before the teas were distributed. Four. Next time you criticise my lads, I will put you in a body cast. Are we clear? Now piss off. Do not bother me again until after four today."

The connection cut, offering no opportunity for Terry to apologise, explain, or justify his actions. "Arrogant Welsh cunt!" Looking at his phone, wishing he had not spoken aloud, his wish exacerbated by several pairs of eyes trained on him, universally Welsh, including the two constables due to accompany him on the execution of his search warrant.

Hastily departing the station, taking the rear seat, he provided the destination to the driver. Closing his eyes, trying to erase Emyr's threat of physical violence from his mind, seeking a simple method of appeasement, none coming to mind.

Parking directly outside Bangkok Massage, the police car livery offering protection against the double-yellow lines, Terry jumped to the pavement ahead of the constables, warrant in hand, ready to impart his authority. Planning to teach the old bag a lesson, he was met with a homemade sign on the doorway, in large font on paper double the size of A4, advising "Closed today. Family illness. Sorry. Please come back tomorrow."

"You have to be fucking shitting me!" He tried the door, shaking the framework, the entrance obviously locked. Seeking a bell, finding none. He tried knocking on the glass, loudly, to no avail. "Look for a back door." Barking at the constables, bile rising in his throat, knocking again, shouting "Police!" repeatedly, attempting to open the door, meeting only resistance. The returning constables confirming their identification of a rear entrance, also locked, same sign taped to that window.

"Kick it in. Kick the fucking door in."

The constable stood his ground. "Can't do it, Serge. Our warrant doesn't allow for forced entry. All we can do is continue to ring the bell."

The second constable, emboldened by his colleague, adding, "Or we can wait around, see if anyone turns up."

Removing the card found at the victim's house from his pocket, Terry dialled the printed number for Bangkok Massage, hearing three rings before a recorded message cut in. "We apologise for the closure of our facility in Wrexham today. This is due to an unexpected illness within our family. Please leave your name, with your number, and we will contact you tomorrow. Thank you for your understanding. Khob khun kha."

"This is Detective Sergeant Terry Holmes from North Wales Police. I have a warrant to search these premises. I insist that you come to these premises immediately. You must open these premises to search, by law." His shouted message failed to relieve his stress. Further violent banging on the door, insistent ringing of the bell, everything failing. The watching constables stared, open-mouthed, at the DS meltdown, concerned to be a component in this embarrassment, seeking an exit strategy, expressing relief in their body language as he signalled that they should return to the car.

DS Holmes activated his phone again. "Hello. I wish to speak to the doctor involved in the Mark Forrest post-mortem, please." Listening. "Yes, I can hold."

"Dr Tay? This is DS Holmes at Mold CID. Do you have any initial findings from the PM on Mark Forrest?"

"DS Holmes. The PM is scheduled for this afternoon."

"Afternoon? You've had the body since yesterday. What's the delay?"

"DS Holmes, your paperwork is inconclusive as to the likely nature of the suspicious death. Hence you take lower priority than an obvious homicide, or similar case. You know this."

"Yeah, but…" Terry was interrupted by the pathologist.

"I have to go now. Your details are in the file. I will send you a preliminary report when I complete the examination, and a full report within three days. Goodbye."

"Fuck! What the fuck? Is today Fuck Terry Holmes Day? Is it?"

Both constables looked away, avoiding eye contact, excited to get back to the station and share this one with the troops. DS Holmes, anti-Welsh, mental, falling to bits, dissed by forensics, hung up on by the pathologist, no access with his warrant. Losing the plot. Sometimes you had to love this job.

Taking a breath, seeking calm, wishing he understood yoga, he instructed the constables to wait for fifteen minutes and watch the streets for anybody remotely Asian-looking.

Reviewing his day so far. One continuous fuck-up. Recalling the first words he heard that morning, Doris on the phone, "inconvenient", "stay closed". Surely not. Coincidence?

Eleven
Tuesday, 12th February

The Mancunian was unhappy.

Having successfully imported twenty-seven Asian women into the country as replacement staff for some of his ageing masseuses or expansion staff for his soon-to-be-opened facilities, his attention had been diverted from business, instead focused toward the single dead lady and the reasons for her demise. He had that useless piece of shit Harris restrained in a warehouse, almost certain he had been responsible, awaiting irrefutable confirmation. He had instructed his network to maintain business as usual, not wishing to draw attention to his empire, and desperate to avoid any suggestion of a link between the deceased woman and his facilities. He was fortunate in that she had nothing to identify her when she was discovered, his established procedures dictating the "passengers" and their luggage remained apart until arrival at their specified destination.

Requiring a simple answer from his flagship Wrexham premises, related to the dead lady's personal effects, he had called the facility reception to be greeted by a recorded message advising a full-day closure, contrary to his instruction. Attempts to raise the manager via her mobile remained unfulfilled. His happiness quotient was reducing. Frustrated, he addressed his employees, delegating duties.

"You. Find the Mama San from Wrexham. Get her to call me. Urgently."

"You. Visit that prick at Vodafone in Chester. I want forty of our special arrangement mobiles, sim cards, credit, the usual shebang. Get a price out of him first and keep it under ten grand. Tell him I need delivery by the weekend."

"You. Bring Nesbitt to the warehouse. I want him face to face with Harris to see how their stories hold up."

"You. Get onto our friendly policeman. I need to know if they have DNA on the body of Madam Nattaporn. And if they do, can they identify the guilty party from it. If he gets twitchy, offer him an exchange of information to our mutual benefit, intrigue him. Last resort, you call me and put him on loudspeaker; do not give him my number."

Addressing the group collectively. "Any questions?" Their shaking heads indicating none. "Okay. What happens next?" They waited, knowing he enjoyed this game, ready, willing to play along. "Now fuck off!"

Pause, two, three, in unison. "How shall we fuck off, sir?"

Despite his mood, he managed a small laugh. "Off you go, lads."

Alone in the spartan office, The Mancunian reflected on the origin of his professional name, accidentally given to him by Madam Nattaporn, his friend in Thailand, the best massage manager he had ever known. He had brought her to Wales to improve his business; now she lay murdered and cold in a mortuary. Remembering being with her and friends at a bar on Soi Bintabaht in Hua Hin, mixing her Thai and English, explaining her relationship with "The man, khun Ian", meaning dear Ian. His origins being from a Manchester suburb just too much of a coincidence.

He was annoyed that his troops were assuming she was a hooker. She had given that up years ago, moving into management. She created establishments which welcomed anyone and everyone. Premises which were nicely furnished and brightly lit, staffed by attractive ladies of clearly legal age. She arranged discreet rooms for elongated treatments, subtle innuendo rather than blatantly advertising extras for those who wanted or expected their happy ending. He was devastated that she was dead and had already decided the punishment for the perpetrator, irrespective of his or her identity. He suspected Dai Harris but would wait for proof. Reflecting that none of this would have happened if the United Kingdom government had processed her legitimate visa application, fully sponsored by his registered shell company.

Rising from his desk, he kicked the litter bin deliberately, snarling "twat" as he took a position allowing him to monitor the street, scanning the vista for suspicious people or vehicles. The pavements were quiet, the ground dry, a hint of midwinter sunshine jousting with cumulonimbus cloud patterns. Light traffic polluted the air, mild temperature evidenced by punters wearing open coats. With nothing attracting his attention, he called the warehouse. "What's happening with Dai?" he demanded, his authority producing a prompt response.

"He's okay but sticking to his story. Consistent. His face is a mess. No attempt to abscond, though we have tied his feet together."

Content with the reported status, he lowered his voice. "Nesbitt will be coming in later. Keep them both there until I arrive, no matter what transpires. Okay? Remember, only I make the final decision, so go easy on the heavy stuff. Intimidation is fine, but you should keep the physicality down."

Again, a prompt reply. "Of course. Understood. Do we restrain Nesbitt, too?"

This option unconsidered, quickly decided. "Yes, you do."

Hanging up, he tossed his phone onto the desk, the Apple device sliding across the smooth beechwood laminate surface before falling across the edge, landing on his chair. The musical ringtone activated, disturbing the quiet within the room. Striding to his chair, lifting the phone, he stabbed the green button. "Yes?" Listening, brows furrowed, concentrating, concerned, interested. "Why did the Heddlu bring a warrant?" The conversation one way, inward, his only reaction a variety of facial expressions. "She did the right thing. Tell her, from me. Bye."

The Mancunian was curious. Why would North Wales Police present a search warrant to turn over the Wrexham facility, on the pretext of investigating a regular customer? Something was not right, happening one day after Nattaporn's death. Coincidence? The situation unknown, which was not to his liking. The name Mark Forrest meant nothing to him. He had been advised Forrest was a regular in Wrexham, with a preference for the younger girls in the house, always demanding intercourse after his rub down. He was unpopular with the girls, not as gentle as he could have been. *Paedo investigation?* Something to be avoided. He remained confident all the Wrexham facility ladies were of legal age, some not by much, but certifiably okay. For reassurance, he opened his employee file list, assembled in Excel, password protected, all hundred and thirty-one employees sorted by location, with their legitimate dates of birth highlighted, seeing no issues at that location. Two flags at Prestatyn, another at Llandudno. Glancing through the data, he observed the increased prevalence of Vietnamese staff, their numbers approaching that of the genuine Thais. The quantity of Burmese and Cambodian girls was gradually eroding, having proved difficult to manage, while prone to outbursts of petulance. The punters were led to believe that all the girls were Thai; it suited their fantasy and was company policy. But cost savings were necessary, even in the sex industry, and the Vietnamese staff worked for less money, complained rarely and reportedly performed to satisfaction.

He closed the file. The document could convict him should it fall into the wrong hands. It contained passport data, National Insurance numbers and other personal information, some of it genuine. Taken as a whole, the document could be interpreted as indicative of people trafficking, a subject currently newsworthy, trending with the media and declining celebrities and resulting in exaggerated sentences for anyone convicted.

He didn't think of his masseuses as trafficked. They were recruited. Their role was clearly explained. The monetary rewards were honestly indicated, the illegality intimated. He treated them well, they were paid on time, accommodation was provided for them and they were free to enjoy the area on their time off. Encouraged to be discreet, they were never forced to perform any act against their will beyond the basic expectation. His retention of their passport and other identification a fair and reasonable protection against his investment.

Locking his drawers, hearing footsteps on the stairwell, he prepared for the next interruption. Politely knocking before entering, Boris the Orange greeted his boss with a muted smile, combined respect and sympathy expressed, enhancing their handshake with his other hand cupping those conjoined. "I'm so sorry for your loss. If there is anything I can do, you only have to ask." Boris was one of his trusted employees, inner circle, respectful, professional, careful. His language skills gaining him his role as a translator, able to speak Mandarin, Thai, Vietnamese and Malay, the Chinese-based ability the source of his nickname. His above-average height contrasting with his Asian features, a hybrid Eurasian exception to the rule that such combinations inevitably produced beautiful people.

"I have the ladies. Shall I bring them in?" Receiving a nod of assent, he left the office, providing an opportunity for The Mancunian to prepare the office to receive guests. Placing glasses and sparkling water on the circular table, arranging five chairs evenly around the perimeter, he took a position beside his desk, defining his role as the boss. Boris returned with four young ladies, having accessed the premises via the emergency exit at the rear of the building, each standing within the office, clearly coached to allow the boss to perform a visual inspection. Having scanned them, he invited everyone to sit, his verbal invitation supported by gestures.

"These are the girls who shared the car with Harris and Nesbitt?" he asked Boris.

"Yes, sir. All from Vietnam, all have some limited ability in English. But we will save time if you ask questions and I translate. Is that okay with you?"

"Do they know anything about what happened to Madam Nattaporn?"

"Nothing, sir."

Pouring water for everyone, offering a smile, he sensed a relaxing of their initial tension. They knew what he was, if not who he was, making their nervousness understandable. He invited the ladies to join Boris for dinner at the Slow Boat restaurant in Chester's Frodsham Street, explaining that the restaurant's menu consisted of Thai, Malaysian and Vietnamese food. He knew that Boris would enjoy the experience, entertain them, demonstrate some of Chester's highlights, inserting an element of loyalty into their arrangement.

The conversation was complicated. His English wording occasionally interpreted by the ladies, partly more than fully. One seemed to have a superior English ability in comparison to the others, still limited, but showing some potential to accentuate her attractiveness. If she could develop these skills, she had potential to move upwards, perhaps into his premium escort service. Mostly, Boris translated in both directions.

They established that Harris and Nesbitt had collected five ladies from the truck. Their journey had been mostly comfortable, food and drinks were provided regularly, but the final truck ride had been cold.

The car had been a gold colour, the short man had sat in the centre row, the taller one driving, the Thai lady sitting in front. The little man had asked for a volunteer to give him a blowjob, an internationally recognised phrase and act, but had not touched anyone. The driver had not touched but had looked at the Thai lady a lot. They described being dropped off, two first, holding their hands up, then two more, raising their hands in turn, unaware of any incidents after that. They expressed appreciation of the Mama Sans at their locations. One had asked why the Thai lady was absent, assuming this meeting was normal for every arrival.

Suspicion confirmed, he had excused the ladies, thanking them, welcoming them, touching each hand in turn as he bowed lightly. Slipping a bundle of cash to Boris, he instructed him to ensure they had a good time tonight.

Isolated again, he reflected on these latest recruits. They had sharper features compared to the softer-featured Thais, more obviously Asian, eyes generally smaller in appearance. As always, the quality varied; one certainly pretty, one with stunning long hair but a figure like a prepubescent boy, one curvy with poor skin, one plain yet with a tantalising expression. Their story supported those of Nesbo and Dai, as far as it went. Their confirmation of Dai's interest in Nattaporn was crucial, supporting his suspicion without providing proof.

Placing another call, he learned that he would receive thirty phones on Sunday, ten more within another week, at a total cost of eight thousand pounds. The financial solution acceptable, the delivery less so. He instructed his employee to insist upon thirty phones by Thursday, with the balance by Saturday, no later, payment in full on Thursday if agreed.

Calling the warehouse, he received confirmation of Nesbo's arrival. He was apparently unhappy at being tied to a chair and had taken to shouting obscenities at Dai, distancing himself from his former friend.

Overloaded on conversation, he sent a message, seeking an update on contact with their friendly policeman. The reply disappointing, no contact so far, still trying. Resisting the urge to issue a warning, he postponed a sharply worded message until the next time. Peckish more than hungry, he locked the office, preparing to visit his favourite café, wondering which skirts the girls in No Chips No Garnish would be wearing today.

Twelve
Tuesday, 12th February

Limited by a lack of immediate choice, they selected Muffin Break as the venue for their initial encounter, the simple coffee shop offering an enticing odour from a selection of baked goods. Amy was internally amused, recalling her pontificating former boss at No Chips No Garnish, who seemed to think she had invented this atmospheric environment. She smiled as Rob withdrew a chair, inviting her to sit, assisting her, before taking the seat directly opposite. His simple gesture making her feel appreciated and unfamiliarly feminine.

Watching her browse the menu, he neglected his own, taking the opportunity to look at her. Her overall impression was a contradiction of independence balanced by an undertone of vulnerability. He admired her smooth skin, gently adorned with enhancement, her eyes enigmatic.

"I think I would like English breakfast tea. Are you eating?"

Her words ending his observational reverie, affording him a new opening to engage with her, taking that chance. "I would like to. I hope you can join me."

Amy suddenly relaxed, releasing a little laugh. "You are so polite." The *so* being extended to four syllables. Continuing. "An apple bran muffin, please. Could I ask for lemon with my tea, instead of milk?"

"If they don't have lemon, I will get one from the supermarket for you myself, so long as you promise to still be here when I return."

Unable to stop smiling, he left the table, turning to glance at her as he walked to the counter. He placed her order exactly as requested, adding a skinny cappuccino for himself and a savoury zucchini muffin, forgoing his usual cheese and ham toastie. He contemplated a further item, looking for a way to extend his time with her, scarcely believing his luck. Paying in advance, he returned to their table.

Waiting for their elevenses to arrive, they began the inevitable exchange of information associated with coming to know a new person.

Taking the lead, traditionally the male responsibility, she offered information about herself, then asked for his.

"My name is Amy, surname withheld, and I'm twenty-six. You?"

"I'm Rob, thirty years old, having an awesome day, delighted to meet you."

"What do you do, Rob?"

"I was a journalist, but now I'm an editor, meaning I spend less time in the field, more time correcting and arranging content." His tone and manner suggesting enjoyment, an element of pride in his role. "Your turn?"

Composed. "I am between roles. I resigned my previous job a few days ago. I need to go there today and pick up my outstanding payment. The owner of No Chips No Garnish and I never saw eye to eye, and it was a stop-gap role anyway." She had been prepared to continue, noticed his amusement, eyes widening as he attempted to restrain himself. Curious, she paused, allowing him to speak.

"Oh, my. I almost suggested that place when you agreed to join me. That would have been," he thought for a second, "awkward."

They looked at each other, mutual interest increasingly evident. The moment interrupted by the arrival of their order, neither speaking as the items were placed on their table, the waitress efficient, finishing quickly.

Amy broke the silence. "It would have been awkward, for sure. It would be worse if you were now imagining me in the uniform that they wear there." Her light-hearted insinuation amusing her, enjoying his momentary discomfort.

He changed the subject. "Where did you go to school?"

Teasing now, in full flow. "If I tell you, will you be imagining me in my school uniform as well?"

Realising she was tormenting him, he laughed, found something interesting in his muffin, addressing her indirectly, his expression hidden. "It's hard to imagine you looking any better than you look right now. Truly." Quickly continuing, "So school, college?"

"Balwearie High School, in Kirkcaldy. University of Bradford. Logistics and distribution." Belatedly acknowledging his compliment. "Thank you. Again." Seemingly searching for additional words, finding none, enjoying his appreciation.

"Salford Uni, English Literature. Boring, sensible, relevant to my limited skillset. Why Bradford?"

Squeezing the lemon, she placed the segment in her cup, pouring tea while ignoring the superfluous milk, disregarding the sugar. Encouraging him to taste his coffee, she removed a pinch of muffin, tasting it, finding it delightful, better than it probably was. Her positive mood exaggerating everything, internally setting her count to one, good one, for emphasis.

"No specific reason. They had a course in which I had an interest and they had places. I qualified, the student halls were economical, I knew some people studying there. I wanted to be away from home. It just came together. Bradford is not as horrible as people expect."

He tested his muffin, unsure of the flavour. Unusual, unexpected, unnatural, unsweetened. Seeing her expression, he made an admission. "I've never had a savoury muffin before. It tastes weird and I'm not sure if I like it. I usually have a toastie. I thought that the healthy muffin might assist me to make a good impression."

"Don't worry. You are." She hesitated, ensuring her message was received. "Try mine; we can swap if you prefer. I like the zucchini muffin." Switching the plate positions, offering the traditional muffin to him, sipping her tea while meeting his look, unconsciously fluttering her lashes as she became increasingly relaxed in his company. Taking a sample of the apple bran muffin, his instant response suggested it being more to his liking, a careful sip of coffee following quickly.

Taking her phone from her bag, she punched a few buttons. Catching his look of surprise, she further compounded his reaction. "Okay, Rob, would you like to give me your phone number?" Listening as he dictated the ten digits, repeating them in four, three, three phrasing, typing the number into her device. "Your turn." Watching with amusement as he fumbled with his Apple, almost dropping it, hastily attempting to negotiate the password, then ready, expectant, his finger poised.

"Amy…?" Indirectly asking for her surname.

"Let's leave surnames for now. Avoid the Facebook and Google searching. We'll get to know one another the old-fashioned way, face to face." Offering her number, his fingers scrambling to keep up, her face revealing her delight at his frantic effort. Further teasing. "Assuming you want to see me again?" Rewarding him with a radiant smile. "Go ahead, call me, test it."

Contrary to her invitation, he typed a message, sending a short SMS, looking at her. Her device beeping on receipt, her attention briefly diverted by the message content, accepting the intent, flattered by the three simple words: 'You are gorgeous.' Attempting to dial down her now glowing smile, seeking self-effacing but failing, her features further displaying her delight. Internally, she increased her count to two. She mimed a "thank you" to him.

"You can ask me one more question, then no more today." Confirming his optimism. "Save some for the next time we meet."

Contemplating the importance of this final question, he gave an impression of deeper thought, settling on a query of significant gravity. "The Kardashians. Like them or not?"

Her giggle contagious. "Oh, absolutely not!"

Their breakfast over, exchanged muffins and warm beverages consumed, he risked a quick glance at his watch, the first since they met. "So, when can I see you again, Amy?" Encouraging her. "How about tomorrow?"

"I have plans tomorrow evening." His disappointment evident. "Morning? Lunch? Afternoon? All good for me."

His relief burying his momentary disappointment. "Lunch. Twelve thirty?"

Standing, she accepted. "Send me a message. Where? Dress code. Confirm the time. I'm looking forward to it."

He stood with her, remembering his manners, his gesture noticed. "Can I walk you anywhere?" he asked.

"I'm staying here. I came in to buy a dress. And I am now a little behind schedule."

"Then I should return to work. I'm behind as well." He appeared reluctant to leave.

Aware of his likely indecision, she took control of the situation, stepped towards him, placing a gentle kiss on his cheek. "Till tomorrow. Thank you for making my day. Bye." And she was gone.

Thirteen
Tuesday, 12th February

Constable McGarry took a seat, twin mugs of steaming coffee before her, supplemented with an unhealthy range of biscuits. DS Beecham took his place at the desk, facing her, grateful for refreshments. His head was buzzing with random thoughts competing for priority. He required an outlet, an additional cranial analytical resource, a devil's advocate, someone to assist in separating the complicated strands of suspicion. Scanning the range of snacks, appreciating the selection, paracetamol the only missing ingredient.

"Thanks for coming in, Flick. I really need a second opinion on this." His earnest tone intensifying the words, welcoming her back to the case.

"Glad to be back, sir. Looking forward to catching the bastard this time!"

They consumed coffee and biscuits as they discussed previous case activity, raising impressions from their individual reviews. The old flipcharts and flow diagrams provided a visual reminder of their earlier work, timelines and suspect photos once again adorning their situation room. Manila folders spread across desks, almost re-enacting the original set-up, the most significant difference being the absence of Chappell and Holmes. They were undertaking a case review with potential to become an investigation once again; their task deemed no longer worthy of a full investigative team.

Doris ambled to a clean flipchart, selecting a green marker pen, then annotating the page with the date and time, his and her initials and the case number, underlining the entire heading, ready to begin. He added "suspects" below the line, the following hyphen becoming an arrow, two names inserted alongside. Flick watched with amusement, already sure of the names likely to appear, her suspicion immediately confirmed.

"Amy Meadows. No surprise there. Jenny Coleman. Is that it?"

"I know you think I am blinkered, but Meadows is top of my list, even after review. But Coleman keeps rearing her head for consideration. Your comments?"

She stood, injecting physical energy into her person, prepared to commit to the case, any thoughts of subservience abandoned. "Well, if you discount the fact that they both have an alibi, I could agree they are the strongest suspects from our original list." Waiting for a reaction, nothing forthcoming. "We need to expand the list, promote further suspects from that long list you created. Open mind, remember?"

"I think we can break their alibis. I don't believe the Meadows story, not for one second. Too convenient. So many other elements of her interview point towards guilt. And we never really checked the Coleman alibi in detail. There is absolutely nothing in the notes unless Holmes did it and forgot to update us. These alibis require further investigation."

"Despite one of them being from the live-in girlfriend of a DS who was working on the case." She gave him a direct look. "Have them on the list, but you have to consider others, remove the blinkers, sir."

He added a series of question marks below the two names listed. Put in a new heading, "When", again adding an arrowed hyphen, listing Friday 26/1, Saturday 27/1, Sunday 28/1, each split into 'a.m.' and 'p.m.'. "We focused only on a limited window, based on an informal testimony presented by DS Chappell, with CCTV suggestive of corroboration. We need to widen that period of investigation. Remember, the pathologist gave us a broad estimation for the time of death. It is much tougher to pinpoint time of death accurately when the body is a week old."

McGarry responded defensively, having been involved in the CCTV analysis. "We definitely saw the victim come home with a woman on Friday evening, and we saw her leave on Saturday morning. We can't discount that."

Doris interrupted her. "Agreed. But that only tells us he pulled a bird, took her home, got lucky, released her in the morning. It only proves he was too lazy to take her to her home. What about later? The pathologist window allows for somebody else to come to his home later that day, come in, kill him, then bugger off. In that scenario, we have no idea if we are looking for a male, a female, whatever."

"I thought we had agreed it was a woman?"

"We still suspect that. Or I do. However, we became convinced of the female angle only after we had to discount the gay sex theory. You said yourself, we need to broaden the scope of the enquiry; we need to consider male suspects, too. Even though I think we will find that it was Amy Meadows."

She ignored his attempt to elicit a reaction from her. Thinking beyond Amy Meadows, a thought surfaced, one almost too obvious in hindsight. An omission that bordered on collective stupidity, even approaching negligence. Reluctant to say the words, hoping she might be incorrect, she found her voice. "We never had an identity parade. We never had Chappell's witness look at Coleman, McGarvey, Meadows, etc. Surely we should have done that?"

His expression betraying his realisation, diverting his attention to the flipchart, writing 'ID Parade', listing the initial five principal suspects, completing the annotation with 'witness'. Considering her words, he had to wonder how the investigative team had missed such a step in their process. Curious as to the absence of any official criticism related to such an omission. "What was his name?"

Flick performed a software search on the case computer. "I'll look it up. He lived in Saltney."

"For fuck sake. He lives close to the victim. How could Chappell and Holmes fail to set up an ID parade? He admitted to knowing the deceased, claims he saw him with a woman. Christ, he could even be the fucking killer! Tried to throw us off the scent." A further idea germinating, roots forming, maturing. "There has been too much inside bullshit in this case. Fucking Holmes protecting Amy Meadows. Chappell keeping his so-called witness away from the station, away from scrutiny." Creating a space for the name below the others, expanding the suspect list, smaller letters to fit into the limited space on the flipchart page.

Under the newly added heading 'Next' retaining the green pen, he bracketed the listed previous suspects, Jenny Coleman, Susan Grey, Jasmine Kemp, Ruth McGarvey, Amy Meadows, using a cursive bracket to group the names, annotating the link with 'ID Parade', further adding 'Expanded Alibi'.

Nodding her agreement, enjoying the opportunity to brainstorm with the new DS, no longer burdened by inferiority, she joined him beside the flipcharts. Opening an adjacent chart, leafing through the pages, she located a list of names, some marked with a red asterisk, others with a green exclamation mark, some without annotation. Pointing at the list. "This is where we start. Those you marked in green, we interview first, plus the witness, plus that Vodafone guy. The Guv had a concern about him; even I thought he was a tool. Plus, the original suspects, of course."

Doris deliberated briefly. "Okay. You start inviting these new suspects to come to the station, today or tomorrow. Any resistance, we send some uniforms round to bring them in. I'll set up the ID parade, invite the ladies to come back and see us, bring our witness in. Once he does that, we question him. I can get his details from Chappell. I imagine Miss Meadows will not be happy about returning here. It will be interesting to see if she enlists DS Holmes for assistance. This is good."

Tasks assigned, they returned to their desks, working together yet separately, a common goal uniting their disparate activity. Beecham, quietly impressed with McGarry, brought in for her case familiarity, accentuating her involvement with relevant observation, her potential further apparent. McGarry, appreciating the DS's intention to be more thorough, prepared to take the necessary time, willing to consider her input, welcoming his involving personality.

"I've found the complete contact details for the witness, and his mum. Isn't that weird?"

"Thanks, Flick, scribble them down for me. I'll chase him, try to get him in here soonest."

Taking a toilet break, DS Beecham released tension with his urine, his exhaling breath transforming into a satisfied sigh. Having held on almost too long, the act of urination became enjoyable, a peculiarly male reaction to a natural function. Thoughts continued to percolate, less scrambled than before, the likely challenge of recalling all five female suspects to the station welcomed, the confrontations eagerly anticipated.

His reverie was brought to an abrupt end by the voice of DS Holmes seeking his attention. "Doris. A word?"

Staring ahead, replying, "You'll need to wait, Terry; see you upstairs."

Hearing Holmes come closer. "I think you might prefer this conversation to be private."

Shaking before zipping up, turning to confront his equally ranked colleague, he asked "Okay. What's so urgent I can't enjoy a leak in peace?"

Several inches shorter than Doris, Terry couldn't muster any sense of physical intimidation. "Did you advise the Bangkok Massage to close today, to prevent the execution of my search warrant? I heard you on the phone this morning. It took me a while to put it together. Are you the immortal Commissioner Graham?"

"Fuck off, Terry."

"Is that all you've got? What am I going to find? That you spend time there getting your rocks off. Or is it deeper? Are you assisting an immoral industry to avoid police detection? Is it money, sex, what?"

"Informants."

"What?"

"I have a couple of informants working there. Providing the occasional snippets of information. That probably never crossed your mind, eh? Jump straight to conclusions. Assume the worst. Sometimes you are a total wanker."

Suddenly unsure, hesitating. "You expect me to believe everything is above board? You're not dipping your wick in the honey pot, in exchange for protection?"

"That's no business of yours. I'm divorced, making me single. Who loses sleep wondering whether or not I enjoy a massage on occasion? Who bloody cares if I get a complimentary happy ending? It's none of your concern."

"I care. I care if your behaviour impedes my investigation. You tipped these people off about my warrant, which impacted my investigation. You just got promoted, why the hell would you risk that for a quick wank?" Thrown off balance by the lack of denial.

"Really. You are one to talk, you dozy bastard. Impacted my investigation?" His voice imitating Terry's, the parody perfect. "What about you and your girlfriend providing Amy Meadows with a false alibi? No impact there? You needn't look so surprised; of course, I know the alibi is pure bullshit. Shall we get this all on the table? Sort through this right now. Before I put your head down that toilet and flush you away." Threat spoken, absent of any emotion.

"Are you serious?"

"Yes, to both assertions."

Confronting one another, righteous indignation and defensive concerns on both sides.

"Okay, why?"

Doris raised his left hand, fingers closed. "One." His pinkie raised. "I enjoy a nice massage; it helps me relax. Note I say massage, nothing else. Two." Ring finger uncurling. "I have an informant within the premises who has been valuable in the past. Three." Middle finger extending, the impact lessened by two adjacent fingers. "It's a bullshit warrant with no probable cause. Using a warrant to ask about a possible customer. How the fuck did you get away with that?"

"I'm following a trail in a possible murder. I do whatever needs to be done."

"Possible murder? When you and I discussed it, you weren't sure what the fuck it was. Murder or thrill sex?"

"No confirmation. Still awaiting the FP report. Until then, I keep an open mind and follow the leads."

Beecham referred to the massage facility, offering an olive branch. "What do you need from the warrant? I'll get it for you. List of questions, photos, whatever. Quick and easy."

"How about you take me there, get me in and allow me to do my job?"

"Yeah, that works. But here's the thing. Going into a massage parlour in the morning will yield you the square root of fuck all. If you want to learn anything, you go in during the evening, when they are busy, when the girls are all there, when they want to avoid any distractions in front of the customers."

"Seems to me you know way too much about these activities."

Doris reacted to the insult. "You know, you might be correct. Or it may just be that I am a much better policeman than you, with more experience, more awareness of people and more insight. You know, the police skills that they can't teach you from a textbook. The skills, in my opinion, that you just don't fucking have."

At an impasse, neither entirely comfortable, facing each other, conflict in the atmosphere, antagonism overcoming the background reek of toilet smells. Neither willing to concede, both considering compromise.

"So, will you take me there, tonight? Get me the access I need?" Terry, voice a half octave lower, anger relegated to the background of his tone.

"I can. But I want something from you. I want to know if the alibi your young lady gave to Amy Meadows is genuine. Trade?"

Taking a moment, selecting his words, seeking an appropriate explanation. "I have doubts about the accuracy of the alibi." His deadpan delivery appropriate. "I can't say more."

DS Beecham regarded DS Holmes, both suited and booted, surrounded by porcelain, paper, and piss. Undisturbed by any third party. "So, where does this leave us, Terry?"

"If you can resolve my issues re the warrant, if I can get the information I need, then I see no reason why your relation to the massage parlour needs to be raised or mentioned at all."

"To nobody. Yes? Your word?"

"Agreed. But I have a condition. A *fait accompli* to offer."

"Go ahead."

"If you reach a situation in your case where you can overturn the alibi given to Amy Meadows, even if you are only close to doing so, then you contact me and you allow Holly to come in and advise you that she was mistaken on the dates provided in her alibi. You give her the opportunity to clear herself before you close on Amy Meadows. Those are my terms." Folding his arms, indicating an air of finality, Terry waited for Doris's agreement.

Doris thought this was an acceptable compromise. It was workable, an honourable draw. He wanted a win; his dislike of Terry Holmes having grown during this confrontation. Poised to accept, he asked a further question. "Where is the weak link in the alibi? Where should I start?"

Terry, close to a conclusion, uncaring of Amy's fate, offered, "Her hair colour. Get access to her phone, selfies, Cloud, whatever. It's inconsistent. Failing that, I would look at how Holly made her way to and from Amy's apartment. Car? Taxi? Public transport? Proof, or lack thereof."

"I think we have a deal. Seven thirty tonight. Outside the chippie about a hundred yards from the massage place. Bring your photos and anything else because this is a one-time access. If any future access is required, you come through me." Agreement secured, a handshake unnecessary, they escaped the toilets, heading outside for fresh air, Terry through the rear door, Doris via reception as he thought to himself, 'I knew it. I fucking knew it. Lying bitches.'

Fourteen
Tuesday, 12th February

Barry Chappell and his forensic investigation resources were fastidious. Completely closing the layby, the area abundantly taped, they were dressed in paper suits as they trawled the ground, performing a precision fingertip search. Anything of marginal interest marked with a numbered tag and routinely photographed. All data assimilated, the potential value yet to be discovered. An area of grass on the verge, close to the tarmac, demonstrating clear signs of a struggle. Heel marks in the softer areas of ground, unexpected fibres, suspected bodily fluids, blood, vomit and more. Beyond the fence at the place where the body had been discovered, the ground was almost buried in tags, evidence abundant. They were now bagging and tagging, Barry demanding everything be carefully annotated, ensuring any prospect of a mistake was eliminated. Following procedure to the letter.

The site investigation complete, the evidence stored for transport, he invited the troops to head back to the station. Dialling Emyr, who sounded weary when he answered, he expressed his appreciation. "All done. Your guys were awesome. Found lots of stuff; just need to try to process it quickly. Thanks for helping."

"Glad to hear that, much appreciated. Not like Holmes, who was critical of the lads yet expects our undivided support. Anyway, got a bit of bad news for you. We had the semen compared to our database, but no hit, I'm afraid, so not an existing pervert. What we do know is that the killer will have a severely scratched face. We found a lot of skin extracted from under the fingernails. The next watch will be asked to look out for anyone scratched to bits; best we can do for now."

"Thanks. Do we know who she is yet?"

"No hits on her fingerprints, no identity documentation, no belongings discovered. All we suspect is that she is from Thailand, and that's only based on the pathologist. Complete mystery. I'm wondering if she has been a victim of people traffickers — just my gut feeling."

"I'm with you on that. What industries smuggle Thai women? Massage and prostitution. But she really didn't look the type."

"Follow the evidence, then follow the money. Tried and tested. Got to go. Cheers."

****

Standing in the car park, in an area frequented by smokers, Terry reflected on his exchange with Doris. On the upside, he would get access to the masseuses and had negotiated a level of protection for Holly. On the downside, he had likely sacrificed Amy to Doris's suspicions and damaged his relationship with a fellow detective sergeant.

Hearing an incoming SMS, he checked the screen. Holly. 'What do you want for dinner tonight?' About to reply, a further message: 'Nude? Wrapped in a towel? Mini skirt and stockings?' He remained astounded by her recent behaviour, swaying between confrontational and insatiable. Again, he intended to compose a response, interrupted by another incoming: 'Not sure why I asked. Stockings it is.'

Frustrated, fearful of telling her he would be home late, he wondered if she could retain the horny for an extra hour or two. 'Sounds amazing. Might be late at work. Will come as quick as I can. Xoxo.'

A few minutes passing, the inevitable beep. 'Piss off then, toss yourself off before you come home. No dinner for you. See you next Tuesday.'

Unable to compose a response, he dejectedly returned to his desk, consoling himself with the knowledge that Holly could change her mood in an instant. There remained some chance he would see stockings tonight.

Seeing an email from a former colleague at Bradford, he double-clicked, reading the wordy message. Intrigued, he opened the PDF attachment, initially skimming the document. Repeating the exercise more carefully, he absorbed the content, registering the impact, gaining insight into Mark Forrest, thought-provoking and concerning. Sending the attachment to the communal printer, he went back to the email text.

Following a brief polite introduction, he read that Sandra Forrest had separated from her husband eight months before. At that time, she had raised a request for a restraining order against her husband, citing domestic violence against her person. No charges were ever made, resulting in the request being denied by the court. A month later, she reported being verbally assaulted in a public place, fearing for the safety of her daughter and herself. Witnesses confirmed the severity of the verbal abuse, although charges again were not laid. Days later, she applied for a protection order for her daughter, citing concerns of her estranged husband's behaviour in the company of their daughter, thinly veiled suggestions of improper expressions, distasteful comments and threats. The daughter was eleven at the time and had informed the social workers that she was frightened by her father. On this occasion, the courts granted the order, although Mark Forrest was not placed on any register.

Composing a professionally grateful reply, adding an element of personal interchange, Terry hit Send.

Processing the information, he related it to his case. Certainly, there were circumstances which could induce depression, lending support to the suicide option. Much of the content indicated the deceased to be unpleasant and liable to outbursts of anger, providing potential reasons for revenge, lending credence to the murder option. Unsubstantiated insinuations about his relationship with his daughter added unwelcome complications. Making a trip to the kettle, he collected the print-out, re-ingesting the official report.

Sipping the lukewarm hot chocolate, he concluded that none of the death options could be eliminated.

****

Amy admired the dress, the way it sat on her body, already committed to the purchase. Her intention had been to find something she could wear day to day. Discovering the essential little black dress had been accidental, fitting as if designed for her. She remained reluctant to remove the garment, her vanity rendering her arms useless, her toes tiring from supporting her weight, simulating the higher heels she would wear to complement her new outfit.

Completing her exorbitant purchase, prohibiting further spending, she left the shopping centre to walk to her next destination. Enjoying the exercise, she welcomed the occasional appreciative glance confirming her rather excellent day.

Arriving at her former place of work, she hesitated for a few seconds before entering.

She was greeted by Brenda, the youngest of the waitresses, friendly, immature, welcoming. "Hi, Amy. How are you? Welcome back."

"Hey, Brenda, I'm okay. How are you, and the other girls?"

"Oh, we're okay. She hasn't been in much since you faced her down. But she is through in the back of the café."

Feeling some satisfaction, Amy asked, "Can you ask her to come out? We need to speak."

Brenda expressed a momentary concern, her ebullient enthusiasm returning immediately. "She left instructions that she would not see you. Absolutely not. But we should give you an envelope from the drawer. I'll fetch it."

Suddenly alone, feeling slightly awkward, aware of the other diners' attention being drawn to her, the customer not being shown to a table, curious if unconcerned. Receiving the brown envelope from Brenda, she became amused, wondering if anybody suspected her of receiving a bribe, perhaps a microfilm in an espionage movie. Revealing the contents, reading the folded sheet of paper transcribed with an explanation of the calculation, corresponding exactly with the cash contained, everything per her entitlement.

"Thanks, Brenda." She leant forward, giving the younger woman a hug.

"What are you doing on Friday?" Without pause, providing no opportunity for a response, Brenda continued, "There's a party thing at a pub I go to regularly. Why don't you come? Have a few drinks together, check out the talent?"

Amy resisted her eager friend. "Maybe, but unlikely. I have a new boyfriend, so I'm hoping he will take me out on Friday. But if not, then maybe." Avoiding outright rejection, leaving the door ajar.

"Okay. I'll text you the time and place. Reply me if you're coming. I hope you can. See you."

****

Felicia McGarry prepared to leave the station, having had a fruitful day on the restarted case. Feeling valued, she had changed in the locker room, releasing her growing hair, her skin-tight jeans capitalising on her height and proportions, attracting some surprised looks from the front office. Surprise or appreciation? She planned to head into Chester directly to catch happy hour at the Liverpool.

"On the pull?" She had not heard Doris arrive beside her.

"Depends. Have a good evening, sir."

DS Beecham meandered to the incident room, the revelation from Terry fresh in his mind. Unable to officially include it in the file and unwilling to share with Flick, he nevertheless permitted the news to influence his thinking. *Amy Meadows. Watch yourself.*

He made the call to the witness. Reticent, the witness was reserved, objecting to attendance at the police station, claiming work pressure. Familiar with this process, Doris reminded him of his civic responsibility, suggested appreciation for his compliance, veiling a threat regarding mandatory attendance. Eventually, he gained agreement for him to present at nine tomorrow morning, confirming one hour maximum would be required.

Armed with this commitment, he easily achieved agreement with Susan Grey and Jasmine Kemp. Supplying a precis of their role, endorsing their innocence, simply following procedure, they both agreed to attend at nine.

The conversation with Ruth McGarvey was fraught with tension. Adamant she would not attend, she threatened legal action, claimed harassment, protested about her previous treatment and her false arrest. Maintaining a calm demeanour, he encouraged her support, suggested her assistance could only benefit her outstanding charge in Cheshire. Permitting her to bring her lawyer should she choose to do so. Eventually achieving her consent to participate.

Receiving no answer from Amy Meadows, he tried Jenny Coleman. The lively persona he had witnessed on video, especially when Terry interviewed her, demonstrably absent. She displayed her indignance, her assumption that she was free from this situation. Firmly, he demanded she attend, intimating her continued involvement, her continuance as a person of interest. Overcoming her final objection, committing to send a car to her home at eight thirty to bring her to the station.

Shuddering with excitement, he made a further attempt to reach Amy Meadows. Succeeding, he heard the acute disappointment in her voice, pleasing him. Foreseeing her resistance, relishing the challenge, he was surprised at her acquiescence, the lack of drama extracting some of his gratification.

Reflecting on a successful hour, six people attending at nine tomorrow, the previously omitted identification parade scheduled for remedy.

****

The Mancunian arrived at his warehouse, still adorned in his motorcycle leathers, helmet, gloves on, visor down. Entering the building by the six-digit pin code, all heads turned to him, apprehensive, aware of him despite his dress. He performed a panoramic scan of the area, two restrained employees tied to chairs, four minders, two standing, two seated.

Removing the helmet, displaying unkempt hair, his face remained impassive.

"Nice of you to join us, Nesbo. Don't get up." He made a quarter turn to assess the other restrained employee. "Dai? Have you confessed yet?" Addressing the minders. "What have we got?"

"Nothing new, boss. They both broadly maintain their story, though Dai has suggested that Nesbo might be involved."

"I've had enough of this. Give them both a slap. Don't be gentle."

A large man stepped forward, muscles bulging beneath a tight dark blue tee-shirt, matching a bruise on his jaw. Without forewarning, he unleashed a right hand to the middle of Dai's face, rocking his head backwards, the recoiling face almost reconnecting with the fist. To his credit, Dai did not scream. He groaned at a moderate volume, issuing a small quantity of blood from his nose and mouth.

Sensing his own impending pain, Nesbitt screamed in advance, unable to prevent a similar punch distorting his face, snapping his neck to the rear, the off-centre impact turning his head to the right. His hands wrestled with the binding, the reflex futile, incapable of providing comfort to his pain-ravaged face. Spitting blood, his chin sagging.

"Now ask them again. I'm going to change." Walking away.

Entering a room designed as a warehouse office, housing two metallic desks, two barely cushioned chairs, a small filthy window and a grey three-drawer filing cabinet in the corner. The linoleum floor was torn in several places. Clipboards hung, attached to cup hooks on the wall, wrinkled documentation attached via the spring clamp. *What a total dump. Needs cleaning. I'll tell the boys before I leave.* Placing his gloves and helmet on a desk, he began the laborious process of removing the leather jacket and trousers, needing the opportunity to reduce his core temperature. Sweat dripped from behind his ears, his neck saturated.

Contact with their friendly policeman had failed to materialise. Aware of his regularity at the Wrexham facility, he called Mama San Nan, informing her of his wish to speak to the copper, reminding her not to issue his mobile number. With the instructions delivered and his temperature approaching normal, he selected a Diet Coke and a Sprite from the fridge, removing the corrugated lids from the bottles. Returning to the warehouse, he was aware of his entry provoking a negative reaction from Nesbitt, while Harris remained impassive. Damaged but impassive, almost admirable in the circumstances.

"Is there anything either of you would like to tell me?" Waiting for a response, expecting nothing, proven correct. "Untie their hands." He gestured confirmation of his instruction. "Remember, lads, if you try to run, we will take you down, so let's be sensible here. I want to explain something to you." He sat on a vacant chair, holding the untouched drinks, observing their reactions as their limbs were released, the standard stretching, shaking, accompanied with mumbled moans. Stepping forward, he handed the Cola to Dai, the green bottle to Nesbo. Waiting for them to drink, indicating they should, restricting his internal fury, intimating they should drink more, rewarded with their compliance.

"The lady you collected from the truck, the mature woman who seated herself in the front of the Volvo, a woman who is tragically no longer with us, was a personal friend. Madame Nattaporn and I met in Thailand, some four years ago, give or take." Making a semi-rotation of his straight hand. "I invited her to come here to assist in the development of my business. I even applied for a visa for her, legally. But that was rejected because she is from beyond the European Union, and her university qualifications are unrecognised by the UK. She was not a massage girl, not even a madam. Her role would have been at my office, helping me redesign our chain of parlours. She had intentions to brighten the décor, install open-view massage chairs in the receptions, make the outlets welcome to both genders, to reduce the somewhat murky reputation that we have." He smiled, seemingly amused at his admission. "I blame myself. I should have collected her from the truck. I should not have left her to be transported with the working girls. It was late, I was tired, I was lazy. I will live with this regret for the remainder of my natural life." Taking to his feet, he turned away from the gathered men, suggesting his sadness, potentially displaying weakness, turning again to face them with his features distorted in anger, his next words spoken loudly, with venomous intent. "She was not for fucking!"

Nesbo and Dai flinched as he approached them, anticipating assault. Instead, he removed the drinks from their grasp, carefully, using napkins, retreating to place the bottles on a vacant chair. Further lowering his tone, the menace clear. "If I can prove either of you fucked her…" The remainder of the sentence unsaid; the inference clear.

Fifteen
Tuesday, 12th February

Uneasy allies, Doris and Terry met outside the nominated chip shop, the emanating odour of vinegar inviting, initiating hunger reflexes, competing with resistance of the calorific content.

Walking together to Bangkok Massage, Terry shortened his stride, inviting Doris to enter first. Upon entry, the lady at reception greeted the larger policeman with hysterical delight, effusive joy at seeing him. An inordinately warm welcome extinguished instantly on seeing Terry, instantly cold to his presence.

"Madame Nan, please don't be concerned. This is my colleague. He needs to ask a few questions." Holding his hand higher, quashing her interruption. "He has no interest in this business, nor in the ladies, nor in what goes on inside."

Joining the conversation, uninvited. "I only want to ask you about the man in the photograph. Nothing else."

"Mister Graham. You know we respect our customers. We are private. This is not good for our customer. He will be angry with us. He may not come back."

Concurring visually, Doris explained. "Nan, the man is dead. He cannot be angry with you. We," indicating Terry, "are trying to find the person responsible for his death. We have some doubt about the death being accidental." Adding a lopsided grin. "Can we ask the girls? We won't interrupt their business."

Complying, she offered, "Okay. You can take an empty room; wait there. I will send the girls to you when they have quiet time. Having the police in reception is bad for business." Fixing Terry with a look, suggesting his stupidity. "If you had told me the man is dead, I would have allowed you access when you first came here. Remember for next time."

She led them to a room furnished with a double bed, two chairs and an unmatching bedside table. A pile of blankets along with several towels lay on the bed, as well as a wooden tray holding bottles containing a variety of massage oils and related lubricants. A solitary discarded condom foil lay on the floor below the nearly level wall mirror. "You can wait here, Sergeant Holmes. Mister Graham, please come back with me. I have someone who wishes to speak with you."

Abandoned in the massage room, Terry hastily appraised his surroundings, conceding the contents were in accordance with an adult massage experience, his earlier suspicions confirmed by the condom wrapper, an exclamation point provided by the smell of stale ejaculate. Having no desire to sit on the bed, not wishing to stick to the sheets, he sat on the nearest chair, muttering, "Why does anyone come to a place like this?" Wishing his erstwhile colleague would return, hearing the door open, the entrant at once challenging his established opinion.

A young Asian lady entered, petite, with everything in proportion. Wearing a tight white tee-shirt with a wraparound multi-coloured sarong, the join providing glimpses of a shapely leg. Barefoot, she wore her long black hair pulled behind her head, swirled to appear over one shoulder, flowing downwards to cover one breast. She gave a small bow as she raised clasped hands towards her face, indicating her respect.

Now aware of at least one reason to come here, he invited her to take the other seat, appreciating her delicate movement, his concentration drifting. "Can you tell me your name, please?"

Initially reluctant, clearly present under instruction, she answered softly. "My name is Hoi. H.O.I."

"Is that your full name, or a nickname?" Engaging, seeking clarification.

"My name is Hoi. In Thailand, we use our short name." Spoken quietly, clearly, lightly accented.

Enduring her limited response, he progressed the interview, introducing the photo of the deceased, inviting her to look, revealing her familiarity with this man. "His name is Mark. He is a regular customer. I don't like him."

Encouraged by her openness, asking, "Why do you say that? Is he violent?"

Shaking her head, her expression close to a smile. "No, not violent, he is not crazy. We have protection against violence." Deferring a response, he waited for her to continue. "He always wants boom-boom, after massage." Placing one pointing finger within a circle formed by her opposite thumb and forefinger. "He wants to do it every time, not happy with regular happy ending. He always asks for the youngest girl. I am the youngest girl. He is not gentle. He tries to pay lower price after agreement. He is not a good man."

Interest piqued, ignoring her blatant admission of providing sex for money. "How many times would you say he came to you, for boom-boom?"

"Many times. Nearly every week. After the first time, he complained I have too much hair, ask Mama San to make me shave for him. He said he would pay more, but he only paid the same." Intending to guide the conversation, a question forming, hearing her continue. "He always asks not to wear the condom." Seeing his expression conveying his shock, she misunderstood his reaction, attempted to remedy her confession. "Sometimes, he takes off his condom, tries to finish in my mouth, but I don't like."

He asked further questions, learning little about his victim. The relationship was transactional, nothing else. She did not know his surname, his occupation or personal details. Pillow talk was clearly not part of the package. He asked the only remaining relevant question. "How old are you, Hoi?"

Relieved to hear her say, "Seventeen."

Giving his thanks, he released her to her duties, warmed by her smile and excessively excellent manners, saddened at the role she had to play in this establishment. Terry made notes, summarising what he had heard, aligning it with the report he had received from Bradford, confused as to where the revelations led him in terms of the case.

The following two ladies provided little about Mark to progress the investigation. Jum, older but still attractive, with ridiculously long hair, had seen him but never provided any service for him. Joy, with a fuller figure and a naughty smile, had massaged him on a single occasion, denying her provision of additional services, suggesting his interest lay only in the younger girls.

Wondering where Doris had disappeared to, he contemplated everything he had learned, wishing some of it had failed to penetrate his consciousness.

DS Beecham had been taken behind the reception counter, advised by Mama San Nan that an important man wished to talk with him on the landline. She had stressed the importance of taking the call, revealing little more. He had a suspicion about the purpose, possibly thanking him for his warning about the search warrant, mentally preparing to be magnanimous. Looking away, permitting her to press the numbers, waiting for the connection to be made.

"Sir, Commissioner Graham is here." She held the receiver for him to take. Placing the ancient device to his ear, listening, detecting the sound of breath, followed by words. "It's Ian." The voice familiar from previous occasions.

"What can I do for you?" Undecided whether there was a pause or a delay on the line, holding.

"I am hoping we can do something for one another. You are aware of the dead woman found on the side of the road?" Assuming concurrence, continuing. "Is there useful DNA on the body?"

Doris replied, "I am not involved in that case. It would be improper of me to divulge details to an outside party. What's your interest?"

"Have you identified her yet? Do you have a suspect for her murder?"

"As I said, I am not involved, have little knowledge, and could not reveal that to you if I did. Sorry. I doubt I can help you here. Do you have information pertinent to the case?"

"How about we offer mutual assistance. An acquaintance of mine has identified as possible, I stress possible, involvement in the cause of death. I can provide you with a sample of DNA for comparison purposes. If it is unrelated, no foul. If it matches, then you have a breakthrough. How does that sound?"

Considering the implications, Doris raised the obvious question. "What's in it for you?"

"I could give you some bullshit about my civic responsibility, supporting our excellent police force. Or just admit that I might want this piece of crap removed from circulation. All I ask is that I get feedback on the DNA. A yes or no. Does that seem fair?"

"Let me get this right. You only want to know if there is a DNA match, nothing else?"

"I will be providing you with two samples. I need to know if there is a match, and which one is the match. That is all I need."

Seeing an opportunity to assist in breaking a high-profile case, failing to detect any negative impact, he agreed. "Fine, I'm in. How do I obtain the DNA?"

"Simple enough. When you leave my premises, head back to Chester along the A483, stop at the layby where the body was found. My man will meet you there and give you the samples. Do I have your word you won't attempt to detain the messenger? I need your commitment. His vehicle will be sporting false plates, so don't waste your time tracing the registration."

"Agreed. We should be leaving within an hour."

"I assume Madame Nan has been supportive of your requirements?"

"She has, as always." The old-fashioned click signalling the end of the conversation.

Walking towards the door, preferring to leave Holmes to conduct his own investigation, seeking a modicum of privacy, he made a call to Llay reception. Identifying himself, he asked for the investigating detectives on the roadside murder case, advised that DI Jones was leading, assisted by DS Chappell. Thanking the duty lady, he cursed Chappell's involvement, contemplating his options. A little brown nosing with the DI, mend a few fences with the DS; either way, DS Beecham wins.

Nan proffered an ornate glass containing a vaguely clear liquid, the odour reminiscent of jasmine. Taking it with good grace, shrugging his substantial shoulders, tasting, blowing, mouthing 'hot'.

Unable to justify his absence further, he joined his colleague in the inactive massage room. Entering, identifying distress in Terry's features, he avoided the bed, remaining on his feet, enquiring, "How goes it?"

The reply immediate. "Brilliant and effing awful at the same time. I'm almost done. Can you get the Mama San to talk to me as we leave?"

Interrupted by the arrival of another masseuse, another young one, barely older than Hoi. "Hi. What's your name?" Terry maintaining his professionalism despite a growing sense of repugnance at the exploitation of these young women.

"Pui. P.U.I."

Adjusting the order of questioning. "How old are you, Pui?"

Her response brief, instant. "Nineteen."

Upturning the photo of Mark, his image clear. "Do you know this man?"

Unusually, she lifted the photograph, giving an impression of concentration. "Yes, he is a customer." Placing the photo back on the table. "This man is not nice, asking me to wear clothes he brought with him. He promised to pay higher price. I said no."

"Oh, Jesus." Doris watched in dismay as Holmes extracted further evidence of a fantasy sex life, thankful when the interview ended. "I see what you meant now. Are you sure you want any more?"

"Might as well. I'm never going to sleep tonight anyway."

Fortunately, the interchange with Mama San Nan was brief, providing testimonial confirmation of the claims made inside, adding miniscule extra information. Remembering his manners and his commitment, he offered his gratitude to the Mama San, promising to stay away as he made his way to the external door, desperate to escape from the premises.

Arriving at the cars, Terry watched Doris enter the chippie, figuring he may as well join him. Burdened by two generous fish suppers, they ate in the elderly Mazda, exchanging token conversation, each absorbed in separate thoughts. The chips were excellent; handmade and chunky, soaked in vinegar, adequately salted and hot. In contrast, the fish was coated in a soggy batter coating limp flakes of grey fish, infirm flesh from something barely related to cod, clearly cooked earlier and reheated.

Doris deliberately failed to mention his planned rendezvous, settling for a strained goodnight, their earlier confrontation remembered in the absence of suspects or witnesses to interview.

Terry watched him go, belatedly entering his own car, desiring sanctuary and distraction from the statements tonight. Trying not to picture Hoi naked, seeking to control his impulses. The Ford roared into life, attracting looks from the chippie customers. He made his way home.

Seeing the motorcycle as he drove into the layby, Doris assumed this was his contact, flashing his lights as the Mazda came to a halt. The rider stayed on the bike, pointing towards a package seemingly abandoned on the verge. Doris left his car, stepping to the plastic carrier bag, looking inside before touching, absorbing the image: two soft drink bottles, each enclosed in separate transparent zip-lock envelopes. Continuing to avoid contact with the evidence, he addressed the messenger.

"Is this from Ian?"

Raising the visor, allowing limited access to his features, he pointed again at the package. "This is the DNA comparison package, as promised. Take it. I can't leave until you do."

"Thanks for the confirmation. I need to follow the evidence protocols and tag these items. It's going to take a few minutes."

Dropping the visor, lingering on the saddle, offering no indication of a desire to depart, the messenger watched the policeman extract an assortment of paraphernalia from the boot of his car. Plastic bags, marker pens, gloves, dust mask. Watching, he had zero desire to anger the big boss, overcoming his distaste of forcibly remaining in the policeman's presence.

Placing everything in his car, Doris signalled his completion, before starting the hoarse engine, pulling ahead into the empty road, aware of the bike having ignited, observing movement in the rear-view mirror. Transaction complete, he detoured to the Llay facility, submitting the evidence to the shift forensic investigator. Providing an explanation, anonymous tip-off, DNA comparison, for the attention of DI Jones and DS Chappell, two items. His final task, a text message to Chappell: 'Tip off on your case, DNA at Llay, two bottles, compare to the semen on your victim. Let me know if there is a match. Doris.' He should have phoned but preferred to avoid direct contact, alluding to their strained relationship.

Sixteen
Wednesday, 13th February

Listening to her significant other wash himself while releasing an occasional bubble fart from the shower, Holly contemplated getting out of bed to begin her heavily scheduled day. A full day at work, an evening with Amy and whatever may come after.

Terry had arrived home earlier than she had expected in the previous evening. His revelation that he would work late had mightily pissed her off, especially as she had intimated her desire by offering to wear stockings for him. Hearing his car pull into the garage, her itch unscratched, she had restored the sheer black stockings to her legs, swept her abundant hair into a wild frenzy and lain otherwise naked on top of their bed, showcasing her hour-glass curves, the central heating ensuring she avoided hypothermia.

He had come immediately upstairs, more in hope than expectation, walking into their room, seeing her. Stripping frantically, he had dropped beside her, his interest and intention clearly visible, finding her body reciprocating that interest, ready, willing, welcoming, warm.

He was unaware of her early-evening activity, considering himself the source of her sexual anticipation. Ignorant of her extended use of a pornography website where she had researched examples of girl on girl, a precaution against inexperience should Amy be receptive to her advances, should she make those advances. The predominant activity had appeared to be reciprocal oral, accompanied by absurd levels of moaning, the participants adorned in make-up probably applied by trainees from clown college. To maintain balance, she had also watched some regulation heterosexual porn with the obligatory ridiculous plot, amused at the surgically enhanced breasts, astonished at the inappropriately proportioned male. Despite the dubious quality, she had found herself stimulated by the content.

She had no insight into his motivation, the impression that had been made on him by the young massage girl, his arousal inspired by her relaxed attitude to physical pleasure accentuated by her stunning appearance. Dismissing his concerns regarding her treatment, her situation, he had wondered how much she charged as he spent a considerable percentage of the journey home imagining Hoi naked.

Their joining had been immediate, foreplay surplus to requirement, the act regulation, missionary, familiar. His moves predictable, her response encouraging, a solid performance, mutual satisfaction achieved without undue effort.

Recalling his little squeal at the end, she reminded herself of the need to have an elongated douche, to make herself clean and fragrant, to ensure no embarrassment if Amy decided to go down on her. No need for a spunky residue to infringe on the moment.

Seventeen
Wednesday, 13th February

The time had slipped past eight o'clock on a horrid winter morning. The night sky had evolved to a dark grey, before returning to an ominous shade of black. The rain had transformed from initial droplets to an angry, intense wall of water, vindictively smashing into all surfaces, drenching everything in its way. Inflicting misery as it overpowered any residual morning happiness.

The *Leader*'s reporter remained ensconced in his vehicle, his vision impeded by the torrent, the windscreen wipers battling to cope. His visual monitoring of activity at the local police station was being restricted by the seasonably normal weather. Nilesh sipped lukewarm tea, his flask having failed to maintain the original boiling temperature. The sugar assisted the flavour, the milk irksome in the cooling brew.

Having received complimentary feedback from the editor, he had permission to follow up on his story. Yesterday had been wasted at this location, seeing nothing of interest. He had been unable to access any detectives, and comments were not forthcoming from the press office. His scheduled commitment this morning wasn't until eleven, an assignment at Wrexham Football Club, a press conference likely to announce a change of manager, as if anybody cared, but mandatory coverage for a Wrexham-headquartered newspaper.

A small Toyota hatchback pulled into the staff car park, his carefully selected location allowing him a direct line of sight into that area, the rain blurring his view without obliterating it. Watching the occupants extract themselves from the vehicle, running for the secure rear entrance, he was amazed that the compact vehicle could deposit five adult females from its limited capacity. Four of the females were dressed in active wear, without coats, implying recent gym activity, perhaps arriving directly from there. Instinct aroused, attention refocused.

Constable Felicia McGarry, continuing her CID secondment, led the trail of women across a minimal stretch of car park, laughing as her dishevelled friends fought a losing battle to remain dry, the inclement conditions hindering progress. Her requirement to enter the password a second time meeting with high-pitched protests. Hardly an auspicious start. She had persuaded the ladies to come to the station, to act as distractions in the forthcoming group identification parade. Her reasoning was sound, the suspect being a slim brunette, the Pilates class containing numerous examples of the slim brunette, including herself, albeit barely. They had willingly agreed, strangely excited at the prospect of being involved in the investigative process. Five gym bunnies, five suspects, two other constables already drafted, the round dozen as determined by PACE.

Minutes later, a liveried Heddlu hatchback delivered another clone: young, slim, dark-haired, already damp as she was led through the secured entrance. Six extremely similar-looking women at a police station, attractive-looking generally, if you liked slim women. *Interesting!* His preference was for a rounded figure, something to hold on to, something to keep you warm in these freezing winter nights.

Further people arrived at and departed from the station, force and civilian, understandable at this time of the day. Diverting his attention to the main entrance, he spotted a couple arriving, the woman barely discernible but familiar, her male companion unimportant. Another brunette, another clone, perhaps older. The woman from the press conference, Ruth McGarvey. The one charged then released in that murder case. Her husband with her. He wondered why she would be here, having been exonerated only days ago, in a blaze of publicity. "What is going on?" he wondered aloud. An abundance of similar-looking women arriving at a police station, early morning. "Identity parade?" Confident he had uncovered something, his energy levels inflated, his tea forgotten, he intensified his attention towards the public entrance of Mold police station.

The next arrival came on foot, suitably drenched due to being unsuitably dressed, her uncovered hair darkened by moisture, contrasting with her pale complexion, dismissed as unconnected by the journalist. Followed by two concurrent arrivals, again similar-looking, dark-haired, needing to eat a decent meal, in his humble opinion. They exchanged words at the doorway, braving the elements, perhaps a greeting, maybe words they preferred the police did not hear.

Glancing back to the staff car park, he observed the entrance door swinging closed, raising the possibility that he had missed somebody important. He decided to wait for the departure of Ruth McGarvey, planning to approach her to ask the questions the readers demanded, to determine today's circumstances and report them after suitable embellishment. Rearranging his position within the car, entirely immersed in the situation, foreseeing development in his story, Nilesh exercised his renowned patience.

Within the station, Doris regarded the chaos before him. Stereotyping on a gender basis, he supposed that herding twelve women into a room would be an achievement akin to corralling two hundred wild horses on a five-hundred-acre estate. The situation was complicated by the initial need to maintain separation between the suspects and the decoys, having to explain the process twice, similar words with an altered emphasis. Abandoning Flick and her sequestered lady constables, he adjourned to interview room one, joining their star witness at the table. Sitting alongside to avoid any hint of conflict, he assumed he was issuing a sense of comfort by his presence.

"Thanks for coming in. DS Chappell sends his appreciation for your assistance." A lie, Chappell being ignorant of the man's presence, unaware of the procedure unfolding. "Are you sure you understand what we are about to do?"

The witness nodded, his growing hair partially obscuring one eye. "I just sit here and watch a room full of women through this window."

"That's correct. We are hoping you can identify the woman you saw with Jeremy Campbell-Foulkes on that Friday evening. The one he was kissing at the bus shelter. That's all we need from you; then we can let you get back to work."

"You know I didn't see her clearly?" His statement ended with a rising inflection, accentuating the inferred question. Technically true, he had limited sight of her that night although he had a better view the following morning as she spoke to his mum. The big copper had specifically mentioned the bus shelter so he would respond based on that.

Interpreting the expectations of the police usually resulted in complications.

Doris elaborated, seeking to improve his witness, without leading him. "You stated in your previous statement that the lady with Jeremy had long dark hair, a slim build, her facial profile suggested she was pretty. You intimated she was likely in her twenties."

"I also said she had amazing legs. Really nice shape, slim, high heels."

"Yes, you did. That is a subjective observation, which we cannot use in a court of law. You see amazing, another man might say skinny, or chubby. We have to concentrate on the indisputable facts. Is that clear?"

"Okay. I also told you what she was wearing." Recalling the short dark skirt, the pale blouse, lightweight jacket. Her nice bum. "Will the ladies be dressed in the same way?"

"We are unable to dictate what they wear. That would be sexist, regrettably. You know how things are nowadays, political correctness, media spotlight." Seeking to bond, establish a common opinion, unsuccessfully.

Along the corridor, Ruth McGarvey had Flick's attention. "Explain it to me again." Flick's mouth opened then shut as the irate former suspect continued, "I was released from here, wrongly accused, your top brass said. Fully exonerated, he said. So," drawing breath, preparing to unleash, "what the fuck am I doing here?" Preventing the police officer from responding. "I have proven my innocence, so what can anybody gain by my presence? Or perhaps you are just a bunch of vindictive bastards! Getting your kicks from making innocent people suffer?" No opportunity to speak, Flick internally commented, *Innocent, yet facing an assault charge in Cheshire.* The tirade continued. "I reiterate my objection to being here, in front of these witnesses," indicating the other women. "I would like to leave now, or you fuckers will be hearing from my lawyer!"

Amy Meadows and Jenny Coleman stood against the wall, watching the angry woman, seeing the constable battling to control herself. Sharing mixed emotions, they enjoyed the spectacle, nervous at the forthcoming exercise. "She must be the one they charged," whispered Jenny. "I was interviewed as well. I used to date the dead guy."

Sharing the intimate moment of reciprocal confidence, Amy admitted. "Me, too. I dated Jed as well; not for long, though. Luckily, I had an alibi."

Jenny looked at Amy, then Ruth, then Amy again, then the gathered crowd. "Seems old Jeddy boy had a type. We are quite similar-looking, most of us."

"Do you think they will ask us more questions? Eh…?" Inviting Jenny to reveal herself.

"Jenny. I was told they had a further question to ask me. I think we will be here for a while."

"I'm Amy. Nice to meet you, Jenny. I'm getting sick of this. But she must be furious." Pointing at Ruth.

"Tell you what, let's have some fun. If they ask us questions afterwards, we agree to say nothing. No comment to every question. I will if you will. That should make life annoying for them. They can't trip you up if you say nothing." Jenny's enthusiasm was infectious, akin to childlike.

"They can't trip you up if you are innocent, either. Okay. No comment to every question."

"Here we go." The assembled women were ushered into a room, suitable for a group of thirty, providing adequate space to mill around. They had been told to work the room during the preamble, instructed to move around, spending time at the rear as well as close to the window, where the witness sat assessing their similarity to whoever he had seen, hidden by the partition.

Behind the closed door, the suspects were immediately obvious. The decoys were infinitely more relaxed, secure in their non-involvement, exacting pleasure from the excitement as they casually circulated the room, concern absent from their expressions. The suspects, following primeval self-preservation, naturally drifted to the rear of the room, coming forward only when coaxed.

The witness and the detective watched from their secluded vantage point. The detective observing in abstract, following Amy Meadows, seeing others while dismissing them, taken by how different Jasmine Kemp looked, her fine blonde hair strikingly incongruous in this environment. The witness was impressed, reflecting on the quality of the ladies gathered before him, his interest drawn to the oddball, younger, blonde Jasmine, unknown to him, desirable, lovely.

"Anything?" Doris asked.

"Not yet." No need to rush, this was proving enjoyable, like his own personal beauty contest. The witness concentrated, squinting.

"What about this one?" Doris suggested, as Amy approached the viewing area. "She fits your description pretty closely."

Assessing her, medium-length hair tangled from the rain, clad in a warm sweater and jeans, flat shoes, accepting her similarity to the woman he had seen, but feeling something about her being incorrect. "She doesn't look right. Her hair is too short."

"Maybe she had a bloody haircut?" Allowing voice to his frustration, he unleashed at the witness, his behaviour indicative of bullying, possible to interpret as leading the witness, devaluing any positive identification which may be achieved.

"Not just that, she's not right. Now, maybe this one." He pointed at Jenny Coleman. "She looks familiar; I've definitely seen her before." He sat upright with triumph etched on his face.

"Keep watching. I'll make a note."

The group identification parade continued. The ladies within the room circulated, the novelty over, boredom entering their persona. The witness and the detective persisted with their observation, eliminating some candidates, motivation gradually declining, close to requiring a break, when the door behind them opened, revealing a woman in uniform.

"What's going on, Sergeant?"

Still adjusting to his new rank, Doris failed to respond immediately, hearing an unfriendly reminder. "Well?"

Standing, turning, confronted by the DCI from Wrexham. Straightening, demonstrating his respect for superior rank, he addressed the newcomer. "Ma'am. A group identification parade, Jeremy Campbell-Foulkes enquiry. This man witnessed the deceased sharing intimate moments with a young woman around the time of the murder."

"Did the witness see the murder take place?"

Replying. "No, Ma'am."

"Can he place the person he saw at the scene of the crime?"

Admitting. "No, Ma'am."

"Is it possible you are using the witness to confirm the sighting of a person whom you regard as a suspect?"

Denying. "No, Ma'am."

Choosing this inopportune moment to ring, Doris's mobile chirped, the vibration on the desk surface adding further noise. The DCI's words guiding his instinct to decline the call. "Do not answer that phone in my presence, Sergeant! Wrap this up! Now! Your old DI's office in five minutes!"

The witness failed to contain his amusement, seeing this hulk of a policeman being reprimanded like a child. By a woman. A smile escaped, captured, already noticed by the humiliated policeman. "You can go." Remembering etiquette. "North Wales Police thanks you for your co-operation." Escorting him to the reception area, he stopped on the way to instruct Flick to release the extra participants, reminding her to hold the five suspects. Advising her he had to see the DCI, he left her to handle everything, forgetting his intention to retain the witness for further questioning.

Entering the absent guv's office, he stood before the desk, awaiting the attention of the DCI.

"When you come to my office, you knock and wait to be invited before you enter. Is that clear?"

Stiffly. "Yes, Ma'am."

"What the fuck was that all about, downstairs?"

Confused. "Ma'am?"

"How many of those twelve participants were actually suspects?"

Informatively. "Five of them, Ma'am."

"Five? Five? Five out of twelve?"

Confirming. "Yes, Ma'am."

"For fuck sake, you can only have one per group of twelve. Any idiot knows that, or apparently not. Anything you gained from that event is null and void, do you realise that?"

Questioning. "Are you sure, Ma'am?"

"Tell me. Suppose your witness identified that little blonde girl as your suspect. Identified from a group of twelve, eleven of whom are dark-haired. How well do you think that would stand up in court?"

Defensively. "He didn't pick her. He picked another of our previous suspects. The blonde girl was interviewed before, her attendance was valid. Ma'am."

"Shut up with the fucking Ma'am. If you wanted to include her, she should have been placed in a group of similar-looking people. Same applies to everyone. Each suspect in a group of twelve, different group make-ups. Not this pile of crap. I saw three constables in there, so only four neutral decoys. Absolutely no chance of getting anything from that. Why?"

"The previous investigative team didn't do an ID parade of any kind. I thought I should correct that."

"The previous team, of which you were part, should have held an ID parade, subsequent to selecting Ruth McGarvey as the suspect you intended to charge. Doing it at that time would have been professionally sound, prudent and correct. Not doing it was negligent; doing it now, in this fashion, was bollocks."

He noticed that the DCI was prone to outbursts of profanity, sometimes inappropriately, suggesting to Doris that she was trying to be tough, to act like a man, to be treated with respect and accepted by the lower ranks. Withholding this sentiment, he phrased a careful response. "Thank you for your guidance. I feel we have achieved something useful that can develop the investigation, accepting that it may not be presentable as evidence, but producing a lead which could help resolve the case. On this basis, I feel the exercise was worthwhile." Wishing to avoid confrontation. "To an extent."

"This had better not come back to bite me, Sergeant."

"I'll do my best to ensure it does not, Ma'am."

She dismissed him with a wave of her left hand while holding an impressive, monogrammed pen in her right, the gesture indicative of her arrogance, annoying DS Beecham excessively.

Finding Flick in the incident room, eager to hear of anything positive, he summarised the identification process. "Well, the DCI says none of it is permissible. She chewed my arse out for failing to follow procedure. Slagged us all off for failing to hold an ID parade on McGarvey before we charged her. Says this one is too flawed to use. She went mental at the blonde girl being included. Oh, and the witness picked

Jenny Coleman from the gathering as the girl he saw with Jeremy. Result, I think."

"Not Amy Meadows?"

"He reacted to Amy Meadows as well. These two are the new updated current shortlist."

"Reacted?"

"Says it could have been her, only the hair was too short. Remember she has been blonde as well in the last few days, so we can't rule her out."

Flick looked suspicious, pondering whether Doris had heard what he wanted to hear. Organisational skills assuming control, she asked, "When do you want to start the extended alibi interviews? Is there a particular order you want?"

"Give me ten, I need to call Chappell. Then Kemp, McGarvey, Meadows, Coleman, Grey. Thanks."

DS Beecham wandered to a quiet corner, tapping the missed-call icon, automatically returning the call, promptly connecting to DS Chappell. Their conversation was strained, tinged with a modicum of grudged appreciation. He learned that the DNA from the bottles had been fast-tracked. The Sprite bottle yielding saliva identified as belonging to Joseph Nesbitt, a known small-time crook, while the Diet Cola bottle yielded an unidentified DNA, a DNA which matched the semen found at the scene of the mysterious Asian woman's death. Chappell pressed for further details of the source, Doris explaining the complexity of his contact, committing to performing his own fast-track to process this finding. Having ended the call, he called Mama San Nan, asking her to urgently contact Ian. Snapping his attention back to his own case, he swaggered towards interview room two.

Eighteen
Wednesday, 13th February

Sporting a clean-shaven appearance, crisp white shirt, neatly ironed trousers and a blue striped tie, DS Terry Holmes began the day with a degree of optimism, reasoning that this day had to be an improvement on yesterday. A day so terrible, saved only by the welcoming attention of his stocking-clad girlfriend.

He assumed his seat in the detective room, opening his laptop, tapping his fingers as he waited for Windows to come out of hibernation. Entering his password across a background of waves crashing against rocks, he hoped for some form of salvation from his email inbox.

"What's this?" Surprise evident in his tone as he scanned the emails. Seeing a report from Doctor Tay, the little icon suggesting an attachment. That message followed by a forensics report from Emyr Christopher, also indicating the presence of an attachment. Further scanning finding an email from Sandra Forrest, titled 'I can come to you today'.

Interspersed with the positive news was an unwelcome message from Human Resources. Accessing this one, learning he had been mentioned in an incident, the blame apportioned to him, relating to a sensitive racist comment involving use of foul language. His presence was expected in a hearing at zero nine hundred on Friday fifteenth at the HR department in Llay. A default button to confirm his attendance emblazoned across the screen, no such button to decline, no button offering a 'fuck off and let me do my job' option. With no alternative, he clicked his mouse on 'confirm'.

Seeking better news, he opened the mail from Sandra Forrest. It was brief, advising him she could come to Mold today around noon, to formally identify the body assumed to be her estranged husband. Terry rattled off a quick reply offering his thanks, suggesting she ask for him at reception upon arrival.

Reading the mail from Doctor Tay, he absorbed the summary offered. Deceased IC1 male, ninety-eight kilograms, estimated time of death on Sunday 10th February between 6pm and midnight. Cause of death asphyxiation by inhalation of carbon monoxide, no puncture wounds, no evidence of assault, no further trauma to the body. Pointedly, no suggestion of suicide, accident or murder mentioned.

Opening the attached report, registering the 'preliminary' stamp, he digested the additional details presented. Traces of Valium located in the deceased's blood. Low-level traces of alcohol. An additional comment in parentheses warning against mixing Valium with alcohol. Details of the damage inflicted by the CO gas. Traces of ejaculate belonging to the deceased found on the body. Signs of accumulative damage to the liver, likely related to prolonged alcohol usage. The lack of bruising or other impact damage suggesting the deceased had not been physically attacked or restrained, indirectly hinting that homicide was the least likely alternative.

Printing the email text and the attachment, he resisted the temptation for coffee, his investigative juices flowing, eager to observe the findings from the forensics team.

The findings were made as bullet points with minimal text, suggesting time constraints on the author, Sergeant Annie Freeland. The stain on the driver door had been identified as semen consistent with the deceased's DNA. Fingerprints in the car belonging to the driver, further prints belonging to the housekeeper, two other unidentified partials found. A trace stain on the leather passenger seat consistent with dried urine, insufficient material to provide identification. Traces of lipstick found on crockery, a common brand and shade unlikely to be of value. Inconsistent pale cream threads found on the sofa, possibility of origination from an overcoat, nothing similar found within the possessions. Footprints unremarkable, their large size indicative of male traffic. An iPad search history indicating an unsurprising interest in pornography with a preference for Thai and Filipina ladies. His mobile phone yielding little of interest, available for collection any time.

Printing the email and attachment, reading the expanded report, Terry attempted to co-ordinate the evidence and match the reports to his findings. He found the likelihood of homicide decreasing, despite the deceased being an unpleasant person. Trying to maintain an open mind, he arranged for delivery of the mobile phone to his desk, interested to read the history, see the contacts and perhaps find some unlikely inspiration.

Transposing his notes from the Bangkok Massage interviews, updating the case file, considering the reports and emails already consumed this morning, Terry accepted the need for a second opinion. Conscious of the presence of a seconded DCI in the guv's office, he chanced an unscheduled visit. Knocking on the closed door, hearing a faint invitation to enter, he facilitated a tidy entrance, standing at ease, biding his time, extracting her permission to sit.

"What's the news on our body in Rossett, Sergeant Holmes?"

Providing an abridged description of the information gathered to date, respectfully inviting her to submit an opinion, surprised and unsettled by her response.

"Are you telling me that we do not yet have a formal identification? He died on Sunday. This is Wednesday. Get your finger out and sort it. Jesus. What kind of shop is this?" The last question rhetorical.

"With respect, Ma'am, we have several informal identifications of the deceased, visual and documentary. We know who he is. His wife will be here today to close that loop."

"You know what I dislike? I dislike it when detectives short circuit due process. Cutting corners leads to mistakes, and mistakes screw up open-and-shut cases. And I really dislike it when people say 'with respect' when they do not bloody mean it."

Internally celebrating his discomfort, the benefits of her superiority, she allowed the awkward silence to continue a few moments longer, eventually deigning him worthy of receiving her wisdom.

"It seems to me that there are no compelling reasons to assess this case as a murder. It is unclear if it is a suicide, but that is most likely, in my opinion. Being a perverted fucker, it might be a sex game gone wrong. Either of those options could apply. North Wales Police has a high number of open serious crime cases awaiting results. We could do without another murder case on the books. Consequently" — drawing the word, elongating the third syllable, ensuring his focus — "the guys with the brass buttons would look kindly on this case being an accident or a suicide. That decision would not be harmful to your career, so long as you have sufficient reason to assign it that way. In my view, you have ample reason to close the case, write it up and move on, with the blessing of the higher ranks."

Assimilating her suggestion as confirmation of his own determination, Terry considered asking for her ruling in writing. Immediately understanding it would not be forthcoming, he swallowed the question, thanking the crabby-faced DCI for her input as he rose to leave her office.

"Sergeant?"

"Ma'am?"

"Do fuck-all until you have that positive ID from the wife."

Feeling a response would be irrelevant, he left.

Nineteen
Wednesday, 13th February

In the process of closing a selection of loose ends, a task requiring intense concentration, he was annoyed to hear his phone ring.

Employing mental arithmetic, a dying art form, he estimated the lost value of the shortfall in his drug delivery. Every shipment had minor errors, usually tasting samples or a gift to a busy Customs officer. An allowable percentage loss was understood. Twenty-seven travellers, twenty-seven cases, thirteen point five kilograms, one percent loss in transit should ensure a minimum of thirteen point three six five kilos, at two hundred thousand pounds wholesale per kilo, yielding two million, six hundred and seventy-three thousand. If this consignment weighed an aggregate of thirteen point two six five, he calculated an additional transit loss of twenty thousand pounds.

Pondering his options, he accepted the call. "Yes, Nan."

"Policeman Graham wants to speak with you, sir. He says it is urgent and asks if you can call him, please."

Astounded at the police turnaround time, suspecting other motivation involved, he issued instructions. "Call him on your mobile, put the call on loudspeaker, then call me on the landline. Place the handset close to the mobile. Do it now."

Minutes later, Ian and Doris were in communication, indirectly, the contact quality impaired by the airgap between devices, the legibility nevertheless sufficient for them to converse.

"We have a result on the bottles you gave us. The green Sprite bottle contained DNA known to us: Joseph Nesbitt, one of your unofficial employees, we suspect. That DNA is not a match for the evidence found on the deceased lady." Careful to say "on" rather than "in". Continuing. "The sample from the clear glass Cola bottle does not match any person in our system. However, it is a perfect match for that taken at the crime scene. I can say for certain that the source of this DNA is our prime suspect in the rape and murder of an unknown Thai lady."

"You think she is Thai?" Ian, fishing, nonplussed by their insight.

"We do. It's time for you to hand over the suspect. We will do the rest. There is already enough to charge him." Doris, coercive, bordering on demanding.

Ian, stalling, in receipt of the confirmation he required, aware of his obligation to share some knowledge with the plods. "I need some time. He is an outsider, there are wheels to turn. Call Nan at the parlour tonight at nine o'clock; she will give you an anonymous tip on where to find this person."

Comprehending the difficulties facing both sides, Doris agreed. "Nine pm."

"Is there anything else I should know?" Betraying his personal interest, a momentary lapse.

Filing the revealed interest for another time, DS Beecham shared the unofficial rumour circulating at the police station, sourced from a horrified loose tongue at the mortuary, emphasising the unofficial.

Removing an item from his locked drawer, he donned his leathers before tidying his desk and placing everything in a lockable filing cabinet. Turning the key, removing it, he placed it behind the stem of his fledgling cheese plant. Lights off, office door locked, he carefully descended to the reserved parking area, appreciation of his powerful Honda a contradiction to the darkness of his mood. Slinging his right leg over the bike, key in, kick start, the roar muted, experience ensuring a moderately quiet start, attracting less attention. Helmet on, ready.

Having slept better, being permitted to assume a horizontal position, Dai Harris gave thought to his predicament. He was being blamed for the death of the old woman, correctly he conceded, facing a severe form of criminal justice. With his clearer mind, he understood he had occasion to push the blame towards Nesbo, whose alibi did not exist, who had only Dai's word that he was dropped at home, who could have remained in the car after the deposit of the other four ladies at their workplaces. Working on this scenario, he sought to imagine a situation whereby Joe attacked the woman and killed her while Dai was unable to protect her in time. He cajoled himself to develop this story and build a defence, dump on his colleague, minimise the potential impact on himself.

Nesbitt had been removed to another area of the warehouse, separated from Harris, assigned his own dedicated pair of guards. His legs were secured to the base of a metallic shelfing system, a series of interlocking cable ties ensuring his restricted mobility. He feared for his future, understanding the anger present in the boss, unsure if he would be apportioned blame for the death of the lady which incorporated a risk of severe to fatal punishment. His risk mitigated by being absent when the incident occurred, his role in locating Dai, and being honest throughout his imprisonment. Hopeful, not confident, wondering what the day ahead would hold.

Hearing the motorcycle suggesting the impending arrival of the boss, one guard took a position at the warehouse entrance, prepared to open the door as a courtesy. The second guard in this area kicked Dai, encouraging him to stand, despite his feet being tied together, using the wall for leverage towards a vertical posture. Responding to this activity, Nesbo was coaxed into an uncomfortable sitting position, legs remaining secured, minimal capability to defend himself.

Announcing his arrival, The Mancunian removed his leathers, throwing the crash helmet to the floor, emanating an emotional outrage. Pointing towards the partially obscured Nesbitt, "Keep that fucker secure until I am ready for him. Plug his ears." Turning to Dai, addressing the guards, "Strip him naked. Retie him, call me when he's ready."

Using electrical cable cutters to remove the cable ties, Dai was released, presented with his opportunity to fight or attempt escape, challenged by the guards to do so, their expressions intimating their wish that he would try. Accepting the futility, he remained *in situ*, removing his clothes, preparing for the impending humiliation, his self-consciousness compounded by the winter temperature coupled to a lack of heating in the facility. Psychologically impaired by nudity, he prepared for the interrogatory barrage.

"Last fucking time, Dai. Tell me everything that happened from collecting the ladies until the death of Madam Nattaporn. Don't leave anything out."

Dai recounted his modified story, maintaining solidarity with his previous dissertation, up until the point where Nesbo left the car, before presenting a revised sequence of events. "Nesbo was supposed to go home. He went inside but came back saying he wanted to stay with us. He got back in the car. He was acting funny, restless, then he asked me to pull over in the layby, said he needed to relieve himself." Nodding, pleased with the words, the avoidance of crudity giving credence to his explanation. "He opened the car door, telling the lady to get out of the car. When she didn't, he hit her, hard. Then he pulled at her before hitting her again. Reached in to undo her seatbelt. I had no idea what he was doing, I thought maybe he had spoken to someone, and been told to do this." Looking around, seeking understanding, assessing response. "He threw her down, attacked her, punching her. He grabbed her dress, tore it, yanked it up." Pausing for effect, applying concern to his expression. "He put on a condom, then mounted her, really pounded her, grabbing her throat. I was shocked, frozen to my seat. When I understood what he was doing, I left the car to run around to help her, but I was too late, I could see she was dead. And he was still banging away at her. It was horrible. I'm sorry I couldn't stop it. That poor woman."

The Mancunian listened, displaying an indication of concentration, silently fuming, patience evaporating as his temper spiralled. Pure fabrication. Barely containing his physical inclination to inflict pain, glancing at the guards to gauge their disbelief, he stared into Dai's eyes. "If Nesbo was wearing a johnny, as you said, then how did your spunk find a way into Madame Nattaporn's twat? Explain that to me?" With no reply forthcoming, he instructed his minions to leave Dai naked but to tie his hands together, tie his feet, gag and blindfold him.

Wandering to the corner location, indicating the earplugs should be removed. "Nesbo. Dai has just told us that it was you who raped the lady, killed her, then asked him to help you cover it up. What do you say to that?"

Startled. The words unfathomable. Adrenaline coursing into his metabolism. "No fucking way! I told you, he dropped me off, insisted on it. He had the hots for her, he wanted to be alone. I didn't do anything. I swear. I didn't."

Patting his shoulder, commiserating with him. "I know you didn't do it. He did. The cops have the DNA." Observing Nesbo's shoulders slump, relief evident in his expression. "Don't get too relaxed. You failed to follow your designated instructions, thereby enabling this situation. You will be punished, though less severely than him." He indicated Dai. "Get your clothes off, let the boys rebind you, and we'll get this completed today."

Retreating to the internal office, he left his people to their tasks. Gathering his protective clothing, placing it on a desk, donning lightweight gloves, he assessed the item he had brought with him. Impressively heavy, with a long barrel, the sight mechanism reinforcing the impression of craftsmanship, the trigger precise. All identifying markings had been removed, a significant element in the overall cost. Fully loaded, safety catch activated. The silencer lay beside the gun, an optional accessory, innocent in its solitude.

Scrutinising the internal office space, the corkboards mounted on the walls, door and ceiling, supposedly offering protection from the noise of delivery trucks during normal operations. The floor was carpeted in a layer of thick polyvinyl opaque sheeting, held in place by strategically positioned furniture, furniture to be disposed of after the event. Content to an extent, his emotions compromised by circumstances.

Opening a small toolbox, the red paint peeling around the edges, he extracted a pristine pair of garden secateurs. The blades illuminating the room, reflecting light, the grey handles immaculate without blemish. Testing the device on a nylon cable tie, snapping the thick plastic instantly.

Nesbitt first. A beating. Then a finger. A final warning. Release.

Dai second. A beating. A finger. A toe. A final warning. Another finger. Another toe. A bullet. Dispose.

The guards brought Nesbo to the office. Now wearing a blindfold, his mouth was duct-taped, his ankles and wrists encased in nylon wraps. Pressing him onto a chair, The Mancunian explained his ruling.

"You fucked up. You sneaked off early against protocol, leaving a valuable member of my staff at the mercy of a predator, a scumbag who killed my friend. Your failure is mitigated by your assistance in finding him. On that basis, I will allow you to live. But I will take a finger, as a token of your future loyalty. It won't be as bad as you think. You have already been given strong painkillers which will help you tolerate the residual pain. Of course, it will hurt like a bastard when I do the removal, but only fleetingly. Oh, and Billy here doesn't like you, so he is going to hit you a few times. Let us begin."

Suppressed cries emanated from behind the tape, his body wrestling for free movement, tensing in anticipation of impact, pain realised as the punch crashed into his lower left jaw. Reeling from the assault, he felt hands in his armpits, lifting him from the seat, confusion surrendering to torment as a gut punch folded his torso, his balance subsiding, head glancing against the chair as he went down. Reactively curling inwards, preserving his vital organs a reflex compulsion. Unseen hands once more lifting him, his agony ignored, placing him on the seat again. Two hands pressing his left wrist to the table, gripping, immobilising. Denied visual confirmation, senses responding to pressure, cold, above and below his little finger, caressing the joint, settling into the groove, the sound of a snap the precursor to abject, excruciating, debilitating trauma. Nerves seeking response from previously conjoined fibres, their unrequited signals sending uncontrolled pain messages to the brain. Half a finger lay on the desk, the volume of blood significant, reflexes agitated, screams muffled but audible.

Dispassionately watching, he rolled the cylindrical device onto its host, matching the thread to achieve unity. Unable to tolerate the scene before him, the agonised thrashing of the restrained detainee, his blood splashing across the room, limbs spastic in their movements, he knocked the suffering underling to the ground and kicked him onto his back. Pressing a foot on his chest, inhaling a long voluminous breath as he disengaged the safety mechanism, exhaling as he took aim at the chest, squeezing the trigger. The sound depressed by the appendage, a softer sound accompanying the impact of lead into chest. A second impact, a second spout of blood emanating from the wounds in the upper torso, spreading along fat lines in the naked flesh, unimpeded by movement, the suffering over.

The room was silent. The shots unexpected. A smell in the atmosphere. Cordite? Burning? Charcoal? Joseph Aloysius Nesbitt had passed.

The guards exchanged looks, they had both assumed the wee guy would be released.

"Boss? What shall we do with him?" Billy had voiced the question, his surprise evident, trying to adjust to the revised circumstances. The boss replied, curtly, "Leave him as he lies. Bring that other cunt in here."

Leaving the office, the guards exchanged positions with those assigned to Dai, forcefully bringing their prisoner into the office. Similarly gagged and blindfolded, restraints on every limb, Dai was positioned within the office, upright, unsteady, unsure of what had transpired earlier. Receiving a signal, one guard removed the blindfold, the sudden increased luminance forcing Dai to blink, look away from the source of light. Facing down, he recoiled as he saw the body on the floor, unable to vocally announce his shock, his countenance demonstrating his strained emotions.

"Dai. Dai. Dai." The Mancunian walked around him, reappearing behind, their faces close, guiding his vision towards the corpse before them. "Two things have saved you, my friend. Changing your story to incriminate Nesbo was the correct thing to do. And. My police informant told me that my friend was assaulted by a well-endowed man." Coming around to face him again, gaze falling to his groin. "You have been naked for a while now, and that little thing has barely grown past an inch. Clearly you couldn't have been the attacker, your dick is way too small. Lucky for you."

Permitting Dai to observe the body, inviting him to look around, the finger on the table, the bloodstained secateurs, the warm pistol, the guards, the doorway, the sound-proofed walls, he continued, "Now that you are cleared of the attack on Madame Nattaporn, we need to resolve the issues between us, issues of false accusation, of trust, of our future working relationship." Addressing him directly, seeking his agreement. "I need a display of trust from you. A simple one. Something we can do now, together, ending this situation. What do you say?"

Shaking, fearful, his circumstances fraught with danger, he inclined his head, his taped mouth unable to present his agreement.

"One thing only. Not negotiable. To prove your loyalty. I want you to shag that body."

Scarcely able to comprehend the instruction, unable to process the expectation, he battled to withhold the vomit circulating in his throat. Scanning the office, seeking a colleague, an expression of sympathy or support, finding none, only impassive faces hiding any horror they might harbour, loyal and steadfast with their employer.

"Are you horrified? Why? I heard this was your thing, shagging dead people. I expected you to have a monster hard-on at the prospect."

Dai knew he would not survive. They knew. Had known. Turned in by the police, fucking ironic. Ironical?

"Go on, do him. If you can, if you fully consummate your relationship with him, you might get out of here. Otherwise..." The shoulder shrug confirming the lack of alternative.

Mustering some vestiges of pride, showing defiance, he shook his head, turning away from the body before him. Emotions closeted in tears, he prepared for what was to come, glad to have the gag, permitting him the dignity of not pleading for his life, certain any plea would be refused. Standing upright he looked at his adversary, issuing defiance in his expression, mumbling behind his gag. "Go fuck yourself."

Suggesting an admiration at the defiance shown, the bravery in hostile circumstances, The Mancunian grinned as he lifted the gun. Walking beyond Dai, then stepping closer behind him, he placed the cold metal against Dai's flesh, pressing it between his shoulder blades, dragging the hard weapon lower, using the spine as a guide.

Dai waited, resigned. Feeling the chill of the metallic silencer sliding across his skin, aware the shot could come any time. The physical discomfort combining with emotional dread to dilute his resistance. Urine dribbling from him gently, dampening his upper legs, gradually forming a small puddle between his feet on the plastic-covered floor, the plastic belatedly understood. Still moving lower, the circular aperture created indentations in his flesh, cool, cold, firm, hard. The movement ceasing as the gun rested against his anus.

Senses heightened, touch aware of the gun traversing his body, smell analysing his urine, his fear, sight recognising the cruelty in the faces of others, hearing a small click. The gentle sound unprocessed as heat tore through his body, impact upon impact, internal tearing, ripping, shredding, burning. The foreign object ejected, his senses shutting down, nerves oscillating as life extinguished, signals to the brain unheeded. The defiant body remaining momentarily steady, before falling lifeless to the floor.

Justice achieved, he calmly disengaged the silencer, taking a tissue from the table to carefully wipe the tip of the gun, followed by the barrel and the entire weapon, despite gloves being worn, unnecessary risk contrary to his beliefs. "Remove all the binding, wash him down, leave no traces of yourselves, then wrap him in plastic. I'll let you know where I want him dumped. Get the others to do the same with the other body. Thank you for your diligence and support." He left unsaid the likely monetary recognition, mutually understood, his appearance devoid of compassion. "Then let's get this office stripped down, remove everything, especially that shitty cork panelling. Recover the bullets, Polyfilla the walls, wash it down, repaint the entire place, I want new furniture in here before Monday."

Twenty
Wednesday, 13th February

Permission to occupy five interview rooms had been denied, leaving Doris and Flick with no option but to store the spare ladies in one room while they interviewed each in turn. This presented the suspects with ample time to talk amongst themselves, far from ideal during an investigation.

They had planned to start with Jasmine Kemp, the least likely candidate. Instead, driven by circumstances, they began with Ruth McGarvey. Sitting together, facing their former suspect, Doris commenced the interview, stating the parameters of this discussion, offering a caution.

"Thank you for coming in today. Your co-operation is appreciated." A gentle start.

"I was released on Monday, after evidence proved my innocence. I would like to know why you people have brought me here again. I agreed to the identity thing, now I'm back in here, under caution, being recorded. I would like to leave immediately."

"Rather than argue with you, I'll make this brief. You have an alibi for Friday twenty-fifth, provided by your husband, and Saturday morning twenty-sixth from Asda CCTV. I found that footage." Introducing an element of sarcasm to his tone. "You are welcome." Short hesitation, for effect. "We would now like to know your whereabouts for the afternoon and evening of the twenty-sixth and the duration of Sunday twenty-seventh. In your own time."

Without consideration, she provided a response. "As I previously intimated, my husband was unwell that weekend. After shopping, I spent the day preparing a delightful home-cooked meal, which we followed with a packaged dessert, some red wine, and an early night. I remember it clearly, as Jim was on good form that night; he brought me off three times with his tongue." Her turn to infuse her tone with fluctuating emotions. "On Sunday, we slept late, for obvious reasons. We spent the remainder of the day at home, together. I assume you will ask him, please go ahead, with my permission."

"You are telling me that your movements cannot be verified by a third party?"

"That is correct."

Invited to raise a question, Flick declined. Doris ended the interview. "We will check your story and get back to you if we have further questions. Interview terminated." Indicating the door. "You are free to leave."

Flick escorted Ruth to the reception area, keen to accelerate her departure and escape from the tricky situation. Exchanging few words, Flick discharged Ruth before collecting Amy Meadows from the assembly area, taking her to face Doris. He performed the routine advisory statement for the recording device's benefit.

"Hi, Amy. We meet again."

"We do, Detective Beecham, and I would like to say that I am not delighted about it."

"I am sorry to hear that. Nevertheless, we have uncovered new evidence which may negate the value of your previously submitted alibi." Flicking through his notes. "You provided a statement concerning Friday twenty-fifth of January, where you spent an evening at home in the company of Miss Holly Dryburgh. Do you stand by that statement?"

Not bothering to reply, Amy inclined her head, indicating her confirmation as well as her disdain for this process.

"For the benefit of the tape, Miss Meadows has confirmed her statement by nodding. What about Saturday? How did you spend your day? In your own words."

Exasperation displayed on her features, performing a caricature of seeking to extract a memory, Amy stared directly at both officers. "I went shopping in the Grosvenor Mall, then I took a bus home. You can find me on CCTV, certainly in the bus station."

"What time was this?" Flick interjected, unhappy with the latent aggression within the room.

"No idea. Afternoon some time. Then home. Alone. The curse of the single woman."

Resuming the questioning, DS Beecham asked, "And the Sunday?"

"At an industrial park, buying a barbeque and accessories. Maybe an off-licence to buy some wine. Again, alone, no family locally, no boyfriend, or girlfriend." The timed glance at Flick, coincident with girlfriend, intuition?

Suddenly interested, Doris focused on her statement. "Why would you buy a barbeque in February?"

Laughing as tension released from her, perceiving his question to be ridiculous. "Anybody with even half a brain would buy a barbeque in February; they are half price compared to summertime. Surely you should have asked me why I would buy a barbeque when I live in a flat. That would have been an appropriate question." Meeting his gaze, certain she had struck a chord. "Before you ask, after the fact, the flats in my building have a common garden area which we can use for gatherings, including barbeques."

"Does it take all day to buy a barbeque?" Frostily, bordering on harsh.

"It can take a while. Shopping around. Comparing products, prices, ensuring stock availability. It's not like buying clothes where you might go to one shop, see something suitable and buy it. I like to spend time, seeing what is available, comparing features, evaluating the items, making a considered decision before spending my money wisely. I am sure Constable McGarry will understand."

"Where did you buy the barbeque?" Abrupt now, civility erased, accusing.

Amy opened her handbag, removing her purse, searching the pockets within, removing two paper items before perusing their content, placing one on the desk and pushing it towards the police officers. "There's the receipt. You can copy it if you like, but I need it back; it provides my twelve-month warranty. The date and time are on there, along with the store address."

Flick took a photo with her phone, returning the receipt to Amy.

"If there is nothing else, I would like to go. I have a date which I hope turns into a relationship, so that I will be able to provide alibis in future, when you guys harass me again. By the way, I consider your behaviour as harassment, and I will be writing to your Chief Constable, or whatever you call him here. Are we done?"

Having escorted Amy to the station entrance, Flick considered the recent interview. Doris had performed poorly, his blinkered suspicion floundering against Amy's strong personality, clever to the point of being arrogant. She had suggested that Doris should be more open-minded about Amy; now she thought he might be on to something. Her behaviour was erratic, at times intelligent, always combative.

Collecting Jenny Coleman, the process recommenced.

"Hello, Miss Coleman." The first deviation. "We would like to expand our knowledge of your movements relating to the weekend commencing Friday twenty-fifth of January."

"No comment." Her response raising eyebrows across the table.

"You previously stated that you were at work on the Friday, then had dinner with friends at the Grosvenor hotel in the evening. Would you like to confirm those statements?"

"No comment."

"A simple yes or no would suffice."

"No comment."

"Can you confirm your personal activity for the full day on the Saturday?"

"No comment."

"Miss Coleman, are you willing to answer any questions that we put to you today?"

"No comment."

Flick interrupting. "Jenny. Is something wrong? Can you just help us here? We are seeking to eliminate you from suspicion. Please?"

"No comment."

Patience having evaporated, Doris stood, his impressive stature intended to intimidate the suspect. "Miss Coleman. You were selected from the identity parade today as having been seen with the deceased around the time of his death. By failing to talk to us, you are making your situation worse."

"No. Comment." Each word phrased independently.

"If you continue to impede our investigation, I can arrest you. I can detain you here, or I can rip your private life apart for the time in question, and a few weeks either side if I desire. How about you help us, so we can help you?"

Jenny stood, located the ceiling mounted camera and addressed it, making signals with her hands. Upon completion, she took her seat again, offering a longer response. "For the benefit of the recording device and as a precaution against faulty equipment, I have just used sign language to your camera, stating that I have no comment."

Seeking to avoid an incident on camera, Flick ended the interview, leading Jenny from the room, leaving Doris to vent his frustration on a teaspoon, hurling the steel cutlery against a wall.

The interview with Susan Grey was completed in minutes. She presented her breakdown of the entire weekend, seventy-two hours of her life laid bare, every aspect available for follow-up. Her performance again devoid of any suspicion, her only shortcoming having been in a relationship with Jeremy Campbell-Foulkes.

The Jasmine Kemp discussion was instantaneous, as she presented boarding cards for airline flights she had taken, proving she had been outside the country on those dates, rendering further questioning inconsequential.

Sitting together, five follow-up interviews concluded, comparing impressions, they agreed that Jenny Coleman and Amy Meadows were suspects, and their alibis should be fully investigated. The remaining three could be dismissed from the investigative process.

Following her interview, Ruth McGarvey had taken a stance outside the police station. Her temper barely contained, she considered the building, the organisation housed there, the impact they could have on innocent lives, their entire process built upon intimidation. Popular wisdom had condemned all United Kingdom police forces as interested in generating revenue from speed cameras, preferring to forego complicated investigative work which required resource and expenditure. Her personal experience contradicted that wisdom, bearing repeated interference in her private life, making accusations against her, placing her marriage at risk. Unable to contemplate a method of recompense, short of suing them for wrongful arrest, she considered vandalising the building, potentially gaining a minor degree of satisfaction.

Approached by a man of Indian appearance as she prepared to leave, Ruth remained still as she heard her name. He introduced himself as a reporter from the *Leader*, and he wondered if she might wish to talk to him about her treatment by the police. He had attended the press conference, thought it might be appropriate to inform the public of her side of the story. Resisting her initial instinct to protect her privacy, sensing an opportunity for vengeance, she agreed to join him at the nearby newspaper office, to conduct an interview on the record.

She welcomed the chance to clear her name, to explain explicitly that she had been wrongly accused. She had accumulated additional information from the waiting room about the other ladies under suspicion in the same case. Concerned that people would continue to suspect her, assuming no smoke without fire, she could deflect suspicion away from herself, onto these other women. Perhaps a selfish act, but understandable from the way she had been treated.

Nilesh suggested they walk to his office, the weather having brightened, their vehicles already securely parked. The stroll providing the chance to enhance their relationship, remove some barriers, permit a fast start when the recording device was enabled. Confident of a story, forming questions in his mind, he beamed at everybody.

Twenty-One
Wednesday, 13th February

Driving towards Chester, J Lo on the radio, the Clio passing a cap-wearing pensioner in a new-looking Mercedes, Amy reflected on her performance at the police station.

Clearly, Detective Beecham disliked her, possibly suspected her and harboured doubts in relation to her alibi. Having intended to be quiet, even polite while offering an apparent humility, she had lost her resolve. His focus on the barbeque was hilarious, revealing his lack of any coherent evidence against her, fishing only, seeking anything which could return her to suspicion. Confident in her performance, certain she had garnered the female cop's support, she provided a tuneless backing vocal to the ageless Latina performer.

Glancing at the digital clock, she calculated the time against the distance she had to travel. Dressed in warm winter clothes for the benefit of the identification parade, she needed to change before she met with Rob. Wanting to look nice, wishing him to find her attractive, hoping he would appreciate the effort she had made, ensuring their gently developing relationship could continue to prosper. Wanting to look nice for herself, her vanity insistent.

He had suggested The Yard. Lunch, possibly drinks. A nice touch: the invitation SMS had requested her presence. She had avoided the Boardroom, located below, since the slap incident with Kirsty, insuring herself against the possibility of being barred, allowing memories to fade. The combined venue providing another reason for her to look good, the premises habitually attended by poseurs: men and women whose sartorial elegance was essential to their ego. The venue presenting a platform to denigrate the appearance of anyone falling below their esteemed yet inadequate standards. Amy intended to wow him, cause heads to turn, inflate his personal pride, intimate an out-of-reach notice to the wannabe yuppies.

With time of the essence, she invested in the valet parking, taking her large carry bag and purse, the carry bag a gift from Holly on her return from Phuket with Terry. The bag was adorned with a ridiculous luminous elephant holding its trunk aloft as it saluted a golden, seated Buddha. The bag contained her change of clothing, make-up pouch, perfume, hairbrush, and shoes. Essential shoes.

Rob had informed his staff of his impending departure from the office. He had scheduled an abundance of time, returning home to change, making the effort to look smart, taking a second shower, polished shoes awaiting him. Despite his planning, he was late. Nilesh had accosted him at the door, gushing about an opportunity he had, dirt on the local police, a development on his previous story. Minimally listening, he had encouraged his reporter to follow his nose. Eager to be away, excited to meet Amy again, his attention less than it should have been.

Ninety seconds late, he gave his name to the waiter, his window-adjacent table reserved. Failing to see her, he was relieved that she had not been waiting and forced to stand due to his tardiness. Now he became concerned that she was late, that she could not attend, she would stand him up after realising that she could do better. He took the chair offering him an unobstructed view of the entrance, his confidence diminishing with every passing second. His attention became distracted by a woman arriving from the rear of the restaurant, dressed immaculately in a classic sleeveless black dress, intriguingly short, further enhanced by flattering black heels and a simple elegant gold chain adorning her neck. He absorbed these details, admiring her figure, her slim tapered legs, raising his eyes to risk a glimpse at her face, recognising the hairstyle he had appreciated only yesterday. Her face perfection, he struggled to reconcile this vision before him as the woman joining him for lunch.

Entertained by his reaction, Amy offered a demure smile. "Hi, Rob."

He stood to greet her, stepping around the table and taking her hand as he leaned into her, accepting her offered cheek, lightly kissing her soft skin, whispering, "What an entrance." Resisting his innate urge to blurt *Oh my God, you are beautiful.*

Assisting her to her seat before joining her at the table, they exchanged smiles, mutual nerves apparent. He tried to thank her for coming, discovering he had forgotten the entire English language, praying he hadn't drooled, then rescued by her voice.

"You look nice. Thank you for inviting me."

Offering him a simple auto-response. "I'm glad you could make it. You look lovely."

They endured an irritating interruption as the waiter brought menus and drink recommendations, coercing them into breaking eye contact. The intrusion offered an opportunity to gather themselves, ameliorate the overwhelming excitement of new dating. "What would you like to drink?" he asked, simply.

Taking her time, perusing the cocktails, inviting him to demonstrate patience, she settled for, "A glass of red wine, please."

Aware of the proximity of the waiter, relieved to have a concrete task in hand, he requested, "Two glasses of the Adelaide Hills Cabernet Sauvignon, please," portraying some knowledge of wine, fervently hoping he had selected well, having chosen a red from the middle of the price list.

As they waited for their wine to arrive, they shared small talk, asking about their respective day, how they felt, their shared relief at the improvement in the weather. Amy, inventing a relaxed day updating her résumé and performing online banking transactions, while avoiding any mention of attending a police station or being interrogated and placed in an identity parade. Under his breath, he suspected she had done none of the things she had mentioned, instead spending the entire day making herself unbelievably gorgeous. These thoughts occupying his mind, he almost missed her question.

"Do I need to be careful about what I say around you? Being an editor. That's like a journalist, isn't it? I mean, do I have to say 'off the record' when I speak to you, or can I relax?" Her manner was friendly, her expression open, her voice light.

Unsure how to read her, he followed his nose. "Tell you what, in your honour, I will regard everything you ever say to me as off the record. This means I could never quote you in print or verbally without your permission expressly granted to any specific statement."

"Ooh, that's nice, I like that."

The wine arrived, glasses placed before them, the white tablecloth contrasting beautifully. Other diners irrelevant, unnoticed. Ordering different pasta dishes, solid, safe bets, touching their glasses, sipping the wine, his choice evidently excellent, they concentrated only on themselves.

Continuing to explore one another, seeking preferences, finding commonality, exchanging likes and dislikes, becoming comfortable in their proximity. He found subtle nuances in her appearance, her eyebrows marginally uneven, her earrings dancing horses, a crinkle on her nose when she smiled. She found his respect for her endearing, his manners, his pleasant looks, wondering how she might fix his hair, enjoying his appreciation, a level of emotional intimacy already developing.

Their food was delivered, twenty minutes having passed effortlessly. Typical Italian food, over-hyped, overpriced, simple fare blending tomatoes with garlic and green herbs, boiled pasta, grated cheese, ground pepper. Tasty, reliable, unremarkable. Requesting a bottle of chilled sparkling water, he returned his attention to the woman before him.

Enjoying his attentive behaviour, she found herself fighting an urge to blush. Cautiously consuming the food, determined to avoid staining her expensive new dress, she responded to the challenge, finding a delicacy she was unaware she possessed. In her mind, singing to herself, unheard, Ray Wilson half growling *Take It Slow*, the song a cautionary reminder.

Finding her fascinating, he attempted to control his instinct to look at her body, to assess her physically. He listened to her every word while eating more carefully than he ever had, savouring the shared experience, scarcely believing his luck to be taking lunch with this delightful person.

He asked about her plans for this evening, gently cursing her companion, relieved to learn she was a friend from university, a friendship maintained. She explained they would be having a girls' night in, laughing as she explained her conundrum, her commitment to cook when a pasta dish was the limit of her culinary artistry. Having had pasta for lunch with him, she wondered what she might prepare for her friend.

"You could make a platter," he offered, "a selection of finger foods; you know, chicken wings, spring rolls, wedges, stuff like that."

"Excuse me. We are girls — that is very definitely boy food. At least I know what to prepare when you come to visit."

"Oh?" Trying to remain casual, to conceal his excitement. "You plan to invite me to your place? Nice."

Leaning forward, engaging him with her smile, distracting him with her movement within the dress, she clarified. "Did I say *when*? Sorry, I meant *if*." The way she said it, her body language, her sparkling eyes, he wasn't disappointed, understanding she was teasing. Revelling in her closeness, the hairs in his nose tingled with her scent.

At the conclusion of their lunch, he reflected on a successful event. He had avoided verbal stupidity and she had failed to catch him enjoying her figure in the fitted dress. He liked her, without doubt. The bill settled, the amount irrelevant and barely noticed as he slid a card across. Already anticipating seeing her again, even as she remained before him.

Withdrawing her chair, he assisted her to stand, curious where these instincts came from, mentally thanking his parents for inducing manners into him at some point in his life. Delighted as he was rewarded with a smile, ecstatic as she took his hand in hers, walking away from the table while attracting glances from other patrons, their togetherness reinforced by the hand contact. Rob worried he might burst as he swelled with pride. Negotiating the occasional narrow space by slipping behind her, then returning to her side, hand contact unbroken, sneaking a subtle glimpse at her rear as she stepped forward, stunned at her stunningly stunning figure.

She complimented herself that this dress had been worth every exorbitant penny, feeling his look upon her, aware of the appreciation she was receiving. Responding to the doorman as he held the door, making his day with a demure "Thank you". Rob's "Thank you" barely registering.

They waited together as her car came via the valet, surprising him. "Parking can be difficult sometimes, and I really did not want to be late. Well, only a few minutes." Her unrequested confession inflating his joy, understanding she had taken their lunch seriously.

"Your entrance was incredible. I doubt I will ever forget it. Thank you for that, and for joining me, and for being exceptional company. And for looking beautiful."

She responded to the compliment, touching her lips to his, gently without pressure, without outward indication of passion, contrasting intensity unmistakable in her open eyes, the contact electric.

As she stepped into her car, tantalising him by displaying most of her slim leg, she spoke. "Meadows." Seeing his confusion, explaining, "My surname. Amy Meadows. I think you deserve to know my full name. Thank you so much for today. I really enjoyed it."

"Can I call you tomorrow?"

"Of course. Maybe we can meet if you have time." Fastening her seatbelt.

"Dinner?"

Shaking her head. "Maybe a movie? I'll leave it to you."

Waving their goodbyes, her door closing, the Clio moving ahead as he watched her disappear, sad to see her departure. His thoughts were interrupted by the valet. "Mate. Wow."

Facing the stranger, unable to prevent himself laughing. "I know!"

The valet lightly punching his arm, their joint appreciation undisguised. "So, which is it?"

The question asked, Rob unsure of the meaning, querying. "How do you mean?"

The valet maintained his grin. "There are only two ways guys like you and me pull women like that. Loads of money or a big cock. So, which is it?"

Understanding, having had the same conversation with friends in the past without being the butt of the accusation. "For someone like that, obviously it's both." Enjoying the laughter from the valet as he walked away, swaggering, barely aware of the developing winter chill.

Twenty-Two
Wednesday, 13th February

Sandra Forrest made a positive first impression on her arrival. She stood at the station reception desk confidently, her voice emphatic, explaining her appointment with DS Holmes for the purpose of identifying a deceased person. That impression continued in the detective room, Terry appreciating her assertiveness while sensing an absence of grief.

"You understand that we have a deceased person in the morgue, who we suspect may be your estranged husband. We cannot be certain until he is formally identified. There is a possibility that our suspicions might be incorrect." Selecting his words carefully.

"I understand. If it's Mark, I will confirm it."

"The morgue is in Wrexham at the Maelor Hospital. It won't take us long to get there. The Forensic Pathologist will meet us and present the body to you and answer any medical questions you have. Other questions, you can ask me." He intimated the invitation would remain open.

She appeared older than her stated age of thirty-seven, the grey in her hair more suggestive of mid-forties. Physically tidy and smartly presented, her expression revealed little emotion, likely to activate at the identification. Questions unforthcoming, he suggested coffee or tea, the offer declined.

"Can we just go there, and get this over with?" Her first sign of anxiety. Impatience? Apprehension?

"Okay, let's go," he said, suspecting she might become more expansive in the privacy of the car.

The journey passed quickly due to light traffic, supported by moderate weather, limiting the opportunity for conversation. Terry had parked in the area reserved for the doctors; his police ID sufficient to persuade the uniformed attendant that complimentary parking was appropriate for a grieving widow. Raising the barrier manually, with a wave, the attendant had guided the vehicle towards a convenient vacant space.

Holmes introduced Doctor Tay in his allocated office, his ponytail resplendent in a blue scrunchy, completing the formalities before adjourning to the morgue. Terry and Sandra remained outside the main work and storage area, behind a glass aperture which provided them with an unobstructed view of the trolley containing the deceased.

"Please don't be alarmed." Ponytail's voice sounded clearly through an intercom system. "I will turn back the blanket, you will only see a face. Take your time. Please be sure of the identity before you confirm. If you are unsure, and that can happen, you can provide details of distinguishing marks elsewhere on the body and we can seek to confirm those. Do you have any questions or concerns?"

Calmly, she confirmed her lack of questions. Taking his guidance from DS Holmes, Tay commenced the procedure, turning the blanket slowly with reverence in consideration of potential emotional impact, revealing the head and shoulders of the deceased.

"Oh, thank God!" Her words initiating unexpected responses from both the pathologist and the detective. Each sought direction from the other via the glass, neither proffering an opinion to guide the other. Sandra spoke again, decisive, certain. "That's him. That is Mark Forrest, my husband, legally at least."

Again startled, their expectations tested, her responses eliciting confusion. "Mrs Forrest. Can you confirm that the deceased body before you, is that of your husband, Mark Forrest?" Terry, seeking confirmation, her contradictory statements bemusing him.

"Yes. I confirm that is Mark Forrest. How did he die?"

Having achieved physical identification, they were able to furnish information freely to the spouse of the deceased. "He died of asphyxiation" — Ponytail, accurate, professional, devoid of emotion — "caused by the presence of carbon monoxide in an enclosed space, eliminating ingress of oxygen, resulting in loss of consciousness, followed by death." Adding a momentary consideration. "I suspect that his death was painless."

Turning to Holmes, she asked the same question. Offering a different perspective, he said, "He was found in his vehicle, engine running with a hose from the exhaust into the car, causing suffocation." Observing her nod, seemingly agreeing, he continued, "We remain uncertain of the exact circumstances. Possibly suicide, possibly a sex game, we do not think there was foul play involved." His final statement normally a source of comfort to the relatives of the deceased.

"Knowing Mark as well as I do, you have to think sex game. He had unusual sexual inclinations!"

Preferring privacy as details of the deceased were released, Terry indicated to Doctor Tay to cover the corpse, ending the identification process. He led Sandra to a table.

"Tell me about Mark." An open question asked with a layer of compassion.

"We have been separated for quite a while. Our relationship disintegrated and I had to seek court orders to keep him away. But you probably know this?" She raised her face to him, seeking silent confirmation, achieving oral verification.

"I have read the file. You expressed concerns related to him and your daughter." Barely able to conceal his disgust. "You don't need to give me details, just explain what type of person he was. Help me to get inside his head, to assist me in making the call about his cause of death." His manner and posture inviting her confidence, portraying his understanding of her situation, his acceptance of her reaction. Observing her continued absence of sadness.

"He was a show-off. Always trying to be the comedian, wanting to be the centre of attraction in any crowd. Be the funny guy. Act like an ass. He tried to cultivate his image as a good guy, always fun to be around. But it was different behind closed doors. Moody, angry and resentful. He had a massive chip on his shoulder. He believed the world was against him, that his abilities were under-appreciated. He never had a good word to say about anyone and was perpetually jealous of others. To his mind, he was always unfairly overlooked for promotion." Her words were captured via the recording function on his mobile. She had silently agreed when he placed his phone on the table, their conversation outside a police facility, Sandra beyond suspicion rendering any caution unnecessary.

"Did he ever abuse you?" Phrased gently, suggesting he suspected something.

"Verbally, all the time. Has done so for years. Always criticising, sometimes threatening. Physically, there have been occasions where he threatened to use his hands on me. Sexually, he has taken advantage of me if I have had a few drinks, indulged his fantasies. Usually apologising if I confronted him, explaining how it was a compliment to my sexuality."

Concealing his increasingly troublesome impression, Terry continued, "And with respect to your daughter?" Incapable of finding words to complete the accusation.

"No! He never had the chance. I made sure he never had that opportunity." Pride evident, her expression aggressive. "But there were times when his actions were questionable from a father. He didn't and I cannot be sure he would have, you know, but it became the final straw, and I left him. I would like to leave it at that."

"I think you did a very brave thing. From a personal perspective, I would say that you acted correctly, protecting your daughter and yourself. Without revealing incriminating information, I can say that some of his actions recently support your decision to leave." Leaving the statement before them, open to interpretation.

She pointed at his phone. "Does this conversation count as my statement? Can I go home now?"

"You can. For the recording, can you just confirm again that the body you saw was that of Mark Forrest? I will have this conversation written up while we are at the station. If you sign it, we are done, and you can go with my thanks."

"My name is Sandra Forrest, and today is the thirteenth of February. I confirm that I have identified the body of my estranged husband, Mark Forrest, at the mortuary in Wrexham, in the presence of Detective Sergeant Terry Holmes and a pathologist, whose name I have forgotten, but he had his hair in an elaborate ponytail."

"Thank you, Mrs Forrest. I am sorry for your loss." The trailing six words an automated response cultivated by the coaching manual. A meaningless stereotypical statement as an adjunct to the situation, offering closure for the police officer without providing anything positive to the recipient. He ensured Sandra saw him cancel the recording function.

Having previously indicated a desire to leave, she remained in her chair. Terry sat again, joining her at the table once more. "Is there something else?"

"My daughter and I are the beneficiaries of a life insurance policy he had. It isn't huge, though it would support us for a while, since the money from him will stop now. Suicide is an exemption."

Terry considered the situation, understanding her concern. He balanced the likelihood of suicide against accident, factoring the pressure from the suits to avoid considering homicide, hinted incentives to close the case. Compensation to the family could be denied if he declared suicide as cause of death. Who benefits? Who suffers? When is justice served? Collecting his impressions, his distaste towards Mark tempered by his own reaction to the young masseuse, the spunk stain in the car, the historic tension in the family unit. Contrasting and confirmatory concepts competing within his mind.

Taking her hand, he spoke gently. "Leave it with me. I will let you know as soon as I can." Indicating his predilection to assist her, the words unsaid.

Twenty-Three
Wednesday, 13th February

Buzzing with explosive information, itching to tell someone, anyone, Nilesh stalked the corridors of the office at the *Leader*, unsuccessfully restraining his urge to gloat.

The interview with Ruth McGarvey had gone extremely well. She had shared elements of the investigation which he could scarcely believe. Reconciling her story with the recent press conference suggested the police were inflicting a gross deception on the public, a deception he felt obligated to expose.

Failing to find his editor and denied his opportunity to shine, he returned to his desk to apply his attention to the story. Mildly curious at Rob's whereabouts, he wondered where his editor could be during peak office hours, considering and rejecting any notion of Rob working on a story.

She had been astonishingly frank, confessing to enjoying a purely sexual relationship with Campbell-Foulkes, of which her husband was now aware. The affair had been without personal warmth, a purely physical indulgence meeting her needs at the time. The police had latched on to her self-defence skills and possession of a letter opener considered a relevant substitute for a knife. Her alibi had been an inconvenience brushed aside in their haste to prove her guilt. Her minor assault on her husband on an unrelated matter deemed more pertinent, her anger expressed during the pressured interview process deemed demonstrative of her murderous intent.

She had admitted that she and her husband were in financial difficulty. They had discussed allowing the wrongful arrest and charges to proceed, their end game being to expose the false charges and extract monetary damages from the police. The scheme had been abandoned as unfeasible, unworkable.

Under further questioning, she had expressed her resentment at being dragged into the police station today. Having been publicly exonerated only days before, she had resented the police demand to attend an identity parade involving several former girlfriends of the deceased. It had struck her how four of the five were similar in appearance, at least superficially, the exception being a frail blonde girl in her teens.

He had extracted the names of the officers involved: Holmes, Chappell, Beecham, the latter now leading the investigation review while the others had been reassigned. Amused at Ruth's description of the WPC involved, a "bitch of a bull dyke", something he could not use, not in print anyway.

Sensing her interest waning, he had expressed sympathy with her situation, indicated his outrage, suggesting her story could be an inspiration to others, that the police actions should be brought to public scrutiny.

Guiding her towards the other suspects, she knew only first names for Amy and Jenny. The young blonde one was Jasmine Kemp, learning her surname as she provided a shoulder for the young girl to lean on. Susan Grey had revealed her name and little else, maintaining her distance from the others, potentially suspicious in Ruth's estimation.

Using a series of yellow Post-It notes, he displayed everything he had learned, sticking the tabs to a paper desk calendar, adding solid and intermittent lines between tabs with highlighter pens, making connections, seeking further lines of intrigue.

Promising drinks with a co-operative constable, he had expanded his knowledge of the suspects, acquiring their full names and grainy second-generation photographs. He learned that the investigation had initially focused on a possible gay angle, before being redirected to the former girlfriends.

Speaking quietly to an empty room, he summarised his findings. "Inconsistent statements from the force. Signs of incompetence. False arrest and charges. An unsolved murder. A killer roaming the streets. The public's right to know." He assessed the photographs of the suspects, understanding their inclusion would sensationalise the story, surely outweighing any possible privacy issues.

Retreating to the office pantry, he used the dilapidated microwave to warm his homemade thali, the vegetarian dishes conducive to reheating without completely losing their taste. The continued absence of his editor now beginning to annoy him, delaying his chance to impress, and be appreciated. *Where are you, Rob?*

Oblivious to the time, Nilesh began to draft his article, testing the facts while weighing the contradictions as further concerns emerged. Seeking to expand the core story, he introduced the primary areas of concern, suggestive of a killer loose in the community and a lack of confidence in the authorities, finding a way to introduce the photos, asking 'Could any of these be the surprising face of a vicious killer?' The dramatic content exemplified.

His progress was interrupted by the editor's arrival. Taking his opportunity, he grabbed Rob before he could reach his desk, enticing him with an intriguing outline. The editor's feelgood factor simplified the task. As Nilesh explained what he had, along with what he thought he had, Rob listened while scanning the summary, his trained eye sensing levels of inadequacy, content likely to deflect the public while simultaneously alienating law enforcement. The risks unjustified as it stood.

"Nilesh. You have something here. Clearly. But your excitement has exceeded your discipline. I can't use this as it is." The editor adjusted his voice to a conspiratorial tone, inviting his colleague to access an imaginary inner circle. "Broaden the story, clean your sources, name where you can. I agree with you, it is really good; we need to publish, but we need to do it properly." Holding his gaze, embellishing their conspiracy. "Get this right, and we could go national with this story. Forget tonight's deadline for tomorrow, aim for tomorrow night's deadline; bring it to me early afternoon, we can finish it together." Seeing concern, he added. "Relax. Your story, your name." Glancing at the photographs of the alleged suspects, deterred by the quality, moving on. "Try to get those photos cleaned. Ask Bryn for help, he's good at that stuff. Nice work, Nilesh, really good." The praise satisfying the reporter's ego, ensuring he would accept the publication delay.

Twenty-Four
Wednesday, 13th February

Both men exercised patience as they sat in the black nondescript car. Aware of the expectations, they were determined to follow their instructions exactly. The vehicle remained inside the warehouse, a carefully wrapped package in the trunk fastidiously prepared for later disposal. Displaying interest in their mobile phones while sharing only token conversation, they occasionally assessed the sky through the open roller door, seeking signs of dusk. Their mentor had been adamant they should perform their role only under cover of night, but with a deadline of 8pm.

****

"Fuck it, Doris. I can't wait until after nine. Can't you get the information now?"

"Like I told you, Barry, my source said nine and not before. Feel free to continue investigating yourself, but I get the feedback at nine, so that's when you get it."

"The DI is asking questions."

"Not my problem. I'm solving your bloody case for you. A bit of gratitude would be welcome."

****

Navigating the afternoon traffic with little difficulty in her little red hatchback, she wished the radio would play a song she could sing along with. *Five Hundred Miles* by The Proclaimers would work. *Una Paloma Blanca*? Tones and I was just not cutting it for her.

Reflecting on lunch, the acceptable food accompanied by delicious wine, the appreciative companion, the overall experience approaching wonderful. She had enjoyed herself, delighted at the relaxed ambience, the simplicity of their conversation, feeling natural together. She muttered his name, relishing the sound in her mouth as she recalled his lips against hers, liking that feeling also.

****

Emotionally complicated. A summary of his assessment from the force's psychoanalyst.

Cheeky bugger, making these snapshot judgements. His opinion of the cardigan-clad weirdo diminished further. These "professionals" allocated their opinion to personnel files without contemplation of any potential career impact, untouchable in their domain. They had no interest in an officer's distractions at home, a daughter injured at school sports day or a toddler who hadn't slept a whole night since birth. *Come to my house, dickhead, then assess me. See what I handle every bastard day.*

Senior Sergeant Emyr Christopher had been surprised to receive a summons to the psycho, his conjecture being a necessary assessment to ensure he could cope with demotion, a means to determine his likelihood of resigning. *Resign? Fat chance. I'm skint with three kids. A family who enjoys overseas travel. Two weeks in Dubai last year, fucking expensive sandpit.*

Reflecting on his caseload, the overall team seemed to be improving again. DS Holmes' case with the dried urine in the BMW had intrigued him. An unusual discovery on a car seat, possibly expected from a child, but kids should be in the rear. A random thought nudging him, recessed but persistent, driving him to open Google. Initially searching for ejaculate, he refined his search to female ejaculate, the invisible light bulb in his head suddenly illuminating. "PSA! Prostatic Specific Antigen. That's it."

Calling the forensic subcontractor, he connected with his preferred contact. "Listen, do you still have that sample from the car seat, the dried urine?" Receiving confirmation, resuming. "Can you test the sample for PSA? Thanks. Just a hunch. Let me know."

****

Bowels spectacularly evacuated, Puss-Puss sat in the stall, perspiring, praying for continued solitude, astounded that she could create a smell as bad as this. She considered possible causes of her indisposition. Dodgy food? A bug in the bank? Nervous about dinner with Miss A?

About to stand and escape the toxic atmosphere, her stomach gurgled, prompting a return to the seat. "Oh, no." She felt the barely viscous liquid expel from her rear, increasing her discomfort as she felt herself become increasingly tender.

****

Taking advantage of his supervisory role at the telecommunications giant, Simon excused himself from the premises without bothering to inform his colleagues of any reason. Opening the hatch of his Audi, he placed the final rucksack inside, completing the consignment.

Changing radio stations as Tones and I was introduced, finding Marillion halfway through *White Paper*, acknowledging the brilliance of the guitar playing, his tension receding as he entered the meeting place to his navigation system.

At first, these meetings had made him anxious. Dealing with lower-level lowlife criminals had intimidated him. Having become experienced, he maintained a moderately relaxed approach to each instance. Always a different place, usually a different person, only occasionally tense.

Carrying thirty assorted mobile phones composed of traded-in devices, budget models and out-of-contract handsets, he had located each in a plastic zip-locked bag. Every device was provided complete with charger, USB cable, battery, sim card and a credit voucher for ten pounds. Random brands, inconsistent features, untraceable, registered as donated to charities. Ten more to follow, those packages almost ready.

****

DS Holmes escorted Mrs Forrest to her car, complimenting her on the way she had handled a difficult situation, expressing his appreciation for her co-operation. Comprehending the silent question in her eyes, her tears barely withheld, he became more certain of his decision.

"I plan to suggest to my superior officer that we classify Mark's death as an accident, caused by indulgence in a dangerous sex act without supervision. That should assist you, and your daughter."

"Thank you, Terry. Thank you so much."

He expected the DCI would be amenable to his decision, providing he took some time to present a solid justification for his reasoning. He planned to do so this afternoon.

****

The black car rolled slowly forward from the warehouse, both front seats occupied, the trunk full. Their intention was to take a leisurely drive to the nominated location, arriving early to wait for full darkness before committing their task.

"Where are you going, lads?" The Mancunian had signalled they should halt.

"Thought we'd make an early start, boss. Beat the traffic."

"Are you simple? Don't answer that. Why would you want to leave the warehouse and drive across town earlier than you have to?"

"You gave us an eight o'clock deadline. Eliminate an element of risk. That's what we thought."

"You've got a body in the boot. The longer you are exposed, the higher chance of being pulled over. Get back inside."

Knowing that argument would be pointless, the driver engaged reverse, returning the Vauxhall to the warehouse. Relieved, The Mancunian diverted his attention to the painting of the office.

****

Closing her office door, Barry presented himself, upright, earnest, drawing her full attention.

"Anything pressing on your desk?"

Her reply, coquettish. "Nothing that can't wait. Why?" Red lips parted, anticipating, curious.

"Fancy joining me for a matinee performance at my place?"

Sergeant Freeland reflected on his inexplicable offer. "Are you asking me to leave the station to go to your place, for an afternoon of shagging? Seriously?"

"Yes, Annie, I am." Undeterred. Defiant.

Collecting her keys and handbag before standing, looking into his eyes. "Just so happens I'm in the mood; your timing is perfect."

****

Carefully removing her new dress, she hung the garment on the dedicated padded hanger, admiring the simplicity and elegance of the fabric and design. Her replacement blouse and tracksuit trousers providing a startling contrast.

Raking through her fridge, she sought inspiration for a dish unrelated to pasta, her thought processes inefficient, drifting to her date and his respectful treatment of her. Her body reflecting the emotional pleasure she received from his attentiveness.

Trawling through the freezer, she found a variety of unsuitable ready meals. Hesitant to go out to the supermarket, yet wanting to cook for Puss-Puss, short of alternatives, she conceded that she may have to eat pasta for the second time today.

The underlying agenda for tonight forgotten, for now.

****

Felicia McGarry hung up. Intrigued by the development, she wondered why they had not checked this alibi before. She consoled herself that she was a constable, seconded in, working below three detectives. Any fault did not lie with her.

Finding DS Beecham helping himself to a hot drink, she shared her news.

"I spoke to the Broughton medical practice, checking the alibi for Jenny Coleman."

"Oh yeah, does it stand up?" Doris only half-interested, his focus on Amy Meadows enduring.

"No. She was not at work that Friday afternoon, which, in her words, is the busiest period of the week. She took a half day, had booked it two weeks in advance."

Interested now, he asked "So, where was she?"

Flick spread her arms. "I think we have to bring her back in. Lying to us about her alibi, what else is she lying about?"

"Send some plods round. Get her lifted right away." His sentiments mixed, high that they had a lead, low that it wasn't Meadows.

****

Emyr passed Annie's office, noting her absence, trying the locked door, seemingly gone for the day.

You haven't got my job yet, he thought, *but already benefitting from the perks.*

Aligning the wall clock behind her desk within his phone screen, he snapped a picture, showing the empty office during working hours. Weak, easy to explain away, nevertheless bringing him satisfaction.

****

"Are you okay, Holly?"

The teller absorbed the sweat-streaked face, the pale skin, the unsteady gait, showing concern for her colleague.

Seated, Holly wiped her brow with an aloe vera-coated tissue. "I'm okay, thanks, feeling a little bit sick. I hope it passes."

The colleague approached, touched the back of her hand to Holly's forehead, taking her temperature. "You're flushed. Be careful. Maybe you should go home?" Coming closer, she dropped her voice. "Avoid the toilets. Seems someone has contaminated the ladies, big time."

****

Feeling like the proverbial spare prick, Simon watched as the customer inspected the merchandise. The thug was counting everything, checking the credit vouchers, ensuring sim cards were present, admiring the superior phones while dismissing those of lower specification. The money had yet to be exchanged or even offered.

"What about the numbers?"

"Included. Written on the sim cards packaging." Resisting the urge to add "as usual".

"Some of these phones are shit. I mean, really shit. Are you ripping us off?"

Impatient, unhappy at the attempted interrogation, he responded roughly. "What do you expect for these prices, the latest iPhones? The top concern is traceability, and these cannot be traced. Ask your boss."

Placing the items in his car, the customer returned to Simon, producing a stuffed envelope, presumably the money. Indicating that Simon should take it, he caught Simon's wrist. "Watch how you speak to me. I can break you."

Backing away, releasing his wrist, opening the package, he forced the customer to wait while he meticulously counted the wad of cash, taking his time and repeating the exercise before being finally satisfied that full payment had been forthcoming. "Eight thousand. Tell your boss thank you, the rest of the mobiles will be ready on Saturday."

Mutually uninterested in shaking hands, they departed.

****

Desisting from animalistic passion, Annie and Barry each assisted the other in undressing, before adjourning to his bedroom. Engaging in polite conversation interspersed with light kissing, they explored each other, their pleasure heightened by the naughty factor, sneaking away from work to indulge their mutual attraction.

Condom applied, they copulated slowly, gently, considerately, unlike their previous encounters, sharing a perceptibly higher level of intimacy.

****

As Holly's scheduled arrival approached, Amy's nervousness increased. Her anticipation tempered by anxiety, intrigued yet bewildered about the possibility of sharing her bed with another woman. The situation could be further complicated by their close friendship and the risk posed to their future relationship. If the experiment went badly, would they become uncomfortable with each other? If it went well, would they elongate the experiment and establish a relationship? Convinced of her own heterosexuality, Amy had nevertheless dressed nicely, retained her make-up from lunch and attentively prepared her intimate areas, subconsciously inviting the interaction.

****

The black vehicle paused at the edge of the road, a short distance beyond the designated layby. A casual observer might question the wisdom of passing an authorised parking area, then stopping shortly after. However, casual observers were absent from the scene. Working together, the men removed the cargo from the boot, carrying it to the edge of the foliage, before swinging the package up and over the fence, hearing it land solidly beyond the wire boundary. The descending dusk ensured that visibility was limited; seeing no vehicles in proximity, they drove ahead.

Parking in the next stopping area, they crossed the boundary fence before hiking in the direction of the abandoned package, ducking down as a precaution when they heard an approaching car. Their caution impacted the time taken to return to the covered item lying behind bushes, unmoving. Pulling the heavy cargo away from the fence, they made their laboured way towards the destination layby, compensated for their efforts by full winter darkness enveloping the area.

Still obscured from the road, several metres from the layby, they deemed their position close enough for the appointed task. Unzipping the bag, unwrapping the contents, they revealed a naked male corpse, blood staining the abdomen, eyes closed, skin pallid, the centre of gravity adjusted by rigor mortis. As directed, they laid the body on the ground, hidden from casual view, face upwards, uncovered, available for predator attack, tender opportunities for the adventurous forager.

"This is why we do as we are told." The villain voiced his recognition of the circumstances surrounding the death of the person before them.

"Grab the bag; we need to take it with us." Walking back to the car, he added, "Do you have the legitimate number plates?"

"Yeah, we'll fit them back at the warehouse, then dump this thing in the usual place. Are you driving the replacement?"

Receiving a nod of assent, he moved, joined by his partner, progressing through the dark bushland, avoiding headlights, puffing as they climbed into the car. Without discussion, they joined the road, heading for Wrexham.

****

The text messages made The Mancunian smile. The body was in position. The vehicle was en route for disposal. The phones had been received. Everything was in order.

He surveyed the office within the warehouse. It had been jet-hosed extensively, industrially bleached, hosed again and was now in the process of being painted. The unwanted furniture and cork soundproofing had been removed, deposited in a skip whose contents were burning brightly in the gloom. The bullets and casings were recovered and all damage to the walls and floor were repaired. He reflected on a successful day.

Calling the Mama San, he gave her the message for the friendly copper, saying she could pass the message at any time, but only when asked.

She asked him to repeat the message. "You'll find what you are looking for at the scene of the crime."

****

Nilesh worked late, refining his story, cross-referencing his sources of information, providing a template of corroboration for the editor. As he developed the text, he admitted to himself that it had improved immensely. Rob had been correct: get it right before publication. Dreaming of national syndication, he prepared to head home.

****

Flick dispensed the frustrating news to Doris. The uniforms had been unable to locate Jenny Coleman. She had not returned home, was absent from work and her mobile was switched off. Without any means to apprehend her, Doris called an end to the day, inviting Flick to join him for a drink. Surprised at her acceptance, they took their coats and headed to the nearest pub. Doris, absorbed in his own case, completely forgetting his instruction to call the massage place for an update on the suspect in the Asian lady's murder.

Quaffing his first pint in three swallows, he ordered a repeat, encouraging Flick to keep up, disregarding her gender, treating her like a mate.

****

Barry Chappell, empty, satiated, happy, had fallen into a light sleep. Annie Freeland lay beside him, enjoying the respite from his libido, relishing the soft mattress, her tenderness below, pondering the change in their physicality, unsure if she understood. This relationship had begun as a physical outlet, a rebuttal of her reputed frigidity, unconditional, emotions optional. The changes were suggestive of an increased co-dependence, feelings becoming more ardent, rewarded by significant improvement in the bedroom.

Ambition dictated that she should keep this relationship casual. Emyr was facing a board, she was positioned to accede into his role, the promotion and remuneration expected, anticipated. Anything prejudicial to her promotion could not be risked.

****

Recalling Holly's intention to visit Amy, Terry reconsidered his plans for the impending evening. Holly would probably get drunk and stay over, hopefully disposing of those incriminating photos before she did. The empty house unenticing in the winter chill, he steered his Ford towards Wrexham, justifying his intentions as a reward for closing a complicated case to the benefit of all interested parties.

Trotting from his vehicle to reduce the impact of the drizzle, he entered the reception area at the massage premises. Received without a warm smile, he hurriedly explained his situation. Off duty, no case, seeking a relaxing massage, willing to pay without expectations. He asked if Hoi might be available.

Delighted minutes later when the petite masseuse appeared, inviting him to follow her, suggesting he might like to take a shower, assisting him in removing his jacket.

The shower had been lukewarm, insufficient to revive his tiredness. Entering an unfamiliar room, he carefully took his position face down on the blanket, modesty assured by his damp towel, her hands on his shoulders instilling a sense of relaxation. Her movements slow and precise, imparting gentle pressure, increasing as she located tightness in his muscles. After twenty minutes of mellow pleasure interspersed with short sharp pain, she asked him to turn on to his back, the masseuse making deliberate adjustments to his towel, continuing to preserve his modesty.

His modesty deserted him as she massaged his upper leg, moving to the inside of his thigh, the rear of her hand brushing his scrotum. Her actions eliciting a spontaneous reaction, obvious beneath the towel, twitching. Unsure of the situation and how he was expected to react, he heard the words he wanted, gently whispered as her cheek brushed his own. "Would you like a happy ending?"

Dressing afterwards, settling the account for the extras in cash, Terry exchanged a bow with the beautiful young lady, before paying for the standard massage out front. Analysing the receptionist's expression as mischievous, he exited the premises, feeling wonderful, meditating on the level of pleasure achieved from such a simple act. *It certainly doesn't feel like that when I relieve myself at home.* Revisiting her technique, arousing him with her lightly oiled hands, touching him, then touching below him, extracting stimulated responses, taking him close. Then settling him, before slowly building again, positioning herself to allow him to appreciate her, teasing him towards release, climaxing with a joyful yell, his ecstasy almost painful.

****

The superintendent found an unexpected file on his desk. Opening the manila binder, he exposed a case file from Police Scotland, family name Meadows. Puzzlement conceding to recall, he remembered asking for the file after the press conference. Flicking through the pages, confirming the file as the one he had wanted, he returned to the front page, reading with increased intensity, the information gelling with his own memories.

It had been a contentious case, observed from a distance, relevant personally due to it being his former territory. Marjorie Meadows had been sentenced to twelve years for killing her husband Michael, convicted of manslaughter. The Fiscal's office had campaigned for a murder charge due to evidential indications of premeditation. The defence lawyers, supported by the press, had campaigned for release, citing extended ongoing spousal abuse. "Political hot potato," he muttered, remembering the coverage.

The defence had petitioned for a non-custodial sentence. Marjorie had been in fear for her personal safety and increasingly frightened for her daughter, Amelia. The child was approaching sixteen, sufficiently mature to be unable to avoid awareness of her mother's suffering and her father's physical domination of the family. The child had told the court of her father issuing every ultimatum with a precursor. He would count to ten and if unsatisfied, punishment would follow. The lawyers presented pictures of discreet bruises she had incurred, located below clothing, invisible to school friends or teachers.

The psychologists had enjoyed a field day, earning substantial consultation fees from the government to assess the family, including post-conviction sessions with the child, warning of possible latent anger-management problems.

"Definitely relevant." Closing the file, labelling it with a Post-It marked for the attention of DS Beecham at Mold, he scrawled his signature, applying the date. As an afterthought, he stapled his card to the file, ensuring top priority would be given. Having made another important intervention, he buzzed for tea and biscuits.

****

Welcoming Holly at her front door, she instantly sensed an issue. Her friend was pale, drawn, dishevelled, untidy. Sharing a short hug, Amy stepped back, closing the door, preserving the warmth in her home while repelling the winter assault on her comfort. "Puss-Puss, what's wrong? Are you okay?"

Holly flopped on the settee, coat on, bag to the floor. "I've had the donkey trots all afternoon. I feel like shit, literally."

Amy sat beside her, allowing space, taking her hand, providing comfort through contact. Seeking words of support, failing to locate them.

"Look at you, all dressed up. Just for me. I'm flattered. I must look horrible."

"You never do, Holly. You're always glam and gorgeous. Can I get you anything?"

"Cola and crisps. I need to get some electrolytes back in me. Or similar; lemonade and pretzels, anything sugary and salty. Thank you. Sorry. How's your day been?"

Offering no response, Amy retreated to her kitchen, seeking refreshments as she contemplated the evening ahead. Pouring Coke into two glasses over lemon and ice, she delivered them to the lounge table, placed within Holly's reach, seeing her friend gratefully gulp the sparkling drink, sighing with appreciation, retaining her grip on the glass. Locating crisps and snacks, Amy poured ready-salted crisps into a bowl usually reserved for salad, leftover from Christmas salted pretzel sticks added to an adjacent bowl, sealing both half-empty bags with plastic clothes pegs. Depositing the snacks on the table, laughing inadvertently as her friend grabbed a handful of crisps, dropped half, tried to suck the remainder from her hand, fumbling for the dropped items on her skirt.

Their early exchanges suggesting any intimacy unlikely, Amy felt her anxiety reduce.

Holly explained the photograph demands from Terry, seemingly embarrassed. Amy understanding, relieved at the professional insight, performed the task immediately, confirming Holly had already deleted her copies.

Presenting wine and the gargantuan cider bottle, both declined by Holly, Amy suggested food, again politely declined. Replenishing the Cola and snacks, she took a seat beside her friend, closer this time, their knees brushing together. Taking her hand again, Amy stroked the soft fingers, feeling heat emanating from Holly's body. Concerned, she offered to take Holly's coat, her intentions misinterpreted.

"Amy. I know what you want." The statement spoken, inviting discussion. "I think I want it, too. I think." Shaking her tousled hair, uncertainty physically indicated. "What if it affects our friendship?"

Blindsided, her intentions only having been to accommodate her friend's advances and respond if approached, Amy instead being suggested as the aggressor, not quite an accusation. "Holly, you made the first indication, suggested you thought about making a move on me."

Vigorously denying the claim, Holly said, "I don't think so. I mean, I do fancy you a bit. But I'm straight."

Amy caught her eye. "So am I, but I would try it for you, only for you."

Mutually appreciating an escalating tension, both withdrew, maintaining visual contact, smiles forming reluctantly, escaping, releasing. "So, we've both been thinking about it, and we're both hesitant, and now we're blaming each other. That's funny." Holly, displaying signs of recovery, raised herself to a sitting position, moving forward on her seat, half turning. Returning her friend's soft touch, their fingers intertwining, appreciating Amy's delicate features revealing her confusion, disarming her with a raised hand, touching her hair, appreciating how it had been restyled, improved.

Inclining her head, tilting her face as she moved forward, her hand holding her friend's face steady, she placed her lips on Amy's. Gently at first, gradually applying pressure, opening her mouth, feeling the reciprocal action. Flicking her tongue, tasting her friend, persisting, pulling Amy closer to her, an alien tongue tasting her, the moment immortalised. Reducing the intensity, releasing the contact, retracting from the physical proximity, she re-engaged visually.

Betraying a hint of breathlessness, Holly enquired, "How was that?"

Without hesitation, mildly flustered, replying, "It was a lovely kiss." The response ambiguous.

"Okay." Thinking, forming a further question. "How did it make you feel?"

Lowering her expression, considering her reaction. "Confused." Receiving encouragement to continue. "It reinforced how I feel about you." Ambiguity persisting. "You're my friend. I love you. You know that."

Frustrated by her friend's continued ambiguous interpretation, Holly became specific. "Did our kiss make you want to go to bed with me, experiment with me, go further. Are you hornier now than you were five minutes ago? You said you would be honest."

Her eyes moistened as she prepared her reply. "I don't want to hurt you." Wiping with her hand. "No, it hasn't aroused me, though I did enjoy it. But it didn't work for me." Uttering the white lie. Suddenly embraced by her friend, lips against her ear. "Thank God. I just didn't feel it. You are so lovely, I have fancied you for ages, but, while kissing you, I felt nothing sexually." Increasing space between them. "Are you okay?"

"I think we need that drink now."

Twenty-Five
Thursday, 14th February

Hearing a uniform sarcastically wishing him a happy Valentine's Day, he issued a brusque "Fuck off." In no mood for banter, silently cursing just about everyone he knew, Barry Chappell stared at the crime scene before him.

Doris had called him this morning, sharing the information he had expected at nine the previous evening. The useless bastard was twelve hours late, selfishly omitting to consider the gratitude he owed. Arriving on scene alongside the A483, in the same layby as where they had found the deceased Asian lady, he was supported by a pair of constables, taking their time to find the object of the search, a heavy early morning mist deterring any urge to rake among the bushes and soak his recently ironed trousers.

They found the naked body, displaying a rain-smeared bloody pale abdomen, the victim unfamiliar. He issued instructions to the constables to preserve the scene, closing the layby, the police car angled to discourage vehicles, striped tape stretched above the tarmac, beyond into the bushes, closing off a substantial area of land.

He had called for medical support, already certain of death, following the established procedure. He had requested forensic support from Emyr, the Cardiffian seemingly jovial today. Lastly calling DS Beecham, advising him of the find, asking him what else he knew.

Meandering through the layby, resisting the temptation of his warm car, he surveyed the crime scene, seeking foreign bodies, disturbed ground, assuming the body had been brought here by vehicle. Remembering, calling the station, asking for somebody to chase up CCTV for the stretch of road for the last twenty-four hours.

Understanding the weather could compromise the recovery of forensic information, Barry was comforted that DNA would not be problematic, expecting confirmation of a match with that taken from the slain Thai woman. Idly wondering if Dr Tay would come to the scene. Hoping Emyr would send Annie, helping to brighten a dismal situation.

Unsure of the exact geography, he placed a courtesy call to Cheshire CID, informing them of the discovery of a body, on a lead received in Wales, referring to the proximity of the border. Cheshire agreed to send a liaison detective to the scene, precautionary, procedural. Hearing sirens in the distance, Barry awaited the first of many arrivals, the scene likely to develop into an orgy of police activity.

Returning to the proximity of the body, he snapped a few pictures on his phone, expanding the pictures to seek clues to the body's identity and the cause of death. The abdominal damage looked likely, reminiscent of a gunshot wound, the residual blood mostly washed away to reveal torn tissue, muscle and flesh. Attempting a long-range close visual inspection, still unwilling to soak his clothes and reluctant to contaminate the scene, he scanned the photos for clues, noting the fingertips remained intact, seeing a face that was bruised and battered, but potentially still identifiable.

An ambulance, the source of the siren, pulled alongside the recess, two paramedics extracting themselves from the front seats. "Where's the body?" they asked as they continued their approach, despite receiving no answer, wrapping their hands in medical gloves, one producing a highly powered flashlight to combat the gloom.

"Over here." Barry indicated the location with his hands, guiding the paramedics to the site. Spotting the body, they climbed over the fence, one squatting as he checked for a pulse, failing to find one at the neck, again at the wrist. Wordlessly agreeing with his colleague, addressing DS Chappell. "Confirmed, no sign of life, suspicious death, gaping wound in the lower midriff. You guys can start your processes."

Expressing a gratitude that he didn't feel, Chappell escorted the ambulance crew to their vehicle, internally belittling their contribution, *stating the bleeding obvious*. The departing ambulance replaced by a hatchback carrying two forensic investigators, accompanied by Annie who was presumably assuming the supervisory role. Instinctively, they approached the fence, locating the deceased without guidance, their professionalism evident.

Controlling his reaction to Annie's presence, he conceded the crime scene to the forensic investigators, monitoring progress from his vehicle. Distracted, he failed to notice the latest arrival. Ponytail knocked on the window as he passed Barry's car, striding purposefully towards the protectively clothed technicians. Irrationally pissed off, Chappell extricated himself from the vehicle, joining the activity surrounding the body, feeling any residual heat withdraw from his extremities, particularly his toes.

"DS Chappell, what do we know?" Dr Tay's question posed with a chirpy inflection.

"Tip off. I suspect this person may have been involved in the death of the Asian woman you dissected recently; hopefully Annie's guys can confirm that. Meanwhile, it looks like another murder, likely caused by the gunshot wound to the gut. Annie?"

Sergeant Freeland offered her opinion. "The body has been here a while, overnight maybe. The rain has partially cleaned the body. My early impressions are that the body was killed elsewhere, then brought here after the fact. I concur that the gut wound is the likely cause of death, subject to further investigation."

The pathologist crept closer to the deceased, assessing the wound while checking for latent signs of life, continuing a career-long habit. "There is just one problem. That abdominal wound" — he indicated the obvious site — "that is an exit wound. Cause of death remains unknown." Recognising their surprise, pointing at the edge of the opening. "The skin puckers outward around the edge of the wound, indicating the bullet or other object travelled from inside the body to the outside. We need to turn him over. I suggest we bag and tag him, take him to my place and have a proper look at him. Are we all agreed?"

Annie, rattled at missing such an obvious condition, quickly agreed. Barry, processing his revised opinion of the doctor, *arrogant twat*, seeking any source of warmth, concurred.

Waiting for the technicians to perform their remaining tasks, and for the body to be claimed, Chappell exchanged a short conversation with the Cheshire detective, explaining the situation, describing the highlights. They shared an opinion that a dead criminal was one less thing to worry about in their thankless profession. The Cheshire cop had a look at the body, agreed jurisdiction belonged to North Wales, before leaving the scene in his sparkling new Toyota.

Watching the body being loaded into the recently arrived mortuary van, Barry departed, heading for Maelor Hospital, mentally preparing himself for the ordeal of watching the post-mortem. Annie joined him, leaving her technicians to complete the site works. Once on the road, with his speed approaching sixty, he reached across to touch her hand. "Hi, gorgeous."

His attempted flirt rejected with a prompt response, louder than she intended. "Piss off, Barry, we're at work!" The remainder of the journey was mostly quiet, the heater providing no respite from the frosty atmosphere.

Dried and refreshed by caffeine, the interested parties assembled in the post-mortem suite, as the mystery naked body was placed on the stainless-steel surface. The pathologist began his recording, setting the required parameters, explaining his decision to turn the body onto its front immediately. Inspecting the corpse, he came to a quick conclusion.

"You might want to see this, guys. Like I said, the belly wound is an exit, the actual bullet entry wound is round here, at the rear." Hesitating, waiting for Barry and Annie to join him. "Our deceased man was shot in the rectum, from extremely close range; there are burn residues evident around his bottom. This would appear to be an execution. I have never seen anything like this." Stepping back, inviting Barry to make a closer inspection, closely watching his hands for improper handling, appreciative of the delicate manner displayed.

"Was the gun fired, eh, internally?" Horror evident on his features.

"I would say no. I suggest the gun was placed against the rectum, then fired from a barely external position. Thankfully. The internal examination will confirm conclusively."

"Thanks, Doc. Could you hazard a time of death?"

"Give me a couple of hours, I'll have a preliminary report for you. Estimated time. Blood type, prints, DNA, all that good stuff. You can assume cause of death is gunshot wound. This might be one worthy of publishing."

Retreating to the exit, wearing their masks, they were eager to leave the suite, anxious to maintain protection against the odour, leaving the Forensic Pathologist to his work.

Outside, mask removed, Barry excused himself while inhaling fresh air from the open window, calling DS Beecham, who picked up on the second ring. "We've got a real fucking issue."

"What is it now, Barry?"

"The tip-off you provided as the DNA match for my dead Asian woman. He's only turned up dead as well. Shot in the fucking arse! Yes, up his arse. Bullet came out through his gut. It probably happened last night, which is when you were supposed to give me the information. We could be facing an enquiry here!"

"You have the time of death confirmed? Nine pm or later last night? Absolutely sure?"

"Well, not yet, but the pathologist indicated…"

Interrupted by Doris. "Indicated? But not confirmed? Why don't we wait until the information is official, then you can poop your pants?"

"I need to speak to your informant. Now!" Hearing the sound, deep inhalation, from the other end.

"Not going to happen, Barry. Way too complicated for that. I need to work my way up their system. It might take a while."

"Not good enough, Doris. Get him quickly. You have put me out on a limb, again. This is not good!"

"Take your head out of your backside for a minute and try thinking like a senior officer. Put yourself in PJ's shoes. You have the guy who raped the woman, probably the murderer, and he's dead, too — case closed. And a lowlife off the streets as well. He won't give a flying fuck about when we got the message, or who the informant was, or how quickly we reacted."

"Who the fuck is PJ?" Barry, exasperated, feeling like an outsider, not privy to the inside track, his self-control tenuous.

"Your gaffer. DI Jones. Peter. Joined us from Australia a few years ago. I know him quite well, obviously better than you. He'll be stoked, his word, to solve this so quickly."

"What do we do now?"

Doris, dismissive. "You wait until you have all the facts, consider what you have, play with it, present it to your DI, select your angle. Meanwhile, I will get back to my own case, for which you have provided zero assistance, to try to catch a killer. Yours would appear to be caught already."

Pondering a sharp response, unable to voice it as the connection had already broken, Barry headed to his office with plenty to think about. His morale lifted by the likely solving of the Thai immigrant murder, removing the rumoured potential political pressure from himself and his DI. He understood that the PM report would be the decisive element in his reporting of the case.

Unlocking his glovebox, he poured a small shot from a pewter flask, the spirit camouflaged in a plastic cup. The liquor assisting the return of calm, his normal emotions resurfacing, confidence swelling, a requirement to pee slowly manifesting itself.

Twenty-Six
Thursday, 14th February

Surprised at being summoned to this location, Boris the Orange stood beside his car, extracting warmth from the rubbish skip smouldering at the boundary of the site. The adjacent premises remained without tenants, ensuring adequate privacy for their activities. Lighting a cigarette from an oversized Zippo replica, he waited.

The roar of the motorcycle preceded the appearance of the boss. Tossing the half-smoked Marlboro into the skip, he stepped forward to greet Ian, receiving an enormous grin as the helmet was removed.

"Boris! Good morning. It's a fucking beautiful day. How are you?"

"Feeling good, boss. Glad to be here, surprised maybe?"

Indicating the building, Ian led the way to the office within the warehouse, producing keys to access each entrance, punching buttons on the keypad. Sniffing the air, detecting fresh paint, feeling comfortable.

Boris complimented the boss, "I like what you're doing to the place."

Invited to sit, he dropped onto a stool, avoiding a paint tray. His employer selecting a chair behind a pristine-looking desk. "We found out who killed Madam Nattaporn. It was Dai Harris. Probably assisted by Joseph Nesbitt. They have been punished. The matter is closed."

"Okay?" Unsure how to respond to this information.

"I want you to come up with a strategy for how we explain to the girls what happened — in a way that they feel safe, but also aware that justice has been served. I think you can do this. You know the girls better than anyone. You've fucked most of them anyway."

"Come on boss, you can't say that."

"Really? Which one did you hump on Tuesday after the meal? I'm guessing the taller young one with the decent English. Was she good?" His face revealing amusement, an absence of malice.

"The small one. She speaks almost no English. The tall one was reluctant, the little one eager to please. Good food, a few drinks, back to my place, kit off, legs akimbo." Seeing that he had provided enough detail, he asked, "What have we done with Harris and Nesbitt?"

Appreciative of the "we", The Mancunian explained. "Dai has been handed to the fuzz." Perceiving concern on Boris's face, he elaborated. "Already dead. We allowed them to find his cleansed corpse, so they can match his DNA and close the case. Nesbo is in the skip." He made the revelation casually, almost as an aside. "Should be pretty crispy by now, almost like a part of the furniture." Pleased with his own comedic genius, laughing. "The site is clean, as you can see. No evidence."

Sliding open a desk drawer, the new fitment squeaking from unlubricated hinges, he extracted several plastic bags, presenting the latest batch of mobile phones and accessories. "You can distribute these to the new girls. Explain the rules and our expectations." His hand remained over the phones. "I have other things I would like to discuss with you, Boris." Scrutinising the face, seeking signs of interest or reluctance. "We should consider increasing your profile in the organisation."

"You know me, boss. Always keen to help. On the lookout for new ways to earn some cash."

"This incident with the woman has impacted my trust levels. I want future shipments to be more tightly controlled, handled by my closest allies. That includes you, my friend. I want you to be my go-to guy, whether that be trafficking important people or moving the Ice around the network."

"I've never been involved in the drug side. You would need to teach me."

Staring intensely at Boris, The Mancunian growled. "That's why I want you. Your honesty. It's like any other logistical exercise, just with extra precautions due to the value of the cargo. Pour some coffee, and I'll give you a summary of what we do."

Sharing coffee and inside knowledge, The Mancunian explained the business to his increasingly trusted employee. "We source our ladies for the massage business from Vietnam, Laos and Thailand. They are gathered in the Golden Triangle in Thailand's North. We separate the ladies from their belongings, shipping the people via Pattaya to a ship bound for Yemen, where they are divided into smaller groups and brought to Albania, then by road to France. Their belongings are modified to carry a quantity of crystal meth and are transported through a similar route on different vessels, deviating to Holland, before delivery to Great Yarmouth on an oilfield support vessel. We take the ladies through the Channel Tunnel in trucks, documented as asylum seekers as a precaution. Separate lorries deliver to the Chester area, where the luggage and ladies are reunited at their new homes, the drugs already evacuated from the bags."

Nodding his understanding, expressing his admiration, Boris posed a few questions. Learning that the Ice was an irregular regular activity, while the ladies were more *ad hoc*. Airports were avoided at all costs for the drugs, due to security equipment constantly evolving, improving, and European Customs agents remaining impossible to bribe despite the relative simplicity in developing Asia. Seaports, especially smaller ones, were reliant on antiquated technology and sniffer dogs, while restricted by budget-limited operational hours. The mantra being to minimise risk and maximise profit.

"How much are we talking about?"

"Oh, we are small-time on the Ice. Maybe fifteen million quid a year wholesale; we resell at a fifty percent margin, then the dealers top it up to establish the mythical street value. Do the sums. Too small to warrant attention from the Task Forces. The massage parlours turn over more than twenty million, but with higher overheads, so smaller margins. Nice business, lower risk, lesser sentences. The high-class escorts business is fledgling, beginning to pay, having more potential than I realised."

"I had no idea our empire was this large. It must take a lot of managing. And reporting to the ultimate owners." Boris displaying interest approaching fascination.

Ian sat back, pride overcoming caution. "I am the ultimate owner. And you would be working directly for me. That's the opportunity I am presenting to you."

Standing, extending his hand, smiling, Boris the Orange accepted the challenge. "I'm in. Thank you for your faith. When can I start?"

"The phones first. Come back at four. I have five kilos of Ice to move to Llandudno; you can handle that. Details to follow. And leave a few of the girls for others, especially the one who knocked you back last night; I might try her myself. Your new role is between you and me for now, confidential. Understand?"

Twenty-Seven
Thursday, 14th February

An open packet of Mr Kipling lemon slices before them, Flick and Doris shared a moment of respite from the incessant interviewing of second-tier suspects, conceding that none looked as likely as Jenny Coleman or Amy Meadows. Hoping for a surprise break, they continued perusing the list of outstanding persons of interest yet to be seen.

Off the clock, Doris changed the subject. "The guv's getting better. Doing well." Referring to DI Catt, their absent leader hospitalised after a suspected heart attack. "They stuck a device through his wrist to check his plumbing; seems he wasn't as bad as first suspected. Instead of a bypass, he had an ablation, whatever that is, to stop his heart rate shooting through the roof."

"That's great news." Flick liked the guv, also aware that Doris was close to him. "Will he be going home soon?"

"They said he could go home tomorrow if he behaved himself. So possibly next week." The joke lame, affection clear in his voice. "I spoke to his wife this morning." Explaining his knowledge.

"Let's hope we solve this case before he comes back."

"You met this guy at Vodafone, Simon, with the guv. What was your impression?"

Chewing frantically to swallow the remnants of her third cake, feeling crumbs escape as she spoke. "I thought he was a complete tool. A bit of a smartass. Seemed full of his own importance, then became quite helpful. I can't see him as a killer, though he was evasive about his relationship with Jed."

"And you're sure the gay angle is not applicable?"

"Sure? Fucking certain! Jed preyed on women, vulnerable women."

"Come on, we'll go around to Jenny Coleman's place of work, rattle her cage, shake her up, then bring her here. Everything I have ever learned in this job tells me it's either her or Amy Meadows. One of these two. Don't look at me like that; at least it's a partially open mind."

Excited to escape the station, to break the monotony of interviews, PC Felicia McGarry bestowed her warmest smile on DS Grahame Beecham. "Can I be bad cop?" Walking together towards the car park, passing Terry Holmes, sitting at his desk enclosed by a mountain of documentation, wearing a perplexed expression as he listened to his phone, casually acknowledging their presence with a wave.

****

"Can you say that again, Emyr?"

"Let me explain it in words of one syllable, for the benefit of the English twats in the conversation." Score. "The sample we analysed from your BMW passenger seat, remember I said it was like urine." Accepting the imaginary agreement from Holmes. "I had it further tested, and we found traces of PSA, a chemical consistent with the residue from the female orgasm."

"Where's the relevance here?"

"It may be nothing. But it could indicate that there was a woman in the car, perhaps at the time of death, enjoying the spectacle so much that she had an orgasm, and squirted on the upholstery."

"Wouldn't this woman have succumbed to the fumes if she was in there?" Scarcely believing his ears.

"Depends how long she was exposed for. Even if she waited until he passed out, she could still escape. There was Valium in his blood, so he would have been sleepy first. It is only a theory. You're the detective — I just provide the inspiration."

"Could she have had her orgasm a day before?"

"Sure. We have so little to work with, I doubt we can carbon date it; we can't even get DNA out of it, unless we had something to compare it to. Imagine that forensic test." Putting on a pompous accent. "Madam. I just require you to orgasm, on demand, so we can compare your ejaculate to the one we have on file. If you need help or stimulation, please ask."

"You're mad."

"Agreed. Is that an improvement on arrogant?" Emyr teasing Terry. "We've both got meetings tomorrow, any chance we can both get away with it?"

"No chance, we're both fucked. I wish you well, and thanks for this. I'll put it in the file, though I already suggested accidental death on the report."

He pondered this new information, filing it in his head, omitting to introduce it to the file which he had mentally closed pending confirmation from the DCI, ready to record as solved.

****

With a file as far away from closed as could be imagined, Doris barged into the medical practice in Broughton brandishing his CID identification before him, Flick following in his turbulent wake. Catching movement from the periphery of his vision, he turned, addressing the scrawny man hastily standing. "Don't you move! Sit down, now!" Taking his lead, Flick positioned herself at the exit from the waiting room, challenging anybody to leave without permission, her height and challenging expression compensating for her gender.

"I need to speak to Jenny Coleman." Placing his ID on the counter. "Nobody moves until she is standing here in front of me." Rising to his full height, his stature and attitude in intimidatory harmony, inviting co-operation.

The receptionist, suitably impressed, found her ability to speak. "I'll get her for you." Slipping from the chair, inelegantly finding her feet, retiring to the rear of her imaginary empire.

Multi-tasking, Doris approached the man who had tried to leave. "Identification, now!" Accepting the driving licence, he studied the data, the name unfamiliar to him. Using McGarry's airwave, he contacted the station. "Do we have anything outstanding on a John Williams."

Hearing a crackle-infested response. "You'll need to be more specific, sir."

Glancing at the card. "John Rhodri Williams. Date of birth nine February, nineteen ninety-seven, dirty brown hair, scrawny." Imparting his menacing expression, standing over the man, smelling fear, garnering a response worthy of his suspicion.

"Person of interest in a suspected breaking and entering in Pulford."

Faced by two now adjacent police officers, John Williams stood, presenting his wrists for restraint. "Can I assume this is not your first time, Mr Williams?" Flick, applying her handcuffs to his wrists, polite, aware of a multitude of people watching her. "North Wales Police thanks you for your co-operation. Please take your seat again while we settle this other matter."

"You weren't here for me, then?" John asked, revealing a combination of disappointment and frustration. Her shaking head endorsing his complex emotional reaction. Playing to the audience, he belatedly protested. "I haven't done anything. This is a stitch-up." Seeing no interest from the assembled public, he returned to his seat, allowing Flick to return to her post.

"Miss Coleman. You are a difficult lady to find." Immune to her attractiveness, further enhanced by her uniform and thick dark hair swinging as she approached him.

"You could have called instead of embarrassing me here, at work. This is not acceptable. What do you want?"

"We did call, Miss Coleman. Seventeen times yesterday, four times today. Would you like to see the log on my phone? Perhaps we could share it with the ladies and gentlemen? Or would you like to join Constable McGarry and I at the station in Mold? Your presence is humbly requested."

"Am I under arrest?" Her agitation obvious.

"No. But that can be arranged if you prefer." Doris presenting her limited options.

Lifting her chin, drawing attention to her looks, locating a level of bravado, she faced him directly. "Always happy to assist our brave policemen and women. I'll collect my coat."

Reluctantly impressed, watching her go, he indicated that Flick should follow. Doris grabbed the collar of the disgruntled Mr Williams. "Come on, John, we'll take a ride, clear up this matter for now. Maybe it's all a misunderstanding." Escorting the cuffed patient from the waiting room, he strode purposefully towards the practice exit. Pushing his chin to the left, speaking into the borrowed airwave again. "I have John Rhodri Williams at the Broughton Medical Practice. Send a car to collect him. Be quick about it." Adding as an afterthought, "Please."

Inclining his head, straining to hear the response through the crackling, he deciphered the confirmation. "ETA four minutes."

Watching Flick and Jenny arrive together without restraints, he considered the unfair comparison, the police uniform considerably less appealing to look at compared to the crisp and clean health worker clothing. "Waiting on a car for Johnny boy here, then we can go."

Scanning the surrounding neighbourhood, his view dominated by the bulk of the Airbus factory, the site employing lots of people making wings for that mammoth aeroplane. Private housing, mostly detached on two levels, the impression being of a high-income successful area, contradicted by crime statistics suggesting otherwise.

Delegating responsibility for Williams to the occupants of the recently arrived panda car, Doris invited Jenny to sit in the rear of his Mazda, suggesting Flick join her. Holding the door, he ruined his gentlemanly action by enabling the child lock, securing both women in the back seat. Bringing the coughing engine to life, Doris commenced the journey to the station, aware of a question from Jenny Coleman but neglecting to respond, Flick following his example. Having her next question ignored, Jenny conceded defeat, sulking. Looking through the rain-streaked window, she reflected on her situation, effectively arrested at the surgery before her colleagues. She could imagine the rumours already circulating, hoping her boyfriend would allow her to explain before jumping to conclusions.

****

Making his way to the toilets with an increasingly urgent need, Terry Holmes was waylaid by the lady DCI. She carried his case file, the number visible and familiar. Following forced pleasantries, he responded to her queries about his findings, expanding on the written content. Ignoring his intensifying pelvic pressure, he confirmed the positive identification from the deceased's wife. Referring to the results from the post-mortem, he added his own conclusion that foul play was not suspected, his full groin imparting a tingle to his gums. He watched as she scribbled her signature on the folder, listening gratefully as she confirmed the case as closed, her insincere congratulations irrelevant as fluid began to infiltrate the funnel. Accepting the file, he tucked it beneath his arm as he resumed his journey to relief. Arriving, unzipping, releasing, flowing, splashing, chasing the sanitation brick as the intensity gradually subsided, trickling, shaking twice, done.

Using the new air-flow hand dryer, he reflected on how the technological development was fundamentally flawed. *Brilliant at hygienically drying hands, useless for wiping excess perspiration from your forehead.* Manually wiping the sweat from his face as he walked into the reception area, muttering about pampering to militant environmentalists, he watched Doris and Flick shepherd the lovely Jenny Coleman towards the interview rooms.

****

Entering interview room five, Jenny surmised that each interview room must be nearly identical, the only differences being the uneven state of the décor. Ushered to the seat facing the camera, the routine familiar, the officers' attitude hostile, she vented her anguish. "Why am I here again? What is it with you people?"

Again ignored, she slumped in her seat, impatiently watching as the big cop enabled his monitoring equipment, eventually making the statements about recording, her rights, her status, *ad nauseum.*

"Please state your name and date of birth for the record."

"Jennifer Clarissa Coleman. Seven, ten, ninety-five."

"Thank you. I remind you that you are currently not under arrest, and you are not under caution. You do not require a solicitor, although you may demand to have one present at any time. You are presently assisting us with our enquiries. Do you understand?"

"Yes, I understand. I should also like to state that I am here under protest, having been pulled from my workplace and humiliated in front of my colleagues. So, you'd better make this quick, or I am out of here. Do you understand?" She emphasised the "you" with a pointed finger directed at DS Beecham.

Doris smirked. "Yes, I understand. I am also delighted that you have deigned to speak with us on this occasion. In our last interview, you declined to comment. Definitely progress."

"Get on with it."

Flick opened a file on the desk, providing Doris with access to the contents. Retaining his smile as he reminded himself of the content, he turned to Jenny. "Miss Coleman, when we interviewed you with respect to the death of Jeremy Campbell-Foulkes, we asked for your whereabouts on the day in question. You informed us that you were at work, and you emphasised that response with a claim that Friday afternoon is your busiest time of the week. Do you recall saying that?"

"I do. Because it is true. Every single person with a sniffle waits until Friday afternoon, then wants to see a doctor in case they feel worse over the weekend. Bloody annoying. That's why I remember so clearly."

"And for the evening, you stated that you attended a dinner in the Grosvenor hotel, with several friends, going home around ten thirty. Is that correct?"

"That is correct. And?"

Doris reclined, turning to Flick, offering her the opportunity to assume control.

"Jenny." Her voice softer than her colleague's. "I checked with the practice. You took a half day on that date. You were not at your place of work; your practice manager has confirmed that. Much to their annoyance, as it was a busy day." Having laid the facts on the table, continuing, "So, where were you?" Softness evaporating from her voice. "The truth. Please."

Watching Jenny descend into silence, Doris asked another question, diverting her attention, deliberately loading the pressure. "I need a list of all of the people at that dinner, their full names and telephone numbers. I need a confirmation of the venue, a copy of the bill or reservation. A taxi or rideshare receipt to establish the time you departed and where you were taken to." Passing a sheet of paper and a pen towards her. "I am placing you under caution. You might want to call a lawyer."

"I haven't done anything!" Her protest akin to a plea.

"Hmm. You have given a false alibi to a police officer during an interview. I would not call that nothing. You see, everything you now tell us is tarnished by a suspicion of your dishonesty. Anything and everything you tell us will be recorded and checked for authenticity until we establish a mutual trust. When we factor in your whole 'no comment' performance, you have given us a lot of reasons to suspect you.

"I'm still waiting for you to tell me where you were on that Friday afternoon," Flick reminded her, increasing Jenny's agitation.

"You own a knife. You told us. Jeremy was killed with a knife. Your alibi is non-existent. You are a suspect. Make it easy on yourself, tell us why you killed him. You will feel better; we can ask the judge for leniency based on your co-operation." Doris using his reasonable voice.

"What did you use to smash his skull?" Flick again. "At least solve that mystery."

The constable allocated the task of monitoring the interview in the screen room sat aghast, watching the DS and the PC lambast the pretty woman, tearing her in two directions, destabilising her. Impressed, he took notes, planning for his next promotion opportunity.

"Come on, Jenny. Who else was at that dinner? I don't see any names."

"Come on, Jenny. Where were you that afternoon?"

"Why should we believe you, Miss Coleman?"

"Did you kill Jeremy?"

Leaning forward, placing her head on the table, closing her eyes as her head spun, Jenny Coleman accepted her need for assistance. "I want to contact a solicitor."

Twenty-Eight
Thursday, 14th February

Her urge to rise and shine continued to diminish, losing the battle with her inclination to remain warm against the expected winter elements. Her phone had pinged, the device beyond her reach. *Alone in bed on Valentine's Day. Sad, but hardly unique.*

She reflected on the evening with Holly, the mutual apprehension, the declared attraction, the relief. That kiss. The little white lie. The denied reaction she had felt, unmentioned. The lingering suspicion. Her confusion. Transferring her thoughts to lunch with Rob. His kiss. Her reaction. His reaction to her. *Quite a day for kisses*, she thought, meditating on the conundrum of sharing kisses with two people, yet waking alone on the supposedly most romantic day of the year.

Admitting her extremely unlikely return to sleep, her pressing need to read the incoming message, she unfolded her quilt, exposing herself to the cooler temperature. She swung her legs to the floor while achieving upright in a singular smooth motion. Placing her feet into conveniently located slippers, lifting her phone, noticing only eight percent remaining battery, she accessed her device.

The text message proposed a movie, as she had intimated. An unusual choice, a period drama slash comedy with three female leads. Rachel Weisz, Emma Stone and Olivia Colman, whoever she might be. *The Favourite* was the name of the film and it was showing at 6pm and 9pm. She recognised his selection of a chick-flick as a demonstration of his consideration.

"He is trying so hard." Voicing her appreciative thoughts. "I could get used to this attention."

Replying, she agreed with his choice of movie, stating her preference for the six o'clock showing, leaving the other arrangements open for him to organise.

He responded within seconds. 'When are you available? Shall we eat first or after? Drink?'

Withstanding her desire to issue an immediate reply, she strolled to the kitchen, laying her phone on the counter as she inserted the charger. Taking a frivolous tour around her home, making him wait as she hid her enthusiasm, keeping him guessing. Balancing the options against the bus schedules, she offered her first response: 'Any time from four.' Sending that. Composing her next message: 'Let's eat before.' Holding the message, releasing it, composing her final response: 'Yes to the drink.'

His immediate confirmation. Four o'clock, location provided. Sending him a smiling emoji, intending an end to the SMS conversation. *Ha-ha, so keen*, she internally commented as she opened her wardrobe, seeking inspiration in selecting her clothes for tonight. Informal for cinema, warm for winter, contradicted by her urge to look a little sexy, her instinct to tone things down from yesterday. Fresh new undies, just in case.

A further ping on her phone revealing a further text from Rob: 'Happy Valentine's Day'.

Twenty-Nine
Thursday, 14th February

Armed with new insights, Barry was convinced he could now hear the faint trace of Aussie in the DI's accent, sandwiched between foreigner English and an inherent residential Welsh twang, the result a complicated hybrid.

DI Peter Jones remained in his large swivel chair, exuding authority tempered by interest, surveying the documents placed before him. Consuming the facts, the assumptions, the insinuations. Looking up, he paraded a satisfied smile, seemingly pleased.

"Congratulations, DS Chappell. It seems we have solved the rape and murder of this Thai lady. Great result. Fast, excellent police work."

"Thank you, sir. But we still don't know who she is, or why she was killed. What motivation the killer had for doing what he did."

Motioning Barry to sit, Jones sat forward. "Break it down into bite-size pieces. A lady was raped and murdered. You found the person who did it. That case is closed. Result. Who was she? Pass that to the Missing Persons people. That's their area of expertise; let them take it away from our desks. Why did the killer do what he did? Who knows? He's a criminal. He's a pervert. He performed a sexual assault, had a panic attack, killed her. End of."

Admiring his superior officer's attitude, simplifying, abbreviating, closing.

"You say the tip-off came via DS Beecham. Can he give us access to his informant? Do we want that access, or need it? Probably, because we now have a new case. A murdered criminal-cum-rapist-cum-killer. New case, new file, no effect on the previous case being closed. Dai Harris, you say?"

"One of the uniform constables recognised his photo. No DNA on file, no prints in the system, but the PC is certain. Harris's mum is on her way to make a formal identification."

"Dr Tay has produced an excellent preliminary report. Shot through the bottom. That is a first in my career. Do we have another pervert on the loose? Where do we go from here?" DI Jones read the relevant section of the pathology report again. "Seems he took a beating before death as well. Looks like gangland to me, infighting maybe."

"That's why we need access to Beecham's informant. I would like to know which bunch we are looking at."

Jones picked up his desk phone, inspired by a sudden thought, speaking to his secretary, asking for the direct line to Cheshire's dog handling inspector. Having written the number on his desktop calendar, he made the call. After exchanging pleasantries, he made his request for canine resource, describing the location, making a schedule for late afternoon, suggesting direct liaison with DS Chappell. "Let's allow the pooches to have a sniff around the scene, see if they can pick up anything. It can't do any harm. Chase the CCTV from Roads for that stretch, expand the search to the most recent thirty-six hours."

Barry further appreciated his DI, his ability to get things done, get resources moving, despite his overwhelming reluctance to leave his desk.

"Treat this as a new case. I will write up the old one, delegate the new actions. Try Beecham again. If he remains intransigent, tell him to call me and explain himself. That should do the trick."

Barry offered suggestions. "This could be a punishment killing for actions within one organisation. Or it could be rival organisations agitating each other. We need more information, for sure."

"If villains want to kill each other, I say we fucking let them. We can sweep up the effluent later. Investigating the death of a murdering rapist is not something I expect to incur an overtime bill for." Exchanging glances, ensuring the message was understood. "But it does require diligent investigation. Thank you, Sergeant. Excellent work."

Leaving the office, passing Emyr in the corridor, he knocked before entering Annie's office. "Have your guys found anything relevant?"

"We're analysing some traces found at the scene, possibly washed from the body. Hair, fabric, a potential skin sample within the broken nose, damage around the bum. Fingers crossed." Rewarding him with her brilliant smile. "If it is Dai Harris, I hear he works for that brothel-keeper

Ian MacKenzie, also known as The Mancunian. Runs a chain of massage parlours throughout North Wales."

"Annie, you're a genius." Allowing her to mouth "I know" before continuing, "Massage parlours, a dead Thai woman, there has to be a link. That's where I look now."

Making his way slowly to his own temporary office, acknowledging Doris had been correct about DI Jones's lack of concern regarding the source and time of the lead, only interested in the result. Elation entering his psyche. A quick result and praise from above, a new case already in progress, his blossoming relationship with Annie. Things were improving for DS Finbar Patrick Chappell."

Thirty
Thursday, 14th February

Nilesh faced his editor across the desk, observing Rob's conflict but unaware of the reason, convinced he had presented an excellent story. It was worthy of the front page, with solid background and first-person quotations, while controversial and in the public interest. His grammar immaculate.

The editor was complimentary about the article, the journalism skills were beyond anything Nilesh had ever produced. The story was likely to invite an emotional response from readers, possibly an outcry. This woman had been wrongly charged with murder, her relationship with her husband tarnished, her life likely blighted for years. The police chasing a gay crime of passion, then suddenly switching their attention to five former girlfriends, those women all remaining involved to various degrees. Nobody charged close to three weeks later, society potentially at risk; everything a story needed was there.

He had to print it, knowing he had no choice. As a manager, as a journalist, as an employee of a struggling publication, he knew he had to. Only one reservation, personal, preventing him from endorsing the story and sending it to the printer. One of the former girlfriends involved, her digitally cleansed photograph removing any last vestige of doubt from his mind. His new girlfriend, Amy. Amelia Grace Meadows.

Conceding to his responsibilities, he praised his journalist. "Nilesh. This is the best story you have ever produced. Absolutely first class. We run it tomorrow on the front page. Congratulations. I am thrilled for you, and for the *Leader*. Do you want to deliver it to the typesetter?" Stamping and signing the completed document. "Get it done."

Isolated, conflicted, intrigued, frightened. Rob sat alone, wondering what would happen when he confronted Amy, when he advised her of the story due to appear tomorrow. Her inclusion was unavoidable, being integral to the story; her picture would be printed with the others. He was unable to imagine her reaction. Would it be indifference, possibly anger or resentment? Would she accuse him of betrayal? His promise to be always "off the record" with her had been technically honoured as she remained unquoted. Technically.

He attempted to control his simmering personal reaction, his unwarranted jealousy. The relationship was from her past, before they had even met. It was an irrelevant albeit recent episode. His thoughts drifted to consider her possible involvement. Impossible. She was normal, friendly, feminine and beautiful. It was inconceivable that she could be a factor in the investigation, yet she had been recalled for the identity parade and re-interviewed, a person of interest. Her impact on him, his emotions inflamed, infatuated, her image permanently prominent in his mind.

Remaining excited to see her at four, cinema tickets pre-purchased online, he was dreading the possible confrontation. It was his duty to inform her, surely better than waiting for her to read the paper in the morning. Better for him? For her? His distress confirming his feelings for her, the extent of her influence, his attraction to her. Already caring, his emotional instinct wanting to counter his decision to allow publication.

*****

Having achieved a consensus with herself on her outfit for the evening ahead, she now endured indecision about her footwear. Comfortable, sensible flat shoes, practical for cinema and public transport, against black boots adding an element of style, or high heels maintaining an element of sexy in her attire. A decision yet to be made.

Further choices to come. How to wear her hair? Her choice of make-up, bold or delicate lipstick, shoulder bag or clutch, floral or herbal perfume, regular bra or push-up.

Welcoming her indecision, she gave credence to her unspoken but intimated suspicion that she liked Rob, cared that he should like her appearance, generating her undeclared compulsion to please him. Forcing herself to reach decisions, she started again, returning her jeans and figure-hugging sweater to the wardrobe, the dress-down comparison too huge from yesterday, seeking a closer compromise. Having settled on a skirt, sensible shoes were not an option. Blouse, pale in contrast to the dark skirt. Tights, warm, unsexy, not required if she wore her boots. Boots confirmed! Bra and panties — matching, of course, white, the chosen pale blouse eliminating her default black selection. She chose a figure-enhancing bra, acknowledging that slimmer girls needed a boost sometimes. Cognisant of the temperature requiring a jacket or coat, the longer coat offering protection for her body and un-stockinged legs. The thought of stockings flitted across her consciousness, discarded, too early in the relationship, for another time. Coat selected, worn open, ensuring he could see her in her entirety. A shoulder bag more suitable when worn with a long coat. To contrast the conservative clothing, her hair tied back, lifted, exposing her cheekbones. Make-up light but precise, with delicate lipstick, allowing his attention to be shared across her entire face. A scent test producing a winner, the light floral perfume.

Delighted, she had permitted each decision to influence the next. Selecting a shortish dark blue skirt, accessorising in sequence. Contemplating a gin and tonic to calm her nerves, accepting she was nervous. She deferred the drink, nibbling four squares of Galaxy Crispy instead.

****

Seated on an Arriva Cymru bus, attempting to watch the passing landscape, the difficulty increased by running condensation from the windows of the heated bus interfacing with the low temperature outside, Amy looked forward to the planned cinema event. She had added a loosely fitting soft hat to her ensemble, keeping her head warm, intending to arrive early and comb her hair in the ladies' room before Rob arrived.

The winter sun had battled bravely to make an optimistic appearance. She had been the only person to board at the Butchers Arms, observing little joy on the faces of her fellow commuters, only lots of fatigue accompanied by random impressions of misery.

Anticipating an enjoyable evening, probably a drink after the movie, maybe two, she had chosen to leave her car at home. She was unsympathetic to the cretins unable or unwilling to resist the temptation to drive while intoxicated, believing they deserved the punishments they incurred. Wiping the window, clearing a partial space, she realised her journey was approaching a conclusion.

Entering the cinema foyer early, she had charmed the ticket clerk into permitting her to access the washrooms. Removing her hat, she had teased her hair into position. Unbuttoning her coat had ensured she revealed an interesting amount of leg. Ready to devastate, she returned to the foyer, seeing Rob immediately, quietly approaching him from behind and surprising him with a gentle "Hello."

Startled, he turned, expressing delight at seeing her, scanning her from head to toe, toe to head, subtly, respectfully. "Amy! Hi."

Sensing his uncertainty, she offered her cheek, inviting a kiss, rewarding him with a smile. Appreciating his cleanliness, his smell enhanced by something expensive, she admired the quality informal shirt hanging over skinny jeans, a lightweight jacket folded across his wrist.

Third time with her, third time blown away, stunned by how effortlessly she presented herself, always different. His enjoyment compromised by the news he required to break to her at some point, his impulse to defer until later, understanding that he should clear the matter as early as possible.

"How are you? Have you had a good day? You look lovely." The phrases rushed together.

"I'm fine. Happy to see you. Excited to see the movie. Are you okay? You seem, I don't know, tense or preoccupied?"

The opportunity there, leaving him with no option but to accept it, to step up and explain his concern to her, then hope she would understand. A lump forming in his throat. "Something came up at work today. Awkward, placing me in a difficult situation. Can we step outside for a moment? I need to tell you something, something away from casually listening strangers."

Agreeing, she led him to the front entrance, stepping back as he opened the door, holding it for her, before following her through. They faced one another in a quiet space just metres away, the ambient light unsure of its destination, darkness competing with light. "Okay. What is upsetting you, and how does it involve me?" Her question obvious, her tone one he had not heard before. Not cold, not indifferent, more not warm.

Unable to think of an excuse, he began. "Today, one of my reporters presented a story to me. The journalism is excellent, and the story will run tomorrow. Online from midnight, in the first editions of the paper in the morning." Her expression remained neutral, waiting for the kicker. "It relates to the death of Jeremy Campbell-Foulkes and the way the police have bungled the case till now." Pausing, sensing her comprehension developing, her empathy subsiding. "Unfortunately, your name has arisen, with a picture." Her expression changing, beyond his knowledge. "Amongst others. Indicating the police are maintaining an interest in you. There's more, but that is the gist of it." Seeking to engage with her, failing to elicit a response, her smile a distant memory. Faltering, he continued, "There is no accusation towards you. It's more about the police incompetence. But you are named. I'm sorry."

Maintaining her silence, taking time to assimilate what she had heard, she considered the implications, selecting her response position, to defend or attack. Experience advised her to allow the silence to prolong, increasing his discomfort while providing her with additional time to decide upon a strategy.

"Say something. Anything. Amy."

Her thoughts clear, she spoke. "He called himself Jed. I dated him twice; there was no spark, nothing to like, so I ended it quickly. As relationships go, it was almost non-existent." She halted, giving an impression of being thoughtful. "Am I still off the record, as you promised?"

Relieved to be able to offer her something, even something so minimal, he replied, "Of course, Amy, anything you say to me is off the record."

Continuing, her tone low, her manner distant. "Because I dated him, the police interviewed me; actually, they interviewed all of his former girlfriends. We were all at the Mold police station this week, parading around for some witness who has surfaced." Addressing him, their usual mutual warmth absent, elaborating. "I have not been charged, I was not identified by the witness, I have a cast-iron alibi for the date and time in question. I cannot see any relevance for you to include me in your article. Can't you remove me from it?" Her final words betraying her appeal.

"I can't change the story as it is. You are a component in the ongoing situation. I can offer you media space to counter with your side of the story, I can coach you and assist you with it. If you choose to ignore it, nobody will remember you in a few days."

She snapped, upset by his ignorance. "Rob. I will be in the paper! My name, my reported involvement in a homicide enquiry! I am unemployed! I am actively looking for a job! Employers check the press and social media nowadays. Who would want to hire a murder suspect? You are ruining my prospects of finding work! I will be all over the Facebook accounts of my friends and acquaintances! Have you considered the impact this could have on my life? Really? Have you?"

Her tirade had been anticipated, the words as expected, her anger more controlled than he had envisaged, suggesting the possibility of resolving this issue, with effort. His optimism supported by the sudden advent of sunshine, splitting the clouds, illuminating the winter landscape. About to issue a response, recognising she had more to say, he ceded to her.

"You had a choice. You have chosen to side with your job. You have selected the *Leader* over me, your girlfriend. Why?" Her expression disjointed, elements of frustration, sadness, disappointment, irritation. The "why" revealing a weakening in her voice, the sound slicing through his emotions.

"I didn't choose my job over you, Amy. I had to maintain the journalistic integrity and support the efforts of my reporter. Hurting you was never my intention."

"But you have hurt me, Rob. Badly." Tears forming in the inner corners of her eyes. "I hope you find happiness at work, with your reporter and your story." Sniffing, her tears obeying gravity, moving down her cheeks. "I thought we had something. We hardly know each other, yet I feel a connection with you. Felt that connection. Our time together has been wonderful, really lovely, I should have known better." Opening her bag, removing a tissue, mopping tears. "Don't you feel it? Don't you feel something amazing between us?"

"Amy." Unable to find suitable words. "Amy. Please don't cry." His turn to plead. Reaching for her, belatedly, reprimanding himself for his hesitant physical approach.

His movement rejected, Amy stepping back, declining his comfort as she ignored his instruction, allowing her tears to flow, her sorrow becoming dejection. "Don't!" The word causing him to freeze. "I hope you enjoy the movie. You and I are over. Bye."

Her message surviving interference from her tears, her intent unmistakable. Turning, she walked away from him, making no attempt to hide her distress, paying no heed to the expressions of concern from strangers. Aware she was walking the wrong way, unwilling to change direction, unprepared to offer him any satisfaction.

He stared after her, this beautiful woman he had unbelievably become involved with, unable to comprehend that she was gone, so quickly. Hearing a sad song in his head, pertinent, relevant, the gruff throaty vocal of Ray Wilson, "I can see your tears, in a lemon, yellow sun." He had seen her tears, could see and feel the sun. He had supported his newspaper and his reporter, been diligent to his vocation. In return, he had hurt someone he already cared about. Aware of a dampness on his cheeks, reflecting the pain inside, the value of his impending loss became apparent.

Instantly deciding to follow her, catch her, tell her he was sorry, offer her whatever he could. He ran towards her, covering the short distance easily, impervious to the staring strangers, opening his arms, inviting her to him.

Amy saw what he was doing, feeling a moment of hope, wondering what he would say. She could not condone what he had done. Further attention from North Wales Police was not what she needed; her picture circulating mainstream media could jog somebody's memory. The only acceptable thing he could say to her was that he was cancelling the story. She did have feelings for him, her reactions providing confirmation. Stopping short, avoiding his proffered embrace, fighting her emotions, she asked, "What?"

"Amy, we can get through this. Together. I care for you. I want to be with you. But I can't block the story. I'm sorry."

Stepping aside, preparing to walk past him, her disappointment complete, she uttered the only suitable phrases in her vocabulary, designed for maximum impact. "Happy Valentine's Day, Rob. Now fuck off and leave me alone. Goodbye."

Thirty-One
Thursday, 14th February

Presuming they would be in for a long evening, Doris had placed a delivery order for the three-person banquet from a nearby Chinese restaurant, figuring the quantity would be sufficient for Flick and himself. They had abandoned the interview room to Miss Coleman, granting permission for her to make any necessary calls, including one to arrange the presence of a solicitor at the station.

During the brief hiatus, he had briefed the DCI on their progress, expecting some positive acknowledgement, instead enduring a combative response which even alluded to his motives being questionable. Careful not to voice his suspicions, he wondered if the transiting DCI may be entering the PMS phase of her cycle.

Fumbling in his pocket, he eventually retrieved his ringing phone, swiping the green button to the right. "DS Beecham."

"It's me." The familiar voice, the source of the tip-off relating to the Asian woman case.

"I'm surprised to hear from you. That was quite a bombshell you left for us." His voice cold.

"Listen. He was alive when I was last aware of him. I have no idea what happened after that. You know what the Skemarooneys are like, ruthless bastards."

Doris placed the phone on his desk, applying the loudspeaker function with the room otherwise empty. "Are you seriously blaming the Rooney family? For fuck sake, Ian, I am getting real heat on this. I submitted the bottles for DNA comparison. I gave the lead to check the location, and you give us a naked dead body. What the hell?"

"All right, Sergeant, keep your hair on. I'm calling to help you. The dead lady was working for a competitor of mine, the aforementioned Rooney family. She was killed by Dai Harris. I assume you have identified him. Harris has done occasional work for me in the past. I needed to distance myself from him, which I did by helping you. They took him out very quickly. I'm just suggesting you have your Scouse colleagues have a look at the Rooney family."

"Sounds like bollocks to me." Grahame was unsure; certain elements of the situation were consistent, others very convenient. "And what about Nesbitt?"

"He's gone to ground, I believe. Check it out or don't, it's up to you. Oh, and tell your mate Holmes that he pays full price at my facilities. There is only margin for one cop to enjoy mate's rates, and we both know who enjoys that privilege."

The screen on his phone went blank as the connection was broken, leaving Doris to consider what he had heard, to try and balance the content with possible reality and select which components of the story he should share with Chappell. Releasing a gentle burp, unwitnessed, he heard his phone ring again. Sighing, wishing the food would arrive, he checked the caller ID displaying a known local journalist, reluctantly accepting the call.

"Detective Beecham. Can we talk?"

"Depends." Cautious. "What do you want to talk about?"

"We are about to run a story about the NWP's handling of the Campbell-Foulkes murder, with some new information in our hands. I wondered if you would like to comment."

Doris considered. "Sounds to me like you are fishing."

Doris could hear something in the caller's voice, sniffing, suspecting a head cold. "We have an extended interview with Ruth McGarvey, where she revealed a lot of previously unknown detail. You can imagine that she has been less than complimentary about the police in general, and that includes you."

"Is that it?"

"We have photographs of Jasmine Kemp, Susan Grey, Jennifer Coleman, Amy Meadows, and Ruth, of course."

Now interested, Doris resumed his questioning persona. "Where did you get those names? And the photos? Who's your source? You should be careful here."

"Thank you for confirming the accuracy of our information, Detective Beecham. We intend to run an expansive story about the questionable competence of North Wales Police. We will name the suspects, we will refer to your wasted efforts searching for an angry gay lover, we will focus on the false arrest, the breaches of protocol. Need I go on?"

Taking a moment, Grahame weighed his options. He knew there had to be a leak in the station. Permitting the story to be published could be damaging, for himself and the force, possibly the case. Wondering how to play the situation, he allowed his experience to guide him. Dropping his voice, introducing an earnest tone, he replied, "You need to watch what you print here. You are entering an area of judicial influence. You could affect ongoing due process, to which a magistrate might take your interference very badly. What do you want from me?"

"Bullshit. There is no judicial process."

"Wrong, dickhead. Off the record! Can you confirm what I am about to say is not for publication?" Knowing the journalist would be unable to resist, hearing the confirmation. "We have a person of interest currently assisting us with our enquiries. That person has requested a solicitor to attend the station and on arrival we will resume the Q and A. Seems to me that you could run your story tomorrow and already be out of date. You risk your criticism of the NWP being printed as we close the case and charge our suspect. Go ahead."

"Which person of interest?"

"One of the five you named. I won't say more."

Neither spoke. Beecham waiting to hear if his defence of the police had succeeded. Continuing. "Look. Run your story. I don't make deals with reporters. I don't know what you've got, but from what you have said, I don't think you have much. The risk is on your side and you'll look very fucking stupid if we announce a charge tomorrow. Do whatever you like."

"Maybe we could meet. Talk about things. Get your side of the story?"

"The Drovers Arms on Denbigh Road, one thirty tomorrow. You're paying. No recording devices. Off the record, unless I agree otherwise. Yes, or no?"

"Okay." His 'thank you' unheard as the detective hung up.

His eyes lit up as Felicia walked in with a substantial box of Chinese food, the box a former carton for twenty-four packages of MSG. "Trough time, Doris," she stated brightly. "You're a busy boy. The restaurant called twice to tell you the food had arrived. Reception called me, saying that only you ever order the banquet for three. All good?"

"All good. Let's eat before Jenny's brief turns up."

Opening the cartons, surveying the contents, both reaching for the salt and pepper ribs, Flick asked the obvious question. "Do you think she did it?"

Stripping tender meat from a thin bone, munching and swallowing, he replied, "Maybe. She has certainly done something. The witness picked her out. Let's see."

"She's lied to us throughout. For me, she ticks most of the boxes. All that 'no comment' nonsense. The way she tried to play DS Holmes. Yeah, there is something about her."

Indicating his agreement, the mention of Holmes reminding him of the comment from earlier, suggesting Holmes had returned to the massage parlour. He wondered if the dirty bugger had gone for the nineteen-year-old masseuse. Something to be checked, prospectively useful information for the future.

Hearing his phone ring again, he rejected the call without registering the caller identity, paying full attention to dinner.

Thirty-Two
Friday, 15th February

Holly prepared for her latest assignment within the bank, interviewing a couple for a mortgage, their borderline application requiring insight from an experienced assessor. Her mood did not bode well for the prospective buyers. Terry had smelled different when he came home on Wednesday evening, an oil or lotion residue? Sexed up? He had also been distant, this attitude continuing into Thursday, having displayed no inclination towards her at bedtime.

Her evening with Amy had been strange, starting badly, improving later. She could remember the touch of her friend's lips, physically pleasurable leading to consciously conflicted, the awkwardness gradually retreating. They had shared cider, their relationship seemingly unaffected, allowing her to go home early and take medication to finally fix her stomach problem. There had been no contact from Amy all day Thursday, no response to the messages she had sent, causing her to wonder if there had been a latent reaction to their interaction.

The file for this loan application had come to her on the previous afternoon, decision deferred, the file large and complex. Differing assessments were expressed throughout the notes, inconsistent declarations related to the ability to pay. The standard smiling loan assessors, the pleasant public face of the bank, the artificial personable financial expert reliable only in that they did what the algorithm told them to. In cases like this, where the algorithm was indecisive, they sent for Holly.

Preparing to enter the closed room where the couple were already waiting, she detected their nervousness, palpable even through the heavy glazing. Her phone buzzing, she saw a message from Amy. Opening the text: 'Going to a country pub rave tonight. Interested? Let me know. Cheers. Amy.' Pleased to receive the message, relieved at the renewal of relations, relaxing, the couple's prospects of securing a loan suddenly improved.

****

Arriving early at the new facility in Llay, Terry sought interaction with a friendly face, becoming increasingly aware that he knew few of his supposed colleagues here. Preferring to avoid Barry Chappell, strategically prudent to avoid Emyr Christopher, he joined Annie Freeland in the canteen.

"What's new, Annie?"

"Not a lot. Surprised to see you here; I didn't expect you lot to transfer over for a few weeks. I'm just waiting on Emyr's disciplinary meeting. Hope it goes well for him."

Liar, thought Terry, knowing she was waiting on her opportunity to move up. Joining the pretence. "I hope so, too. He's the reason I'm here as well. Human Resources demanding my presence, for something I said publicly, allegedly about him."

"Oh, yeah, the 'arrogant Welsh cunt' comment." Unable to contain her amusement, she embellished her statement. "He didn't give a shit about it, but some of the sheep-shaggers were quite irked by your choice of phrase. Don't blame him."

"I don't. I'll just smile and say sorry, lesson learned; they like that bollocks. How's Barry?"

"Why would I know, or care?" Her reaction overplayed, transparent. Draining her cup, excusing herself, leaving the table, her crockery remaining on the simulated Formica surface.

****

Doris was in a hurry. Crossing the car park, ploughing through puddles, his multiple obligations coursing through his consciousness. Share information with Barry bastard Chappell. Restart the interview with Jenny Coleman, accompanied by her irritating fucker of a lawyer. Lunch with a fuckwit reporter, with his own wanking agenda. Hoping to see his guv'nor, DI Catt, due to be released from hospital today. Most importantly, unwrap and devour the bacon roll held against his body, the van's reputation for a great buttie going viral. Enjoy it while the butter remained melty, the bacon salty, the roll soft.

Relieved to find the office empty, he unfolded the bacon roll, revealing a thing of beauty: large, round, thick, melted dairy oozing from the lower side, the bread cut unevenly. Properly made by hand. Raising it to his mouth, he indulged in a substantial bite, delighting in the flavourful combination. Chewing and swallowing, repeating.

He had released Jenny Coleman reluctantly the previous evening. Her lawyer had made a strong case for permitting her to return home on her own recognisance. PC McGarry had indicated her support of release, quietly reminding him of the recent McGarvey scenario. Earning a minor victory in the exchange, he had agreed to the release on condition the solicitor accepted responsibility for the timely return of the suspect in the morning, reminding everyone that a man was dead. The lawyer accepting as he explained directly to Miss Coleman the responsibility and liability involved, all recorded on camera.

Finishing the delectable breakfast roll, he wiped his hands on a tissue, placing the evidence in the bin under Flick's desk. Job one complete, he called Barry Chappell.

"What have you got for me, Doris?" Barry, abrupt as usual, devoid of courtesy.

"I've got an ID for your dead guy." Doris, pausing for effect, preparing to place DS Chappell further in his debt.

"Dai Harris. Right?" Enjoying stealing the big guy's thunder, Barry continued, "Works for The Mancunian. Unless you know otherwise?"

Surprised. Doris replied, "That's him. Dai Harris. My information is that the woman was working for the Rooney mob. Rumour is, they took him out." Offering information which he had intended to retain, unsure of the accuracy or relevance. "Apparently, Nesbitt has gone to ground. You can't rule out his involvement in some way."

"Have you got direct access to MacKenzie? If so, I need it."

Denying such access, honestly, suggesting, "You can always rumble one of his massage places, shake up the staff, maybe get to him that way?"

"But not Bangkok Massage in Wrexham. That's yours."

"Fuck off, Barry, you can go where you like. I've helped you a lot on this. A little gratitude wouldn't go amiss." Expecting a reaction, getting nothing, goading him further. "Though I'm sure you get what you need from the frigid forensic sergeant."

Pleased to hear the connection broken, Doris refocused his priorities, checking the clock, mentally adjusting for the arrival of Jenny Coleman.

He found the envelope bearing the markings of the Superintendent's office on his desk, beneath the Jasmine Kemp file. Professional curiosity aroused, he slid a finger under the seal, accessing the copied case file, the Lothian Police logo eminently displayed in the letterhead. Clearly an old file, prior to the regional amalgamation into Police Scotland.

He focused immediately on the name, Meadows, assigning instant importance to the package, unsure if he had time to digest the contents in their entirety. He closed the file, hiding it in his desk drawer, narrowly resisting the urge to rip it apart and consume the constituent information.

****

Feeling refreshed, having slept decidedly well, her distress from yesterday consigned to memory, Amy operated her Nespresso machine, preparing an extremely strong two-capsule coffee. Her mobile's indicator flashed, intimating messages or missed calls, the device set to silent mode. Opening the phone, not uncommonly surprised to see she had twelve missed calls from a single number. Accessing her messages, seeing five in total, again from a single number, the same number. She deleted them all, their content unread.

Extending an olive branch to Puss-Puss, she invited her to come along to the pub rave she would attend with Brenda. Not expecting a positive response, she hoped the gesture would be appreciated. She intended to call her later, time permitting, to seek some comfort should it be necessary.

****

Entering the extravagant meeting room, the décor reinforcing his impression that HR departments really knew how to treat themselves,

Holmes took the assigned isolated seat on one side of the table, facing the impressive wooden surface capable of seating twenty. Only two seats were in position on the opposite side, confirming his suspicion that they were incapable of challenging him one to one. A young woman had escorted him to his seat, placing a bottle of Evian water before him with a glass and coaster, before departing the room, her functional smile lacking any hint of warmth.

The door swung inwards again, introducing another young woman, her lack of height reinforcing her immature appearance, emanating the impression she had barely graduated from whichever institute awarded qualifications in Human Resources. Battling his prejudice, Terry stood, extending his hand as he stated his name and rank, confident he could control this exchange.

"Nice to meet you, Detective Sergeant Holmes. Of course, under different circumstances would have been better. My name is Carole Leadbetter."

Hearing "ankle-biter", Terry smiled, nodded his implied agreement, inviting the lady to sit before he did. Immune to his charm, she continued, "We will be joined by the head of Human Resources for this division of North Wales Police. She will attend the meeting as quickly as she can." By way of explanation, "She is extremely busy."

Internally processing the situation, Terry assessed his prospects. Two women, typical. A young one, possibly inexperienced, attempting to portray a strong personality. The one to come being the local head of department was a bad sign, countered by her being busy, impatience potentially to his advantage.

The door opening and closing, presenting an attractive blonde lady, professionally dressed, permeating authority as she greeted him. "Good morning, Detective Sergeant Holmes." Walking towards the vacant seat at the table, proceeding. "Thank you for coming in today to resolve this matter. I hope we can expedite a solution and return to our duties." Reaching across the table, she offered her hand, taking his in a firm grip, presenting her business card, rewarding him with the smile of a predator. "Shall we begin?"

Reading her card, initially recording a sinking feeling before making the link, using his natural mental agility to identify an opportunity. "I have to raise a point of order here, Mrs Christopher. Surely you cannot supervise this meeting, related to Emyr as you are."

"Why not?" Her voice confident, mildly quizzical.

"Correct me if I am wrong, but I am here because of a comment I made at the end of a conversation with your husband. Doesn't that disqualify you?"

"Terry. May I call you Terry? This is Carole, and I am Charlotte. Did you read your requested attendance at this meeting, properly?" Enjoying his discomfort, watching him search for words, seeking an improvised response, prevented from doing so as she provided the explanation.

"Terry. At the end of a conversation with Senior Sergeant Emyr Christopher, you made an offensive statement within the station at Mold. Senior Sergeant Christopher has already dismissed your comment; therefore, he has no active involvement in this matter. This is about numerous staff who were offended by your remarks, disturbed by the unmentionable word you used, and upset that a supposed colleague would use such a phrase. Due to the quantity of complaints, as head of HR, I must be involved."

Unable to present a counter argument, Terry remained quiet, inviting Mrs Christopher to continue. "This meeting is not being electronically recorded, though Carole will take notes and present minutes of the meeting within a few days."

Resigned to the waste of time, Terry braced himself.

****

Tossing fractured wood from a mountain of discarded pallets into his skip, he added half a can of petrol, before lighting a rolled newspaper and tossing it in with the rest, hearing an audible surge of flame from within the faded blue metal structure. He reckoned the remains of Nesbitt should be virtually disintegrated by now, still intending to feed the flames for the remainder of the day as a precaution.

Boris the Orange was late. The Mancunian suspected that he knew why. Precisely five kilograms of Ice had been despatched to Llandudno, but four grams had not arrived. Boris had also employed the services of an unauthorised driver, introducing an unnecessary element of risk. The customers had reported that he had appeared to be under the influence of something, their displeasure recorded. Knowing how easily people became hooked on this pharmaceutical, MacKenzie considered his potential error in bringing Boris into his inner circle. He considered that his employee might have run away, rejecting the idea, certain he had not betrayed any concern when he arranged the meet. The idiot was probably feeling like crap.

Boris the Orange was closer to yellow, lying in a massive pool of his own vomit, his metabolism having rejected the infiltration of the foul chemical. His body was alive with antibodies trying to protect the vessel, battling the invasion of impurities from the addictive pharmaceutical. The sickness an unappreciated positive signal in the battle to dilute the illness pervading his entire physiology. Boris had fucked up, was fucked up, knew he had to get to the meeting with the boss or he could be even more fucked up. Achieving a sitting position, feeling then hearing himself shit his pants, his stomach retching as it expelled simultaneous vomit, valiantly fighting to cleanse his body.

****

Confused by the polite welcome he had received, he was relieved that he had taken time to groom himself, his dress uniform immaculate. His intention had been to accept his punishment with defiance, go down in style.

Joined in the expensively furnished refreshment room by two senior officers, warm drinks distributed in a convivial atmosphere, Emyr silently wondered, *What the fuck is going on here?*

The Superintendent joined them, selecting a single source brand of coffee bean for his refreshment. Suitably cupped, everyone standing, he addressed the Senior Sergeant.

"Emyr. Thank you for joining us. We would like to discuss your career in the North Wales Police Force." Flummoxed, he thought, *this has to be the weirdest fucking career demotion in the history of mankind.*

"As you are aware, throughout the United Kingdom there has been a trend towards making the scene-of-crime investigators into a contracted civilian unit, rather like the subcontractors we use to analyse evidence. Sadly, this trend has now reached Wales."

Emyr internally assessed the statement, surmising, *they are going to make me redundant. Bastards. Dress it up, have some tea, now piss off with six weeks' pay and our best wishes.*

"I was aware of that, sir. Of course, I remain unsure of the viability of the intimated change, but I retain an open mind and I can see some positives from the proposal. I would be interested to hear the opinion of senior officers such as yourselves." Politically excellent, possibly too late, Emyr felt a pinprick of pride at his handling of the situation.

"Notwithstanding that we have no choice, I remain optimistic with reservations. Which is why we have asked you to join us today. You have presumably been wondering about that?"

Saying: "That is correct, sir." Thinking: *I assumed I was in deep trouble!*

The Superintendent glanced at his senior colleagues, collecting their positive affirmations. "Emyr" — continued use of his first name — "there will be a nine-month implementation of the change. Forensic Scene Investigators or SOCO's as I prefer, are to be transitioned into a civilian resource, the procedure to be managed by the NWP under a senior specialist officer." Noting the confusion on the relatively junior officer's face. "We would like you to be that specialist officer, with the rank of Inspector and a suitable salary review, of course. Reporting directly to me during the transition, then joining the established hierarchy thereafter. What do you say?"

Employing further separation between his thoughts and his mouth, he thought, *Fuck me gently with a ten-foot barge pole.* Orally, "I would be proud to accept that challenge. Sir. Sirs."

Embracing the congratulations bestowed upon him, Emyr thought about the reaction this announcement would receive, already anticipating Annie's stunned disbelief. Enabling his newly awakened political gene, he asked, "What operational milestones have you identified, sir? How many core staff should we consider retaining within the force?"

"Excellent questions, Inspector Christopher. Sounds good, doesn't it? Let us pencil in a strategy forum next week, all of us in this room with a couple of DCIs, maybe the new Forensic Pathologist, and brainstorm the nonsense from this situation." Refilling his cup. "I'll send out an invitation after the weekend. Meanwhile, your new contract will be ready on Monday morning. Once you sign it, I will make the official announcement. Until then, just between us, yes?"

"Absolutely, sir. Timing will be important. I might suggest the announcement of the strategy, followed by my new role. Until then, I shall keep it close to my chest."

"Good man, Emyr." Suddenly amused, breaking into a pompous laugh. "You may wish to discuss the appointment with your wife. After all, she will be preparing the contract for you. Should be an interesting weekend in the Christopher household."

Aware that his presence was no longer required, Emyr requested permission to leave, citing cases necessitating his input. Granted, congratulated, back patted, he left the privileged office with his head spinning, wondering what had just happened. Making a conscious effort to remove the smile from his face and the satisfaction from his persona, he loosened his tie as he walked to his office.

Thirty-Three
Friday, 15th February

Arriving at the company premises in Mold, the editor of the *Leader* faced a tirade of questions. Feeling below average, he struggled to address the multiple issues being raised by various members of his staff. Walking away from them, he closed his door, seeking refuge at his desk, reassuring himself that he had taken prudent steps to alleviate a burgeoning clusterfuck. Even if nobody believed him. Even if they accused him of fear. Even if they questioned his decision-making.

His door flew open, the wooden panel smacking against the rubber stop on the floor, rebounding, almost striking the furious reporter present in the doorway.

"I need to know what happened to my story. Why did you pull it? What the fuck, Rob? What happened to you? Who got to you?"

Overly tired and sick of the questioning he had received, he addressed his irate reporter. "Get everyone into the meeting room, right fucking now. I'll be there in five minutes. You can ask your question again and I will answer it in front of everyone so that I don't need to repeat myself all day. So that there are no channels of Chinese Whispers through the publication, everyone hears my explanation at the same time. Go on, set it up."

"No, sir. I want a private conversation with you. This was my story!"

His patience evaporated. "I don't care what you want!" Convinced he could be heard throughout the office, unconcerned. "Gather everyone in the meeting room. Now get out of my office!"

Chaos enveloped the publication with rumours abounding about overnight changes, a major story dropped, questions related to the impartiality of the Editor. They gathered in the meeting room, some seated, others standing, all waiting for the expected whitewash, yet hoping for the truth. Rob walked in, taking a position before the white drop screen, clearing his throat, holding his arms aloft, asking for quiet.

"Ladies. Gentlemen. Colleagues. I shall now make a statement. I'll keep it short, then you can ask your questions. Let's keep it orderly, please. Nothing is off the table, but I insist on reasonable behaviour, or this meeting ends. Are we clear?" An anticipatory quiet descended, allowing him to commence his statement.

"Yesterday, we had the paper set up to lead with a story detailing the incompetent performance of North Wales Police, particularly with reference to the Flint CID, on the homicide investigation into the death of Jeremy Campbell-Foulkes at the apartments alongside Boundary Lane. The online version had been authorised and the printed matter was ready to go. At a point in the evening, I pulled the story, causing lots of rework to be required, resulting in a hastily prepared publication which has failed to meet our usual standard. Are we all agreed that this is what is causing so much anguish this morning?"

A general murmur pervaded the room, indicating assent. "Good. Okay. Nilesh, you can repeat the question you asked me in my office a few minutes ago. Feel free to use the same words, the same disrespectful language. We are all friends here."

Nilesh stepped forward, confidently. "I asked you what happened to my story. I asked why you pulled it." Looking around, seeking support.

"What you actually said was, and I quote, 'I need to know what happened to my story. Why did you pull it? What the fuck, Rob. What happened to you? Who got to you?'"

"Yes, those are the words I used."

Retaining control of the room, pausing for effect, he ensured everybody had the chance to digest the exact situation. Sensing the time to be right, he attacked.

"This little exchange has been indicative of the situation I found myself in yesterday evening. We spoke five minutes ago, yet Nilesh has already paraphrased his own statement, rather than honouring the integrity of his initial questions." Attention grabbed. "Having written an excellent article and had publication agreed, Nilesh decided to take the evening off. Is that correct?" Without waiting for a response. "Whereas I contacted a source inside the police station and asked for an update on the case." Setting the audience thinking; experienced, they understood the merits of keeping tabs on a story. "I learned that North Wales Police had a suspect under caution at the station with a solicitor present. It was one of the names in our article. What I want to know, Nilesh, is why did I learn this from the police and not from the reporter investigating the story?"

Some heads turning, the crowd momentum swinging towards neutral.

"You can imagine the situation. Today, people buy our paper and they read our story about NWP, the police are useless, a killer in our community, blah blah. Then they turn on the radio at lunchtime to hear that somebody has been charged this very morning. How would that make all of us at the *Leader* look? It's a rhetorical question — we would look fucking stupid!" Taking a short break. "It would make us look as if we are running an antipolice witch-hunt."

"Were you placed under pressure to pull the story?" From the receptionist.

"No. It was a decision taken based on the circumstances. Purely my decision."

The intensity of the audience had noticeably dropped, their righteous indignation ameliorating to mild annoyance.

"What's the latest at the copshop? Are they still holding this person, and do they plan to charge her? Where are we on this?" This from one of the formatting technicians.

"Maybe our ace reporter would like to answer that one? Nilesh, what can you tell us?" Dumping on his journalist, petty revenge for the shitstorm this morning, already certain his authority had been restored, his thoughts drifting to his mobile, wondering if any of his messages had received a reply.

"I'll head over there now." Defeated, Nilesh only wanted to escape the room.

"While I have your attention. Does anybody know anything about a naked man found dead on the A483 yesterday morning? Nobody? Why the fuck not? Why is a major story developing in front of us, but you are all in here accusing me of quitting on a story. Priorities, ladies and gentlemen. Get them right and you will do well here."

His unstated threat hovering, the mood darkening, the rebellion crushed. "Are there any further questions? If not, get back to your jobs.

I would prefer that nobody disturbs me as I need to prepare for a meeting with a senior policeman later today. If you do choose to disturb me, it had better be for a very good reason."

The staff commenced their exit, slowly filtering through the only door, generally subdued. He heard one voice say, "Thank you, sir." That felt good.

Returning to his office, he reflected on a mission seemingly accomplished. His decision had been clarified, his explanation accepted, even understood. Away from the accusations from his staff, he performed an honest assessment of his decision. Had it been the correct thing to do, from a journalistic perspective? Yes! Would he have made the follow-up on the story without the Amy factor? Unlikely! Was his criticism of Nilesh justified? Based on one good story in eight months, yes! Would his action withstand inspection from the owners? Certainly; they were money men, without interest in the truth. Had the chance to repair his relationship with Amy been a factor? Absolutely!

He was curious why she had still not returned any of his calls or messages. She must have read the paper by now. Surely, she would know he had chosen her, pulled the story, shown his commitment to their fledgling relationship.

He tried again, her number first in the redial log. She did not answer the call.

He sent another message. 'Amy. I pulled the story. For you. Please call me. Or just please answer when I call you.'

He spent an hour searching for her on Facebook, finding a few potential Amy Meadows, including one of sublime proportions in Niagara Falls, Ontario. None matching her, frustrating him. Recalling Nilesh's file, he grabbed it, scrolling through the content and finding her full name. Amelia Grace Meadows. Back to Facebook. Locating her and sending a friend request, hoping for a positive response. Her limited photographic history reminding him of how pretty she was.

Thirty-Four
Friday, 15th February

"I would like to read a statement prepared by my client, under advisement from her representation."

DS Beecham and PC McGarry reclined in their seats, the recording devices already rolling, entertained by Jenny Coleman now speaking through her solicitor. "Please proceed."

The pinstripe-suited legal representative placed a single sheet of paper on the table, the large print clearly visible from across the desk but difficult to read due to being upside down. Removing foreign bodies from his throat, indicating his client with a limply hanging raised left hand, a pictorial confirmation of his physical handshake, wet and weak, reminiscent of a defrosted halibut.

"My client, Miss Jennifer Clarissa Coleman, would like to state for the record that she had no involvement in the death of her former boyfriend, the late Jeremy Campbell-Foulkes. She has provided considerable co-operation to North Wales Police and in return she has been subjected to incessant interference in her personal life to a level consistent with police harassment. She would like to receive a guarantee that her further co-operation will result in a cessation of investigations against her. She will proceed only on that basis."

Folding the paper, the lawyer invited a response from the officers. PC McGarry spoke first, incredulity in her voice. "Co-operation? Are you serious? Come on, Jenny, you have been anything except co-operative." Turning to the lawyer. "You have not attended any of Miss Coleman's previous interviews. She may not have informed you of their content. Perhaps I should bring you up to speed." Now speaking to the entire room, to Doris's amusement. "One entire interview saying only 'no comment'. Providing a false alibi to a police officer. Failing to provide the names of the people she was claiming as another alibi. Admitting to possession of a knife. Obstructing the process of a group identification parade. Flirting with a policeman. Do I need to continue? That statement was the worst case of misrepresentation I have heard in my entire career. You must feel quite foolish to have delivered that statement on her behalf."

Interjecting, Doris added further comment. "How are we supposed to guarantee to cease investigating her when she remains our primary suspect? Enough of this. I am resuming the interview, and remember, we permitted Miss Coleman to leave the station last night, so the retention clock is reset. We can keep her here for thirty-six hours if we need to. Nobody is going home until I am satisfied.

"Where were you on the afternoon of Friday twenty-fifth of January, when you claimed to be at work but were proven to have been absent? Where were you on the evening of the same date, where you claim to have attended a dinner with multiple people whose names you have yet to provide? Where were you on Saturday twenty-sixth January for the entire day?"

Jenny tossed her hair, releasing a half smile, sitting forward. "On that Friday afternoon I was with my boyfriend in a local hotel. He is married. I was trying to protect his reputation, as well as my own."

"Name and contact details." Immune to her feminine charms, Doris remained brusque.

"Like I said, he is married. I prefer not to release his personal information."

Playing her role, Flick offered an insight. "If we don't have his information, then he is not an acceptable alibi. You need to provide further details."

"That's difficult. He's a doctor at the practice. Nobody knows about us."

Beecham's turn. "Seems you have a choice. Give us his details to allow us to check your alibi. Or I could go to the practice and ask the administration lady who else was absent from work on that Friday afternoon. That should narrow it down quite a lot. Or, and this is my personal favourite, I could go into the practice and just ask everybody if they are the one shagging Jenny Coleman. And you might be amazed at how many people know what you are up to. People see more than you realise, especially when it is a bit scandalous."

Flick again. "Remember that time we asked that group of engineers about who was doing the payroll girl. Five of them raised their hands. Five. So funny." Invented, dishonest.

Her solicitor leaned across, speaking to her behind his hand, offering guidance, earning a portion of his two hundred per hour. Accepting the advice, relenting. "Dr Mohammed El Masri."

"Which hotel?"

Her reply. "The Royal Oak."

"Did you check in together?"

Her reply. "Yes."

"His credit card?"

Her reply. "Yes, his."

Indicating for the door to be unlocked, Flick left the room with the intention of checking that element of the alibi. Doris continued the questioning.

"The dinner at the Grosvenor on the Friday night, who was there?"

Her reply. "There was no dinner."

"Where were you? The truth this time."

Her reply. "At the Royal Oak. We stayed there throughout the evening. We had dinner there."

"Did you stay the night?"

Her reply. "He had to return to his wife. He left around 10pm. The room was paid for in advance, so I stayed over. I was quite tired." Her face increasingly red.

Stretching, loosening some of the stiffness in his back, Doris softened his attitude. "Jenny. We are the police. We are not your priest, rabbi, whatever. We investigate criminal activity. We couldn't give a shit about what you do in your private life. All we ask for is honesty. When I did my sergeants' exam, I don't recall any law being passed which makes it illegal to have sex with another person, so long as they are of legal age and a consenting participant. Morally, sleeping with a married man is questionable, legally there is nothing of concern. From my personal perspective, you are an attractive woman, you don't need to be involved with married men."

With a congenial atmosphere developing, the lawyer made his unwelcome input. "Your personal opinions are irrelevant, DS Beecham. I suggest that we are done here. Come, Miss Coleman."

"Miss Coleman remains under caution. She stays here until her alibi is checked. You," indicating the lawyer, without respect, "are welcome to go at any time. Sorry, Jenny. We have more questions, and we have to ensure you are being truthful this time."

"It's okay." Her voice softer, her manner friendlier, her attitude improving.

He extracted the remainder of her weekend activity. Having stayed overnight at the hotel, she slept late, then enjoyed a hotel breakfast, leaving before eleven and heading straight home. During the day she had taken a bath, completed a laundry cycle, watched rugby on the tv and had a takeaway delivered around 6pm. In the evening, she had spoken to her mum on the phone, watched more tv and drunk two bottles of beer, before retiring to bed. On Sunday, she had attended church at ten fifteen, spoken to lots of people, their names unknown but their faces familiar from the congregation. She provided names and numbers for two men she shared a drink with at a pub close to her home in the afternoon. Her evening had been spent cooking and cleaning, alone.

Lots to check. Enough activity to reduce her level of suspicion, should it all check out. Reviewing his handwritten notes, he sought a basis for raising further questions. Flick returned, whispered to him, confirming the room at The Royal Oak had been reserved for and paid for by Dr El Masri. He had been accompanied by a younger woman, approximately fitting Jenny's description. The doctor had agreed to come to the station, expecting to arrive between one thirty and two.

Pausing the interview, inviting the young woman and her lawyer to take a refreshment break, arranging for the door to be unlocked, he allowed them to leave the room, before bringing Flick up to speed.

"We need to check every part of her story, step by step. There are some potential gaps. Do you think we should hold her?"

"I think we may have to release her," Flick said. "But let's see what the dirty doctor says before we decide."

They took a break, tracking the elapsing time, both with further commitments to service later in the day. They discussed what they needed from the doctor, with Flick allocated the interview. Doris's schedule commitments in conflict with the doctor's expected arrival, his phone available as back-up should she need it.

Having wandered around the station, finding DS Holmes free, Beecham asked him to sit in on the interview with the doctor, but to allow McGarry to lead the questioning. Terry was indifferent, warming to the request when informed that there could be a follow-up exchange with Jenny Coleman. He recalled interviewing her during the initial enquiry, the rapport they had established, her little upturned nose.

Thirty-Five
Friday, 15th February

Taking facing seats at a table in the rear of the bar, they exchanged pleasantries while perusing the limited lunchtime menu. Chips were the only potato option available, offered with every item including the curry, as a half and half with boiled rice. The pints were delivered, the journalist sipping his dark ale, the copper slurping his lager, while the waiter hovered in expectation of their food order. Responding to his silent request, they chose their meals, allowing him to depart before resuming their discussion.

Placing the printed A4 document on the table, the journalist invited the policeman to read the article that had been scheduled for publication. The reproduced photographs were included, the text in a reduced font to fit the pages. Effortlessly gulping another quarter pint, he scanned the document, raising his eyebrows occasionally, a mixture of grins and grimaces released at potential misinterpretation. Absorbing the content, the policeman identified the underlying agenda, observing mistakes, along with some occasional inspired comment. Finished, he handed the article back to the originator.

The policeman delivered his opinion of the withheld article, citing several important inaccuracies while complimenting some of the insights, simultaneously lamenting the lack of instinctive policemen coming through the ranks. He highlighted two elements of the article, suggesting the paper could have been open to libel had they gone ahead. The journalist's disagreement easily parried, naming a high-profile media case in London only months ago.

The journalist considered the policeman's comments, wondering what he might receive in exchange, his thoughts halted as two substantial plates of food arrived. The steam rising from both plates raised suspicion of microwave involvement. Presented well, the food stimulated their primeval urge to eat, consuming fuel to generate energy. The policeman had selected Balmoral Chicken, the white breast meat and haggis covered in a gravy which also moistened the mealie pudding. The dish was finished with bacon, traditional public house peas mixed with carrots, and chips from a freezer bag.

Assessing his cube of congealing lasagne embellished with unnecessary chips, the dripping white sauce tarnishing everything on the plate, the journalist asked about alternative stories he could follow. Seeking an informal, confidential, off-the-record guide towards the inside track on a current case, he wanted something which could permit the paper to praise the NWP while compensating for the story they had withheld.

****

The people trafficker elaborated on his emerging disquiet with the performance of his translator and newly designated mule. Two physically imposing underlings listened, providing their opinions only when demanded, otherwise performing their roles of sounding boards to the head of the organisation. Concerned that he may be over-reacting, he sought their input, welcoming their insights, understanding those were calibrated by their caution against aggravating him.

Pausing from his outpouring of concern, he followed the lads, taking a tour of the warehouse, impressed to see the office completely decorated, renewed, and furnished. Genuine paperwork for their legitimate business had been filed in the cabinet, while clipboards adorned the desk with imminent shipments listed. All traces of the previous contents had been removed and destroyed, much of it burning in the still-smouldering skip in the yard.

Admiring the renovated warehouse, the recently installed metal storage racks around the walls, the small component storage bins mounted on industrial shelving, every rack and shelf labelled with an RFID identifier tag to ensure efficient stock tracing. Genuine business products had been situated on low-level shelves, massage tables complete with cushioned body and head support with the viewing aperture, carefully wrapped in cellophane. The floor was painted, walking paths marked to comply with Health and Safety, routes marked for pallet trucks, signs to firefighting equipment and emergency exits. A proper warehouse, for a legal business, capable of surviving any council inspection.

****

Having reaffirmed the conditions of the discussion, nothing on the record, the journalist listened wide-eyed as he learned the intricacies of a live case that his team were completely ignorant of, reaching a decision relating to Nilesh's future, deferring his thoughts as he attempted to mentally record what he was hearing. An illegal immigrant, possibly trafficked, certainly raped and murdered, her attacker identified then executed, his accomplice disappearing. Rumours of a territory conflict developing, with potential crossover into the Liverpool underworld. The lasagne largely forgotten, as it deserved to be.

He asked about the suspect at Mold, receiving another anonymous tip that Jennifer Coleman had become the prime suspect, though not necessarily the policeman's first choice. Hearing that she had been evasive throughout, escalating herself from fringe candidate to potential killer solely through her consistent inability to tell the truth to the police.

Unable to resist, curiosity overpowering rational thought, he asked the policeman about the other women from the list in the article. Hearing that two had been immediately dismissed from suspicion, that one had been wrongly charged, one was under caution now, leaving one on the fringes remaining under suspicion. Unwilling to reveal his relationship with the fringe suspect, uncertain if he had a relationship, his attempts to extract further insight were blocked by the policeman. Noticing that her name induced a different reaction in comparison to the other names.

****

Proud of the warehouse achievement, his anger subsiding, he asked one of the lads to source lunch from somewhere nearby, providing two twenties to cover the cost. He left the choice to the lad, not caring what was selected so long as there were chips.

The skip remained hot to touch, the contents continuing to burn fiercely. He tried to imagine what condition the body of Nesbitt might be in by now, incinerated probably, with minimal identifiable remains and further burning to come. Anticipating lunch, he hoped to enjoy the food before the translator arrived, to further inflate his mood and induce tolerance into his persona. He needed to balance his level of remaining faith in Boris against the danger of the business insights he had revealed.

All three sat around the office table, consuming cod and chips from greaseproof paper, white napkins used to protect the integrity of the furniture, plastic bottles of sparkling drink on offer. The boss selected Lilt, the quiet underling singing the old jingle in a terrible Caribbean accent, bringing amusement to the table. Licking his condiment-soaked fingers, he asked directly what the lads would do about the translator, if they were in his shoes. Hearing the consistent replies, he took their opinions on board.

The translator arrived at the office, seemingly recovered, with evidence of his returning personal confidence on display. Sitting without being invited, bemoaning the lack of leftovers, the smell of cod tantalised his ingestion cycle. Helping himself to a Pepsi Max, complaining it was lukewarm, missing the sarcasm as the boss asked if he would like some ice, barely aware of the declining atmosphere in the room since his arrival. Expressing surprise as tie wraps secured his wrists to the armrest of the new office chair, the brown drink overbalancing, messing the newly installed desk surface, irrationally inflaming the business leader's temper.

****

One empty plate removed, along with one barely touched, fresh pints arriving at the table, their purposes largely achieved. The paper agreed to publish pictures of the Asian lady, requesting the support of the public, subject to the case investigating officer's agreement. Raising their own profile while being seen to support the constabulary. They would also receive the inside track on the development of the current suspect's situation, either way. The removed article would remain unpublished. A consensus achieved, they took the opportunity to enjoy their drinks, their business concluded. They debated the lingering uneasy relationship between law enforcement and journalism, blaming political interference on one side and financial blinkers on the other.

Taking a break, each accessing his mobile, the journalist searching for incoming messages, finding some but none from the person he wanted to hear from. His disappointment pervading his manner as he struggled to think of further alternative approaches. The policeman finding his device crammed with unwelcome messages and an urgent voicemail request to call the station.

Explaining his need to depart, the policeman exchanged a polite handshake with the journalist, providing him with a final snippet revealing further inconsistency from their current suspect, suggestive of guilt. Thanking him for an excellent lunch, he suggested the Balmoral Chicken over the lasagne in future. Emptying his glass, he turned to leave, hearing the journalist express his appreciation while leaving close to a third of his drink unconsumed.

The journalist placed two further unsuccessful calls to her number, followed by two text messages, simply asking for a response, even an angry one. Calculating his alcohol breath to be just about under the limit, he drove to the office, calling ahead to demand the investigative reporters be in the meeting room when he arrived.

The policeman, an institution in North Wales, had no concerns related to his alcohol blood percentage, knowing it would require considerably more than two pints to take him above the limit, especially following a substantial lunch. Hands-free enabled, he accepted a call from Flick, listening as she summarised the interview with Dr El Masri, the confirmation of the affair and the trip to the hotel, before arriving at the discrepancy. His departure from the hotel had been around 10pm, his lady friend having deposited the key at the reception drop box, effectively checking them both out of the hotel. It was his impression that she had also gone home.

****

The translator confessed to consuming a small quantity of the pharmaceutical taken from the shipment he had been entrusted to deliver, his apology fuelled by panic as he sat secured to the chair, facing three hostile colleagues. Forced to listen as he was treated like a child, the addictive nature of the product highlighted, the rapid deterioration many users had endured. His position of trust in the organisation being inconsistent with becoming a user. Expressing his understanding, his regret, his future intentions, recalling his own suffering without an urge to vocalise his torment. He listened as his debt was explained, indignant at the calculation, the amount chargeable much higher than he had taken, the unit price beyond market value. He had suggested a staff discount would be fair, withdrawing the suggestion as he accepted that his situation was not conducive to negotiation.

Placing a real value on translation skills was difficult. Many massage room transactions had become universal, the words understood globally, thereby undermining the skill of the language expert. But poor decision-making by a leader was another concern, a concern necessitating minimal spread, something to be nipped in the bud before it became universally known. Forcing the translator's lips apart, they inserted a handkerchief into his mouth, suggesting he bite down, then smearing a length of duct tape across his mouth, inhibiting his ability to speak. Cutting the securing tie wraps, freeing his wrists, they encouraged him to induce circulation, allowing him to stand, positioning themselves to discourage any attempt to abscond.

Signalling his confidantes to remain behind, assuring them of his control, he led the translator outside. Walking around the perimeter of the warehouse, he pointed out the recent improvements, the benefits ultimately destined for their bottom line, the improved security against random police activity. Explaining the reality of a career beyond the limits of the law, the requirement to remain low-profile, the absolute need to stay away from the merchandise, especially the narcotics, but also the escorts and the massage girls. Indicating the likely consequences for failing to adhere to the standards demanded. He described the penalties for skimming from inside the organisation and also from the customers.

Placing five hundred pounds in the hand of both underlings, issuing words of thanks, verbally justifying his decision and their collective actions, the leader departed from the scene, content with the manner he had selected to resolve his situation. Stealing the product could not be tolerated, must be seen to not be tolerated. A severe financial penalty, a final warning, a demonstration of the price to be paid for further indiscretions. The silencer-enhanced pistol against the translator's temple had ensured the message was clearly understood, the urine stain on Boris's trousers testament to his comprehension.

As was his habit, the leader left the warehouse, heading to his office, enjoying the instantaneous surge of power from the motorcycle, certain the translator would cease to be a problem.

****

Having resolved the situation with the journalist, the policeman had exhausted his reserves of patience. Standing before Jenny Coleman, he summarised her situation. "Another inconsistency, Miss Coleman. I have had enough of you and your lies. You will be remanded in custody overnight while we investigate every microsecond of your alibi. If we find that you have misled us in any way, we will bring in the CPS and ask them to charge you with the murder of Jeremy Campbell-Foulkes." Issuing a threatening stare directly at the solicitor, he voiced his frustration. "Do not dare to request her release." Returning to the suspect. "Get out of my sight." Without conceding an opportunity to protest, he left the suspect in tears, returning to the incident room.

Thirty-Six
Saturday, 16th February

The room remained dark, offering little ambient light. Unfamiliar. Her mind roamed, attempting to rationalise where she was, where she could be and how she had come to be here. Uncovered, she understood she was on a bed rather than in one, no bedclothes providing warmth. Cool to the point of cold, she traced her fingers across her body, naked from the waist up, her skirt in position around her middle, her legs bare beneath the skirt. No indication of anyone beside her.

Turning her head gingerly in both directions, confirming her solitude upon the bed, inflicting discomfort to her forehead and cheekbones, she simultaneously attempted to cope with the pain while endeavouring to recall why she was here.

Recollecting being at some sort of countryside bar, attending a bumpkin version of a rave with Brenda, her former work colleague. Feeling old at twenty-six, while younger adults danced to louder than necessary music, their enjoyment influenced by a spectrum of coloured alcopops, blowing their minds while laying a foundation for diabetes in later life.

She paused her thought processes, unconcerned for the link between the bar and this strange room, her missing clothes. She pressed her hand against her upper skull, easing the ache momentarily, aware of an unpleasant taste in her mouth, urgently requiring liquid. Gently, she brought herself to a sitting position, her skirt riding higher as her legs dangled from the bed. Vision adapting to the low light, she located her bra on the floor, adjacent to her wrinkled blouse, which lay outside in, as if there had been difficulty in its removal. Extending her leg, she snared the blouse with her toe, dragging the fabric towards her, allowing her arm to reach, grab, secure. Repeating the process, she hooked a strap on the bra, her toes bringing it home.

Feeling the headache marginally recede, she risked standing. Feeling no adverse reaction, she donned her upper-body clothes, bringing a level of warmth while reducing her exposure and her physical frailty. At full height, she saw her underwear, the pants and tights intertwined, again indicating clumsy or difficult removal. Lifting them with her feet to avoid unnecessary bending, she sat again on the bed, beginning the process of separating the items, donning the pants over her ankles, pulling them to her knees, before inserting her feet into the black tights, positioning the heels and toes correctly, partially raising them to her calves. Standing, she completed her ensemble, less tidy than yesterday, better than when she had awakened.

Covered, with her confidence improved, she left the bedroom, passing another as she searched for the kitchen. Once there, she opened the tap to pour cool then cold water into an empty mug found sitting beside the sink. She sipped the water, gradually increasing her intake rate, gulping as she finished. Refill, repeat, the beneficial properties of the water rehydrating her body.

Her pain levels impacted, uncertain whether she was hungover or had taken a pharmaceutical, she assumed inner caution. She noted the time on a wall-mounted clock — just shy of five in the morning — listening for sounds of activity, the presence of people or animals. Making her way to the lounge area, she located her handbag, relieved to see the contents meeting her expectations: purse, mobile, mascara, perfume, tissues, all the usual paraphernalia. A different mobile phone lay on the coffee table, dark and dormant.

Seating herself in an expansive armchair, she gave thought to her circumstances. She could recall being at the bar where Brenda had taken her. She could remember the loud music, remembered drinking cider, unusually for her. Enough clarity for her to concede that she had probably not been roofied. Good news. She had been approached by an older man at the glorified children's party, even older than herself, though hardly old. He had joined her to talk, sitting with her, buying her a drink. All okay till then. He had asked if she would like something to raise her spirits, the exact wording her returning memory confirmed. Agreeing that she would, she had taken the pill he had offered, assuming it was Ecstasy. She was now sure they had left the bar together.

Summarising her situation, her count set at zero, she questioned her state of undress when she woke. Had she undressed herself? Had she received assistance from somebody? Had her state of inebriation resulted in her divesting some of her clothes before collapsing onto the bed? Could she have been undressed by the bloke, gotten frisky, put out on the first date. Despite being physically tender, she remained emotionally strong, her uncertainty eliciting a burning need to know what had occurred.

Taking the mystery phone from the table, she walked to the other bedroom. She found it occupied by a solitary male sleeping on his side, one arm raised above his head across the pillow, mouth slightly open, snoring gently. His tangled hair revealing signs of thinning, baldness marching inexorably towards domination. She gauged him as not ugly, not handsome, kind of forgettable. Reaching forward, she touched his shoulder, shaking gently. "Hello," she said, barely above a whisper. "Are you awake?" About to use his name, realising that she could not remember it, forgotten somewhere in the recesses of her mind. "Hey!" A little louder, still no response.

Folding back the duvet, she saw his nakedness, not definitive but surely not a positive sign for her. Their mutual nudity increasing the likeliness of having had a carnal event with this unknown person. Her intrigue increased, her concern mounting, she considered her next move.

From a vague recollection, she shook his phone, achieving the enlightened screen. Touching it against his exposed thumb, she smiled to herself as his mobile unlocked, allowing her access to his life. Retreating from the bedroom, she took the same seat in the living area, opening the device's apps. She identified a default Gmail email account with nine unread messages, a Hotmail account containing only one unread message, his regular SMS messages folder and a WhatsApp account. Finding nothing of interest to her, she opened his gallery, planning to look at his pictures and see what she could learn about him.

Immediately, her attitude changed. From the small thumbnails gathered under the previous day, she could see her image within several photographs. Clicking on the first photo of her, she was fully clothed, lying on her back on a bed, the same bed where she had awakened a short time ago. Second photo, her unbuttoned blouse exposing her bra, her skirt higher on her thighs than previously. Next, blouse and bra removed, her eyelids tightly closed, clearly below consciousness, her nipples hard from the temperature or from stimulation, she could not be sure. Next, still topless, underwear at her knees, skirt covering her privates, she almost looked sexy, would have been sexy if she had been awake. Next, a different orientation as the photographer had relocated himself at her feet, underwear at the same position, her skirt raised, displaying her pubic hair. Fortunately, her upper legs remained together. Next, her undies removed, the skirt up to her waist, legs pushed apart, the camera closer this time, gynaecology one oh one. The next photo was a selfie, showing his face beside her pussy, his lips pursed as if preparing for a kiss.

Shocked. Violated. Angry. Horrified. Returning to the beginning, she began to count, increasing her count with each picture. One. Two. Three. Four. Five. Reaching the exposure of her personal femininity, she doubled the increment count, six, seven. Again, on seeing the selfie, she doubled up, eight, nine. Her pulse raised, her hands shaking in agitation, she allowed her temper to consume her, liberating her. Any feelings of tenderness and fragility gone, a visible vein on her temple pulsing furiously, her rage overcoming containment.

Restraining her emotions, reigning back her instincts, controlling her simmering fury, she assumed control once again, logic replacing passion.

"Nine," she whispered. "Nine." Again, for emphasis.

She reopened the apps on his mobile, now seriously interested in the content. Reading his recent emails, his recent messages, she discovered nothing untoward. Repeating the exercise, concentrating on his sent messages, looking for anything outgoing which might have her photo attached, any of these recent invasive pictures. Finding nothing, surprised yet relieved, it appeared her immodesty remained unshared for the moment.

Confirmation that he had not shared any pictures of her was essential. She required to awaken him to confirm that information. She also needed to ask, needed to know, if he had had sex with her. Remembering a folder not checked, she accessed his videos, again relieved to find nothing incriminating her. Once more, surprised.

"Maybe these are just for his spank bank?" she wondered aloud.

Aware of her count, how close she was to ten, how important it was that she remain stable, she contemplated her next move. He enjoyed a physical advantage over her; not significantly, but enough to challenge her. She had the element of surprise, she was already sharp, thinking ahead. He would have the advantage of being at home in familiar territory. She had her knife, within the folds of her handbag. Moving around his kitchen, she continued to assess the pros and cons of her situation, while seeking inspiration from the contents of his drawers and cupboards.

She discovered a lone opaque nylon tie wrap, more than a foot long, maybe a third of an inch wide. She garnered the item, hoping to find more. Accepting that a single tie wrap would only restrain one limb, insufficient for her requirements, she sought rope, string, anything suitable to hamper movement from his arms and legs. A temporary restraint until she had the answers she wanted. Hearing sounds from the direction of his bedroom, she became still, listening intently for movement or evidence of activity. Silence followed. Continuing her search, she found an old-fashioned ball of string, beige and thin, unravelling at one end. Not strong, she assessed it may provide a temporary solution, bringing it with her. Stepping lightly towards the lounge, she accessed her handbag, extracting her small ornamental knife, the blade sharp, a realistic precaution for her protection. In possession of the knife, the string, and the cable tie, she walked to his bedroom, pausing in the doorway to gauge his breathing, satisfied he remained asleep.

Appreciating that she was invading his privacy by skulking around his bedroom as he slept, she reconciled her actions as fair; her own privacy had been severely infracted, photographic evidence providing indisputable evidence. Close to his head, she gently lifted his wrist, bringing it closer to the wooden slats of his headboard. Placing the wrist atop the angled pillow, she slipped the tie wrap around the vertical wooden bar, bringing the ends together around his wrist, securing the nylon mechanism. Drawing the cable management device tighter, she secured his wrist within the loop, attaching his arm to the bed, limiting his future movement. She worked slowly, gently, ensuring he remained undisturbed, the tie closed but not exerting undue pressure on his flesh.

Retreating to the foot of his bed, she cut a long length of string. Withdrawing the quilt from his legs, she prepared a bowline loop, slipping the string across one foot above his ankle, drawing the tail of the string around the castor at the foot of the bed. Having completed one loop of the castor, she reached up, tugging the bowline closed, tightening the string around his ankle, pulling the string tighter around the wheel of the bed, tying the string to itself.

He came awake, unsure of his situation. Groggy, his eyes only partially open. Not waiting for him to become fully aware, she grabbed the tongue of the cable tie, pulling it hard to tighten the mechanism, disabling his right arm completely. Coupled with the weaker restraint on his left ankle, he was immobilised, at least temporarily.

Partially awake, feeling discomfort in his arm, he tugged against the securing tie wrap. Unable to release the limb, he turned his focus towards the woman standing before him.

"What's going on, Jess?"

Despite herself, she smiled. She had given him her alias, had avoided providing her real name to him. Still smiling, she replied, "You have me at a disadvantage. I cannot recall your name. But I was about to ask you that same question."

Bewildered, he gave his name. "Si. Simon. I did tell you." He looked straight into her eyes, acknowledging their prettiness, despite the smudged make-up and obvious tiredness. Brown, shaped like perfect almonds. "What are you doing?"

Regarding him at his disadvantage, tied, she removed the blue striped duvet, further weakening his position, leaving him naked and exposed, his penis flopped lazily against his thigh. Superior, clothed and armed, secure in her advantage, she softened her tone, seeking to engage him in a meaningful discussion. She began with a straightforward question.

"What was the pill you gave me last night at the pub? You hinted it was E, but it made me drowsy. I would like to know in case I have a negative reaction later. Can you tell me, please? And please, Simon, be honest."

"I thought it was E. Honestly. The bugger that sold it to me must have lied. I'm sorry. I wanted us to get high and have a great time. Really. But you got dopey, and I brought you home, for safety."

"For safety?"

"Yeah, to ensure you didn't wander off. Get into trouble. You know."

Wandering around his bedroom, venturing in and out of his eyeline, she appeared to be considering his explanation, reconciling it in her head. Simon, horizontal, with restricted movement, attempted to follow her.

"Okay. Good start. I believe you. You gave me some form of sedative, accidentally. But you took action to protect me. Brought me here. By the way, where are we?"

"My place." Seeing her exasperation, her smile disappearing. Continuing. "Buckley."

Her smile returned. Her facsimile of a smile. Her lips parted, exposing even teeth. Closer inspection revealing a lack of warmth within those eyes.

"Could you elaborate on our arrival here, at your home? Did the pills make us both drowsy or was it only me? What happened when we got here? Was I up for it? Did you try it on? Did you get into my knickers? I am curious." Her timbre superficially indicating frivolity, betraying a darkening undertone, warning Simon, demanding explanations.

"God, no!" He was adamant. "I didn't try it on. I offered you my guest room, helped you sit on the bed, gave you some water. Then I left you to sleep. I was tired, too. I came here." His plea for understanding almost believable. He tugged with his left leg, further tightening the knot around his ankle, the thin string holding for now. Seeing the frailty of the string, Jessica chose to add redundancy to the bond, cutting a further piece of string, displaying her knife to Simon as she formed a new bowline, slipping it across his foot and pulling tight, attaching the end to the same castor at the base of the bed. He hadn't resisted, the knife holding his full attention.

Having taken some moments, she approached him, mentally measuring the extent of movement his free arm may have. Satisfied with her position, she continued their conversation.

"I woke up with most of my clothes removed. Did you help yourself to a sneak peak, Simon? Did little Simon want to see under Jessica's clothes?"

Shaking his head, his most vigorous movement yet, indicating that he had not, without verbally confirming. She maintained the pregnant pause, eliciting a comment from him. "You probably took off your own clothes. Duh."

Without warning, she raised her voice, reaching a shout, her strained emotions apparent. "Don't fucking lie to me, you wretched cunt!"

Protesting, his own voice raised. "I'm not lying, Jessica. I'm not!"

Unsure if she had accepted his protest, he watched as she turned her back to him, departing from his bedroom, her stockinged feet eliciting minimal sound. Hearing her softly repeating, "Nine, nine, nine."

Simon, utilising his unrestrained arm, tugged on the string holding his foot. He had experience of the string failing before, understood it was weak. He was also aware that two hands would make removal much simpler. He continued to test the string, failing to notice her return to his bedroom doorway.

"Leave it alone!" The words sharp, commanding.

Raising his head, meeting her look, assimilating the vision before him, her furious expression, the object in her left hand, his mobile phone, her right holding the small knife.

"Latest model Samsung. Very nice. Worth a few pounds. Did you buy it? Did you get it through a contract?"

Welcoming a change of subject, any diversion, he mumbled a response. "I got it on a contract with Vodafone."

She tapped a few buttons, turned the screen towards him. He saw the picture, instantaneously arousing panic, understanding that she had gained access, knew she knew he had taken revealing pictures of her, her anger justified, his predicament becoming more serious. The image on the phone showed Jessica still dressed, lying on the bed. The least offensive, much worse to come. Unable to compose a response, he said nothing.

Rotating the phone screen towards her, she swiped, before turning the image back to him, this time topless, apparently asleep, realistically comatose. Again, his voice failed him. Without looking down, he knew his body was betraying him, twitching, reacting to the image involuntarily, blood moving to that area of his physique. He hoped the reaction had not been noticed, her expression suggesting she had seen, recognising her displeasure.

She continued to swipe through his pictures, demonstrating no emotion, extending his concern, confirming her knowledge of his photographic activity. Failing to produce the anticipated temper or revulsion, no scream, no tears, no passionate appealing for an explanation.

Placing the phone on the dresser, she addressed him directly, calmly. "I have a few questions." Sliding the side of the blade across the palm of her hand, simulating a sharpening motion. Seeing that she had his attention, she continued, "Have you sent any of these photos to somebody else? A mate, maybe?"

Rediscovering his voice. "No, Jessica. Not at all. I took them for myself only. Sorry." Feeling a need to continue, assuming the apology had a positive impact, seeing further pacification. "I know I shouldn't have. I couldn't help myself. You're gorgeous. I am really sorry." Seeking a reaction from her, unable to gauge her expression, he stumbled onwards. "I never had any intention of showing them to someone else. I wouldn't disrespect you like that. I thought we were getting along. But when you passed out, the evening ended, I was frustrated. I was, am, attracted to you. I know it was wrong."

"Are you absolutely sure? None of these pictures have been shared? I need to believe you. Do I? That is the question." Accentuating her knife, moving slowly towards him.

"Honestly, I have not shared them. I promise!"

Standing before him in wrinkled clothing, her hair tousled, her cheeks flushed, she saw further spontaneous growth in his nether regions, his body losing an internal battle between fear and arousal. Seemingly satisfied with his answers, she abruptly changed tack.

"When you removed my clothes while I was unconscious, did you fuck me?"

Thirty-Seven
Saturday, 16th February

Occupying his temporary office at the new CID centre of excellence, his casual dress befitting the weekend, DS Chappell surveyed his case, looking for the moment of inspiration, certain it would come.

He had delegated the identity of the deceased Thai lady to the Missing Persons people. No longer his responsibility, he retained some interest in the outcome, aware it may provide a link or a break in his current case.

The information from Beecham was useful, but only as confirmation of the lead provided by the street cops, identifying Dai Harris, the link to the Thai lady established beyond doubt. The formal identification by Dai's mother had been routine, quickly confirmed. Her statement that her son had visited her before leaving early with his colleagues was ignored by the delegated constable. The significance of her impression that he was leaving reluctantly was also missed. Her descriptions were vague, eliciting no excitement from the uniform.

The method of killing Harris had raised concern. Unusual! Unique! Shot through the rectum, the internal damage massive, according to the pathologist. Why? Execution. Who? To be determined. Finding Nesbitt remained a priority, his involvement likely to be important. Where was he?

The dog handling team from Cheshire had scoured the area, determining that the body had been abandoned close to the place where it was found. A vehicle had to be involved. The team had located footprints arriving and departing from the scene, leading to the next layby along the road, suggesting the perpetrators had parked there. There was unanimous agreement that the body had been killed elsewhere.

The forensics team had tested skin and hair found at the scene, rain-damaged, inadequate for conviction purposes, but suitable for confirmation against other evidence. The burn marks around the rectum opening indicative of an extremely intimate assassination.

Seeking to establish a list of known associates of the deceased: he had Nesbitt, of course, plus MacKenzie and his extended organisation. The mother had suggested a list of friends, none of whom had any firm connection to criminal activity. To date. Harris had a clean record. What had led him to rape and murder a stranger? How had he stayed clear of the force when he was involved with a known criminal element?

He had a uniformed constable prepare a comprehensive list of massage outlets in the region, with addresses, names and indications of links to the MacKenzie syndicate. He was surprised at how many places currently operated. Having identified too many addresses to allocate resource for a random door knock, he sought a pattern to suggest a method of preselection, finding nothing obvious.

The natural link would be from The Mancunian to the Thai lady, potentially trafficking Asian women into the country for the purposes of prostitution. If so, where were the others? Could he access outside agency support? People trafficking was a hot topic with politicians currently. Investigating the origin of the Thai lady, possibly tracing her movements, would not only confirm her identity, but could be the route to solving the case. Wishing he had not delegated her to Missing Persons, he recalled the DI instructing him to not waste resource on a dead villain. The circle complete, he began again.

Thirty-Eight
Saturday, 16th February

She rephrased the question, ensuring there would be no ambiguity. "Simon, after taking those intimate photos of my naked body, did you stick your dick in my pussy?"

Anticipating an emotionally charged denial, she was surprised to receive a low-volume, calm and categoric, straightforward answer. "No, I did not." Jessica considered the denial, comparing it with her own body awareness, concluding that she doubted him. Her count remained at nine. Glancing at him now, semi-erect despite his situation, she endured doubt that he had resisted taking the opportunity when it had presented itself. He had wanted her then, he still did, yet she partly trusted his statement that he had not. Maybe he had only wanted pictures to beat off to. Had there been no desire to screw her? Had there been desire, but overcome by his inner decency? Questions formed, remaining unasked, unsure how to proceed, she continued to be stymied by his reaction.

Remembering the foul taste in her mouth when she awoke, initially attributed to alcohol breath, comprehension gradually presented itself. Suspecting she knew the answer, compelled to ask, phrasing the question as a statement. "You came in my mouth. Didn't you?"

He sat on the bed, one arm tied to the headboard, one leg double-secured to the foot of the bed, his appendage showing little sign of subsidence. His gaze lowered, his expression displaying guilt or possibly embarrassment. No words. A barely measurable incline of his head, once only. Unable to meet her gaze, his entire body began to deflate before her. Neither speaking, allowing the dual realisation of their predicament to reach their consciousness. Simon, in a position of weakness, concerned for his welfare, concerned how she might react, concerned that she had a knife. Jessica, enjoying a strategic advantage, confirmation she had been sexually assaulted, processing her level of distress, analysing her options, mentally assessing her situation.

"Well, Simon. Here are my options, as I see them. One. You can apologise for what you did, make me an offer to forget it, and we can go our separate ways. You would need to be seriously fucking generous." Shutting down his enthusiasm for that option, before he could form any words, she continued, "Two. I can call the police, report you for sexual assault. A serious sexual assault. Have them take tests to see if you also raped me. Have you convicted, sent to jail, added to the register of sex offenders. I could basically ruin your life, ruin what is left of your life after you spend ten years inside." Pausing, as if thinking of a third option.

They faced each other, each considering the proffered options. Internally considering more possible solutions to their situation.

Simon looked cold, shivers manifesting on his torso, possibly from fear as much as the temperature. He wondered if he could swing option one. Offer her some money and make an effusive apology, lay it on with a trowel. Option two was not worthy of consideration. There could be residual DNA from him on her and his own photos would incriminate him. He tried to think of an option three, a proposal he could make, his thought processes compromised by his vulnerability.

Jessica, internally phrasing, *Ten*, repeating at regular intervals. Wondering if he would be capable of formulating an option three.

Simon sought a way to persuade her to untie him, knowing that achieving this would allow him to physically dominate her. He would give her a good smack and commandeer her knife. Later, he could destroy the phone, thereby removing her evidence. He applied his thinking to gaining release from his bonds.

She considered securing him further, restraining the second arm and leg, providing herself with additional protection. She expected that he would not co-operate, and she would be unlikely to accomplish it without his acquiescence.

Planning beyond his escape, he considered whether he might shag her again. She didn't know that he had before, bagging up like a gentleman before mounting her, riding her as she slept. He had intended to go again but failed to reignite before fatigue overtook him. He had hoped to cultivate a relationship with her, the pictures his secondary plan in the expectation that she declined to continue seeing him, suspecting she would consider herself as out of his league. His only regret was that he had failed to re-dress her before he went to bed.

He tried. "Jessica, can you untie me. It seems we are both looking for a solution." *Sometimes, simple works best.*

His request remained without response, as if she had not heard, certainly had not considered, maintaining her silence, her pensive expression unchanging.

"Come on. Let me go. We can put this behind us. Pop down to the ATM; I could extract some cash, buy you something nice, say sorry properly. What do you say?"

Her interest piqued, she re-engaged with him. "How about, you give me your PIN number and card, and I go to the ATM and help myself. Three hundred seems about right. I don't really know the going rate for a blowjob, but as you didn't have permission, I think three hundred is justified."

His thoughts raced. *This could work.* Send her to the ATM, allow her to extract cash. She would be gone at least twenty minutes. Enough time to release himself. He considered reporting the card stolen, dismissing the idea; no need for outside involvement. The cash and an apology might sort everything. He sought possible negatives from this solution, finding none beyond the loss of three hundred pounds, an acceptable price to avoid being charged with indecent assault. Totally worth it to have shagged her.

"Although, I should just call the police and press charges for sexual assault."

She let the statement hang in the air, revealing little emotion. Her manner seemed thoughtful. Offering him the opportunity to contemplate this option. Time to reflect, time to panic. Her own thoughts drifting towards the beautiful number, the number composed of the two elements of digital electronics, the one and zero, the high and low, the on and off. A one, followed by a zero. The beautiful number ten. Her number. The cleansing number. The number for justice.

"Eight five zero three," he offered, repeating, "Eight five zero three. My pin. Go ahead. The card is in my wallet. Barclays. I think you should take the cash, buy something nice. I am sorry for what I did. Really sorry. I would like to see you again."

Looking over her shoulder, locating his wallet on the dresser, she made a show of opening the leather. Visually identifying the card, retrieving it from the fabric pocket, raising the Barclays Bank card for him to see. "This one? Eight five zero three? You're sure?" Barely hearing his confirmation, carrying the card, she left the room, leaving Simon alone. Finding the jacket, he had worn the previous evening, she searched in his pockets, finding some coins and three pills reminiscent of the one she had taken. The sedative that was supposed to be Ecstasy. Satisfied, her intention decided, she undressed in the cold, dimly lit room. "Ten." she whispered. Pouring a fresh cup of water, she returned to Simon.

Pausing in the doorway, she permitted him the pleasure of admiring her unadorned body. Extending her pose, legs slightly apart, shaking her hair, deliberately attempting to arouse him, limited success apparent in his midriff.

Extracting another card from his wallet, this one embellished with a Halifax logo, she held it in his line of vision. "Here is my proposal. Simon. I would like the pin number for this card as well. This would allow me to extract a total of six hundred pounds from your accounts. Expensive, I agree. But I am not a whore; I deserve your generosity." She walked around the room, showing herself, teasing, revealing her best features, hiding them again. "I want you to remain here, secured, until I return. I suggest you take a pill and allow yourself to rest, enjoy some quiet time while I collect your generous gift from the banks." She displayed the pills from his jacket, confirming his suspicion. "You take a pill. Once you nod off, I go and get the money, then come back here.

"You won't come back. You'll just take the money and leg it, leaving me here. Why would I trust you?"

"You know what? You might be correct. There are no guarantees. I might take your cards and money. But our mistrust is mutual. You could be lying about the pin numbers, leaving me to waste my time at the banks. But there is something else you should know. When we met last night, after we shared our first drink together, I had already decided that you were not going to get laid, even though I was in the mood. I haven't had sex for ages, but you were not getting it. You are not my type physically, and you come across a bit creepy. But, if you had treated me well, it is possible that I would have considered blowing you."

Letting her comments penetrate his thoughts, she carried on. "What you did to me, while really upsetting, is something I may have done anyway. Taking nude pictures of me was disgusting. That has really annoyed me. You have three minutes." Helping him decide, she approached him, coming closer than before, touching herself, then moving her fingers towards his lips, hinting at her taste. Noticing him pull away slightly, her curiosity became aroused. She held her fingers to her nose and mouth, having already registered some swelling around her intimate lips, detecting traces of a foreign presence. Rubbery? Chemical? Recognition dawning on her. "Condom, eh?" Understanding he had worn one, had obviously penetrated her, lied to her. "You bastard! You fucked me while I was unconscious!"

His predicament having worsened, the extent of his behaviour realised, Simon mentally sought a plausible denial, then justification. Failing to find either, he risked a glance, her expression already hardened, suggesting a fury barely suppressed, his situation deteriorating towards perilous. In desperation, he offered his defence. "When we came here last night, I brought you to the other bedroom. I kissed you, and you kissed me back. Your tongue was in my mouth. I touched your breasts and you responded by touching my cock over my trousers. I told you I wanted to sleep with you, and you told me to wear a condom. I went to get a box but when I came back you had fallen asleep. I was gutted. You had agreed to sleep with me. I thought you might wake up if I undressed you. You had agreed and you were wet, so I did it with you."

"You expect me to believe that? Why did you deny it before?"

Sensing doubt, he persisted with his account. "I was trying to spare your feelings. If you didn't remember, I thought I should act like nothing happened."

Sarcastically, she replied. "Thank you for considering my modesty." Raising a new question. "Why finish in my mouth?"

"I have trouble finishing with a rubber on. When I took it off, I was going to come on your tits, but I gave in to temptation."

Seeing elements of doubt in her expression, he continued. "I'm sorry that I did that. And I am sorry for taking the photos of your body. That was wrong. Please, delete them now. I am sorry for some of my actions."

"Some of them?" she snapped, "only some of them?"

Figuring that he had made some progress, he conceded to her monetary demands. "Okay. The Halifax pin is four nine four one. Help yourself, release my leg, give me the pill, a drink would be welcome. I'll believe you about releasing me. Let's get this done. Thank you for being reasonable, Jessica."

She had been sure he would accept her offer. What choice did he have? He couldn't know the punishment she was planning for him beyond the monetary. Placing one pill in his free hand, watching as he placed it in his mouth, she presented the cup of water to him, the same hand reaching for the cup, taking it from her. Dropping it immediately, he grabbed her wrist, pulling her forward, upsetting her balance, spitting the pill as he released her wrist, entwining his fingers in her hair, yanking the hair, straining the roots. She gave a low grunt of pain, off balance, lying across him, the cup rolling beyond reach, her hidden face expressing concern. Self-preservation overtaking his instincts, he allowed her head to rise above the quilt, her eyes meeting his, pulling her head towards his, bracing before releasing a forward motion, smashing his forehead into hers. The head butt impacting, her head attempting to recoil, restricted by his grasp of her hair, pain exploding across the bridge of her nose.

Satisfaction. Blood leaking from her nose. Inspired, he tightened his grip and smashed her face towards his still-bound leg, raising the knee from his free leg, catching her beneath her ear, her face flaring in further pain.

"Take that, you stupid bitch." She floundered, seeking support, any element of control, finding none. His mobile knee sought to hurt her more, her head suffering, feeling like her hair was being pulled from her scalp, her blood spreading, the increasing flow reflecting the level of pain she endured. "Fucking stupid bitch." He pushed her head down again, her forehead contacting his erection, incongruously aroused in the midst of the fight, his fight for freedom, her fight for survival, fighting to recover her domination.

Feeling her resistance reducing, his control establishing, he made a further glancing contact with his knee, rocking her head. Maintaining his hold, he enjoyed the proximity of her face to his hard-on. Recalling pushing himself between her lips after shagging her, her slack half-open mouth as she slept, rubbing himself as he pressed harder, ignoring the discomfort from her teeth against him, emptying his fluid into her oblivious mouth. Unable to resist, he dragged her head closer to his erection, seeking access to her mouth again, aware of her resistance, twisting her face, battling for survival. His arousal intensifying, stickiness presenting, her physical objection weakening, conceding, her lips touching him, parting, access unavoidable. Savouring the moment, he thrust upwards, simultaneously pressing her downwards, deeper, his breath shortening, chemical reactions taking control of his body, his mind losing traction against instinct, anticipation overwhelming. "Suck it!"

Followed by excruciating pain. His scream, piercing, agonising as he convulsed. His sensitive flesh clamped between sharp teeth, dragging, scraping, shredding him. Tasting his blood in her mouth, sensing opportunity, she introduced a sawing motion with her upper and lower teeth, inflicting maximum pain. Certain she had to end this fight now, sure defeat would be extremely dangerous for her. His fingers relaxed, her hair free from his hold, his hands now desperately trying to lift her head to separate her from his penis, trying to bring an end to the pain blinding him. Roles reversed, Jessica fighting to hold his appendage in her mouth, wanting to inflict further distress, resisting his hands, tightening her mouth around him, ignoring the copper taste, aware of their combined blood staining the sheets around them. His fingers sought her eyes, activating her preservation reflex, her mouth releasing him, her head free, her body unrestrained. Concerned for the proximity of his knee, she rolled towards the foot of the bed, away from him, away from imminent danger. Making no effort to restrain her, his free hand immediately cupping his cock and balls, seeking to provide comfort to himself, unwilling to look, frightened to have the damage he suspected confirmed.

"What have you done to me, you cunt!" The venom in his voice abundantly clear.

She stood at the end of his bed, wild hair knotted, her eyes wide, despite blue discolouration already forming above her nose. Blood running from her nostrils, accompanied by further crimson slipping from one corner of her mouth. Her chest heaving as she breathed heavily, a crazed grin dominating her visage, she appraised him. "Enjoy your blowjob? Ten. Fucker! Ten. You cock-sucking fucking rapist. Ten. Never again, you inadequate twat. Ten. I hope you bleed to death from your tiny little cock. Ten."

His breath came in gasps, his tears evident from the pain combined with concern for his predicament. One arm restrained behind him, his remaining limbs free, the fractured string hanging uselessly from his ankle, his remaining arm protecting his genitals, providing physical protection from further attack.

"You only had to take the bloody pill." Her tone suddenly lacked emotion, simply a statement of fact.

Neither spoke. Neither moved. Both continued to bleed, the rate of blood loss significant without being life-threatening.

His restrained arm fought against the tie wrap, unable to dislodge the improvised plastic restraint. Continued attempts making no impression. Increasingly calm, she watched him, her expression displaying a combination of satisfaction and sympathy. Unexpectedly, her tone softened, her words simple. "I'll get scissors."

Leaving the bedroom, heading towards the kitchen, aware his struggle against the tie wrap had intensified, she increased her pace. Arriving at the sink, she opened the cold tap, splashing water from her hand into her mouth, diluting the blood, spitting into the basin, repeating the process, the taste in her mouth unpleasant. Insignificant compared to her overall suffering, between her eyes, through the length of her nose, her cheekbones, her sinus, her teeth. Her emotional suffering set aside, accepting and dismissing her violation, she diverted her attention to the drawers, opening the top, then the second, locating two sets of scissors. One set for precision cutting: small, sharp, metallic, without any pattern. The second set larger, a typical kitchen implement: blue plastic handle with blades about three inches long, their sharpness indeterminate, showing early signs of rust on the inside of the blade. Selecting both pairs, she ran to the bedroom.

She was confronted by Simon, twisted onto his knees, his back and ass facing the doorway, fighting valiantly with the headboard, the wooden slat bending under sustained pressure. Without hesitation, she crossed the room and climbed onto the bed, spreading her feet for balance as she tossed the smaller scissors to the floor, extending her arms above her head, the blue handles interlocked with her fingers, the blades together. Bringing her arms downwards, shouting "Ten!" as she slammed the scissors into his back, close to the level of his shoulder blades, less than an inch from his spine on his right side. Feeling the impact, her wrists absorbing the resistance, forcing the blades deeper by exerting increased pressure, his crouch position subsiding to horizontal, face down, an indecipherable sound coming from him. Fully focused, she abandoned her position on the bed, collecting the smaller scissors from the carpet, observing the grey pile had a diagonal run, the pattern not noticed before. Reasserting herself on his bed, she sat astride his back, her buttocks resting on his, her knees spread. Evaluating her situation, his weakening attempts to break the tie wrap, the blood spreading from the scissors, his free arm trapped beneath his torso, she assumed her position of domination. She leaned forwards till her body lay along his, almost a reverse spooning, her boobs pressing against him either side of the embedded scissors. Gently, almost reverentially, she raised the smaller cutting device, ensuring the blades were separated, concentrating as she drove a single scissor blade into his neck, overcoming the elasticity of his flesh. Watching as blood spurted from the fresh wound, further contaminating the adjacent bedding. He tried to speak; the words inaudible. She leaned further into him, her ear close to his, asking him to repeat what he had said. Faintly, this time coherent, he repeated. "Fuck you, Jessica."

"You already did that, Simon, without my blessing, so now it's you who's fucked." Enjoying imparting the words to him, still astride him, she felt her release, flowing from her across his flesh, her insides fluttering as her pleasure intensified, the angst retreating as delirium established itself as her dominant emotion. Savouring the release, she let herself surrender to the pleasure.

Her flow reduced to a trickle, then ceased. His movements were minimal, his resistance broken, his requirement for medical attention critical. Returning to her feet, she located her knife, taking comfort from the familiar weapon. Opening the blade, wielding the device in her right hand, she came alongside Simon. She saw his muted reaction, alarm combined with acceptance. His eyes closing as she slipped the sharp blade into his throat, pushing it fully home, turning the handle clockwise through ninety degrees and further, the blood flow slower in comparison to the previous wounds. Retracting the blade, she considered taking an eye, wanting to inflict the worst imaginable damage. Deliberating which to remove, favouring left, reverting right, considering both, she reluctantly abandoned the impulse. Her finger below his nose confirming lack of breath, moving to his neck yet still unable to locate a pulse, understanding he had passed on, his fight over, her victory absolute.

Placing her knife on the bed, beyond reach should he miraculously recover, she used both hands to turn him over. Impeded by his restrained wrist, she was obliged to remove the larger scissors from his back before achieving an acceptable position. Checking his vital signs once more, confirming the end of Simon, her molester. Simon, who had hurt her physically, injuring her face. He lay there, unbreathing. Her anger remaining unfulfilled, she retrieved her knife, imparting several savage stab wounds to his torso, applying various depths and inconsistent techniques to random locations, displaying a cold reality in contradiction to the attacks which suggested extraordinary rage. Blood-soaked, suffering her own agony, she inflicted a final wound, dragging her blade between two existing cuts to form one larger wound, ending the assault.

Adrenaline gone, she was suddenly cold, exposed and suffering intense pain. Disregarding the body, she retreated to the living area, donning her clothes once more, appreciating some warming of her slim body. Searching and failing to find medication, she located the controller for the central heating, switching the function to manual, adjusting the temperature to twenty-four degrees, turning on the heating, hearing clicks, a clump, and a low-level bang.

Revisiting the bedroom, her damaged nose was immune to the smells, her eyes noting the brown deposit between his legs, she found a carton of Ibuprofen in the attached bathroom cabinet, taking the painkiller to the kitchen with her. Popping two pills, resisting the temptation for four, she drank further water to assist in swallowing the chunky capsules, the cold liquid inflicting further discomfort to her mouth, teeth and gums. Survival functions instigated, she stood before his settee, contemplating her actions, perceiving a disturbing habit developing with her.

Does giving a man a hand job constitute having sex with him? Asking herself, mentally, without sound. *I suppose it is a sexual act.* Conceding to herself. *Does a man forcing himself on you while you are unconscious count also?* Agreeing with her psyche. *In which case, I have killed my three most recent sexual partners. That cannot be sustainable.* Her thoughts fleetingly recalling Jed, Mark and now Simon. All having had a form of intimacy with her, all now beyond the realm of the living. Aloud, she gave herself a reprimand. "I need to stop killing my lovers. I must be more selective in future."

Thirty-Nine
Saturday, 16th February

Watching Holly sleep, her rhythmical breathing steady, marginally louder than was ladylike, he felt relaxed to face a Saturday morning without work commitment. No agenda inflicted on him by his resident girlfriend. He wanted to do something different, not shopping, not garden maintenance, not even going for a drink. A break from their usual routine. He abandoned the bed, intending to apply some thought for possible things to do. He couldn't leave the decision to Holly, as she would suggest they get physical again. The woman was insatiable.

Donning yesterday's underwear, fully intending to change later, he slipped into a wrinkled tee-shirt and padded downstairs, seeking caffeine and juice. His mouth dry from their recent morning activity at Holly's insistence.

Waiting for the kettle to boil, his mind drifted to the HR meeting from the previous day. A colossal waste of time, in his opinion. His words had been inappropriate, but hardly unique in a pressured environment, and he felt sure everybody within the police force had heard worse language. The head woman, Emyr's wife, had been fine. She had her authority and wielded it as required, extracting what she wanted from him, ending the meeting cordially with her objective achieved. The little one, the snide little mare, was obviously a closet something with no interest in remaining impartial, seeking any weakness to exploit her personal agenda.

In hindsight, he had been pleased to meet Carole Leadbetter. She had restored his faith, assuring him that he was not attracted to every woman he met. He had begun to wonder. Holly, of course, that naked picture of Amy, Jenny Coleman, Hoi the masseuse, others if he made the effort to remember. But that weaselly little bitch had aroused not a hint of a reaction.

He had been coerced into attending a seminar on tolerance in the workplace; his compliance with the punishment would allow the matter to be closed. He considered whether Emyr had been let off so lightly, curious of any involvement from his HR wife, dismissing the distraction. Adding boiling water to the two heaped spoons of granules mixed with milk, he stirred the liquid energetically, the potent brew providing a comforting smell, the heat warming his hands as he walked to the lounge on a cool winter morning. The juice poured but forgotten.

Flicking the remote, Sky News defaulted to his screen, allowing the continually revolving channel to ramble in the background. Now reviewing the GP interrogation that he had watched yesterday, acknowledging McGarry's improving technique, accessing the information she needed after overcoming the doctor's reluctance to answer. Wondering how a guy like that could be with Jenny Coleman, mentally preparing a list of pros and cons. She, stunning but maybe mad. Him, older, married, triple five o'clock shadow at two o'clock, balding, middle-age spread, kids, arrogant, God complex. He was unable to locate any feature to place in the positive column.

Taking the opportunity, he evaluated the revelation from Emyr about possible orgasm residue in the front seat of Mark Forrest's car. Could it be relevant? Potentially, but the lack of a timeline rendered the information insignificant. The blood analysis, confirming the presence of moderately high levels of Valium: could this be important? Valium plus alcohol plus exhaust emissions, the poor bastard hadn't stood a chance. Both interesting, neither worthy of the case being reopened. He idly wondered what his next case would be.

Forty
Saturday, 16th February

As she waited for the painkillers to commence their magic, she attempted to gather her thoughts.

Her prevailing personality maintained a pragmatic attitude. She had killed Simon because it had been necessary. Her upcoming priority was to clean the area, cover her tracks, destroy any evidence, protect herself and get out of here.

Seeking balance, she projected her natural personality to the forefront. The victim of a predator. A young woman who had been deliberately drugged and sexually abused. A woman who had her intimate privacy invaded and had been photographed in a series of compromising positions. She had been viciously attacked. While enduring a further sexual assault, she had been in fear for her own safety. She retained evidence of these assaults, enough to present a solid case to the authorities, the caveat being to justify her subsequent violent actions as appropriate for self-preservation.

Recent experience with the police had been unpleasant. She had been a suspect in the death of Jed, her former boyfriend. She had been interrogated at the police station, treated like a criminal, forced to submit her fingerprints, and indirectly accused of murder. She was guilty in the opinion of at least one detective. She could see no reason to voluntarily interact with North Wales Police.

The physical battering, she had taken was apparent via already-formed facial bruising, her spilled blood, his DNA in her mouth and likely evidence of sexual activity down below. She was confident the police would accept her story, be sympathetic to her situation, comprehend her fear, her violation. They would offer her counselling, she would be unlikely to face any charges; perhaps her reaction regarded as overly zealous, yet understandable in the terrible circumstances.

Finding her voice in the silent dawn. "Fucking social workers, with their textbook psychology." Opinionated, they would question if her clothing had been overtly revealing; had she invited unwanted attention? Curious why she carried a knife. The prevailing personality saw no merit in following this path.

Conceding that the multiple stab wounds she had inflicted might impair her defence, Amy considered the recent events objectively. Simon was to blame: he had instigated the situation, put his dick in her mouth and pussy without invitation, had hurt her physically and emotionally, had deserved the fate he had suffered. A consensus reached with herself, she discarded the option of making a call to the police for the moment, at least until she had examined the opportunity to cover her presence at this house. Glancing at her watch, shy of seven, she resolved to make no decision until eight o'clock, allowing herself time to reach a logical informed decision.

The central heating was overpowering the winter ambient temperature of the house, inducing a mellow atmosphere, raising her body heat while bringing a flush to her cheeks. The red flush competing with the developing black, blue and yellow bruising taking the opportunity to display their myriad of colour across her features.

Wincing as she stood, she assessed Simon's house. The living room was large, possibly designed as a combined living/dining area, the lack of table providing an expanse of comfortable space. The cream leather furniture unimaginative but appropriate for the location, spacious with an expensive appearance. The open fireplace framed by a marble-effect surround, the ornate wooden mantel adding a touch of traditional class to the premises, supported by the brass tools on the hearth and matching grille. His curtains were typically male, self-coloured, a nondescript grey blending into beige, full length, closed with a substantial overlap. A dark wood entertainment centre, his television front and central, accessories on both sides, modem, router, decoder, DVD, laptop.

'Fuck! How did I miss it? Laptop! Shit! What if he circulated my pictures from the laptop instead of his phone? Stupid! Stupid!' Admonishing herself, she stooped to lift the computer, the charging cable disengaging as she carried the device to the settee. Opening the cover as she sat, the screen slowly awakened before her, offering her the opportunity to sign in. Clicking the mouse to sign in, she was presented with a password demand. 'Fuck, fuck, fuck, fuck!' Compromised, she evaluated her situation again, these new circumstances suggesting a definite incline towards informing the police and presenting her case for self-defence. *No decision until eight o'clock. Stay calm.*

Transferring her presence to his kitchen, she admired the contrastingly ultra-modern appliances when compared with his traditionally furnished living room, all matching, dark grey approaching anthracite-toned appliances. Fridge-freezer, cooker, microwave, coffee machine, dishwasher, washing machine with integrated tumble dryer, kettle, toaster, waffle-maker, rice cooker, all modern, all colour-matched, nothing cheap. The only contrasting item being a medium-sized six-place kitchen table and chairs, the surface composed of a red tile lattice surrounded by wooden edging, co-ordinated red cushions adorning the chairs. Many cupboards, adequate drawers, tasteful accessories. A fake framed blackboard with popular cocktails written in multiple chalk colours. A hanging array of non-metallic cooking utensils, and a beautiful selection of chef knives, including a cleaver and sharpening rod.

She commenced an inspection of the cupboards and drawers, extracting anything which piqued her interest, giving a small squeal of delight as she found a large packet of Marigold gloves, containing four pairs. A full box of giant matches joined the gloves on the work surface, soon accompanied by a bulky manila envelope located behind the assorted chemical cleaners beneath the dual-sink system.

Inquisitive towards the envelope contents, she split the seal with one of her few remaining intact fingernails, revealing a large quantity of apparently identical pinkish bank notes. Pouring the contents onto the table, she recognised the fifties, their denomination conveniently confirmed. "Oh, Simon, what have you been doing? So much money hidden in your kitchen. What do you do for a living?" Unable to resist, she began to count the money, taking only minutes to confirm eight thousand sterling. Exactly. "Eight grand! Well, so much for the police option. You little beauties belong to me!" Returning the cash to the envelope, she placed the package alongside her handbag.

She risked a cautious peek through the living-room curtains. The front garden was large, mostly green, with a gravel driveway to her left, a medium Audi hatchback parked near the house. The street was quite distant, currently devoid of pedestrians, a steady drizzle of rain laminating the surfaces of everything within her vision.

Allowing the curtains to fall together, she repeated the exercise at the rear of the house, seeing a further expansive garden, tidy without colour. Glancing to her right, she located the separate garage, small enough to preclude a second car. The front garage door was an up-and-over type, a side door present towards the rear of the building, white-painted wood without a window. None of the neighbouring houses overlooked the rear garden, providing an excellent level of privacy. Planning to inspect the contents of the garage, she made her preparations. Approaching the front door of the house, she found a key in the mechanism, testing the handle to confirm the door was locked. Opening a door in the vestibule, she found a large blue hooded raincoat, akin to the ancient snorkel parka, offering fantastic protection from the elements and incidental inspection from curious strangers, not to mention warmth.

Donning the coat and raising the hood, she took the keys situated within the rear door, heading for the garage. She successfully unlocked the side door at the third attempt. Entering the garage, devoid of any vehicle, she found the typical detritus of a male householder. Random tools, buckets, a garden hose, one black mountain bike complete with helmet, flimsy metal shelving holding a variety of aerosols, gaffer tape, a bag of kindling, firelighters and twelve bottles of dark ale. An assortment of wooden logs lay loosely on the floor.

She put the firelighters in the parka pocket, tucking two logs beneath her armpit, lifting the kindling bag with her other hand before leaving the garage, awkwardly locking the door behind her.

Divesting the coat, appreciating the increasing warmth within the house while noting eight o'clock was still in the future, she began to build the basis of a fire in the clean open grate. A layer of firelighters supporting a perpendicular lattice of kindling criss-crossed with further kindling, the unrequired logs laying on the hearth beside the matches. Ready to go.

Feeling the return of physical pain, she swallowed two further painkillers. Finding courage, she went to the main bathroom to face her reflection in the washbasin mirror, seeing the dried blood on several areas of her face and neck, her lips swollen and bloody, dried mucus and blood in her swollen nose. The sensitive area around both eyes was already bruising, a lump forming on her lower forehead, her hair loose, with numerous strands dangling from her head, falling free as she attempted to sweep them away. "Fuck me. I look like I have been beaten senseless. I could be a rape victim!" The words comforting her, assuaging any lingering guilt she felt about Simon, reconfirming her decision to proceed as she had decided. "Bastard! He deserved what he got. Ten. Ten." Feeling better. "Ten!"

Coffee had been a bad idea. Unable to resist the fancy machine with the shiny little tubs of potent caffeine, she had used three with milk to craft a giant mug full of warm brown stimulating goodness. Her damaged lips and mouth had protested, instant discomfort becoming everlasting pain, forcing her to abandon the drink to the table, hoping it might be okay upon cooling.

Having donned a pair of yellow rubber gloves, she had commenced her cleaning operation. Her first job had been to launder the bedding from the room where she had slept, every item, including unused pillows as a precaution. His washing machine already performing the hot cycle, allowing her to multitask.

The dishwasher was also operational, containing all crockery or drinking vessels she had found, accompanied by two pairs of scissors and her personal knife. Having prewashed the scissor handles and the cups she had drank from.

The open fire was demonstrating a willingness to catch. She added a log above the kindling, quickly darkening around the edges as the burning kindling provided a persistent source of ignition. The firelighters had blackened, crackling sounds emanating from the flue, sparks dancing against the charcoal background. She straightened the guard. "Got to keep the sparks in the fireplace. We don't want a house fire." A frown forming, a moment of inspiration, considering. *Or do we?*

The snipped tie wrap lay on the counter, beside the torn segments of string. Ready for disposal.

With a basin full of hot soapy water and a dual-sided abrasive sponge, she had carefully scrubbed anything she may have touched. Door frames, door handles, chairs, surfaces, the laptop. Everything except the coffee machine, the fireplace utensils and the surrounds. She had not bothered with drying anything, seeing no reason to do so. *It's not my fucking house.*

Combating exhaustion, she assessed the bombsite that was Simon's bedroom. Bedclothes lay everywhere. One bedside lamp had been knocked to the floor. There was an abundance of blood stains overshadowed by the massive singular shit stain. One unmoving body lying on its back, face turned towards the right shoulder, visible open wounds no longer leaking red. Staring impassively at Simon, not especially tall, not overweight, unburdened by life, she calculated her alternatives for cleaning his body and removing any evidence of her presence. She knew she could clean him as he lay, having performed this task on another occasion. Her intuition suggested that dumping him in a bath full of hot water would be more efficient, requiring less physical effort from her, aside from dragging the body to the bath. A third solution nagged her thoughts, simply setting fire to him, allowing his bedding to provide the fuel to ensure his complete incineration within the flames, with an extra bonus of removing other latent evidence simultaneously.

She sang to herself, assisting her concentration, vocalising lyrics about an eternal flame. The final word beyond her vocal range, the song familiar, the artist less so. "Nuclear Pussy? No, not that, but close." Resisting the option to burn the body, considering the impact a prompt response from the Fire Service may cause, she selected the bath option. Grabbing his ankles with her gloved hands, she tugged hard to overcome the physical resistance of his moderate bulk. A second tug initiating slight movement, she stepped backwards, dragging Simon, his legs leaving the surface of the bed, moving bedclothes assisting her efforts. She heard a thump as his torso tipped over the mattress edge, a louder thump as his head cracked against the floor. Wiping sweat from her forehead, she paused. Grinning, she remembered the group, saying aloud, "Atomic Kitten!"; recalling an earlier, superior version, "The Bangles!" Pleased, she resumed the arduous task of pulling the deadweight towards the bathroom, the effort reducing as she reached the synthetic wooden panels of the hallway floor. She observed the trail of blood on the floor, smudged by her stocking-clad feet, further spread by his hair, a DNA palette containing nothing from her.

Allowing herself some respite, she sat on the bath edge while running the warm tap. She resisted the urge to test the temperature, the gloves rendering this task difficult to perform accurately, conscious of her need to eliminate mistakes as she eliminated traces of herself from poor eliminated Simon. Seeing steam rising, she accepted the water temperature as suitable. Closing the tap, she engaged the plug, operated by a rotating mechanical switch, before fully releasing the flow of steaming hot water into the nearly white porcelain-effect tub.

Regarding him, dismissive of him as an object to be thoroughly cleansed, dispassionate towards his existence, seeing him only as a predator, a danger to women, deserving of his fate. Drawing air into her lungs, repeating the process in readiness for the task ahead, she lifted him by his underarms, twisting as she deposited his upper torso across the bath perimeter. Moving her hands towards his midriff, exerting further energy to raise that element of his torso, achieving a height level with the head, one arm falling into the still-filling receptacle. She used his knees as her next pivot, grunting as she pulled, a splash confirming success as the body slid into the steaming clear liquid. Nudging him as necessary, she immersed her naked attacker, revealing the wounds she had inflicted. His lifeless, flaccid penis bobbing on the surface of the water, the offensive little thing which had invaded her but would never invade anybody again. Placing his hands in the water, she waited for the liquid to fill to the maximum capacity where the overflow became functional. Reaching that point, she ceased the flow of water, leaving the room.

Passing his bedroom, she collected his pillowcases, the neutral fitted sheet, the blue-grey-white duvet cover, an inconsistent patterned throw, and a towel from the floor. Depositing them adjacent to the washing machine, she returned to the open fireplace, flames rising from the wood, their orange tips reaching for the flue, leading to the chimney escape route. The warmth and glow rejuvenated her flagging energy. She added a further log to the furnace, before placing his wallet and mobile phone alongside her handbag, her phone and the eight thousand pounds. Cautiously, she sipped her now moderately warm coffee, the pain less, checking the remaining time on the dishwasher cycle. Searching the house, she found a vacuum cleaner, bringing the appliance to the kitchen.

Glancing at her phone, she noticed a missed call, clicking on the icon to see Brenda atop the list. "Shit, how much did she see last night? Did she see me leave with Simon? Could she even know him? Why is she calling me so early?" Acknowledging that she had an increasing habit of talking to herself, committing to address the problem, she considered ignoring Brenda and switching off her phone as she concentrated on the tasks facing her. Deciding against it, she called her young former colleague.

"Hey, Brenda, good morning. Returning your call?" Curiosity inherent in her tone. Hoping her injured mouth indicated tiredness.

Brenda, bubbly, chirpy, responding. "Hi, Amy. How did you get on last night? Did you pull? Have you got company?"

The basis of the query suggesting a lack of knowledge of her departure from the bar, she dug further. "Didn't you notice the guy coming on to me, trying to load me with drinks?"

"Nah." Her Wrexham accent more apparent. "I was too busy. Got myself picked up, I did. Julian; he's a local musician. Totally intellectual, he is. He says he has fancied me for ages. I wish I had known. We did a bit of dancing, got hammered, then he took me home. Did your bloke take you home?"

Adopting a relaxed manner, her concern abating, trying to reflect the attitude of the younger person, she feigned enthusiasm. "He tried, but I palmed him off. He says he will call me today; let's see if he does." Switching to conspiracy mode. "So, what happened when Julian took you home? Did he stay over?"

"He couldn't. I still live with my folks. Remember? We did some kissing near the house, and he copped a feel downstairs, nice and gentle. That's why I was calling. Any chance I could bring him to your place later today? You know, for sex."

She needed to think quickly. Visitors today were not an option. She could have evidence present. The damage to her face would be obvious. There would be questions. *Think!*

"Sorry, pet. I won't be there today." Her pause, inviting a question, giving her time to align her deception. "I am already on my way to

Holmes Chappell to spend a few days with a friend. I would like to help, but I can't this weekend."

"Don't you have a spare key lying around outside your flat? You could tell me where; I only need an hour or two." Listening to the pleading in Brenda's voice, she almost laughed, the desperate need to satisfy her new boyfriend, the urgency to spread her legs for him, unaware of the concept of making the guy wait. "I'm really sorry. If I could, then I would. Another time?"

Brenda clutched at the offered straw. "You would allow it then, at another time maybe? I could bring a boyfriend round?"

Throwing her a bone. "Sure."

"Thanks. Enjoy your trip. See you soon."

The call had been worthwhile. Brenda had no idea about her and Simon. The possible complications of a visit had been avoided. Task complete, she turned off her mobile, placing the dormant device in her bag.

Responding to an impulse thought, she collected one pair of scissors from the dishwasher, the cycle complete, returning to Simon enjoying his hot bath. With insulation from the Marigolds, she lifted his left hand from the tub, proceeding to cut his fingernails as short as she could, each finger in turn. Right hand next, repeating the cutting, removing nails and debris from beneath the nail as she went. Her anger resurfacing as the mirror reflected the increasing damage to her features, bruising resembling panda eyes dominating her visage.

"Ten." The reminder assisting in settling her emotions.

A clank and a whoosh announced the completion of the washing cycle. Still adorned with her yellow gloves, she removed the first load of bedding, replacing it with the blood-damaged linen from his bedroom. Loading powder, neglecting softener, she enabled the same cycle. Upon hearing the influx of water, she placed the initial items in front of the roaring fire, taking a seat on the floor, armed with the scissors. Betraying no meaningful expression, she commenced cutting the bedclothes into handkerchief-dimensioned segments, prepared for loading into the grated inferno. The cutting was tedious, the scissors blunted by recent activity, the low thread count of the fabric making clean cuts difficult, causing her to flinch in pain on occasion, her hands and fingers firing explosive messages of agony to her tiring mind.

She tossed fabric onto the fire, inclining the fireguard to permit access to the naked flames, typically around six squares of fabric each time, achieving satisfaction as the material smouldered, smoked, then burned.

With one set of cleaned bedding immolated on the fire, she retrieved her knife from the dishwasher, drying the ornate handle and blade before closing the device and returning it to the dedicated recess within her bag. *Till next time, my darling.* Mumbling under her breath, revealing a hitherto unspoken bond with her weapon, unconscious appreciation of the protection it afforded her.

Carrying his phone to the bathroom, she used his thumb to bypass the security again, allowing her access to the contents and insights into Simon's life. Her first task being to delete all photographs of her and any other woman she located in his gallery, the women unknown to her, removed sequentially. Noting that none were named, simply filed by the date and time taken, indicating a lack of intimacy. Only her photos involved nudity, the realisation bringing a limited smile to her damaged face, a backhanded compliment, fatigue preventing her from further obsession with this anomaly.

Deleting all his videos, she continued to investigate his life, her eyebrows raised as she located a contact titled "Jed", the number vaguely familiar to her. The coincidence shaking her confidence, questioning the likelihood of this, suddenly suspicious of this link and concerned about potential consequences. Her mood darkened further when she located Mark Forrest — another coincidence? Impossible, or was it? *Jesus, what the hell is going on here?* She continued to skim through the contacts, backtracking to the beginning, scrolling to the end, repeating, a further contact name attracting her attention, coercing her to speech. "DI Catt? A fucking policeman. Christ! What am I getting into here?" Her inner intelligence attempting to cope with the possibility, probability, of her victims being known to each other, and being known to a senior police officer. The large sum of money adding a further dimension. Her heightened sense of concern sharpening her thoughts, fuelling her efforts with increased motivation, the unknown elements encouraging her to conclude her duties here quickly but thoroughly, without compromise. Finding no further contacts known to her, she shut down the phone and removed the SIM card, tossing the tiny item into the fire. Unsure how she could remove the battery, she placed the carcass of the phone on the floor before attacking it with a wrench she located beneath the sink. Finding a plastic brush and a virgin bottle of Toilet Duck, Amy returned to the bathroom.

Forty-One
Saturday, 16th February

Having spent an unexpected night in the cells, she had developed an anger quotient beyond any rational scale. Demanding to be released, she had berated the custody sergeant, rousing the other remanded prisoners from sleep with her protests. Jenny Coleman was extremely unhappy. Breakfast had been an insult, bottled water served with pre-wrapped bread slices and an apple. Her lawyer had pledged to overturn the overnight incarceration, leaving the station before 8pm, her release failing to materialise.

She had harboured positive thoughts in the afternoon when the big policeman was absent, replaced by the nice one, the butch woman being the only consistency. They had asked her to repeat her Friday encounter with Dr El Masri, every detail, repeating their questions over and over. She had been embarrassed to talk about that relationship in front of the nice cop, the one she believed had a level of restrained desire for her. She had attempted to deliver honesty while trying to preserve some of her dignity.

At exactly nine in the morning, she was summoned from her cell, offered toiletries to freshen up, then taken to interview room three. She wondered if they had a lottery system, drawing a number to determine which room to use. Every interrogation seemed to have taken place in a different room. If their intention had been to unsettle her, it was working.

DS Beecham was back, the tall one. Exchanging a token greeting, he performed the introductions to the recording devices, placing them on pause as they waited for other attendees to arrive. Her lawyer entered the room with the woman constable, seemingly comfortable with each other. Beecham spoke, attracting her attention.

"Jenny, it's Saturday morning and none of us want to be here. Can you just try to stop lying for thirty seconds and allow us to get on with this? Please." Her lawyer protested, fractionally ahead of her, disputing the presence of untruths.

"Dr El Masri has largely confirmed your story, preserving your alibi, except for a few details which are concerning us. You told us that you stayed behind, using the hotel room, sleeping late and taking breakfast. He says you dropped the key at reception, checking out at the time of his departure, which was close to 10pm. So, who is telling the truth? Hmm?"

"Mohammed must have misinterpreted what I told him. He was distracted, on his way home, agitated, as I recall. I stayed at the hotel and had breakfast there. I told you this before."

Doris acknowledged her statement, nodding, writing in his notebook. Glancing at Flick, looking down again, then up at Jenny. "You also told us that you had Friday dinner in the Grosvenor hotel, then told us that you had dinner at the Royal Oak. You told us you spent the Saturday shopping with your sister, then told us you watched rugby on the television. You told us you have a knife. You told us you hated Mr Campbell-Foulkes."

Allowing his words to register, the contradictions laid out, the solicitor showing concern, he continued.

"We operate on a formula in murder cases. You might have seen it on a tv show. Means. Motive. Opportunity. You have admitted to owning a knife — a knife was used to end the life of the deceased. Means! You have stated on the record that you hated the deceased, that he frightened you, that you feared his sexual proclivities. Motive! Your movements on the Friday night cannot be proven; for the time we believe that he died, you have given us many versions of your activity that night. None of them provide a solid alibi. Opportunity! You match the description we received from a witness; that same witness picked you from the group identification parade. You have lied to us and been obstructive to us. Your fingerprints have been recovered from the deceased's apartment, found in his lounge and his bedroom. Opportunity again! I think we have enough."

"But I was at the hotel all night! How could I be in Saltney?"

"Can you prove you were in the hotel all night? Your boyfriend stated that you left the hotel. We can put you there at 10pm, and again twelve hours later taking breakfast. But in between we cannot prove where you were. You intimated that you had been to the victim's Saltney apartment several times, suggesting you are familiar with the area. Perhaps you knew where to park to avoid the CCTV systems in the area. We don't know. And we can't ask you, because you lie to us every single time. Any comments, Constable McGarry?"

"None, sir. I think you have painted a clear picture."

"We are leaving now. You should talk with your lawyer. We'll come back in an hour. Interview suspended." Waving, without subtlety, for the door to be unlocked, they left the suspect and her solicitor to talk, the audio recordings suspended, the video continuing to monitor activity within the room.

Flopping into his seat, he opened the file from the Superintendent. He read the historic case file from Edinburgh, learning about the death of a man he assumed to be Amy Meadows' father, killed by his wife, her mother, to protect their daughter, Amelia, from physical and mental abuse. Absorbing the details, reading about the father counting to ten before distributing punishment, reports of escalating physicality and emotional cruelty. The failure of the social services, who had held meetings but neglected to take meaningful action. It was an interesting insight into her life during her developmental years, potentially influencing her adult behaviour. Any relevance to the current case had yet to be quantified, although it could certainly be interpreted as supportive of the possibility that she would be capable of killing someone. Passing the file, he invited Flick to read it. "Amy Meadows, her mum murdered her dad. That can fuck up anyone. Is it relevant? The Super thinks so; he sent this file to me. Coleman is looking good, but I have this nagging doubt about Meadows, as you know."

"Okay, I'll read it. Objectively. But you understand that killing people is not hereditary, like ginger hair, or bad eyesight." Rearranging the document pages in chronological order. "Have we got enough to charge Coleman?"

"Maybe. I'll make a call to the DCI, see what she thinks. If she is up for it, I'll bring in the CPS. But I want your opinion on this file. And another thing. Terry Holmes suggested to me, privately, that the alibi his girlfriend provided for Meadows may not stand up to scrutiny."

"Holmes said that?" Her question confirmed. "Shit. That complicates things."

Forty-Two
Saturday, 16th February

Applying the toilet-cleaning liquid to her double-sided sponge, her skin protected by the gloves, she scrubbed his fingertips, the cut nails simplifying the process, extracting residual impurities and removing delicate skin from the cuticle area as she vigorously cleaned. Continuing to his hands, the palms already reddened from immersion in the scalding water, she inflicted further inflammation from the rough side of the sponge, harshly treated with chemicals. *As if he could complain.*

Reapplying liquid from the duck-shaped bottle, she washed his knees, as they had impacted with her face, unwilling to forego any opportunity to delete traces of her presence. She considered how enjoyable this bathing could have been in different circumstances. Maybe she would do it for her next boyfriend, without the gloves, of course. Or the clothes and the bleach. She imagined improving the experience, being naked, applying soft soap to his body, with special attention to his sensitive areas. Dispelling the reverie, she committed herself to cleaning Simon's legs from top to toe.

Taking a break, she opened the plug, allowing the water to escape from the bath, the position of the body interfering with the flow efficiency.

Looking at him she considered her next moves. The damage inflicted by her teeth was visible on his dick, less obvious in the current shrunken state, unlikely to become fully evident barring a medically improbable erection. The kitchen knives crossed her mind, offering an opportunity to remove the offending appendage. Could they trace her saliva from the damaged area? Would a cock flush? She applied toilet duck directly to the flexible shaft, rubbing it in, amused at the lack of reaction. *I must be losing my touch. This usually has an instant effect.* Having saturated the area in chemical, she vigorously sponged it, exfoliating to her satisfaction.

Lifting the shower attachment, sliding the tap mechanism lever in the opposite position, she opened the tap again, the shower head spitting, gurgling, becoming a solid hot spray of water. Commencing with his hair, working her way to his feet, she methodically showered his body, rinsing her recent cleaning, pressuring remnants of evidence to the drain, deleting her presence as she cleaned the site. Opening his mouth despite some resistance, she jetted hot water into it, aware of the possibility that he could have tasted her as she slept, squirting the toilet chemical directly into the mouth to mix with the water. The steaming water creating rivulets of red liquid as she crossed the stab wounds, the long slice joining two wounds attracting additional attention. Reaching behind his legs, Amy directed the water jet upwards, disturbing remnants of brown from his rectum, irregular flecks swirling towards the plughole. Rinsing complete, she closed the water flow, replacing the shower attachment before inserting the plug in the drain and restarting the flow of water into the bath. Emptying the remaining chemical into the bath directly below the flow of water, she generated a pathetic replica of a bubble bath, gradually immersing the body in a bleach-based broth. Filling until the overflow activated, she sat on the toilet, relieving herself, carefully wiping the entire suite after use, then flushing her expelled liquid. Flushing again, she left the bathroom.

Pain gradually subsiding, her fluctuating energy returning, she acknowledged the time had progressed beyond eight. Her choice had already been made, her after-incident activity precluding any law enforcement involvement.

With the open fire generating substantial warmth, she disengaged the central heating. Exchanging gloves, she consigned the first pair to the fire, the smell of burning rubber immediate, unpleasant, a mistake impossible to correct. Opening his wallet, she learned about her victim, his driving licence providing essential information, including this address. She transferred his bank cards to the top of the envelope, the pin numbers fresh in her memory. Removing the incumbent cash, she added it to her haul. Extracting his two credit cards, cutting them into fragments, she threw the pieces into the fire. Briefly considering Simon's habits, two debit cards, two credit cards, accepting that she did not care, moving on.

Seeking distraction, she enabled the massive television, finding YouTube, browsing through his recent selections of unremarkable music, settling for excerpts from a comedy show, the amalgamation of *Countdown* and *Eight Out Of Ten Cats*, laughing immediately as the presenter with the tiny eyes roasted one of the panellists.

Hunger announcing an unwelcome presence, compromised by her oral pain, she sipped the now cool coffee, the liquid less abrasive within her damaged mouth, the caffeine likely to dispel the desire for food. She wiped the wallet with a damp cloth, a precaution against previous contact, tossing the item to the sofa, with the contents holding no further interest for her. Walking to the washing machine, she engaged the tumble dryer function again, programming a thirty-minute period to partially dry his bedding, making it easier to cut, simpler to burn.

She placed the cable tie in her handbag, adding the stretched and damaged string, ensuring she would not leave them behind. The money envelope necessitated some adjustment of the bag contents, eventually locating in the central pocket, other items redistributed around the leather bag's interior. She put his debit cards alongside her own. Glancing around her environment, she located his car key, the four circles logo confirming the identity, the device resembling a miniature remote control. Adding the key to her bulging bag, she accepted that she could carry little else.

Finding a heavy-duty plastic bag below the sinks, the dark colour providing a level of protection against intrigued onlookers, she loaded the laptop along with the power adaptor and cable, as well as the remnants of his mobile phone. The phone battery already removed and placed in her handbag.

Glancing at the tv, she admired the numbers girl, her blonde hair and legs from another dimension, her apparent personality enriched with presumably scripted spontaneity. Glancing at the roaring fire, knowing she would require further fuel, Amy made another trip to the garage, returning with four logs. Her garage activity completed, she had locked that door, also locking the house rear door, for now.

Dropping a wet cloth on the floor, she walked along the hallway, using her left foot to steer the cloth across the blood stains, smearing the mess more than she removed, the benefit being to disguise her small footprints, eliminating an obvious clue to her gender. Entering the bathroom, she pushed his head under the water, holding it in position as she used her gloved hands to manually scrub his hair, scalp, ears and nose. Returning to his mouth again, inserting a finger, wiping his gums, teeth, cheeks, tongue, whispering "Ten" as she performed her tasks.

Tired of cleaning, she tossed her coffee cup into the toilet, added a squirt from a new bottle of toilet duck, flushed then flushed again. Removing the cup, she wiped the rim, the action precautionary as her lips were already devoid of lipstick. She dipped it into the bath and wiped again, before taking it to the kitchen and loading it into the dishwasher. Loading any other loose items from the kitchen, remembering the cup in the bedroom, collecting it, dipping it in the bath as she passed, wiping the rim with her gloves, adding it to the dishwasher. After some consideration, she decided to wash the bunch of keys from the rear door in the kitchen sink. Adding a fresh two-tone tablet, initiating the cycle, she restarted the appliance.

Her thoughts turned to home with her work here almost complete. Anticipating the opportunity to take a bath, to cleanse herself from what the dirty bastard had done to her. Feeling her anger return, detecting a hint of emotional distress, she yearned for the chance to climb into bed and rest her weary body, beginning the process of repairing her physical and mental wounds. Understanding her facial damage would require a considerable period of renaissance, she permitted herself a transient consideration of Rob, quickly dismissed for another time.

The comedy clip had ended, the television awaiting further instruction. She selected the adjacent panel, paying little attention, the background chatter providing comfort and a sense of normality.

Adding a fresh batch of kindling to the fire, followed by two larger logs, she fuelled the furnace to capacity. She emptied the remainder of the kindling to the carpet, putting the bag into the fire, the bag she had handled. Repeating the process, dispensing firelighter cubes to the carpet, dropping the cardboard box behind the grate, watching it instantly ignite, curl and burn. The fire fascinated her, a spectrum of colours dominated by yellows and blues, flames altering their shape as air circulated. Moving pieces of wood emanating bursts of heat, embers floating, inconsistent crackling sounds, smoke finding the route to freedom via the chimney.

She contemplated taking the coffee maker with her, valuing the machine at a minimum of five hundred pounds. Desire losing the competition with practicality, accepting the risk as unnecessary, instead cleaning the device, applying extra pressure to the areas she had touched, further cleansing applied by water from a recently boiled kettle. Potentially damaging the device, consoling her, removing residual temptation. She placed the keys from the rear door in the boiling water for a final rinse.

Removing the laundry from the machine, laughing at the residual stain from his bowel evacuation, irrationally amused, internally delighted that she retained her ability to laugh. The blood had faded, imperfectly. Taking the scissors, again cutting the fabric into small pieces, loading every six pieces into the fire, sequentially destroying the primary source of contamination. The process slow, darkening her mood, further affected by the increased joint pain in her fingers, the gloves impeding efficiency.

Placing the scissors on the table, groaning loudly as she massaged her aching digits. "Ow. Fucking Simon!" Walking to the kitchen counter, she selected the largest knife from the wooden block, strolling determinedly to the bathroom, before plunging the big blade into his chest. "This is all your fault, you dirty fucker! All of this! Everything hurts, because of you!" Removing the knife, requiring both hands as the body attempted to follow the blade, the new wound significantly larger than those around it. "Ten!" She left the blade in the bath, pushing it below his body.

Reflecting on her work, the bedding entirely engulfed in flame, the complete house vacuumed, the fireplace tools running in the dishwasher, she acknowledged her readiness to leave the premises. A discovered bag containing ten mobile phones with accessories attracted her attention. She selected an out-of-fashion model iPhone, placing the device and its accessories in her plastic bag adjacent to the laptop, replacing the balance beneath the sink behind cleaning products. Donning the large coat which offered a level of obscurity to her features, she gathered her belongings before exiting the house via the rear door. Feeling no impulse to engage the lock, she tossed the keys into a nearby bush.

Looking around the corner of the house, her visibility reduced by light drizzle, she approached his car from the rear, the yellow gloves contrasting with the balance of her attire. Lifting the driver door handle, hearing the click as the car unlocked, the door releasing under her touch, the presence of the key in her handbag allowing the mechanism to operate. Climbing in, she placed her handbag on the passenger seat, the bag with the laptop resting on the floor. Putting her foot on the brake pedal, she pushed the button, the engine starting first time, as expected from a prestige marque. The vents issued cold air, her acquired clothing protecting her, maintaining her warmth. Adjusting the mirrors, engaging her seatbelt, sliding her seat closer to the windscreen, adjusting the mirrors again, she slowly reversed from the driveway into the quiet street, seeing nobody. Engaging D in the automatic gearbox, she moved away from the house, leaving Simon to his own company.

Adjusting the heat and vent directions, winning her battle against condensation on the windscreen, she appreciated the understated power of the Audi as she drove to one of the Park and Ride car parks. Concentrating on driving sensibly to avoid unnecessary attention, she kept her speed close to but below the limits, the hood of her coat raised to obstruct casual looks from other drivers.

Coming into the parking area, she selected a space in the furthest corner, away from other vehicles and some distance from the buses, achieving a degree of privacy. Reaching into the bag holding the laptop, she removed a wet cloth and sponge to clean the passenger side of the car, assuming Simon had placed her there in her impaired condition. Guessing she would have touched some parts of the vehicle; she scrubbed the entire area with the wet cloth. Following the action with the sponge, covering the same area, being thorough.

Confirming the departure of the bus which had been waiting as she arrived, she concluded her cleaning activities, switching off the engine. Leaving the vehicle, walking around to the passenger's door, she cleaned the external handle, before extricating her bags, placing the key beside the gear stick and closing the door. Removing the gloves, she placed them in the plastic bag above the cloth and sponge, her task complete.

Taking her time, she took a stroll around the edge of the parking area, grateful for the rain making her raised hood appropriate, with her handbag on her shoulder, the plastic bag in her left hand. The unlocked Audi parked in isolation, the position welcoming investigation from joyriders, drunks and drug users. Purchasing her ticket, showing it to the driver, she boarded the bus, selecting the foremost seat, offering other passengers a view of the rear of her head, preparing for the journey to Chester city centre.

Sneaking a peek inside her plastic bag, Amy checked to ensure his recovered condom was inside, the empty prophylactic possibly containing traces of her DNA, requiring destruction at her home in controlled conditions.

Forty-Three
Saturday, 16th February

With his wings well and truly clipped, he sat in an anonymous office, characterless bare walls surrounding functional office furniture, his chair facing another occupied by a bouncer from one of the massage facilities. His presence had been demanded on this Saturday morning with the reason unexplained.

Boris contemplated his situation.

Having paraded his promotion from translator to the inner circle, telling anybody and everybody, he had been publicly humiliated, his demotion spreading throughout the network at all levels. Threatened with a gun yesterday, causing him to wet himself in fear for his life, a substantial debt inflicted on him against a tiny amount of crystal meth, he had been denied fish and chips, then disrespected by the goons backing up The Mancunian.

Seeking to take consolation at a facility, he had been rudely informed that his freebies were over, now required to pay the going rate for massages and extras. Further humiliation.

The bouncer sat across from him, his collar size likely exceeding his IQ, now pointedly ignoring him, having explained that future entertainment of the ladies would require the submission of receipts for approval before reimbursement.

Now he had been delegated with the task of calling the Vodafone geek to organise delivery of the outstanding mobile phones. Given a name and number, he made repeated calls, the presumably specky twat having neglected to answer eight times already. Informing the boss of the non-response, he was told to use his initiative and make a personal visit to collect the phones. Having no idea where Specky lived, he had asked for the address, his request dismissed, further intensifying his resentment. He had a name, a phone number and the knowledge that the supplier worked at Vodafone.

Reaching a decision, a commitment to positive action, he asked the bouncer to arrange a vehicle and a minder, intending to attend the Chester store and intimidate the geek, then extract the merchandise. His profile in the organisation exemplified, the bouncer ignored his request, forcing him to arrange his own transport and support.

He faced a crossroads. Work hard and earn new respect. Keep a low profile and wait for memories to fade. Get out of this business and set up somewhere new. Three options being more of a T-junction than a crossroads.

Locating physically imposing support, commandeering a vehicle, he drove into Chester, defiantly parking on a single yellow. Followed by his aide, he burst into the Vodafone store, signalling his need for attention. Adopting a pose which he imagined to be intimidating, demanding. "I need to speak to Simon."

The employee, a Saturday temp, replied, "He's not in today. Can I help?"

"That's not what I asked." Demonstrating his impatience, confusing the kid. "Give me his home address."

"I can't give out that information. I can give you his mobile number." Eager to please, determined not to break rules, his eight hours at minimum wage too valuable to compromise.

Boris closed the space between them, quietly explaining the situation. "I need the address. Give it to me or my assistant here will beat you to a pulp. Understand?"

Suitably intimidated, the kid wrote an address in Buckley on a pamphlet indicating the variety of monthly plans currently available. "There you go, sir. Please consider these plans."

As they left the store, the kid explained what had happened to a senior colleague, admitting handing over the address, repeating the stated threat. His colleague stepped to the door, watching the men get into a red Kia, noting the registration. Calling Simon's mobile, he heard the message advising the phone was turned off or out of coverage. Next, he called the police, handing his phone to the kid, saying, "Tell the police what happened, then give it back to me. Don't hang up."

As the Vodafone staff spoke to Cheshire police, the process lengthy and complex, Boris and his heavy drove towards Buckley, the quiet aide providing directions to an area familiar to him.

"He said he would beat me senseless, so I gave him the address." The police telephone service woman offered a minimal grunted response. "They may be heading to his address right now." He provided the vehicle plate number. Waiting. The police operator assuring him she would take some action, before terminating the call and following her instincts, forwarding the information to North Wales Police.

Mold station dispatch issued a notification to the mobile units, describing the vehicle and providing the registration, the circumstances of the interaction at Vodafone in Chester and the likely destination address in Buckley. Asking if someone could drive to the address to assess the situation. Three minutes later, she updated the information, advising that a neighbour close to the address had reported two suspicious-looking men seeking access to the house. The priority increased. A car confirming it was only four minutes from the location, intending to attend the scene.

Parking on the street, having extracted his colleague's name, Boris asked Ron to wait out of sight in the driveway while he rang the doorbell. Despite multiple rings, no answer was forthcoming. Continuing to ring while calling the mobile number, he instructed Ron to check for activity at the rear of the house, unaware of the watching neighbour. Ron disappeared, reappearing a minute later as he opened the front door from inside. Boris joined him, closing the door behind them.

"Simon? Hello?" Calling out without expecting a response, they walked into the seemingly empty bungalow. "Nice house. No wonder mobile phones are so fucking expensive." Accessing the living room, finding a real fire roaring, the heat intense as Boris asked. "Did you break in, Ron?"

Ron shook his head. "Back door was unlocked."

Lifting a wallet, checking the contents, seeing the driver's licence belonging to Simon. "Check the bedrooms. I'll look around here." Carelessly opening cupboards and drawers, seeking the handsets.

"Boris." Ron returned to the living area. "You should come and see this." Leading him to the bathroom, indicating the unmoving body in the bath.

"Oh, fuck. Shit. What the fuck. Is he dead?"

Ron pushed the head below the water, meeting no resistance, no struggle, seeing no bubbles rise to the surface of the water. "Yep. He's dead." Emotionless, practical. "We should get out of here."

"Find the phones; we have to find the phones. Then we can go." Leaving Ron to search the bedrooms, Boris returned to the living room, finding himself confronted by two uniformed policemen, one bearing the stripes of a sergeant. Ignoring an instinct to bluff, he ran for the front door, unable to open it before the younger cop grabbed him, restraining him, handcuffing him. "Apprehended in the act of a burglary. You're nicked."

Hearing the commotion, Ron walked calmly into the kitchen, standing passively before the officers, aware of the drill, his extensive record and experience directing his responses. He offered a suggestion that the officers might like to look in the main bathroom. The sergeant did so, turning white, calling for back-up, requesting CID, explaining the presence of a deceased IC1 male at the address, two suspects in handcuffs, preparing to secure the scene.

Boris stood against a wall, wondering if this week could get any worse. The boss would go apeshit if he didn't deliver the phones. The possible consequences of being found at the scene of a killing had yet to register. Ushered out of the house into the rear seat of the Heddlu vehicle, locks enabled, the constable standing beside the car, taking photos of them through the window. A crowd gathering, their intrigue evident, the sleepy town excited to be a place of interest. A mature lady waddled across to the constable, informing him that she had made the call about suspicious behaviour. Asked to wait, informed that a statement would be required from her, she became increasingly agitated, her moment in the spotlight approaching, eager to impress the tv viewers when they saw her on the news.

With the processes initiated, DS Beecham received an instruction to attend the unfolding situation in Buckley. He reluctantly declined the opportunity, explaining that he was interviewing a suspect on a different case. Checking the roster above the photocopier, he advised Dispatch that DS Holmes was the CID standby officer this weekend, suggesting they make a call to his mobile.

Relieved to receive the call, Terry welcomed the excuse to leave his home and escape from his mental girlfriend, her mood having disintegrated earlier. DS Holmes asked for the usual text message detailing the address and other pertinent information. Changing his clothing to something suitable, he made his excuses, leaving Holly to her anger, driving quickly towards the scene in Buckley.

Forty-Four
Saturday, 16th February

Alighting from the bus at the station, slipping Simon's mobile phone battery into a litter bin, she purchased water from a kiosk, washing down two further painkillers to compete against her escalating facial discomfort. Continuing to wear the hood of the jacket, keeping the direction of her gaze downwards to minimise her risk of identification via the cameras, she walked to the platform from where the Rossett bus would depart.

A sense of déjà vu enveloped her. Required to take two buses home on a Saturday, covering her tracks after inflicting fatal injuries on an unpleasant male, wearing the same clothes as the previous evening, the symbolic walk of shame. Her mobile remained off to avoid tracking by the towers, should she find herself under suspicion once more. Ruminating on the unfortunate sequence of events leading to her pain-ridden face, she was unable to reset her count. "Ten." A mumble.

Taking her seat on the almost-empty bus, she found her attention diverted to the teenage boy sitting across from her, understanding that he was scoping her. Her skirt had ridden higher, exposing plenty of leg. Judging by his concerted attempt at subtle examination, she suspected she might be revealing more than leg, his more typical teenage desire to look at her chest prevented by the bulky jacket. Content that he was uninterested in her face, she resisted her reflexive urge to pull her skirt lower, permitting him his immature pleasure.

Faced with a short walk from the bus stop, her spirits rose as she got closer to home, privacy, warmth, sustenance, comfort. Anticipating a warm bath full of bubbles, allowing her battered body the opportunity to relax and commence the healing process. Needing her pyjamas and slippers, a warm drink and mindless entertainment. Opening her door, hefting the plastic bag into her vestibule, closing and locking the door, she allowed her repressed emotions the latitude they sought. Powerful shivers engulfing her frame, tears freely flowing, her restrained anguish finding release, hugging her torso, pointedly avoiding the hallway mirror. She abandoned the shoulder bag, walking into the living area as she stripped the heavy jacket from her body, exaggerated swallowing failing to dislodge the uncomfortable lump in her throat.

Two bottles of red wine caught her attention; conveniently stored at room temperature, they were less likely to impact her pained mouth while providing alcoholic comfort, numbing her emotions until she established her psychological resilience. Twisting the screw top from the Cabernet Sauvignon, Amy poured a half glass into a clean juice tumbler from the dish-drying rack. Sipping tentatively to a tolerable level of pain, sipping again, her recovery process took a first tentative step.

Drawing a bath, she added Ylang-Ylang oil to the running water, adapting the texture of the warm liquid, making it silkier and flesh-friendly while permeating a beautiful odour in the room. Using the toilet, she placed her flush on hold, kicking her underwear free from her feet prior to padding through to the hall. Retrieving his condom from the bag, intuitively squeezing air from the rubbery product she dropped it into the bowl, flushing, successfully disposing of the prophylactic.

Making soft pale toast with lashings of butter, easy on her mouth, she brought it to the bathroom with her glass of red. Adjusting the water temperature, she enabled her mobile, resting it on the basin surround as it performed its multitude of initiation actions.

She discarded her clothes to the floor, risking a glance at her body, finding more bruises randomly emerging, wincing as she placed her fingers on them. "Fucking Simon! Ten! Bastard ten!" Aloud, her anger amplified.

The water temperature now ideal, she climbed into the tub, the oil infusion providing an immediate sensory experience as she encased her weary body in the comforting liquid. The light bubbles already dissipating as she closed her eyes, succumbing to the relaxing environment.

Immobile.

Therapeutic.

The aroma indulgent, her battered nose retaining some sensory ability. The wine symbiotic, her damaged mouth retaining some ability to taste. The oil seductive, her skin responding to the texture, her sense of touch restored. Taking the facecloth from her forehead, she immersed it in the warm water, bunching the material as she applied it to her private place, pressing firmly, performing an internal cleanse, the act functional, devoid of sexuality. Her objective simply to remove every trace of the bastard and his invasion of her, the cleansing equally emotional and tangible. Intending to douche later, she permitted the warmth to further alleviate the agony from her injuries. Applying the damp fabric gently to her face, sensations of torment exploded across her mouth and T-zone. Initially, the agony was fierce, before modulating gradually, becoming bearable, ultimately beneficial.

Overcoming her desire to remain in the bath, aware of her commitments, she brought herself to a standing position, her skin glistening. Wrapping herself within the bath sheet, she dried her torso, then her legs, patting some areas, rubbing others, avoiding contact with her head. Biting gently into the cold limp toast, she used the remaining wine to wash it down. Holding the gargantuan towel around her body, she meandered to her bedroom, extracting cotton jammies from a drawer, neglecting underwear, donning socks, pulling her quilt through to the living area. Leaving the towel to languish on her bedroom floor.

Accessing her previously ignored phone, she read the list of missed calls: Brenda again, Holly, five from Rob. Accessing her messages, eight in total, seven from Rob, one a reminder of credit about to expire. Erasing the messages, reading none, responding to Holly's call her only intention. A news alert appeared on her home page. Curiously opening the link, she caught her breath as she read further about the police presence at a house in Buckley, reporting the suspicious death of a local man. Two suspects already arrested. A picture confirming the house she had recently evacuated. "What the fuck is going on?" she wondered aloud, reading again, confused, understanding her planned actions had suddenly increased in urgency.

Postponing her desire to nap on the sofa, she brought her handbag to the kitchen, repeating the exercise for the plastic bag.

Her first compulsion was to secure the money. Deploying the notes on the counter, she tore the envelope into small pieces, dumping the shredded segments in her swing bin. Distributing the cash around the apartment in bundles of five hundred, she placed it in containers, old socks, a suitcase and at the rear of her bedside drawers.

His debit cards would need to be destroyed. Attempting to use them would now present an element of risk far beyond the monetary benefit. Cutting them each into eight pieces, she kept the fragments in sight for future disposal.

Separating the components of the cable tie, she placed both pieces in the sink, planning to wash them thoroughly, removing traces of his skin from the nylon surface, before disposal with the debit cards. Tossing the string into her bin, the item common, impossible to trace.

The sponge and cloth she had used to clean the inside of the Audi were placed in the sink, joining the cable tie, the gloves joining the pool party. Ensuring the pockets were empty, she loaded the waterproof coat into her washing machine, setting her standard programme, adding powder, starting the seventy-minute cycle.

She tossed his mobile carcass into the sink. Engaging the plug, running hot water while adding an environmentally friendly cleaning liquid, she soaked the items, leaving them immersed. Taking the laptop to her room, she placed it below her bed, pushing it away from the edge of the frame to ensure accidental sighting would be unlikely. She added the power adaptor and cable to a drawer already housing cables and chargers of indeterminate origin. Heaving a monster sigh, she dried her hands, taking the final piece of toast, all her urgent actions now complete.

Exhaustion threatened to overcome her. Reclined on her settee with the quilt covering her, she nestled into the warmth, closing her eyes in anticipation of sleep, beautiful regenerative sleep. The distant rhythm of her ringtone disturbing her, the persistent sound eventually returning to silence. Her physical demand to rest compromised by irregular bouts of agony from her injuries, lightly dozing only, her recovery barely commenced.

Forty-Five
Saturday, 16th February

Wrexham's only female Detective Chief Inspector arrived at the Mold premises, disappointed to be disturbed on a Saturday, prepared to make somebody suffer if her time had been improperly interrupted. Searching for DS Beecham, she found him in a corner of the incident room, studying the case file, his concentration beyond intense. She coughed to attract his attention, watching as he looked up in surprise.

"Ma'am." Registering the presence of the DCI out of uniform, previously unseen, attempting to overcome his reaction.

"Right, Sergeant." Addressing him, her stance erect, her manner conciliatory. "It's the bloody weekend. How about we dispense with the Ma'am and Sergeant bollocks and use our names. A whole lot easier. I'll call you Grahame and you can call me Bethan. On Monday, we return to normal. Agreed?" Considering. "What do we call PC McGarry?"

"Sounds great, Bethan. McGarry is Felicia."

"That's a posh name for a constable. I would not have taken her for a Felicia."

"True, but I wouldn't have taken you for a Bethan, either."

"Watch it, or you'll be back to Doris before you know it. Now, why am I here?"

Beecham updated the DCI on the case and the relevance of Jenny Coleman. Responding to her questions, he embellished as required, presenting his justification for bringing in the Crown Prosecution Service.

Flick joined them, stunned when the DCI addressed her as Felicia, finding herself tongue-tied when invited to refer to the DCI as Bethan.

"Do you concur with Grahame on this?" Bethan asked Felicia.

"Yes. The only consistency with her story is the lies. She fits the bill. She cannot provide any reason for us not to proceed against her."

The DCI stood, walking around the room, reading the flipcharts, considering what she had heard, accepting the positive reasons for proceeding, countering internally with reasons not to. Details which remained vague. Sitting again, this time facing the two junior officers, ready to divulge her findings.

"You have done well. The case is considerably improved, the quality of police work is noticeably better. You have produced information that certainly points to Miss Coleman being a worthy suspect in the killing of Mr Campbell-Foulkes." The compliment complete, the pause uninterrupted, everyone aware that more was to follow. "But" — Grahame caught Bethan's expression — "it is not going to be enough for the CPS, I feel."

Anticipating a protest, raising her hand, making direct eye contact.

"I want you to pursue this. I believe she could be guilty, but we need to prove it beyond any reasonable doubt, and a little bit more just to be sure. The CPS will not risk an unsafe charge after the McGarvey fiasco. Imagine the fallout if we charged two wrong suspects in the same case? Not on my watch."

Grahame asked the obvious question. "What would you suggest? What would be enough to progress this to charge?"

"We don't have the murder weapon, which is often a deal-breaker. Get Coleman's knife, forensic the crap out of it. Is it the right size, are there stains, has she tried to clean it? Anything she owns which could be a possible weapon, get it, analyse it, log it, present it."

Ensuring her message had been received, she continued, "The Friday night in question, the hotel, the two versions of events. We need to try to pin her down. When she finished riding the good doctor — who was my General Practitioner, by the way, not in fucking future — what exactly were her movements? Scour the cameras at the hotel, internal, external, car park. Do a twenty-four-hour sweep, try to find her, anywhere, anytime within that window. If we can't, then we go outside, look at all possible routes from the Royal Oak to Boundary Lane, approach the Roads people for access to their cameras, search for her vehicle on any route. Search for the doctor's car as well; maybe she went with him, maybe that prick is covering for her. Go back through the council CCTV we have already, looking specifically for her."

Felicia making notes, Grahame nodding.

"Get in touch with the taxi firms, the rideshare firms, any pick-ups around 10 p.m. that night anywhere remotely close to that hotel, going in the Saltney direction, single woman pick-up, couple pick-up. I know it's a shit-load of work, but we have to prove she was or was likely to have been in the area."

Bethan continued, encouraged by the lack of protest, "Get Miss Coleman's clothing from that day: what she wore to work, what she wore at dinner, what she wore in bed, what she wore when she took breakfast, what she wore when she left. Every item of clothing: dresses, knickers, anything. Get it to forensics, try to get a match to anything they found in the apartment. If we can place her there on the Friday or Saturday, added to what you already have, we have a case to present to the CPS.

"The final alternative" — smiling, Bethan sought their buy-in — "is to beat a confession out of her. Obviously, I cannot condone a physical beating, but a psychological encouragement to confess would be easier for everyone."

Grahame, thinking aloud. "Get her phone, check her maps, see if she used any type of navigation aide indicating Saltney. Look at tracing her phone throughout the weekend."

"Public transport. Buses. Show her picture to the drivers who were working that night. She is pleasant looking, somebody might remember her, might even have footage." Felicia, joining in, enthusiasm returning, offering suggestions. "Get the witness back in. See if he will absolutely identify her. Wouldn't hurt."

Grahame fixed Bethan with a look worthy of a hungry Labrador mooching for a biscuit. "Can we have some extra resource? We have a lot of ground to cover."

"You can have one more plod. But I'll make it a decent one. And I will help with Roads and the hotel, streamline the camera access. You have done well, guys, but now you need to go the extra mile, see this through to a conclusion, prove it beyond all doubt. You can do it."

"Do we ignore the other suspects, Bethan?" The name sounding foreign in Felicia's mouth, the reply expected, the question requiring to be asked and answered.

"Keep an eye on the others with probable cause. Just in case. Focus on Coleman, watch the others." Glancing at the wall clock. "I suggest another interview with Miss Coleman, apply some pressure, ask for access to her home bypassing a warrant, locate the knife. Give her the usual bullshit about being seen to assist the police. Same with the clothes. Repeat your optimism that charges could be laid, get the lawyer nervous. But, unless she confesses, turn her loose this afternoon. Agreed?"

"I want to haul the doctor in again. Check his story, get him to describe what she wore throughout their tryst together, compare it to what she admits to wearing. We need to go back to the hotel, see if the staff remember. Cameras hopefully will confirm. Lots to do. Okay. Do you want to sit in on the next interview, Bethan?"

Declining politely, she elaborated, "I leave that to the experts. I am a policymaker and a political player, which means I have lost touch with real policing. I find it difficult to determine which is my arse and which is my elbow. Those are a few of the things you say about me. Correct? I need to visit the scene of a suspicious death in Buckley, be seen by the press, say a few words, go through the motions. Then, I've got a bottle of Hendricks, two litres of premium slimline tonic, a lemon and a bucket of ice waiting at home for me, privilege of rank and all that."

With that, she stood, gathering her coat, preparing to leave. "Thank you, Bethan." She was pleased to hear the respect in Grahame's tone. "Thought I'd say it once more before we return to calling you Ma'am." Containing her smile, she swept from the room, leaving two officers encouraged and upbeat.

Watching her go, Grahame commented, "That went better than I expected."

Felicia replying, "She's actually okay. That was quite fair. Not a bad bum for an older girl, either."

Bemused, unsure if he would be allowed to comment, playing safe, he invited Felicia to join him in the interview room, asking if she could locate someone to watch from the monitoring suite.

Forty-Six
Saturday, 16th February

The bungalow in Buckley was a cauldron of activity. A police cordon had been established, beyond which assorted vehicles were irregularly parked on the street, with media vans jostling for prime locations. The local population were huddled across the road, braving the dropping temperature as they speculated about the cause of the massive emergency services intrusion into their community. A freezing constable stood at the perimeter, clipboard in hand, high visibility Police/Heddlu vest raising his physical profile without offering additional warmth.

Within the house, the specialists from the relevant disciplines exchanged impressions, reacting to the situation, hardened by experience yet still affected by the scene portrayed before them. Everyone was covered in protective clothing designed to preserve the investigative environment, blurring their identity, concealing the hierarchy.

"I don't want to move anything until the DCI arrives. She's on her way."

Respecting Terry's wishes, understanding his motivation, Emyr circulated through the house, ensuring his technicians were applying themselves to the established tasks, cautious that the job should be meticulous ahead of his forthcoming announcement. Taking in everything he saw, assessing and evaluating, comparing and noting the state of the bedrooms, the cleanliness of the lounge tarnished by the untidy area around the fireplace. His impression made, he returned to the bathroom to join the DS.

"Are you seeing what I'm seeing?" The question, teasing, inviting a response without waiting for one. "This is very similar to the scene at the Saltney homicide." Paying emphasis to the "very".

Terry agreed. "Multiple stab wounds, some of them possibly posthumous. Could be."

"Could be? Have you checked the bedrooms? No bedclothes. Unusual objects in the dishwasher. Body stabbed to fuck, then scrubbed clean. It is almost like a re-enactment."

"There are a lot of differences, too. The bath for one. No blunt trauma to the head. I don't want to jump to conclusions." Saying the words, thinking the opposite, concerned about the similarities and the expanded implications, relieved to see the DCI arriving. They exchanged minimal greetings as he provided a summary of their findings to date, limiting his suspicions, allowing her to generate her own impression. Her departure to the bathroom was followed by an approach from the pathologist, his ponytail swinging behind his head as he rushed across the room. His face flushed, induced by activity, assisted by the heat from the log fireplace.

"You lot are keeping me busy. Jesus. When can I take the deceased back to the morgue?"

"Let the DCI have a look, then check with Emyr. Once he's finished, you can take it."

Flashbulbs exploding, pictorial evidence being collected, increasing activity agitated by the presence of the DCI, the co-ordinated efforts reflecting well on Terry's control of the scene. Gathering, the senior personnel brainstormed the situation.

The DCI. "What can I safely tell the media outside?"

The Pathologist. "A dead IC1 male, his cause of death suspicious. I have pronounced the death."

The Forensics Sergeant. "I would like to keep the issued statement as brief as possible, with minimal detail. There are a number of similarities to the unsolved Saltney case."

The DCI. "Are you suggesting a possible serial killer? Doris is close to charging someone for that one; I just came from his incident room."

The DS. "Who is he looking at? Jenny Coleman?"

The DCI. "Yes, Coleman. She was held in the cells overnight. Not quite ready for the CPS but progressing."

The Pathologist. "If she was held overnight, then we have a huge hole in the serial killer angle. The victim here has only been dead a few hours. If she was in custody?" The remainder of the question unstated, the implication clear.

The DS. "Go with the minimal information and avoid connecting the cases. Remind the media that the case is being investigated by a DCI, refute those criticisms relating to the Saltney case. Confirm the death has been announced by our senior pathologist."

The DCI. "Okay, carry on, lads. I'll feed some shit to the press and try to disperse them. Keep me informed. Yes?" In contrast to her words, she remained where she stood.

The Pathologist. "Can I have the body? Take it back to my benches?"

The Forensics Sergeant. "We need some time with it after it comes out of the bath. Come and watch if you like. I also need vessels to take the bath water with us — there might be evidence floating around."

The DS. "We need to put that fire out. There might be evidence burning away in there."

The Forensics Sergeant. "I'll arrange that, douse it gradually with a water spray. We can't blitz it; that could destroy as much evidence as it saves."

The DS. "I need to interrogate the idiots found here at the scene. Do we agree they didn't have anything to do with this?"

The DCI. "They could have been involved. Left the scene, then came back for whatever reason. They are stupid enough. I wouldn't disregard them yet."

The DS. "Could be a long day."

The discussion breaking up, Emyr returned to the bathroom, preparing to instruct his team in removing the body from the bath. Ponytail hovering, eager to acquire the corpse. Terry assimilating the volume of information and thinking presented to him, seeking clarity and consistency, reluctant to commit to a link between the cases. Intimidated by the severity of the wounds and the profile of the case, he took comfort from the responsibility ultimately lying with the DCI, aware of his exposure should another case remain unsolved.

Taking a breather from the oppressive internal atmosphere, stepping outside, he heard the DCI update the press. Waving for the first responding sergeant to come over, he asked, "Can you take the two suspects to Mold, toss them into the cells? I'll follow and start the Q&A. As you caught them, I would like you to join me in the questioning. Is that okay?" Receiving a positive confirmation, he went back inside, the contrasting temperatures creating an itch on his skin.

"Have we found a mobile phone?"

A technician held a bag aloft. "Found nine of the bastards. Do you want to look at them?"

"What about his car? Anything?"

"Probably in the garage, which is still closed." Trading expressions, understanding. "I'll take a look, shall I?" Turning towards the evidence co-ordinator. "Where are those keys you found earlier?"

Terry stepped beside Emyr and Dr Tay. "I'm going to question the suspects. Do you need me at this moment?" Realising his mistake, despite the reducing tension between himself and Emyr, anticipating the response.

"Did anyone say that we needed you at all?" Enjoying his moment. "Off you go. We'll call you when we find something."

Hearing an unusual sound coming from another room, followed by cursing and shouting, accompanied by muted laughter, DS Holmes delayed his departure. Moving towards the commotion, arriving in the doorway leading to the bathroom, he observed the deceased body now partly removed from the water, hanging over the bath, arms reaching the floor, semi-rigid midriff folded across the edge of the tub. Unable to phrase a question, his likely query anticipated by the white-clad technician. "He's a bit slippery, being wet and all. We, eh, dropped him as we tried to lift him out of the bath." Turning back to the challenge, the senior officer dismissed from his thoughts as he reacted to something newly identified under the water. "On the upside, I think we just found the murder weapon."

****

Arriving at the station to a nearly empty car park, he took a space close to the rear door, then joined the sergeant and constable in the canteen, ordering tea and cakes for everyone. Discussing the circumstances of their arrival at the address, what they found, heard, saw, he knew the timeline was to the suspect's benefit. Delegating the constable to the monitoring room, assigning the sergeant to join him in the interview room, agreeing with the suggestion to question the old guy first while allowing the younger one to fester in the cells.

Ron was a villain of the old school. He gave his name reluctantly, shrugged his shoulders a lot, denied everything and questioned the validity of his detention. When asked specifically if he was the killer or the accessory to murder, he broke into a smile.

"I never killed anyone, and Boris would shit himself if you asked him to kick a dog. That body had been dead for a while, long before we arrived at the house. You're stretching. You've got fuck all on us, so I would like to leave now."

He described himself as a passenger, providing an intimidatory presence while Boris did as he had been told, collecting overdue mobile phones from the supplier. His calm reaction to the presence of the police in the house supported his claims to innocence. Comparing the timeline, the dispatch records of incoming and outgoing calls, they knew Ron was unlikely to be involved in the death. Continuing to press him, seeking a slip, a revelation, achieving nothing. Exerting their authority, they had him escorted back to the cells to stew a little longer.

Bringing Boris to the interview room, Terry immediately saw an opportunity. Fidgeting and restless, Boris betrayed his discomfort, sweating and stammering as he confirmed his name and address. Asked why he had killed the deceased, straight up without preamble, he showed all the external traits of barely restrained panic. His words confirming Ron's description of events, coming to collect mobile phones, admitting to obtaining the address with menaces, having barely arrived before the police, finding the body in the bath.

"Examine the facts, Boris. There is a dead body in the house, you are in the house, with a known villain assisting you. You threatened a kid in the Chester shop. You made no attempt to contact the authorities, to advise nine, nine, nine that you had found a body. You look guilty, certainly guilty of something. My life is just easier if we charge you. The question is, do we charge you as the killer or the accessory? Ron says he would have to be the accessory, so are you the killer?"

"I didn't kill anyone. He was already dead. Come on."

Persisting with the line of questioning, sensing a frailty emerging from the suspect, Holmes pushed further, digging for anything worthy of extraction. Returning to the bag of mobile phones, Boris admitting he had been unable to locate them, increasingly nervous as Terry explained their find: nine phones, sim cards, credit vouchers and cables, suggesting they were burner phones intended for criminal activity.

Indicating his frustration, the DS ordered Boris be returned to the cells, the frustration exaggerated, overplayed, planting ideas in the interviewee's thought processes. Casually asking the uniformed sergeant about the going rate for murder these days in Wales, hearing twenty years, certain to be overheard as the door was opened from outside.

"What do you think?" he asked the uniformed sergeant.

"Not a chance he did this. But he is cracking already. If we keep pushing, he'll cough to something or sacrifice someone. We should release the old guy. He won't tell us anything. But holding this one, we can leverage that, apply pressure. I'm happy to stay and assist."

"Thanks. I can use the support. Take fifteen. I'll have a chat with DS Beecham, then we can start again."

****

Doris was preparing to authorise the release of Jenny Coleman as DS Holmes walked into the room. He paused, listening intently as Terry explained the circumstances in Buckley, the similarities between the crime scenes there and in Saltney. The inference that the cases could be linked potentially weakening his case against Coleman, since she had been in custody. Holmes careful to balance his description with definite differences between the crime scenes, retaining a perspective.

Beecham instantly questioning aloud the possible whereabouts of Amy Meadows, his enthusiasm for the case seemingly increasing rather than being dampened by the developments. In response to Terry's questions, he admitted a lack of knowledge of Boris and Ron, committing to asking the beat cops when he saw them. Exchanging ideas, informally working together, watched by Flick carrying the papers for the release of Coleman in her hand, still requiring a signature.

Forty-Seven
Sunday, 17th February

He woke early despite having no obligation to go to work nor any desire to exercise. Even his habitual Sunday morning sausage sandwich remained beyond his thoughts. Browsing through his inboxes and social media accounts, he found nothing to create any spark of inspiration, nothing from Amy. No posts, no messages, no calls. Bereft of ideas, he ambled into the shower.

Rejuvenated from a liberal application of frothing lemongrass-scented soap, he banished all thoughts of rejection. *Maybe there is something wrong?* A flood of optimism flowed through his persona, tempered with concern, inspiring him to action.

With darkness remaining dominant in the winter sky, he started his car, the six-cylinder petrol engine purring gently after an initial growl. Enveloped in the comfortable leather seat, he waited for the heater to introduce warm air into the cabin, the backlit instruments indicating plenty of fuel and an outside temperature of three degrees. Releasing the handbrake with his foot, he guided the Grand Cherokee into the street.

Passing a permanently open Tesco, he was inspired to enter the store, buying bread rolls, fresh milk and discounted Lindt chocolates, before resuming his journey to Rossett. Approaching the address, he glimpsed the welcome sight of her red Clio parked at the kerb, feeling a combination of relief and trepidation. Resisting a reflex to second guess his half-baked plan, he committed to follow through, wanting to see her, convincing himself he was worried about her, needing to know she was okay, hoping she would respond to his presence.

Parked nearby, he walked to her door carrying the provisions. Only a few minutes after seven, he was confident she would be home, should be home, praying that she did not have company. Pressing his finger to the bell, he heard chimes from within the building.

Hearing footsteps gently approaching the door, his hopes rose. "Who is it?" The voice low, weary, cautious.

Looking to avoid confrontation or instilling concern, he lowered his own voice. "Good morning, Amy. It's me." Adding what he hoped was obvious. "Rob."

His greeting hovered, unanswered, silence from beyond the door. "Amy? Are you there?" Listening intently, hearing no sound, encouraged that she had not walked away from the door. Still no reply. "Will you talk to me? Please?" Maintaining his lower volume, detecting a pleading tone within his voice. Waiting, his patience rewarded.

"Why are you here? Do we have anything to say to each other?" Unwelcoming words, but words. Progress.

He searched for suitable nouns and verbs to formulate into a sentence she might like to hear; his plan had not prepared for a successful engagement. "I've been thinking about you?" *Not bad*, he thought. "Are you okay?"

"I'm okay. But why are you here? Nothing has changed since we last spoke." Her level tone devoid of emotion, a statement.

Inspiration or desperation formed an idea in his mind, an inquiry requiring a response, her reaction holding a slight possibility. "Have you read any of the messages I have sent? Any at all?" Deciding he could not wait for her answer, continuing, "I pulled the story. It was never published. I cancelled the story because I understood that you had become more important to me than the story. I pulled it. For you. And me." Aware the timbre of his voice had attenuated as he spoke, hoping his words had been clear, he experienced a surge of optimism based on her single word.

"Really?"

"Yes, really. Please check if you want. I couldn't do it. To you." Allowing a pause, lifting his voice for emphasis. "To us."

"Why?" Continuing to reply in monosyllables, barely rewarding his effort.

Licking his lips, about to deliver his recollection, praying it sounded romantic and passionate rather than corny and childish. "When we parted, do you remember that the sun had just come out, brightening the street? You looked so upset. There were tears in your eyes. I hated seeing you cry, knowing I was the cause. And I heard a song in my mind, an old Stiltskin song so relevant to our situation, hearing the song as you walked away from me. The words still haunt me. *I can see your tears, in a lemon, yellow sun.* I knew I couldn't go ahead with the article. I had to pull it."

Hearing her move, her body settling against the door on the inside, so close yet still inaccessible. "I like that song." Hearing her, hearing a complete positive sentence, a short four-word sign of progress, astounded that she might know the song. Wanting to extend the connection.

"Me, too. It's a cool song." Another pause, every microsecond agony.

"You must have woken early this morning. It's still dark." Was he detecting a softening? "What would you have done if I had still been asleep?"

Without hesitation, he replied, "Waited for you to wake up." Saying the considerate words, certain of their truth. He had been willing to wait irrespective of the circumstances, determined to make contact, to remove her ability to ignore him.

"I am grateful that you didn't publish the story involving me. Really. That's a relief. So" — hesitant — "where does this leave us?" Explaining, "You hurt me." Expanding, "Things were going well, then we were over." Wondering, "Is there a risk of being hurt again?"

Waiting for her to continue, giving her voice precedence while forming his answers and his commitments. Hearing her knock on the door, two gentle knocks, repeated. Sitting, the step chilling his bottom, repeating her knock, two then two. Somehow right, reason unknown. "I want to promise that I won't hurt you ever again. I want to. But I can't make that promise; it would not be honest. But I can promise you that I will try. How's that?"

Faintly. "That's a good start."

"I have something for you. Chocolates. And bread and milk." Aiming to coerce an invitation from her, ambition increasing briefly before evaporating, frightened of pushing too quickly. "I could leave them here on the step, if you prefer." Standing once more, his backside chilled, dampened, becoming unpleasant.

Words from beyond the door, hesitant, unsure. "I want to ask you to come in. But I need you to make me a promise. Understand?" Unable to imagine what she might propose, he readily agreed, prepared to promise whatever she needed. "I look a mess." *No way*, he thought. "A druggie tried to steal my bag. I fought him off, but I have bruises and cuts. It looks awful. I need you to understand my situation and support my decision not to involve the police. I need you to avoid freaking out. Can you do that?"

His immediate reaction was concern. "I'm so sorry. Are you okay?"

"Can you do it?" Insistent, her invitation conditional.

Accepting. "I can do it." Hearing the keys operating tumblers, the latches turning, the door opening, with Amy remaining unsighted behind the wooden portal. He stepped into her home for the first time, holding the shopping purchases before him, instinctively respecting her desire to hide her appearance. Hearing the door close, he sensed her approach in the low light, feeling her lean into him with her face partly turned away, resting gently against his chest. Sighing as she felt his arms surround her, lightly embracing her, offering comfort, providing security. Standing together in the dimly lit vestibule, sharing a moment, their embryonic relationship rekindling.

"Thank you," she said.

"For what?" he said.

"This," she said.

"You're welcome," he said.

The hug persisted, neither inclined to end the intimacy. Lightly placing fingers in her hair, feeling her tense briefly, then relax. Saying her name gently, "Amy. Amelia." Considering both variants, appreciating the merits of each, ignorant of Jessica. She stepped away from him, leading the way into her living area, the ambient light remaining low, offering him a seat on her sofa. As he lowered himself into the fabric, she turned to reveal the full extent of her injuries, permitting him to see her at her worst, inviting his concern.

Her eyes waging a battle, hinting at a smile while blackened from injury, providing an alternative perspective hinting at Gothic tendencies unsuited for her. Her nose was swollen, the damage less pronounced than that above. Her lips were scratched, cuts already scabbing over, the healing process underway. Bruising on her forehead and one cheek, blue-black with hints of yellow. Assessing her injuries, he saw significant cosmetic damage with the potential for fractures, igniting sympathy for her, imagining her terror as she fought her attacker. Her hands revealing enlarged fingers and further bruising. Defensive wounds, he imagined. Unsure what to say, committed to the promise he made, finding the words naturally. "I am so glad to see you."

Excusing herself, she went to her bathroom, cautiously cleaning her teeth, finger-brushing her hair, applying deodorant to her body. Abandoning her intention to change into fresh pyjamas, fatigue encouraged her to return to the sofa. Refreshed to an extent, she found him in the kitchen preparing coffee, scrambling eggs, cutting rolls. "Sit," he instructed her. She sat, starting her tv, selecting the YouTube channel, allowing it to awaken and present her with the usual options. He brought coffee to her without asking how she took it, moderately milked with sugar, the temperature below boiling; not her usual way, but surprisingly pleasant. Warming her. Following with an open lightly buttered roll topped with scrambled eggs, the seasoning included within the mixture. Taking a seat beside her, his breakfast identical to hers.

She indicated the YouTube options, referring to the "Listen Again" choices, hovering the selector above Ray Wilson, the box indicating a selection of Stiltskin and Genesis songs. Clicking on it, turning to him. "See. I like Stiltskin, too. I know that song." The segment began with "Take It Slow", live in Germany somewhere. Eating together, suddenly easy in their company, their residual differences aside for the time being.

"You look tired, Amy. Do you want to go back to bed? Do you need medicine?"

She placed her plate on the table, half-eaten, moving into her kitchen to collect tablets — painkillers, he assumed — retracing her steps to the sofa, washing the pills down with her coffee. She sat watching the music videos, waiting for him to conclude his coffee and eggs. Once complete, she presented him with the remote control as she placed a cushion on his lap, leaning across to him, placing her injured head on the cushion. Finding his left hand, she guided it to her shoulder, dragging the quilt over her body. "Just half an hour." Settling against him, projecting an image of relaxing.

"Take as long as you want. I'm here." Enunciating his words, lightly stroking her shoulder and the top of her arm, brushing loose hair from her ear, careful to avoid contact with any areas of lesion.

Looking at her. Wondering how she could affect him this way. Happy to be with her, but seriously worried for her wellbeing, wondering if he could persuade her to present at Accident & Emergency. Aware of his re-emerging feelings towards her, rekindling visions of her in that amazing black dress, the memory pure, raw, stimulating, immediately discarded to avoid an untoward physical reaction. Even now, physically injured, she remained attractive, her vulnerability enhancing her. Very confused but relieved, he relaxed, providing her with an illusion of protection as she drifted towards sleep.

Elusive sleep. Hunting for slumber, images forming in her mind before dissolving, the gentle rubbing of her shoulder receding into the distance, a pleasant song fading away behind her, warm.

Forty-Eight
Sunday, 17th February

Watching footage supplied by the Roads divisions of the adjacent councils, his brain started turning to mush. Endless hours of nothingness interspersed with an occasional snippet of interest, dashed when compared to the reference list. He had played with Excel during the previous day, creating a form with headline boxes for identification, monitoring officer, date, case number and source of data, all headlined at the top of the page. Below, a simple set of columns, detailing the road number, camera number, direction of vehicle, date, time, registration plate and other information.

Starting early, Barry Chappell fastidiously recorded every vehicle seen on every camera. He had footage for the evening of the thirteenth and the morning of the fourteenth courtesy of Flint Council as his priority, further footage courtesy of Cheshire for the same period.

The process was laborious but essential. He listed every vehicle sighting from the first camera location on the form. From the second camera three miles away, he listed every sighting additionally comparing it to the already established list. His interest piqued as he compared the latest observation to the list, the registration plate appearing on both cameras but more than an hour apart, a long time for a three-mile journey. Deducing that the vehicle had probably stopped in one of the laybys, he marked the form with large asterisks, while delegating a constable to check the plate history and owner.

Invigorated by the success, Barry renewed his efforts, monitoring further footage from the road with increased attention.

****

The cell door banged as the duty officer roused the occupants, taking a quick look inside each door via the panel, noting number six had puked on the floor, unsurprising given his level of intoxication. Cold, poorly rested and stiff, Boris surveyed his spartan surroundings, concerned at being detained, but confident of imminent release. Wondering how Ron was feeling, hoping he had slept better.

His impression of detention confirmed, he embraced his probable inability to survive in the prison environment, reinforcing his intention to broker some form of deal with the police. Asking loudly if he could use the toilet, he was equally loudly advised to use the bucket.

****

One leg asleep, unable to move while harbouring no desire to, he enjoyed the uncomplicated intimacy of watching her sleep, his coffee remains long since cold. Fascinated by her diverse taste in music, as demonstrated in her YouTube history. Stiltskin, Disturbed, Biffy Clyro, Supertramp, Manic Street Preachers, Miss A, Nightwish, Avril Lavigne. Symphonic heavy metal to K Pop. Her musical taste a conversation topic to file for when they found themselves facing any future awkward silence.

****

He sensed Holly waking beside him. Cognisant of her increasing tendency for a morning quickie before breakfast, he felt himself growing in expectation of her hand or mouth instigating their passion. Disappointed as she sat upright against the pillows, pulling the quilt over her briefly exposed chest, turning to him, her five words chilling him.

"Where is this relationship going?" Thinking, seeking an escape, considering the early hour, the subject worthy of further considered discussion, accepting he was beyond feigning sleep.

"Pretty heavy for a Sunday morning, Holly. Where has this come from?" Excellent, buying time, precious thinking time. Hearing her voice, opinion predefined, the subject aired, adamant a discussion would occur.

"We've lived together for quite a while now. We sleep together, we both work, both earn decent money, yet we live in a rented house. We don't do a lot together. I want to know where we are going." Fixing him with her stare. "Don't give me your usual excuse about having a case and we can discuss this next week. I know you have a case, and you're not going to it until I have an indication of what you think of our relationship."

Terry accepted the situation, recognised the opportunity to raise some issues, the early hour ensuring he had time to dedicate to the discussion.

****

Appreciative of spending a night in her own bed, superior to a night in a police cell in every way, she permitted her mind to assess her circumstances, the darkness conducive to clear thinking. Recognising that she needed to find a structure to her life, review her career, form a normal relationship, and extricate herself from this ongoing investigation into the death of her former boyfriend Jeremy. Objectively understanding the concerns which the police had about her, she had to provide them with a reason to remove her from their list of suspects.

Her first instinct was to resign from her job at Broughton Health Centre. She had suffered embarrassment there and dreaded attending the facility after the weekend. Being taken away by two police officers was humiliating, compounded by the shame of being identified as El Masri's bit on the side. Her inner devil's advocate cautioned against immediate resignation, realising that some would interpret her action as an admission of guilt. *Fuck! Why is nothing ever straightforward?*

****

Bathed in sweat, uncaring in the empty gymnasium, he contemplated inflicting further punishment on his tiring physique. Checking the screen on the treadmill, six point zero kilometres in fifty-eight minutes, a breakthrough, under the hour for the first time, he felt encouraged to push himself a little more. Seating himself on an exercise bike, adjusting the seat to accommodate legs longer than the previous user, pushing buttons to locate a medium level of resistance, Doris began to pedal, banishing workplace thoughts.

****

Leaving her soon-to-be-promoted husband in bed, Charlotte Christopher prepared a hotel-level celebratory breakfast buffet, catering to the diverse tastes of her three children, not to mention Emyr, whose weekend calorie requirement remained impressive.

Fresh fruit for Suzy: banana, apple, blueberries, kiwi. An overlap with Alicia: banana and berries complemented with cereal, skimmed milk and boiled eggs to follow. Marty had demanded pancakes this week; he would add jam if he saw it on the table. Machine coffee, weak tea and fresh apple juice all prepared, ready for consumption. The grill warming, bacon ready to go, toast on the rack, more in the toaster, butter in a dish, marmalade behind the jam. Boiled eggs and toast for herself.

She had no objection to preparing the spread; it was cleaning afterwards without assistance that drove her mental. Perhaps Emyr would help this week, dismissing the ridiculous fantasy as she sipped warm coffee, allowing the caffeine hit to energise her.

****

Ian MacKenzie, aka The Mancunian, aka Mac the Knife, aka The Candy Man, had the company of an Asian girl from one of his outlets. Pretty thing, but thinner than he liked; he had been disappointed when she had removed her clothes, expecting more. Responding in his usual way, he satisfied his need before permitting her to remain with him through the night. A two-way privilege, giving her the chance to sleep in a nice room with central heating and quality bedding, the caveat being expected to perform again on demand.

The demand was now. Turning her to the position he liked, her slender thighs making entry from behind easier, slipping into her unprotected. The act purely physical, detached, devoid of tenderness, only meeting his need. Her contribution minimal, her role little more than a receptacle.

****

Rolling onto her back, she opened her eyes, seeing him watching her. She detected his conflicted emotions, his smile tempered with concern. Powerless to resist, she smiled back, offering encouragement through the abrasions and pain. Letting her eyes close again, murmuring, "Thank you."

Hearing his soft reply, "Any time," as she surrendered to her body's demand for further rest.

****

His response to Holly's early-morning demands for a serious conversation had been honesty. Voicing opinions, he had refrained from before, home truths, seeing her recoil from some comments, her surprise combining with anger, leading to her expressing her own reservations about him. In retrospect, the discussion had been worthwhile, releasing truth and suspicions in equal measure. Providing both with plenty to think about, to consider their relationship now and beyond, he expected Holly to take the opportunity of a quiet Sunday to think carefully. He accepted the possibility of his possessions being in the garden when he returned from work.

Interviewing Boris the Orange would prevent him from detailed reflection unless he could close it out quickly. Coming home early with some flowers might take the sting out of the situation. It sounded like a plan.

****

Gloved and suited before freshly scrubbed stainless steel facilities, microphone and camera strategically placed, Doctor Tay commenced the post-mortem examination of the recently deceased male. Enunciating carefully, aware of his accent, understanding he could be difficult to comprehend when he became excited. He had chosen to operate through the night, welcoming the opportunity to work on the fresh corpse, thereby increasing the chance of securing valuable insights to share with the investigating officers.

Astounded at the cleanliness of the body, he conceded an admiration for the killer's patience and knowledge. He harboured real concern for their mental state, demonstrated by the ferocity in some wounds and the quantity of incisions. He was professionally intrigued by the mutilated genitalia, seemingly bitten, as well as the acidic residue within the victim's mouth. "I would insinuate that the perpetrator of this murder has detailed knowledge, leading me to suspect their occupation being related to medicine or law enforcement. They have a deep psychosis, probably hidden, possibly identifiable under interrogation."

Completing the procedure, he thanked the student assistant, inviting her to take a rest and enjoy some refreshment, committing to share insights with her. He intended to elaborate on the facts presented to the recording devices, teaching her on the job.

****

On his way home, Doris answered the incoming phone call, using the hands-free device he had self-installed in the slowly corroding Mazda, the number displayed not within his stored contacts.

"Good morning. Beecham?" Inviting the caller to identify his or herself.

"Good morning, Detective Sergeant. It's Jenny Coleman."

His surprise evident as he responded, "What can I do for you, Miss Coleman?"

"I want you to know that I did not kill Jeremy Campbell-Foulkes, that I had nothing to do with his death. I am sick of being interviewed, accused, involved in your investigation."

Interrupting, Doris explained, "That cannot be helped. You are a person of interest, and we have an obligation to investigate every avenue. I'm sorry you are inconvenienced." His voice intimating the "sorry" was satirical.

"I get it. I've been thinking about this. Wondering what I can do." Preparing to continue, interrupted again by the police officer.

"You could try telling the truth."

Ignoring the barbed comment, she divulged the outcome of her introspective review. "Here is my proposal. Forget warrants. North

Wales Police can have full unfettered access to my life. My home, my car, my place of work, my possessions, my clothes, my diary, my computer, my phone, my email accounts, my social media. Come over, take anything you want. With my blessing. Investigate me. Do whatever you need to do. Because, when you are finished, you and only you will prove my innocence. Come right now if you want."

****

Asking for an opportunity to speak to his colleague, he created a fuss when the access was denied. Shouting, banging his cup against the door of his cell, he demanded to speak to a senior officer. Other remanded guests expressed their displeasure at his performance, the duty officer eventually explaining that his colleague had been released during the previous evening.

Reflecting on his situation, he became increasingly worried. He pictured Ron explaining their arrest to The Mancunian. He imagined the boss being concerned at Boris being detained while Ron was released, wondering if he was revealing any of his privileged information. Their failure to secure the phones would not help. Recalling the gun being placed against his head at the warehouse, he reached a decision.

Asking the duty officer, politely, if he could have a word with the detective as soon as he arrived at the station, intimating that he had information which might prove valuable to the police.

****

Barry received the update on a scrap of paper delivered to his desk while he was relieving himself, detailing the status of the suspicious vehicle identified from the CCTV. The number plate belonged to a company, Man Chester Therapy Ltd, the plate inconsistent with the vehicle model. A post office box address had been provided for the company. Further details furnished included outlets for the company which were primarily massage parlours, as well as a warehouse and three offices, all of their addresses listed.

Linking everything. The Thai lady, The Mancunian, Dai Harris. The subterfuge of potentially swapped plates. Enough for him to approach the DI to escalate the case and apply for warrants. He requested the vehicle registration be placed under monitoring, but not to be detained, all sightings to be reported to NWP for his attention.

Forty-Nine
Sunday, 17th February

DS Holmes cast his mind back to his interview for this position at North Wales Police. DI Catt had explained that a detective has two ears and one mouth, and he or she should use them in that proportion. Listening to Boris unload a mountain of criminal insights, he employed that wise advice, providing an appreciative audience for the entertainment unfolding before him.

Boris wanted police protection. Boris would exchange inside information about an expansive criminal empire in exchange for that protection. Boris would provide initial snippets as a gesture of goodwill, those snippets alluding to murder and narcotics.

As the scenario developed, Holmes realised this was big, too big to handle alone. He paused the interview, calling the DCI at home. Initially harangued for disturbing her privacy, her attitude evolved towards complimentary as the extent of the opportunity became apparent. Gladly surrendering control to her rank as she delegated a list of actions for him to complete while she travelled to the station.

Confirming a level of commonality in their cases, Holmes overcame a strained but polite exchange with DS Chappell, relaying the DCI's instruction for Barry and his DI to "move their arses" to Mold, along with two traffic units.

A refreshingly co-operative Emyr expressed a desire to assist, committing a forensics team to attend within an hour. He confirmed that useful DNA could be obtained from a burning skip under appropriate circumstances.

The DCI was arranging the ARU, the likely presence of a firearm at the premises justifying the armed response unit being in attendance. Terry had never been involved with the ARU since his rank was insufficient to instigate their involvement. His escalating excitement was restrained by apprehension about the complexity of co-ordinating the disparate elements in the operation.

****

With the assorted specialties gathered, the DCI presented an overview of their operation. The location was a recently acquired industrial unit within Zone One on the Welsh Road, barely within their jurisdiction. The primary purpose was to secure a skip on the premises believed to contain the remains of Joseph Nesbitt, known associate of the recently deceased Dai Harris, with the possibility of linking both deaths to a local crime lord. When questioned, she confirmed Ian MacKenzie as their ultimate target.

The ARU stated their position: assuming there were four suspects at the location, with one suspected to be armed, they would consider two for safety. The traffic units would set up a roadblock at the exit road from the industrial area with cones, one vehicle and a full-width stinger ready to be deployed. Their additional responsibility would be to divert all traffic away from the area. The SOCOs would follow the armed team, remaining hidden until the area was secured, then focusing on the skip, protecting the evidence within the metallic container. The DCI would act as operational officer on-site, maintaining an element of control over the ARU, with the DI acting as her deputy to provide redundancy in leadership per the risk assessment procedure. Both attending detective sergeants would utilise their knowledge of separate cases to ensure the warrants were utilised to maximum effect. Five armed officers were to access the site, one to remain at the roadblock. The second traffic vehicle to position itself around the corner with the engine running, ready to ram any vehicle attempting to escape the area.

Seventy-two minutes after Boris's revelation, they were ready to go.

****

The Mancunian had arrived at his renovated warehouse, enjoying the refreshed decoration and the enhanced legitimacy of the operation.

Refreshed by his overnight exertions, he was feeling happy with his world.

The two lads on night duty had permitted the fire in the skip to burn out. A casual inspection had revealed the contents reduced to below half of the vessel's capacity, any remains likely obliterated by two days of scorching. He decided to tolerate their carelessness, remembering their support in the previous days with Nesbo and Dai, then later with Boris.

The vacant site adjoining this warehouse provided extra insurance against curious ramblers or similar inquisitive people. The high degree of privacy a selling point when the dodgy estate agent had suggested the location. The lack of weekend activity offering a further degree of seclusion.

Ian took his gun from the drawer, transferring it to the pannier of his motorcycle, the weapon nestled beside a kilo of Ice reserved for a special client expectant of a strategic business development personal delivery. Locking the pannier, he removed the key, placing it in his trouser pocket. His discarded leathers lay across the desk, cooling, airing. The ignition key nestled in his other pocket.

Seated once more at his desk, he dispersed legitimate documents across the surface, while stacking incriminating papers with the intention of transporting them to his regular office. Concentrating, vaguely aware of raised voices from outside, he dismissed the interruption, expecting his lads would take care of whatever it was. Louder sounds, possibly a truck, further loud discussions now distracting him, annoying him. Preparing to venture outside, he reached the door, his body framed in the rectangular opening, an armed man in black instructing him to "Freeze".

Reflexively raising both hands, he complied with the instruction. Visually analysing his situation, he noted the position of the black van within the property perimeter and the presence of several obviously armed personnel securing the site, having already disabled his lads, who were on the ground with their hands secured. His attention diverting to words directed at him. "How many people are on these premises?"

Finding his voice, maintaining calm. "Three. You can see all of us. What's happening?" Jostled to one side as two armed officers entered the office, their co-ordinated movements a well-rehearsed dance of aggression.

Shouts of "Clear" came from behind him.

He turned his attention to the woman approaching him with a folded paper in her hand, introducing herself. Detective Chief Inspector Something, her name inconsequential, advising him that they were in possession of a search warrant for the entire premises, demanding his co-operation. Extending his left hand, inviting the document, accepting it, unfolding it, he began to read as further police entered the building.

"Excuse me. Get out of my office." The DCI stared at him, surprised by his outburst. "Get out of my fucking office! You are in breach of your own search warrant. My lawyer will have a field day with this."

Repeating herself, the DCI countered, "We have a warrant to search these premises, including land and any buildings within the designated limits of the title."

"And I," pushing the document towards her, "have the right to read this warrant in full prior to access by any officer. You are therefore entering the premises illegally. I demand that you remove your team from the building until such time as I have read and fully understood the content of the warrant." Facing her, confident in his position, standing his ground. Passively stating the facts, defying her to challenge his position.

Mobile phone in hand, he pressed a few buttons, raising the device to his ear. "Hey, it's me. Send the solicitor across to the Deeside warehouse on top priority. The police are here carrying out an illegal raid. They have a warrant, but they are not abiding by the conditions stated. Tell him to come prepared. Thanks."

"Mr MacKenzie, you can read the document now." Barry Chappell introducing himself to the conversation.

Skimming the document, able to read it, he put on a show, simulating difficulty. "Says here that employees on the premises are not to be restrained unless they present an obvious danger to the implementation of the warrant. I suggest that you release my colleagues, as you have already invaded their civil liberty. They have been physically manhandled by armed officers when they are clearly not armed. Tut-tut, Mister Plod." Quickly raising his phone, snapping photos of his lads, the officers before him, the armed unit. "Maybe you should just fuck off before you commit any further breaches."

"Your colleagues posed an intimidatory threat, so they were restrained."

"Two unarmed men against a dozen officers, several of whom are armed. That's hardly a threat. I'm sure a jury will be amused by your claims."

The police held their positions, unsure, unable to hear the conversation, experience suggesting the raid was not proceeding to plan. The white-suited forensic team remained beyond the gate, seeing the skip but unable to approach it, the signal to proceed unforthcoming.

"We have reason to believe that a person or persons in this facility may be armed."

"In that case, I consent to undergoing a frisk search, as do my colleagues. And when you determine that we are unarmed, you can release my colleagues immediately. Does that sound fair?" Adjusting his arms, extending them horizontally from the shoulder, the warrant remaining in his grip, he invited the search. "I do not consent to being restrained unless you locate a weapon on my person." A member of the ARU intimating that the frisk should be performed by the DS, under observation by the strategically positioned armed officer.

Chappell performed the search vigorously, ensuring the entire body was covered, failing to find anything except a wallet and some keys. "Clean." Returning the keys and wallet.

The lads were brought to their feet and their hands released, both making a show of exaggerating the discomfort they had endured. They consented to the frisk searches, both confirmed as unarmed, then ushered to the fence, unrestrained but closely watched.

"Read the warrant, Mr MacKenzie!" Her tone had intensified, unhappy at her authority being questioned. "You've got five minutes."

"I think I need my glasses. This print is extremely small. I don't want to fall victim to the small print now, do I?" Enhancing his claim, squinting at the paper, bringing the warrant closer to his face, retracting it to arm's length.

Having established the absence of weapons, the ARU team had noticeably relaxed. Their weapons still deployed, held loosely, barrels aimed towards the ground. Their role largely complete as the CID assumed control of the situation. Circumstances dictating any discharge of weapons would be inappropriate and excessive.

The Mancunian stepped away, offering his explanation. "My glasses are in the box on my bike, I'll need them to read this." Making his way towards the parked motorcycle, the DCI walking alongside him, others watching, some surveying the premises, the situation defusing. Swinging a key in his hand, seemingly casual, he arrived at his bike, turning to place both hands on the DCI, pushing her hard, the force upsetting her balance, causing her to stumble with her palms outstretched to break her fall. Mounting his bike, key in, kick start, already moving as she fell. Disbelieving officers processing the unexpected situation, their response inhibited, movements already late as the powerful bike roared towards the gate, the compromised armed team unable to fire, forced to watch as their primary target fled from the premises.

Holmes shouted into his handset. "Target escaping on a motorcycle, coming to the roadblock. Make sure that stinger is deployed!"

Reacting, the traffic officers at the roadblock deployed the spiked device, covering the entire width of the narrow road, the armed support officer assuming a ready position, unaware that the suspect had been confirmed as unarmed. Hearing the bike before they saw it, bracing, waiting. Observing the rider, clothed normally without a crash helmet, accelerating rapidly, the deafening noise challenging their concentration.

He saw the police roadblock supported by another apparently armed cop, swinging his bike to make a quick directional change, hitting the unseen stinger as he did so, the motorcycle attempting to jack-knife as both tyres blew, only microseconds apart. Bouncing, an irregular motion in three dimensions, the tyres failing to grip on landing, the grit at the edge of the road offering zero purchase, tipping, careering towards the wire-mesh fence.

Maintaining momentum, the rider impacted with the concrete flower display at the corner of the site, separating from his vehicle, tumbling erratically into the fence, his limbs reflexively flailing. The metallic mesh fence bringing the bike and rider to rest, entangled, still.

The armed officer remained ramrod still, his weapon directed at the accident, poised, speaking into his microphone. "Target down. Repeat, target down. I retain line of sight. Clean shot if authorised. Assistance required."

The open ground in front of the warehouse was littered with people wondering what had happened. The lads stood against the fence, offering no threat, figuring something bad may have occurred, minimising their exposure. DS Holmes assisted the DCI back to her feet, asking if she was okay, both shaken. Unsure what they should do, the forensic investigators approached the skip, with nobody impeding their progress, testing the metal box's temperature with the back of their hands, inspecting the ground around the structure.

DI Jones rushed towards the roadblock, joined by the ARU team leader, together speculating on the likely scenario they would find, observing a traffic officer crouched in the distance, his distinctive hat identifying his specialty. Body language from the personnel at the scene suggesting a serious outcome, they increased their pace, already considering where blame might be apportioned. Coming closer, the bike became visible, embedded in the fence, silent, with one wheel continuing to turn. Seeing his subordinate officer retaining his fire position, the ARU leader instructed him to stand down, assume a state of readiness, breathe.

DI Jones was outside of his comfort zone. Standing over the accident, he tried to recall the procedures applicable to the situation, certain that medical competency was demanded, confident that urgency would be redundant. The Mancunian's head rested at an unnatural angle relative to his body, with clear evidence of a severe impact. There were no signs of life.

Turning away from the body, he instructed the traffic cops to secure the scene, suggesting they arrange their cones to completely block the junction from all traffic. Confirming they had tarpaulins in the car, he asked them to cover the body, to protect the scene from the elements and unwelcome curious onlookers.

Fifty
Sunday, 17th February

Coming out of sleep gently, she permitted her eyelids to remain closed, her body relaxed and relatively pain-free. Aware of his presence, grateful for it, her injured head supported on a cushion resting across his upper legs, a suggestion of firmness beneath the cushion. Allowing herself to awake further, questioning how long he had been here, she considered opening her eyes, to discover the time, to tell him she had come around.

Parting her eyelids, rotating her head, looking up, finding him looking back at her, his gaze tarnished with concern, his eyes upon closer inspection displaying affection. Avoiding further movement, she asked him what the time was, hearing after three, scarcely believing yet accepting the update, understanding her fatigue levels. Finding words.

"You have been here for so long; surely you need to use the bathroom?" Attempting to rise to offer him release, finding some freedom of movement, she felt sharp reminders of the suffering she had endured before gradually achieving a sitting position. He stood, confirming her suspicion. "You woke up just in time. I'm close to peeing myself. I won't be long." Watching him go, thinking *that explains the firmness behind the cushion*, smiling, amused. Disappointed?

Reflecting on the recuperative power of sleep, she poured juice from the fridge, swallowing two further painkillers later than scheduled, her pain less invasive than before.

Grateful for his support and attendance, she reflected on her need for privacy, the requirement to dispose of the remaining items from Simon's house, unseen. Pondering ways to politely persuade him to leave, while ensuring he wanted to see her again.

"How do you feel?" His expression revealing continuing concern.

She responded by coming to him, snuggling to him, placing her arms around him. "Much better, thank you. Sleep was exactly what I needed.

And company, of course." Hugging him, welcoming his physical warmth.

"Is there anything you need from the shops? I could go for you. Help you stock up?" His offer providing her with a perfect opportunity to be alone without necessitating any awkward request. "Would you mind? I don't think I am ready to go out yet. There are a few things I need."

Together, they inspected her cupboards, fridge, and freezer, assembling a list of items, moderating some of the considerations. Further ibuprofen and paracetamol, fruit juice, eggs, chicken noodle soup, smoked fish, butter, chicken portions, low-fat milk, asparagus, and broccoli all making the cut. In a moment of inspiration, he added, "Ice cream!" — appreciative of the positive effect the cool dessert could have on her injured mouth.

She suggested he head towards Chester to one of the larger supermarkets, where the choice would be greater and the cost lower, neglecting to mention the increased driving time involved.

She assured him that she felt better and promised to be awake when he returned. Betraying his residual concern, he cautioned her against taking a bath or shower without his presence, hinting that she may have suffered a mild concussion. She jokingly accused him of wishing to see her naked. Apologising for wasting his entire Sunday, she rewarded him with a delicate kiss, inviting him to stay with her for dinner.

Fifty-One
Sunday, 17th February

The mammoth police presence at the warehouse sought direction, their conflicting objectives unfulfilled, their priority to be determined. The apparent death of The Mancunian at the roadblock furnishing a shocked sense of anti-climax. His stunned lads asking for confirmation as they offered to provide authentication of the deceased's identity, their co-operation gladly accepted by the officers as they learned of the man's single status, which would complicate identification by the next of kin.

Resuming control, the DCI delegated DS Chappell to escort the suspects to the body, inviting an armed officer to accompany them from a ten-yard separation. Summoning DS Holmes, she instructed him to supervise the forensics team, ensure the skip was isolated, enclosed, and removed when approved by the white suits. Speaking on her phone, she explained her requirement for DI Jones to remain with the deceased and supervise the activities at the outer site while keeping her informed. Borrowing two of the scene-of-crime investigation team, she instigated a search of the internal office and warehouse, seeking anything incriminating, anything indicating movements of drugs, people trafficking or prostitution.

His lads identified the deceased, asking what had happened, accepting the accidental nature of the incident. Preferring to avoid any confrontation with the law, they remained concerned for their situation, self-preservation their focus over provocation of the police. Subdued, they had returned to a position close to the skip, awaiting instruction, their location permitting a view of the side of the warehouse where Chappell was checking a parked car, the plate consistent with the images from his CCTV search. Being within the physical parameters of the search warrant, Barry began to look through the windows, an additional opportunity garnered.

Holmes assumed control over the lads. Indicating the skip, he began the questioning. "What are we likely to find in there?"

Glances exchanged, the shorter one replied, "Old office furniture, waste from the yard, out-of-date papers. Just the usual shit."

Terry considered the response before replying. "So, nothing unusual. No reason to perform a detailed forensic investigation. No foreign bodies?" Watching them, seeking a flinch, twitch, anything. Seeing it, the momentary panic detailed in the expression of the taller one. "You are aware, with the passing of the gaffer, that you two are now responsible for the skip. Anything we find, it goes against you. Understood?"

"We could make a statement if you like. We heard something. We could tell it to you."

"Let's go inside, exchange some identification, then listen to what you have to say." Holmes invited them to lead the way into the office, without restraints, their movements closely monitored by the ARU. Placing his phone on the desk, he enabled the recording function, stating the names of those present and their location, as well as the obligatory date and time. Indicating they should retrieve their driving licences from the table, he began the informal questioning, as the DCI joined them, sitting alongside Holmes.

"What can you tell us about the skip in the yard, the one where the fire was burning for an extended period?"

The short lad spoke. "I heard that Joseph Nesbitt had been dumped into the skip, while it was on fire."

The statement drawing expressions of horror from around the table. Choking, the DCI asked, "Dumped in the burning skip? Alive?"

The taller lad clarified. "We heard that Mr MacKenzie, the boss, had shot Nesbitt twice in the chest, killing him. Then he had the body thrown into the skip for disposal. That's what we heard. We weren't here, so we can't swear to it, gospel like."

Ignoring the apparent lie, DS Holmes continued, "When did this happen?"

Hearing, "A few days ago." Asking for a more specific indication. "Tuesday, maybe Wednesday. I'm sure I heard about it on Wednesday."

Making a note. "Do you know why your boss would shoot Nesbitt?"

The short lad took over again. "People said that he shot Dai Harris at the same time. Shot them both. Something to do with them killing the old Asian lady. Something about her being the boss's bint. Rumour is, he planted the other body by the road after doing a deal with a copper, some form of exchange. This is only what we heard."

The DCI requested a pause in the discussion, filtering what she had heard, unbelieving of their absence from the scene, uncaring at this time. Recalling conversations, the tip-off regarding the body, Beecham the source. Piecing things together, seeking confirmation. "You are telling us that we might find one body in that skip, that it should be Joseph Nesbitt, that he was shot by MacKenzie. The same person who also shot Harris and arranged his body by the road. Sounds like quite a tale. What else can you tell us about him?"

The taller lad again, figuring the police had further information, sensed that ratification of their information may benefit him. "A couple of days ago, when we were both here, MacKenzie threatened to kill Boris the Orange, one of his trusted people. He held a gun to his head. We thought he was going to do it, so we intervened, persuaded him to take time and think about what he was doing. Maybe we saved Boris's life."

Covering his informant, DS Holmes adopted a confused expression, phrasing a question with incredulity. "Boris the Orange? Who the hell is that?" Receiving no reply, his objective achieved.

"Thank you for your co-operation, gentlemen. We will need you to come to the station to make a formal statement. You can call a lawyer from there if you like. Interview suspended." Adding the date and time before she signalled Holmes to halt the recording. "Sergeant Holmes, can you arrange transport for these gentlemen to the station, separately please, as a precaution." Walking out of the office area, making her way across the yard, finding the nearest forensic investigator. "They say there is one body in there, Nesbitt. Do your stuff. We know what to look for." Turning away, seeing Holmes return, she expressed her appreciation. "Good work. Split them and get them into cells at the shop. Leave them to stew for a while. Talk to your buddy Boris, see what else he has; promise him anything you think is reasonable. This is going to be huge."

"Yes, Ma'am. Is everything okay with you?"

"I'm fine, Sergeant. He took me by surprise. No hurt. A little bit ashamed that he managed to get away, though not far, eh? Once you fuck off with these morons, I can release the ARU, get a few more regular cops in here. We need to find the gun. That would be useful."

Wandering to the end of the road, she joined DI Jones, half-listening to his situation report, while surveying the carnage. "PJ, have you taken a look in the storage box on the back of the bike?"

Hearing, "No, Ma'am. I wasn't sure if the warrant would still apply out here."

Awarding him one of her famous disdainful expressions, adjusting her phrasing, she spoke as if she was teaching a child. "The motorcycle was within the warrant area when we arrived, therefore it shall be deemed to be part of the function of the search warrant. This also applies to the deceased." Checking to ensure her message was understood. "Get the box open and also check the body for anything incriminating." Seeing no movement from her DI. "Maybe do it now, while I watch?"

Seeing Holmes depart, followed by two squad cars, each carrying one of the lads, she was pleased that progress was underway. She watched Jones battle the locked pannier, pushing and twisting, consoled he had at least donned gloves, but frustrated at his efforts. Indicating to the traffic cop to glove up and take over, with a suitable tool in hand he quickly loosened the cover, revealing the contents. Returning to his feet. "Ma'am?" Stepping back.

"Nobody, touch, anything! Son, fetch a SOCO, please. Bingo! You fucking dancer!"

The open box revealed a handgun, an extension resembling a silencer and a plastic bag containing a product visually comparable to partly crushed ice, the origin to be determined, suspiciously resembling a decent quantity of methamphetamine.

Fifty-Two
Sunday, 17th February

Holly carried several hangers through to another bedroom, each adorned with a shirt, one sporting a belt looped around the curved top, placing the clothing in the fitted wardrobe, the order irrelevant. With her anger simmering, she reflected on their early-morning discussion.

She quietly came to realise that she had wanted her relationship with Terry to develop. She wanted more. She wanted to move out of this rented house, buy their own place and furnish it with their choices. She wanted to decorate in bolder colours, she wanted a lawn in the garden, she wanted to consider having children, preferably after marriage, to create a family home. She had access to preferential interest rates from her role at the bank; she was a mortgage specialist, for Christ's sake. They both had solid incomes, without extravagant debts for cars or other luxuries.

She had presumed that he would want something similar. She had enticed him into the discussion, intimating an interest in performing one of his favourite acts. She had not expected the vicious verbal attack he had unleashed, totally unaware of the resentments he was withholding.

He had complained that she didn't cook, just produced anything she could easily reheat. Well, he never prepared anything, so fuck him. She could learn to cook; it was hardly an insurmountable challenge.

He admonished her for the way she dressed, something she had thought he loved. He told her she was getting older, maybe she should try to hide a bit of flesh occasionally, dress age appropriately, stop seeking the ambient attention of strangers when they went anywhere. When did they ever go out now? He was always fucking tired. Boring twat.

His criticism of her house-keeping skills had pissed her off. She worked long hours too, not just him. There wasn't always time to scrub the place, but she kept it clean and tidy, having already worn out a vacuum cleaner since they moved here. When he contributed, if he contributed, he would wash the colours with the whites, having ruined some of her favourite clothes.

Of course, he had raised the thing about the alibi she had given Amy. If he had any close friends, he would have understood that it is okay to assist a friend in need. He was a loner, a typical cop, unable to trust anyone. Then it had gotten worse, accusing her of having a relationship with Amy, admitting he thought they were an item, something he could not compete with, a situation he had no mechanism to cope with. Disbelieving, she had denied the accusation, telling him to get over it, omitting any mention of the kiss. She suspected he had imagined Amy and her together, had enjoyed beating off thinking about it.

He had suggested she learn to moderate her alcohol intake. That was how he had phrased it. When he really meant that she drank too much and should consider stopping altogether. Clearly, he was forgetting the many times he had taken advantage of her drunkenness, performing sex acts on her that he was too shy to ask for when they were sober, like that time he ventured into her dark side. She liked to drink, contending she did not drink excessively, consuming more at home, less when out, compatible with considering that maybe he should take her out more often. Dickhead.

Then he had gone too far. She was proud of her curves, nice boobs, nice bottom, shapely legs, hour-glass figure. She was physically attractive, she knew it and he knew it, in a different way from Amy and others. The slim look seemed to be fashionable again, but she knew her curves were an asset, eyed with jealousy by some, with admiration by others. When the miserable short-arsed twat suggested she should think about losing weight, she snapped. Internally, her tolerance broke; outwardly, she concealed her anger, retaining it for the right time.

That time was now, removing everything belonging to him from their bedroom, her bedroom now. All his clothes to the spare room; his shoes, his watches, cufflinks, to the spare room. His toiletries, to the guest bathroom. His paperback novels, all to the spare room. Removing him completely from her bedroom, step one towards evicting him completely. Surprise the twat when he came home tonight, denied access to her, their former room, her body, her affection. He could wank in peace in the spare room, do his own laundry, feed himself.

Summarising their situation in her head. She had wanted to bear his children, the most amazing gift you could offer to any man. In return, he had told her she was a hopeless cook, a lazy cleaner, dressed like a slut, drank too much, was an attention seeker, potentially a lesbian, a liar he could not trust, and she was fat. He had offered nothing positive. Hadn't said she was beautiful, had not indicated that he loved her, mentioned nothing about a future together. He had not even complimented her on her excellent sexual skills, her ability to make him hard at any time.

Fuck him, she could do better — he had to go.

Fifty-Three
Sunday, 17th February

The revelations were continuously pouring from the interviewee, unstoppable once the seal had been breached.

Misleading Boris, Terry had advised him that The Mancunian had been taken into custody by the NWP, that he presented no threat to anybody. He had been instructed not to mention the demise of the crime lord, the DCI fearing that may discourage Boris from talking.

The lads from the warehouse were fermenting in their independent cells, awaiting interrogation, formulating their cover stories and their excuses. How they would minimise their involvement in activities potentially leading to serious jail time.

Sergeant Annie from forensics sat alongside DS Holmes, the interviewee deemed important enough to warrant two sergeants. Being the only one of her rank available, her nominal knowledge of the case deemed sufficient for her to support Holmes and provide insight from another perspective. To date, she had not spoken.

Boris offered the possibility of retrieving five kilos of Ice from the Llandudno massage parlour if they were quick. The drugs delivered recently therefore unlikely to have been repackaged.

He had furnished further information about the dead Asian lady, providing a partial name, Nattaporn. He confirmed her nationality, her point of origin having been the red-light area of a place called Hua Hin, some three hours south of Bangkok. Enough for Missing Persons to use to approach the Thai embassy. Intimating that MacKenzie owned a holiday home there in one of the gated communities.

He revealed the supply route used for bringing people into the UK, the route for the Ice, mentioning locations, modes of transport, elaborating with the timings used to coincide with reduced border security. Terry understood this could be huge, if it proved to be true, involving multiple national agencies, applying himself to extracting and recording as much as possible, striving to contain his professional excitement.

Terry learned about the burner phones, a deal set up with the Vodafone guy for cleaned second-hand devices with undocumented sim cards and easily renewable credit. The scheme simple, effective, bordering on brilliant. Asking why there had been nine mobiles in the dead man's house, hearing that there had been a short shipment of ten phones. Learning that The Mancunian had prepaid, so was probably angry, that his temper was legendary, that he regularly cleansed his supply lines, often disposed to take out suppliers whom he no longer trusted.

This story reinforced by his removal of a preferred real estate partner. Invited to continue, Boris explained that the properties in the organisation had been sourced through a property agent predisposed to accept unattested paperwork while processing sales.

"The purchased properties were bought by Man Chester Therapy Ltd. It's clever, because the Man and Chester are two words, not one, so searching for the company fails if you enter it as one word, Manchester." Pausing to ensure the officers understood. "They buy the property through the estate agent, he closes the deal, without scrutinising the documentation, then collects his commission. The company sells the property to another company, Man Khun Ian Developments, based in Gibraltar, the agent gets more commission, and the business address becomes harder to trace."

"Was that middle word, um, offensive?" Annie spoke at last.

Boris clarifying, "K.H.U.N. It might be pronounced like 'done' or 'spoon'. I'm not sure."

"So, who is this estate contact? A company or a single person?"

"Single person. Freelance probably, or a small company. Like I said, he was taken out, so they'll be looking to replace him. A bit posh he was, had one of those double-barrelled names. It'll come to me."

DS Holmes felt the tingle of excitement, potentially explosive. "Jeremy Campbell-Foulkes?" Hearing the response, casual, the normality a contrast to the potency of the revelation.

"Yeah, that's him."

"What makes you so sure?" Pressing, seeking confirmation.

"The name rings a bell and I think I met him once. The Mancunian does not like trails leading to him. The phones guy, the real estate guy, he won't keep them open for long. I don't know if he did them personally, or ordered a hit, but I'm pretty certain he would have arranged both. The only other option would be a strike by a rival group. With everything going on right now, I'd bet my left bollock he took them both out."

Overloaded, DS Holmes called a halt, suggesting a refreshment break. Leaving the room, Annie following, they made their way upstairs, looking for Doris, informed he had not come in today. Relieved, given time to think, Terry engaged Annie in a bout of verbal sparring, relating to the Saltney murder case, revisiting the scenario armed with this new angle, seeking a level of certainty before submitting the notion to the DCI.

Fifty-Four
Sunday, 17th February

He had gone reluctantly, not wishing to leave her alone. Endearing, but frustrating. She estimated his trip would take around an hour, her application of a safety factor giving her forty minutes to get the stuff dumped safely and get back to resume her position on the settee. She planned to drive to the parking area where the travellers usually dumped their debris, an easy half hour round trip.

She dressed for the conditions, pulling socks and jogging pants over her pyjama bottoms, a jumper over her pyjama top, sneakers and the laundered parka jacket supplemented by gloves. Collecting the contraband from the hidden location, she loaded her Clio, rapidly leaving her home behind. Already suffering, she obliterated Adele's mumble, unsure if her mental state could cope with further depression.

Impatient arseholes made her journey less than straightforward, though failing to prevent her approach to the parking area ahead of her imposed schedule. "Fuck!" Seeing a police vehicle in the area, both officers remaining in the car, rendering the location useless for a low-profile dumping of Simon's phone carcass, bank cards and other items. Increasing speed, she resumed her journey on the ring road, seeking an alternate location, one eye watching the minutes on the clock seemingly accelerate.

One extra mile becoming two, panic manifesting, she became distracted from her driving, seeking a parking area with a bin. Hearing a horn from behind, she realised she had drifted out of her lane; making the correction, rewarded with a raised index finger. Reasoning that she couldn't risk going much further, she indicated, leaving the road at the next junction, one unfamiliar to her, her intention to perform a U-turn and return to the main road. Seeing a layby ahead, perfect for making the U-turn manoeuvre, she decelerated into the space, spying the litter bin, reminding herself of the purpose of the trip, coming to a laboured stop.

With no vehicles in sight, she alighted from her car, unloading items into the bin. She was concerned about leaving the mobile remains intact, even without the battery or sim card. Opening the hatch, accessing the wheel-changing toolkit, Amy selected the long-armed spanner for loosening wheel nuts. Placing the dormant cell phone on the tarmac, she smashed it with the big metal spanner, the breaking sounds satisfying, the plastic body shattering under the assault. Sweeping most of the innards into the bin, she kicked some into a drain, the remnants beyond recognition, abandoned at the kerbside. Checking the pockets of the jacket were empty, she removed the warm coat, folding it prior to dumping it into the bin, pushing it down as far as she could.

Task complete, she returned to her car, grateful for the warmth from the heater, alarmed to see the time, already thirty minutes and beyond. "Shite!" Turning quickly, she returned to the main road, making her way home, feeling herself accelerate beyond the speed limit.

Recalling the boys in blue parked at the tinkers' layby, she forced the Clio below seventy to pass them legally, feeling developing pressure as her time evaporated, considering possible explanations she could offer, none of them believable. Praying he was in a long queue at the checkout, she fought her anxiety and trepidation, nudging the speed higher, closing the distance to home.

Approaching her place, relief surged through her, converting to disbelief as she found her allocated parking space occupied, evolving to fury as she watched the offending driver locking his doors. Pulling alongside, she opened her window. "Hey. Where are you going? This is my parking space."

Hearing her voice, he turned, addressing her. "I don't think so. I got here first. Try further along."

Unclipping her seatbelt, leaving the car, she faced him. "See that sign. Reserved parking!" Pointing lower. "See that, my registration number. This is my parking space!"

Reducing the space between them, imposing his physical superiority as he asserted himself. "I won't be long. Chill out, miss."

His condescending attitude aggravating her simmering anger, the clock ticking, her heartrate accelerating. "Move your fucking car!" Her low voice unsettling him, the passing time unsettling her. Raising her mobile phone. "I can call the police and have you moved, right fucking now."

He came closer, mistaking her displayed panic as fear. Adopting a convivial manner. "No need to swear. We can be reasonable. There are spaces along the road."

Preventing him from continuing, speaking over him. "Then use one of them. This is my space. Get out. If I hear another word from you, I am going to key your car from nose to tail." Sensing her irrationality, he conceded and returned to his car, suspecting her damaged features were related to drug use, words failing him.

As his engine started, she reversed, permitting him a clear departure from her parking spot. Moving ahead, he rewarded her with an index finger, her second of the afternoon. Immune to the insult, she parked carefully, breathing rapidly, seeing more than forty minutes had elapsed since Rob had departed. Shutting down her engine, she locked the car, running to her apartment, entering, quickly closing the door while removing her sneakers, replacing them in a cupboard, walking to her kitchen. Filling a glass with water, she swallowed rapidly, gratefully, sweating despite the external cold, feeling a semblance of calm slowly return to her metabolism. Forty-nine minutes.

Engaging her defensive instincts, she discarded her clothes to a laundry basket, wrapping her body in a large towel. Running water into her bath, she poured bubbles, certain that the sight of her wearing only a towel would ensure he was distracted. Within six minutes her theory was tested, his reaction to her clad in a towel comedic, conflicted, his urge to compliment her matched by his urge to avoid offence. Placing groceries on the counter, greeting her, he focused on her eyes while trying to avoid looking downwards. "Hi. Are you okay?"

"I'm fine. Running a bath, waiting for you before I take it. Thank you for shopping. Can I get you anything?"

"Take your bath, I'll make dinner. Something light and soft." Watching her walk away, the towel barely covering her bottom, affording him a glimpse of her figure from behind, he became flustered, seeking to cover his agitation. "I must be going mad. I thought your car was facing in the other direction when I left."

Stopping, she turned to face him, her towel scarcely adequate, a smile becoming a laugh. "It appears I am having quite an effect on you. Thank you for the compliment." Bewitching him with a suggestive look, tantalising, her flaws reinforcing her attractiveness. As she moved away, Rob remembered to breathe.

Fifty-Five
Sunday, 17th February

Ponytail confirmed the deceased as deceased. The motorcycle crash had been painstakingly described to him, the collision between head and concrete flowerpot an epic mismatch. He asked forensics to take samples for confirmation as he arranged for the body to be shipped to the morgue.

"Busy first week as head of pathology, Steven." DI Jones stating the obvious.

"I can hardly believe it. I thought I took a job in Wales, not bloody Chicago. I'm losing count of the bodies already."

Watching the deceased Mancunian being loaded, he prepared to drive back to his post-mortem suite, ready to analyse another death, write another report, be asked further questions by impatient detectives.

****

DS Chappell watched the skip being loaded onto the truck. The investigators had sealed the unit with a tight tarpaulin across the open top, securing straps like a cat's cradle across the covering, additional tape applied to seal edges, labels clearly displayed in numerous locations.

He wondered why Emyr wasn't here, or Annie. He had sent her a message, receiving no reply. The big half-Jamaican forensic sergeant was in charge, seemingly in control of events. Gethin. He certainly didn't look like a Gethin. Seeking the DCI, he wandered into the warehouse.

She was at the desk, looking tired. Seeing him arrive, she issued instructions. "Follow the SOCOs back to their lab, impress on them the need to find the leftovers of Joseph Nesbitt. Then back to Llay. Find the narcotics team, we're raiding several of the massage parlours tonight, I want you leading one of those teams. Llandudno is the priority, then Rhyl. Be on one of those raids. Call in whatever support you need."

****

Signing the immunity document, observing the witnesses confirming his signature and that of DS Holmes, the space for DI Jones remaining unadorned, Boris was increasingly confident the police would protect him. He had provided brilliant intelligence, The Mancunian was in custody, hopefully meaning Boris would never have another gun placed against his head. While technically imprisoned, his treatment was fine: takeaway Chinese for lunch coming in, a cold beer already waiting for him. The beer poured into a paper cup; no bottles permitted. Some rules were unbreakable.

****

Soaking in the warm bath with the door open, she listened to him chatter, his insistence that she respond to convince him she was okay, feeling good and not asleep in the bath. He had threatened to come into the bathroom if she failed to answer, and she half expected him to appear at any time. She wouldn't mind; he had earned the opportunity. Her preference was to take things slowly, but she was open to persuasion.

Reviewing her count. Good one for his pulling of the story, another good one for coming to see her today. Another for allowing her to sleep, being her pillow while remaining a gentleman. A fourth for cooking, twice. Four good counts reduced by a bad one against the twat arguing over her parking space. Overall count three, good three. "Three."

****

Gethin bagged the gun, displaying the evidence bags to the DCI. "I'll rush this through, Ma'am." Pointing at the contents, putting emphasis on the bag containing the improvised silencer. "They usually clean the weapon, but often forget to clean the silencer. I can see something on it. I'm optimistic."

"Thank you, Sergeant." The DCI released a softer expression. "Remember, straight to me when you get anything." Reciprocal expressions confirming their understanding.

****

The Immigration Enforcement officers arrived at Llay, demanding dedicated office space, tea and coffee facilities, and the urgent attendance of NWP's senior officers. They were perturbed to have their requests largely ignored, informed that the Superintendent did not work weekends, similarly his deputy, while the duty DCI was at a crime scene. They milled around, fretting about being under-appreciated. They had rushed to North Wales to conduct raids, to snatch illegal immigrants and undocumented workers. Nobody had informed them that the raids would also involve the Priority Intercept Team, the new narcotics division created in Wales, as well as forensics officers, CID, and uniformed constables.

Directed to a vending machine, some sought comfort in vaguely flavoured lukewarm brown water loosely resembling tea.

****

Annie controlled the transfer, taking Boris from the station to a safe house in two unmarked cars, the informant heavily cloaked in a sweatshirt with the hood pulled over his head. Loading was completed in the secure parking area, with Boris instructed to lie across the back seat, beneath a blanket for his own protection, to avoid possible recognition from unexpected pedestrians.

North Wales Police had suppressed the incident near the warehouse, denying access to traffic, arranging urgent removal of the body, the press issued with a gagging instruction. Ostensibly, The Mancunian remained alive and in control of his empire. Boris the Orange remained a trusted assistant. The skip had been removed from the area.

DS Holmes had left the station, sneaking a break before joining the evening raids on the massage houses, leaving Annie responsible for the safe transfer. She enjoyed the diversion, the deviation from forensic duties, while aware that the investigative forensic jobs were lining up. Hoping for good news in the morning, she imagined herself delegating the tasks as the new leader of the local forensic investigation team.

****

His homemade tomato soup was wonderful. Thoughtfully, he had allowed the soup to cool before serving, tearing the soft insides from the remaining bread rolls, scattering the pieces across the surface of the red liquid. Wonderful yet simple, practically a cheat.

Roasting a red capsicum, mixing olive oil with dried basil and fresh basil leaves, sweating a finely chopped red onion. Dicing the roasted capsicum, adding the onion, oil and herbs, blitzing it all in a blender, before adding the smooth result to a simmering pan containing a tin of cream of tomato soup and a tin of chopped tomatoes. Heating together, blitzing again to thicken, ground black pepper, ripped bread, and serve.

Enjoying their informal meal, she joked that he must be hungry, suggesting he should get chips on the way home. Finishing her entire bowl, feeling close to normal for the first time; she was rested, fuelled and bathed, Amy acknowledged her improvement. Enjoying his company, she was astonished at how relaxed she had become with him, and he with her, making her smile with some of his stories, awarding scores to the female string musicians on the music videos. He commented that there seemed to be a hotness standard for violinists, though backtracking after she paused one of the videos on a close-up.

Aware he would depart soon, she had caught him making a couple of subtle glances at his watch as he cleaned the dishes; he put leftover soup into a bowl, placing the bowl in her fridge. Partly relieved as she had several messages from Holly to attend to, partly disappointed having enjoyed his presence. She sought to delay his departure, inviting him to sit, then snuggling into him, cuddling his cheek while resisting the residual pain, accepting his light kiss on her forehead, respectful, considerate.

"I really should go." His words gentle, suggesting reluctance. "I had no idea if I would even see you today. I'm happy I did. I still feel bad. I'm sorry for what happened to you."

Amy explained it wasn't his fault and how he had assisted her recovery. Standing, encouraging him to his feet, bestowing his first reward. "You understand that you are now officially my boyfriend." Following with the second reward, kissing his lips, hiding her discomfort, whispering, "Thank you for everything" as they separated. "Please call me tomorrow?" Requesting or demanding, difficult to tell.

Beaming as he walked towards his car, touching the bonnet of her Clio, cool but not cold, instantly forgotten, his temperament soaring. "I have a girlfriend." The beam broadening as he remembered her clad only in the towel.

****

The raid on the warehouse and yard was over. The skip had gone, the office had been searched, the parked car scoured, the warehouse forensically combed. Evidence bags were labelled and loaded, on their way to the station. The body was at the morgue, the bike had been retrieved for further study. The traffic boys had cleaned the scene of the accident. The two hoodlums were detained at the station. Her final actions being to close the doors, locking the premises, padlocking the gates, and reinstating the premises to appear unpolluted by a police investigation. Two officers hidden nearby, monitoring a subtly placed nanny cam providing a view of the gates and the main door.

Nothing to suggest any form of drastic interruption to operations.

Knackered, she waved to her officers, climbing into her car, planning a short detour home to shower and refresh in advance of the raids tonight.

****

"Where have you been? I've been trying to catch you all day."

"Hey, Holly. What's up?"

"I kicked Terry out. Well, out of the bedroom. He can use the spare room until he finds another place to stay."

"Oh, God. Are you okay? What happened?"

"He told me I was a fat slut. I'm paraphrasing, but basically, he thinks I am unsuitable wife material, so I packed his shit and threw it into the spare room. No more shaven haven for him. Fucker!"

"Oh, Puss-Puss, I am so sorry. I don't know what to say."

"Just say you're getting dressed up and we are going out to break some hearts."

"Honey, I can't. Sorry. I was attacked by a drug addict who tried to steal my bag. I managed to keep the bag, but I am facially pretty messed up."

"Fuck! Really? Did you call the cops?"

"What's the point? They do fuck-all anyway. Before you know it, they look at your short skirt and decide you were asking for it. I just came home to rest, and it is getting better now. Hurts, though."

"I'll come over to keep you company, if you like?"

"Okay. That'll be nice. You can tell me what a dick Terry has been, then we can assassinate his character together."

"See you soon." Click.

Fifty-Six
Sunday, 17th February

An array of locations had been presented to the plethora of team leaders, reinforcing the extent of the empire operated by The Mancunian. Thirteen known locations in Wales, the quantity in England not yet determined and beyond the remit of this operation. Vice officers stimulated by the potential of thirteen active brothels. The Priority Intercept Team excited at five kilos of Ice in Llandudno, expectant of further finds in other locations. Immigration Enforcement anticipating a significant quantity of undocumented overseas workers, optimistic of a people-trafficking network to crack. CID confident of closing several live homicide cases. ARU bullish about their prospects to pull a trigger this time.

Amalgamating their resources, it was rapidly realised they could not support thirteen simultaneous raids effectively. They worked on creating a manageable priority list, understanding that word would spread quickly, and that any location not raided tonight would be cleansed within hours.

The DCI asked everyone for quiet. Taking the floor, she addressed the assembly, simplifying their resource arithmetically.

The room contained eight Vice officers, eighteen from Immigration Enforcement, the Home Office coffers clearly still loaded with bullion, nine from Priority Intercept, six from CID, one DCI, one DI and six weapon response specialists. "Listen! We have forty-nine specifics and sixteen uniforms. That gives us eight teams of eight with one floating, which will be me. Pick eight locations to raid. It is not bastard rocket science, is it? Sort it out, get the teams who will be travelling farthest on their way. Can we be ready to go at eight o'clock? I don't want to go any later than nine. Start talking. I'm waiting!"

****

Llandudno was confirmed as being the critical site. Known as a popular outlet located on the edge of the largest holiday town in North Wales, it was located adjacent to a computer warehouse, an electrical wholesaler, plus a board games emporium. Opening hours were coincident only with the games place, providing temptation to the girlfriend-free geeks as they ended their gaming sessions.

The narcotics resource was doubling up at this location, the intelligence relating to the five kilos the strongest in their possession. One Vice officer at every location, likely insufficient, reliant on the uniforms to assist in detaining those behaving inappropriately. Two from Immigration had been allocated in expectation of multiple targets. The only armed officer was mature and mean looking, his projected air of relaxation appearing to be massively exaggerated. A starry-eyed plod, possibly out of uniform for the first time, his apprehension competing with exhilaration, the weak link, an object of concern for the CID detective. DS Chappell would lead this team, also nominally responsible for the forensics investigators allocated to process the establishment afterwards.

Contacting the DCI, confirming his team were in position with the rear entrance protected, his multi-faceted raiding party ready and willing, he waited on an instruction to go.

Barry traced the second hand on his watch, time passing inexorably, unreasonably jealous of the jackets the IE guys were wearing. *As usual, the best fucking equipment, but no idea how to use it.* He wondered how they would perform in the field, expecting an underwhelming performance while fearing the worst. As operational Detective Sergeant, Barry would lead the access to the premises and present the warrant. The ARU officer to follow closely, discouraging resistance.

Advantaged by the absence of tourists, they would be able to proceed when instructed without consideration for members of the public. Poised, hearing the instruction. "Go! Go! Go!"

Having taken a moment to acknowledge the instruction, Barry found himself overtaken by the enthusiastic Vice officer. Forced to scramble to try to regain his forefront position, he allowed the Vice dick to open the door, pushing past to enter the facility first, closely followed by the firearms officer. Raising his hand, displaying the warrant, he announced their arrival. "Police!"

Striding beyond the reception counter, he saw a woman crouching, reducing her profile. Ahead, a door opened inwards, the bulk of a security steward presenting before him. "Police! Step aside. There are armed officers in…" Unable to complete his sentence, the recipient of an extremely large fist to the centre of his face, his head and shoulders returning in the direction of their arrival in contradiction to the forward momentum of his lower body and legs. His physique almost horizontal as he met the shabbily carpeted floor.

His pride intact, having acted in defence of the premises, the steward exercised discretion in the presence of the armed policeman, kneeling as he interlocked his hands behind his head. Feeling cable ties around his ankles and handcuffs on his wrists, he assumed a position on the floor. Hearing the weapon-toting officer address him. "Nice. Took him out with one punch. Now, I suggest you only move if you want to make my day. Do you understand?"

The woman from the desk crawled forward, allowing herself to be restrained, joining the steward and the unconscious cop on the floor. Stepping back to cover the entrance, the armed officer engaged the lock, taking a position permitting him a panoramic view of the premises, watching everything. Focused.

The Vice specialist could scarcely contain his delight as he stepped over Chappell. Following an impulse, he made for the last door in the corridor, a likely den worthy of disgust, in his experience. Pushing the door ajar, stepping in as shouts of protest came from the bed, identifying himself as "Police!", registering the look of bemusement on the face of a man reconciling the presence of another male in the room. He continued to attempt to pump as the woman sought escape, chasing her as she doggie-crawled forward, his knees unable to keep up, plopping out as she sought refuge behind a pillow. "Oh, dear. What do we have here?" Phone clicking. "Needless to say, sir, do not fucking move; you are under arrest." Turning to the woman, Asian of some description, unsure. "You! Look at me!" Using two fingers to indicate she should look at him. "Do not move! Understand?" Producing cable ties from his pocket, he secured the man's wrists, securing the lady's wrists, joining their wrist restraints together, effectively reducing their remote chance to escape. "Tut-tut, buddy. Bareback? You must be certifiably fucking mental."

The ranking drugs agent stood in the doorway of an internal office, unable to comprehend the sight before him. Setting his phone to video mode, filming the internal space, consigning it to perpetuity and evidence. Plastic bags, gloves, aprons, spoons, spatulas, a precise Avery weighing machine, their presence recorded, ancillary items next to the mound of methamphetamine openly stored on a table. Speaking aloud, for his own benefit and for anyone within earshot. "Five kilograms? And the rest!" Estimating the weight of the Ice before him by eye, resisting his urge to begin weighing the narcotic, that job for the forensics to enjoy later. "At least ten, possibly fifteen. Re-fucking-sult." Hearing an arrival behind him, seeing his Priority Intercept colleague, welcoming him. "Take a look at this. Just laying around. Can you believe it?"

Expecting the younger agent to be impressed, instead hearing, "I found a similar quantity in another room. In a cupboard, hidden by towels. Unbelievable. I reckon we'll be drinking on expenses tonight."

"Is the DS still sleeping out there? Might be an idea to call for an ambulance. Has anyone even gone to help him?"

One of the Home Office staff walked two people to the front of the establishment, encouraging the restrained male to lie on the floor beside the others, naked and humiliated. He invited the petite woman to sit on the bench against a wall, allowing her to cover herself with an excessively laundered grey threadbare towel.

"Why is he nude?" The ARU operative asked.

"Cheeky bastard offered me twenty quid if I would let her finish him off. Said it was the best blowie he'd had in ages." Deeming the explanation adequate, the IE man went back into the rear of the facility.

Engaging the steward, posturing with his weapon, the ARO stated, "You have accepted our warrant to search these premises. Correct?" Receiving a single nod in reply, he cupped his free hand to his ear. "I can't hear you."

A pause, before an audible response. "Yes, I have seen your warrant. I accept your entitlement to search these premises. Okay?"

When the dust settled, nine Asian women had been cable-tied together, wrist to wrist, one duct taped across her mouth, having bitten the officer subduing her. No passports were available on the premises, requiring them to be universally escorted to a police station. Four paying customers were secured, each facing charges, one facing serious questions about the age of his companion. The bouncer, facing a charge of assaulting a police officer, seemingly unconcerned, confident in the organisation he worked for. The criminalists were stunned at the quantity of meth they were presented with, logging the evidence, providing an estimated weight of thirty kilos, needing time to carefully retrieve the content for shipment to their laboratory.

A paramedic used smelling salts to revive DS Chappell. Groggy, posturing, ready to fight with his opponent already tied, fooling nobody. He made a quick call to the DCI, advising her the premises were secure, arrests had been made, rights were being read. Informed of a successfully co-ordinated mission, he was instructed to return to Llay.

Assuming a modicum of control, he issued orders. "Read everybody their rights. Ensure they understand. Inform them they are under arrest. Tell them they will be detained at the Llandudno police station, initially; the more serious offenders will be transferred down to Llay. Any questions?"

Taking a position beside the armed officer, unsteadily, Barry asked in a friendly manner, "Did you get to shoot anyone? Maybe the big cunt that decked me?"

The reply, unsympathetic. "It crossed my mind. But I couldn't hold my weapon steady, I was laughing so fucking hard. Did you even see it coming?"

Fifty-Seven
Monday, 18th February

Rob called Amy at eight thirty, hoping he had not awakened her, harbouring mixed feelings when she advised him that her friend had stayed over. Relieved that she had company, he was jealous it had not been him. He checked on her condition, asked if she needed anything, told her he had a busy day ahead with big developments at North Wales Police requiring his personal attendance. His mood brightened as she suggested that all she needed was a hug from him.

Emyr Christopher negotiated the carnage of his family washing, dressing and the school run, taking significantly more time than usual on his preparation for work. His dress uniform freshly ironed again, buttons sparkling, shoes comparable to black mirrors. His regular heavy shadow eliminated by a new five-blade razor, a hypoallergenic gel, and a soothing Aloe Vera after-balm. His masculine grooming taken to an extraordinary level, reminiscent of an effeminate buddy. He had been advised this would be appropriate for the announcement scheduled for the day ahead.

Three officers involved in the raids the previous evening had been bitten during the activity. Following remonstrations from their respective sergeants, with the origin of the bites having been Asian women operating in the sex industry, each was taken to a nearby clinic for a compulsory blood analysis, including an HIV test, the upside being permitted to take the remainder of the day off on full pay, the downside being a period of uncertainty of up to ninety days. A further downside being suggested restrictions on their sex lives at home, the use of condoms being reinforced as a mandatory suggestion.

The former Border Agency team, now Immigration Enforcement, were having a fantastic day, processing the identities of close to one hundred immigrants with dubious papers. The Mold informant, now in protective custody, had advised the likely location of the employees' withheld passports, his information again proving accurate, reflecting further positivity on DS Terry Holmes.

Terry Holmes was having a busy day, following a restless night. He had attempted to warn the tidy young masseuse to stay away from the Wrexham facility, stopping short of confirming a raid. She had ignored him and subsequently been arrested, now locked in a cell facing jail or deportation, or both. Arriving home, he had found a note from Holly, informing him of her plan to stay at Amy's place, counselling him to stay out of the bedroom they previously shared. Suggesting he should explore opportunities for a new place to live. His attempts to contact her deliberately ignored. "Fucking bitch Amy!" Certain she had been a factor in Holly's erratic dysfunction, neglecting to consider his criticism of his partner as a possible factor.

The stations across Northern Wales and into Cheshire were awash with rumours and stories from the multi-agency raids undertaken the previous evening. Dozens of arrests, street drugs recovered, a reported people-trafficking ring busted, a super-grass dismantling a criminal network. The highlight being DS Barry Chappell being hospitalised overnight with quote severe concussion unquote following an altercation with a massage parlour bouncer. There were rumours of footage.

The Superintendent sat with his deputy, awaiting the arrival of the female DCI. "She's going to be a candidate for a big chair somewhere after this. A hell of a result."

His deputy replying, conservatively, "But do we want the big chairs occupied by the ladies? I thought we had managed to limit them to DCI and below."

Sipping his preferred blend of single-source Peruvian Arabica beans, rediscovering his political correctness. "After a result like this, with the Londoners involved as well, the press will love her. We have to be seen to commend her; believe me, this thing will sprout arms and legs — she will be unstoppable."

Doctor Tay had completed the examination of the remains of Ian MacKenzie. The cause of death had been extremely straightforward, the traffic policeman's witness account vivid and accurate, the injuries consistent with impact at speed, the human head a poor match compared to a stationary four-hundred-pound lump of stone-patterned concrete.

Cuts and abrasions consistent with sliding across tarmac, whiplash injuries present around the neck. Physically, the deceased was fit, his body mass index barely above twenty-five. The surprise had come within the brain, on the side opposite to the crash impact: a prominent malignancy in an inoperable location. Making an educated guess, he would have given the deceased a maximum of three months, had he survived. Speaking to the microphone, embellishing the tumour characteristics, surmising recent behavioural changes likely to have been influenced by the tumour's presence and location.

Holly and Amy sat together, both enduring their problems, contributing opinions and suggestions to the other, largely rehashing their discussions from the previous evening. Holly re-asserting that she had finished with Terry. Amy strenuously resisting any suggestion of involving the police in her assault. Amy reassuring her friend that she was not even close to fat, was still beautiful with a body specifically designed for pleasure. Holly expressing her desire to meet Amy's impressive new boyfriend, intrigued at his attentiveness, delighted at the way they had met. Comfortable together, their bond exceeding friendship.

Having missed the excitement, Doris and Flick had resumed the CCTV analysis, seeking confirmation of Jenny Coleman's movements in the period of interest. They had scheduled a visit to her home at one that afternoon, accepting her offer to collect clothing and other items of interest. Overnight, their media-prominent, high-profile unresolved murder investigation had been relegated to an issue unworthy of resource or effort.

A senior figure in County Lines, the initiator of the Priority Intercept concept, had arrived at the Llay facility, forcing his rank on the forensic investigation team. Their workload was irrelevant to him; he did not care about the body remains in the skip or the corpse in the bath — only the seized drugs were worthy of his attention. Wanting confirmation that Ice had been recovered, an indication of the purity, the total weight, and an estimated street value. Street value impressed the reporters and gave the public confidence. Politically, this was dynamite, a result the department needed following an unimpressive revision to their structure. Allocated only one officer, he liaised with internal and external resources, gathering the sound-bite information he demanded.

Boris the Orange stepped into the kitchen at the safe house, enjoying the view from the window, a brighter day, some greenery rebounding from the harshness of winter. Gulping a large glass of apple juice to satiate a thirst induced by the central heating, he detected movement close to a tree. His nerves triggered, he retreated from the window, aware of his exposure, adopting a cautious posture. Reassessing the area, finding the tree from a different perspective in the middle of the dining room, believing himself invisible to an outside observer, he watched patiently. Observing nothing of concern, telling himself it had been an animal, he revisited the fridge, waiting for the protection detail to get their finger out and make his coffee.

Annie Freeland wondered where Emyr was, the senior sergeant having not yet arrived. She wondered where Barry could be; he had still to appear following the raids on the previous evening. She wondered why Boris the Orange hadn't arrived, wondering if she was supposed to have organised transport for him. She wondered when an announcement about Emyr's future might be made.

Peter Jones endured contradictory emotions. As a Detective Inspector, he frequently accepted credit for the excellent work performed by his junior officers and had expected to continue that trend today following some great results yesterday. Resigning himself to having his achievements hijacked by the DCI, doing to him what he did to others. Poetic justice? Maybe. Fucking annoying? Absolutely.

The Armed Response Unit were weary. They had attended two events on a Sunday, providing their intimidating presence, securing the safety of the regular police officers, without the documentary nightmare of discharging their weapons. There were tales to tell. The officer with his sights trained on The Mancunian as he lost control of his motorcycle, smashing into a concrete flowerpot, the end of his life detailed via a telescopic sight. The observed one-punch demolition of Barry Chappell, the cocky twat knocked out, missing the entire raid. The Welsh madam in Prestatyn, calmly suggesting to an armed officer that long hard things did not intimidate her, and he should put his gun away.

The media scrum had been allocated an auditorium, with tv cameras to the rear, reporters seated beneath the raised platform, an array of microphones spread across the open space, angled upwards. They were informed that numerous announcements would be made throughout the morning, some more newsworthy than others, their patience requested, their co-operation appreciated, a commitment to accepting pertinent questions delivered. The proceedings opened with the news of North Wales Police following the increasing trend of moving forensic services into the public sector, with due diligence and controls, while retaining an in-house management and technical capability. The newly appointed Inspector to oversee the transition was paraded to the throng, introduced, asked to spell his name. Inspector Emyr Christopher, looking severely restricted in the dress uniform, explained the motives behind the strategy, the likely redistribution of expertise from the force into preferred forensic specialist entities, the retention of a core unit within the force. Interesting enough, attracting one question, the Inspector loosening his tie as he escaped the platform.

Walking across the ornate building entrance, projecting an intangible aura inspired by success and confidence, the DCI was immaculately presented, professional. Drawing looks from those on her periphery, respect, even admiration, ascending towards unimagined heights, her hair in the obligatory bun, lipstick marginally bolder than usual. The DCI bathed in her glory, her operational gamble in bringing in the government agencies, drawing resource from every discipline, had all been justified by the astonishing results.

The man asking to speak to a policeman was huge. Tall, wide, rotund, hairy, everything about him was large, dominating the Mold station reception area. He said he had information about the movements of the dead man in Buckley, having recognised the photo of the man on the news. Taking a seat across from Terry Holmes, he spoke. "The guy, Simon, was at the bar where I work on Friday night." Holmes asked which bar. "The Druid. It was the monthly rave night." Displaying confusion, Terry asked him to elaborate. "We put on loud music, one Friday per month for the younger adults, special prices on the Breezers, cider, stuff like that. I recognise him because he stood out." The DS asked in what way. "Too old for the crowd that was in. I watched him awhile, checking if he was perving on the younger ladies; but he left with another older person, a woman." Interested, Holmes sought further information. "They left together about nine. She looked a bit drunk, although she only had two ciders. I keep track." Encouraging him to continue. "Nice-looking she was, out of his league I would have thought. First time I had seen her at the bar." Requesting a description. "Shoulder-length dark hair, stylish and pretty, maybe mixed race, but that could have been her make-up. Nice figure, short dark skirt." Asked to wait for a few moments while the DS collected some photographs for him to look at. "No worries. Take your time." Terry returning with the Campbell-Foulkes file, spreading five photographs across the table, asking the barman if any of them resembled the lady in the bar. "That one is closest, if you remove the blonde hair, make it darker. That's her. Pretty face, nice body. Like I said, she left with him some time after nine."

Priority Intercept took their moment in the spotlight, addressing the assembled TV and newspaper journalists. "I shall make a statement; please refrain from questions until the statement is complete. Thank you. Yesterday, a joint operation between the recently innovated County Lines Priority Intercept team and other agencies carried out raids on a multitude of suspect locations across North Wales. Our focus is removing the scourge of drugs from our streets. Other agencies have their separate objectives. I am proud to announce that this operation has been a great success, and I wish to pay tribute to the hardworking officers whose dedication led to this operational excellence. Across the various premises, we recovered forty-six kilograms of methamphetamine, street name Ice. This batch is particularly unpleasant, containing deplorable additives likely to lead to sickness, distress and ultimately death. The street value of the recovered narcotics is close to eighteen point five million pounds. Everyone should be delighted that these instruments of death and destruction have been removed from circulation. That is the end of the statement; you may ask questions now."

Enclosed in their ivory tower, the senior officers of North Wales Police welcomed the DCI, showering her with compliments and congratulations. Breaking out the single malt, the Glen Garioch crafted in Oldmeldrum, an unusual drop, the spirit served on ice, disrespecting its heritage. They took seats around the extravagant wooden table.

"I must say, Bethan, that this has been quite astonishing. I was unaware of this broad investigation, but the results are splendid." The Super ebullient, his ruddy cheeks glowing. "Give us a summary of what we have closed so far."

Savouring her drink as well as the moment, Bethan gave a summary of their achievements. "Sirs. We have recovered more than forty kilograms of methamphetamine, up to sixteen million pounds of street value, and counting. We recovered more than two hundred and forty thousand pounds in cash, proceeds from crime duly confiscated. At this moment there are more than fifty illegally working immigrants under arrest. Some of these appear to have been trafficked to the United Kingdom against their will, and many have expressed an interest in co-operating with us to shut down this dreadful crime against society." Enjoying their expressions, imagining them recounting her story, word for word, at their club. Continuing. "Our intelligence suggests we may have located another body, allowing us to close a homicide case."

"Yes." The deputy Super interspersing himself. "Shall we discuss homicide? There have been a lot of these recently, an unacceptably high number, and that rather high-profile failure in Saltney."

Knowing the praise could not be allowed to continue, expecting the diversion, Bethan inhaled, swept an imaginary loose hair from her forehead. "Sirs. The rape and murder of the unknown Asian lady beside the A483 has been solved. She was killed by a low-level criminal, Dai Harris, possibly assisted by his sidekick, Joseph Nesbitt. We have Harris's DNA. However, Harris himself was shot and killed, his naked body left at the same location; symbolic, perhaps. We now have evidence that he was killed by one Ian MacKenzie. We have statements to that effect, the likely weapon, possibly DNA to absolutely close it." Pausing, moistening her mouth. "Joseph Nesbitt was also killed by MacKenzie. Forensics are seeking to confirm that at this moment."

"Is this MacKenzie in custody?" The Super, clearly behind on his report reading.

"MacKenzie is dead, sir. He crashed his motorcycle while attempting to escape our raid on his warehouse. There will need to be an investigation, as the crash involved a deployed stinger."

"If I hear you correctly, we have four dead people, and four closed cases. That is remarkable, and possibly, eh, convenient." She nodded her assent, preparing to phrase a response, waiting, as he carried on. "Is there any chance we can close that embarrassing Jeremy homicide as well in Saltney? And that body in a BMW in Rossett? What about the mobile phone fellow in Buckley?"

"Sirs. I'll begin with the BMW. The deceased has been proven to be participating in a deviant sexual act. He died accidentally due to auto-erotic asphyxiation. That case is closed." Receiving their permission to continue. "The deaths in Saltney and Buckley are now inextricably linked to the four homicides already mentioned. The deceased were providing services to this expanded criminal network. We are working hard to conclude both cases, as rapidly as the procedures allow."

"I think I can say, on behalf of us all, that solving these outstanding cases quickly would constitute a phenomenal success when combined with the cases already closed." Raising his glass. "A toast. To impeccable police work." Three glasses aloft, symbolic clinking of glass, refills offered, accepted. "I have to speak to the media today. I would appreciate a short summary before I do so. Would that be okay, Bethan?"

Taking a water break beside her office, Holly encountered one of the mortgage brokers, the commissioned salesmen whose enthusiastic recommendations regularly floundered at her desk. "Hey, Holly. How are you?"

Extracting his name from her mind's recess. "I'm okay, James; how are things for you?"

Adopting his outgoing personality, finding his comfort zone. "Going well, lots of people interested to borrow, low interest rates, seeking impartial advice, you know how it is." Suspicious of his intent, she waited for the sting in the tale. "Hey. You look awesome today. Really nice." Dumbfounded, she watched him stroll back to his desk.

Annie wandered into Emyr's office, confounded by his expansive smile and formal dress. Accepting the offered chair, she half-listened to his explanation while distracted by the potential effect each revelation may have on her career. Hearing of his promotion to inspector, having expected demotion, she sought to determine if an opportunity still presented for her, pointedly failing to offer her congratulations.

Buzzwords floated around her psyche from across the desk, restructuring for positivity, transition management, internal core competency, expertise distribution. Mention of Gethin cutting through her confusion, coming to realise that her perceived position as the department deputy had been usurped, her ambition having become her downfall.

Concussion protocols complete, Barry left the hospital, uncertain where he might find his car. Concussion side effect, perhaps? Unable to locate a parking ticket in his pockets, he retraced his steps, finding the hospital reception. Explaining his predicament, he discovered he had been brought in by ambulance. No car. Taking another look outside, he saw an unfamiliar landscape. Reading the sign above the reception window. "Llandudno? I'm in hospital in Llandudno? Bollocks."

Reclining at home with her pain levels reducing gradually, she heard her phone ring, seeing his name on the display, pleased. "Well, hello." Sharing a casual conversation, the content irrelevant, contact the primary motivation.

"Oh, by the way, I really have to thank you." His words engendering curiosity in her.

"You are welcome. Why? What have I done?" Inviting his clarification.

"When you cried, and broke my heart, I made a sudden decision to pull a story I had intended to publish. You remember. It caused a situation between us." Carefully worded. "I am so lucky that you inspired me to pull that story. North Wales Police today announced an enormous amount of successful case solutions. If I had published the story, I would look so stupid right now. Again, thank you, Amy."

Thinking, *broke your heart*? Saying, "You're welcome. Remember, I always know best."

Fifty-Eight
Tuesday, 19th February

Early morning. A dusting of snow creating havoc on the roads in nearby Chester. An office normally reserved for VIP visits to the station inhabited this morning, warm drinks and pastries paraded on the nineteen sixties sideboard. A sign warning of strictly no admittance at eye level on the external panel of the door, duty officers warned that no calls should be put through to any of the occupants. Reminding everyone that their mobile phones should be switched off, she invited them to sit around the table.

Bethan, the DCI, opened the meeting. "Thank you all for coming. We need to settle these cases and agree on our course of action. I have instructions that we remain in here until we are in full agreement. Are we all clear on the objectives?" Scanning the faces of her three companions, seeing acceptance more than agreement. "Fine. Let's get this shit sorted."

"Good morning. My name is Vincent McKenna. I represent the Crown Prosecution Service, have done for thirteen years. Your task today will be to try to convince me that you have the necessary proof to prosecute your cases. The Superintendent has taken a personal interest in both investigations and he has asked that we resolve our strategy today. Detective Sergeant Beecham, would you like to begin?" He possessed serious features, sharp eyes, heavy brows, a thin dark line across his upper lip.

Doris opened the folder before him, glanced briefly at his crib sheets, conversant with his case, mentally prepared. "I am currently reviewing the murder of Jeremy Campbell-Foulkes in Saltney in January. We are all familiar with the case file, the manner of the killing. The investigation has led me to believe that our killer is one of two suspects: Miss Jennifer Coleman or Miss Amelia Meadows. I expect to firm on one of them in the coming days. I do not support the assertion that The Mancunian criminal empire carried out this murder."

The DCI indicated to her other subordinate. "I am DS Terry Holmes. I was previously involved in the investigation into the death of Jeremy Campbell-Foulkes, so the case is familiar to me. My current assignment is the murder of Simon Williams, found in his home last Saturday. I believe there are significant consistencies between the two crime scenes, strongly suggestive of the killings being carried out by the same person."

"Our intelligence intimates that The Mancunian killed both victims. Your assertion supports that. Does it not?" Twisting his words, the DCI questioned his logic.

"Ma'am. The Saltney case is pinned on a witness seeing the victim with a dark-haired woman, supported by CCTV, psychological evaluation of the wounds inflicted, the meticulous cleansing of the scene. The Buckley case has uncovered a witness who saw the victim leave a bar with a dark-haired woman, similar wounds, removed or destroyed bedding, meticulous cleansing of the scene."

The CPS representative spoke. "You are aware that more than seventy percent of the female population in the UK has dark hair. It might even be more. That percentage will only increase if current immigration patterns are maintained."

"The witness identified Miss Meadows as the woman he saw leave the bar with the deceased. He is extremely credible, able to recall exactly how many drinks she had consumed." Terry, impatient, using a trump card early.

"Miss Meadows has displayed classic evasive behaviour throughout our investigation. Her alibi is weak. She has meddled with her appearance during the process. She is a former girlfriend, the most recent, which ticks another vital box." Doris supporting his colleague.

Addressing the DI, the CPS raised his next objection. "You are united in placing suspicion on Miss Meadows. If your confidence is absolute, DS Beecham, why do you continue to investigate Miss Coleman? For what reason did you hold her overnight in the cells? Are you hedging your bets? Sorry, but I sense you are clutching at straws."

Bristling, Doris responded, "Diligent police work. Reviewing every suspect, maintaining an open mind. It is something we do while we eliminate suspects before we bring the case to your office. Leg work. Investigative procedure. Experience." Leaving the CPS without doubt where his frustrations lay. "Unlike you, we try to identify the perpetrator of the crime. Your department seems mostly concerned with their win loss ratio."

"Enough, Sergeant!" The DCI seeking to defuse the increasing tension. "I want to take a step back here. DS Holmes, you have extracted an enormous amount of intelligence from this Boris the Orange, intelligence which has proven accurate on every occasion. He has led us to a major narcotic bust, to a people-trafficking network, prostitution, the discovery of a body on the brink of absolute destruction. You have presented his claims to me, with confidence, with accuracy. Boris has expressed his opinion that both of the deceased men were killed by The Mancunian. They were both involved in criminal activity, it is an occupational hazard. Why don't you accept his information relating to these two deaths? I mean, two grown men involved in criminal activity, beaten to death by a woman weighing somewhere around seven stones?" Turning to McKenna. "That's forty-five kilos in CPS language."

"Size is irrelevant if you are armed. She is devious; she could have trapped them, attacked them." Sounding desperate, even to himself.

Vincent, his tone lowered. "What's her motive?" Inviting either sergeant to answer. Neither did. Staring at Beecham, challenge apparent. "Did you recover any DNA at the Saltney apartment, or fingerprints, or fibres, which belonged to either Coleman or Meadows? Anything which definitely places them at the scene at the time of death?"

"We found fingerprints belonging to Jenny Coleman at the Saltney apartment." Doris understood the weakness in his submittal, trying to reinforce it. "The place had been wiped extensively, professionally. It is peculiar that we found no trace at all of Meadows, when she has admitted to being there recently."

"DS Holmes. Any evidence of Meadows' presence at the Buckley house?" Terry shook his head.

Pausing hostilities, the DCI stepped to the sideboard, replenishing her cup, accompanying it with an apricot Danish pastry. "Take five, gentlemen. Review what we have heard in conjunction with what we already know. Assess the facts. Consider the circumstantial evidence. We are all on the same side."

Following a few minutes of retrospection, the DCI broke the strained silence. "Vincent. From the CPS perspective, which would you prefer to prosecute? The Mancunian or Amelia Meadows or Jennifer Coleman?" Giving him an opportunity to reveal his thinking.

"The Mancunian has been proven to have killed two of his employees, Harris and Nesbitt. Adding two further employees, Williams and Campbell-Foulkes, would not be a stretch. He is portrayed as ruthless. When you factor in the brain tumour, the potential for behavioural disruption, it is overwhelming. The witnesses are solid. The DNA from Harris on the silencer is the clincher, had there been any doubt. Catching the Mancunian's men in the house with the Williams body, likely sent to clear up, that's another clincher. The Saltney killing is less precise. I would go ahead with prosecution, if we needed to, had he not been deceased.

"Amelia Meadows. Based on a grainy CCTV picture at Saltney, the lack of DNA and prints, their immature relationship, it is weak. If we follow the serial killer assumption, for the Buckley scene, we have nothing indicating she had ever been there. We have an eyewitness that they met in the bar, but it does not place her at the crime scene, and we know that eyewitnesses are notoriously unreliable. Any lawyer would nail us on the photo ID. You only showed five photographs — you are required to show a minimum of twelve, per the PACE regulations, so I would expect it to be inadmissible. As we stand, I would not be prepared to progress a case against Meadows for either homicide; same applies if we prosecute for both. Sorry.

"Jennifer Coleman! If we had to disclose that both crime scenes contain some consistency, we devalue the case against her. She is a possible for the Saltney case, I can see that, but possible, not probable. There is no probable cause. She has lied, she is promiscuous, she is uncooperative. She could not have been involved in the Williams fatality. We cannot prove her to be a killer."

"Thank you, Vincent. Terry, Grahame, I don't see where you can go with these cases. You have definite reasons to be suspicious of both women. I accept that. Whether you consider Meadows or Coleman, you do not have a compelling reason to charge, and you cannot prove that either of them is guilty. What you have is only that they cannot prove their innocence. That is their vulnerability, being incapable of producing compelling evidence to support their innocence. That is not enough to press charges. My decision has to be that we close both cases, we apportion the deaths to the actions of The Mancunian, worded carefully, permitting interpretation that he performed the killings, or he ordered them."

Terry and Grahame prepared to stand, Vincent remaining seated, waiting for his cue. "I think the CPS will be pleased with this result. Have a safe trip, Mr McKenna; give my regards to your supervisor." Rising, extending her hand, suggesting he should vacate the room. Following his departure, she sat again, admonishing her sergeants. "Manners, gentlemen. You might need his support one day. Stop acting like fucking kids."

Rubbing her eyes, tugging at her ear, revealing fatigue, betraying exasperation. "I know you both have gut feelings about these women. You have my sympathy. I wish we could arrive at a better result, but we need to close the cases, blame MacKenzie, keep the top brass happy and enjoy our time in the limelight. I hope I don't have to issue a direct order. You understand where I am coming from. Meadows and Coleman are no longer under suspicion. Grahame, you should inform them personally. Terry, stay away!" Sipping from her cup, the liquid cold, spitting it into the saucer. "We are gradually relocating the Mold CID division to Llay, and there is already pressure to appoint a DI from this resource. That means either of you or Chappell. Don't make me select Chappell. And keep out of those massage parlours; word gets around."

Knowing they should not argue, could not succeed, the decision already made, had been made before the meeting, they conceded their position. Agreeing to follow instructions, move on to new cases, a sense of relief shared that the Campbell-Foulkes case was consigned to the filing cabinet.

Doris turned to Terry. "You can inform Amy Meadows if you want. You know her; she'll be pleased to hear it from you. I'll have the pleasure of Jenny Coleman; no doubt she will lie to me anyway, she can't help it."

Terry turned to Doris. "No, thanks. I'd be happy to do Jenny Coleman, but I am not going anywhere near that bitch Meadows. Best if we do what the DCI told us to do. I'm going for a drink. Do you want to join me? That coffee she served was fucking horrible!"

"Fuck it, why not? I now have two hundred hours of CCTV I don't need to watch."

****

Rob collected Amy from her home, darkness falling in competition with residual light assisted by snowflakes refusing to melt. She had made some effort, applying make-up to her bruised and damaged areas, simple clothing, warm sweater and bootleg jeans, low-heeled boots. A bobble hat providing her ears with protection against the rapidly reducing temperature.

He had booked tickets for the same movie, hoping they would see it this time. She had taken a lot of persuading, concerned about her face, fearing strangers might stare at her, false sympathy based on errant assumptions she could do without. He had cajoled her, explaining how the darkness would help, promising her a giant cola and foot-long hot dog. The chance to hold his hand if she played nice.

Their fingers remained intertwined throughout the movie.

Fifty-Nine
Wednesday, 20th February

She let out a long, slow sigh, arching her torso, stretching her arms above her head. Her long dark hair fanned out across the pillow, her legs spreading, tendons straining as she stretched her ankles as far from her body as she could. Internal excitement building, racing towards an inevitable crescendo, discharging discreet moisture, sweat glistening on her flesh across her breasts and midriff, nipples proud, the pierced stud in her navel sparkling, the cubic zirconia diffusing light. Looking down at his mostly obscured face, only his forehead emerging from her intimacy, tongue performing contrasting gentle circular movements interwoven with urgent flicks top and central. Preparing herself, climax building, taking hold of the familiar item from underneath the pillow, her right arm swinging savagely, embedding the ornate knife in his ear. Thrusting the knife deeper, twisting the blade, blood initially spurting before adapting to a steady flow. His eyes questioning her, why, closing as the blade slammed into his neck, splitting the artery, the crimson life fluid pouring from him.

Amy woke. Agitated. Frantically scanning her surroundings, seeing only disturbed bedclothes. Her nightgown wrapped around her, adhering to her soaked body, gathered above her knees. Her darting eyes confirming her solitude, ears detecting no activity, relief spreading through her, comprehension invading her consciousness. Only a dream; no dead boyfriend bleeding between her legs. Finding her voice in the empty room, releasing her emotions. "Thank God! Oh. Rob. Oh!" A final confirmation, touching her belly button, no jewellery, no piercing, only a dream, graphic but imaginary.

Bringing her rapid breathing under control, she endeavoured to calm her physique while composing her sentiments. Adjusting to her awakened state, banishing the terrible images, returning to normality. Her thoughts refocused, permitting logic to penetrate her thinking, recognising Rob as undeserving of her ire. Sexual activity between them unfulfilled, her feelings for him exceeding expectations, no possible circumstance likely to induce her to apply such extreme justice. Reminding her brain of her count, good four, their cinema date having added a further positive point. Admitting that any boyfriend arousing her in the manner from her dream would most definitely not be discouraged.

Glancing at her phone as she sat up, already past eight, her now regular early-morning headache subsiding, supporting feelings of improvement in her physical health. Building courage to look in the mirror, she hoped for an improvement there also.

****

The private press engagement had been the idea of the DCI, strongly suggesting that her three Detective Sergeants present their united front to the *Leader*. She had an obligation to give the local newspaper additional access to the innards of the force, access denied to the national media. She had instructed them to release some previously withheld information, allowing the *Leader* to report new revelations. The editor from the paper understood his obligation, to portray these three detectives as an example of internal co-operation, working separate cases yet assisting each other to bring multiple cases to fruition. It would have been simpler to write a script, that suggestion quashed.

Four occupants, all reluctantly present. Rob the Editor opening the discussion, while Chappell, Holmes and Beecham did their best to look interested.

Skipping across the already embroidered tale of Chappell locating the killers of the illegal Asian lady, Rob asked how the works of Holmes and Beecham had assisted him in breaking the case. Beecham indicated his having an inside informant within the organisation, while Holmes had interrogated a suspect who had broken under pressure, providing links between all the crimes under investigation.

Moving on to the unsolved death of the estate agent in Saltney, Beecham confirmed the case was linked to the others, releasing the authorised leak that the victim had been involved in property purchases by an overseas criminal consortium. Directly questioned by the editor,

Doris conceded that their previous female suspects were now cleared of all suspicion, confirming all five names, unnecessarily adding that Miss Coleman and Miss Meadows would be formally informed of their removal from the list of persons of interest. Holmes noticing a smug reaction evident on Rob's features

Continuing to the Vodafone employee's death in Buckley, Holmes suggested this case appeared to be linked in a similar way to the others. Unable to fully accept his orders, he intimated that further lines of investigation may be appropriate, maintaining the diligence demanded by the NWP. Rob had asked for a specific reason why he was pursuing this investigation, when the official line was the case being linked to the others. Beecham raising his brows as Holmes suggested that an earlier suspect remained on the police radar, dropping Meadows' name, potentially seen with the victim, that the case could not be closed until this anomaly was resolved.

"Sergeant Holmes, you're saying that Amy Meadows was seen in Buckley with the deceased on that Friday night, and this is preventing you from closing the investigation completely?"

"That is correct." Holmes aware of the disapproving expressions emanating from his colleagues.

"Perhaps I can assist you. On that date, Amy Meadows could not have been with your victim in Buckley since she spent the evening with me." The dishonest revelation stunning the three detectives. "Yes. I have been seeing Amy for a while now, and she was with me for the entire evening. Does that help your investigation?"

DS Beecham was speechless, processing this unexpected sequence of events, giving conjecture to this woman's ability to persuade people to provide her with blatantly suspicious alibis. DS Chappell displayed an acceptance of the statement, seemingly unconcerned, indicating he had already removed Meadows from his list of suspects. DS Holmes said nothing, seemingly angry and incensed with the disclosure, uncertain about the legitimacy, powerless to contest the declaration.

"Now, tell me about the raid at the massage premises in Llandudno?"

****

"Sergeant Holmes. I think we need to edit that section relating to Amy Meadows. It doesn't work for me, or your DCI. Shall we just link the crime to the other cases and leave it at that?" The meeting had terminated, Beecham and Chappell retreating quickly to their duties.

"Whatever you like. You have the same brief as me. All I would say is that you should be careful, really careful, around that woman." Stern-faced, Holmes prepared to leave.

"How can you say that about someone who is a close friend of your girlfriend?"

"Former girlfriend. That's a whole other story, for another time. Look after yourself."

****

Doris and Flick walked boldly into the medical practice in Broughton, their arrival rendering the receptionist apprehensive, recalling their previous visit. Anticipating their need, she advised Jenny of their arrival.

She met the officers in the reception, as rehearsed on the phone, ensuring her curious colleagues could watch and hear the discussion.

"How can I help you, Detective?" Aiming for brusque, achieving obstinate.

"Miss Coleman, on behalf of North Wales Police, I would like to inform you that you are no longer considered a person of interest in the investigation relating to the death of Jeremy Campbell-Foulkes in January of this year." DS Beecham delivering the statement stiffly, as if under duress. Handing her a document on police letterhead.

"Miss Coleman. Thank you for your co-operation and assistance. It has been invaluable in assisting us to find the guilty party. We apologise for any inconvenience caused to you." PC McGarry delivering her first exoneration speech. Exchanging a subtle flash of conspiracy, replacing her hat on her head, the reactions from the witnesses indicating their performance had succeeded.

****

Barry faced Annie in her office, the door closed behind him. She had explained the planned restructuring within the Forensic Investigation department, her fury at being overlooked, criticising Gethin, crucifying Emyr, dispensing anger at anyone and everyone. She repeated her intention to quit the force and move into the public sector, where she could earn more while escaping the bullshit, the phoney respecting of rank and the dreadful hours.

He allowed her to vent, perceiving her need. He had solved three murders in under a week, yet he remained under-appreciated, still tainted from the Saltney fuck-up, desiring to release his own frustrations, prepared to wait for the right moment.

"Annie. The subcontractors will be fighting to get you. You'll be the first person placed, probably in a senior role, earning a shitload more than you do now." He saw her appreciate his supportive stance, deciding to expand his support, gambling. "And there is another massive benefit of you moving out of the force." Pausing, watching her, wondering if she was thinking the same. "We won't have to hide our relationship. We can be open about it. We can tell everyone."

Softening, she assessed him, aware of how difficult those words would have been for him. Grateful. Delighted. Moving to him, neglecting to close the blinds, uncaring who saw, sharing a moment.

****

Returning to his desk, DS Holmes knew he should be pleased. He had made his name, solved several cases and was now in contention for the future promotion to Detective Inspector. He had achieved respect, at last, in this sheep-shagging hellhole. His pleasure quantifiable but compromised.

Being ostracised by his girlfriend, punished for being honest. Women; they claimed honesty was important to them, then spat their dummy out when you gave them that honesty.

He was unable to let go of his suspicions relating to Amy Meadows. He did not believe her alibi from the editor, knew the alibi from Holly was fabricated, felt sure she could be involved in two suspicious deaths. Recalling her photograph on Holly's phone, nude, arrogant, explicit, gorgeous. She was to blame for the strained relationship between Holly and him, he was confident they had shared a bed, angered and aroused in equal measure at the thought. Now she was supposedly dating that prick from the paper. Why?

Terry Holmes called Holly. It was time to repair the chasm between them. She didn't answer.

Sixty
Wednesday, 20th February

The incoming call from North Wales Police had been initially unwelcome. Recognising the voice of the big detective she had faced, she had concerns about his reasons for contacting her. Could it relate to Simon, maybe Jed, Mark even? Cautiously responding, she asked him why he continued to contact her. DS Beecham requested her presence at the station, which she declined. He then suggested coming to her home, to which she did not extend an invitation. Losing patience, he had simply requested a few minutes of her time on the phone, to which she had agreed.

He informed her that she had been eliminated from their enquiries relating to Jed's death. She had responded coolly, acknowledging the advice, internally performing a small jig of delight. Ending the call with minimal courtesy, she reflected positively on the news.

Returning to her dressing table, she persisted with her reaction to Rob's challenge. Inviting her for drinks, he had suggested she wear heavy Goth-style black make-up, hiding her injuries by emphasising them, eager to coax her away from her home, to have fun. She had committed to try, promising nothing. Working on her appearance, welcoming the invitation, enjoying the experiment as she explored an entirely different look, pleasantly confused by the result.

Raking through her wardrobes and drawers to find clothes to match her wild look, she selected a black tee-shirt, naturally, combined with a loose white gymnasium singlet. Inspired, she chose the blue mini skirt from her former No Chips No Garnish uniform, patterned like Taiwanese pirate Burberry, necessitating a bold lipstick, finishing the ensemble with slutty fishnet tights and ankle boots. Simultaneously looking sexy and dirty, she reviewed whether this was an image she wished to present to her new boyfriend. Texting him, asking what he thought, she attached a selfie, nervously awaiting his response. Within a minute she received an encouraging response, devoid of words like pretty or attractive but including a welcome "sexy".

The doorbell interrupted her preparations. Approaching her vestibule, she heard a familiar male voice. "Amy. It's Terry Holmes. I need a word about Holly. Open up, please." Confirming his identity through the viewing aperture, she opened the door, inviting him to come inside, stepping back as he pushed past her, striding into her living room. Securing the door, she followed him.

"I need to speak to Holly, urgently." Scanning the room as he spoke, not looking at her. "Is she here?"

"Does it look like she's here?" Sarcasm betrayed by her tone, her feelings towards him uncertain. Unresponsive, he moved through the apartment, checking all the rooms, coming back to the lounge, seeing her look of disapproval.

"You look different." Not elaborating, neither insult nor compliment. "Do you know where she is? I need to talk to her."

"Sorry, Terry, I have no idea where she is or what she's doing. You could just try to call her."

"She's screening my calls. You call her; when she answers, pass the phone to me."

Unwilling to betray her friend, Amy declined to make the call, offering a suggestion. "You could go home and put some nice flowers on the table. Maybe write a note telling her you are sorry, allow her to find it when she comes home, ask her to call you."

Expecting his consideration, even appreciation, instead hearing resentment. "I know about you two. Your affair. Your little secret." Spitting the words. "The two of you here, probably in that bed. You disgust me." Taken aback, unable to formulate her response, her silence encouraging him, increasing his bravado already inflamed by alcohol.

"Why? You're a decent-looking woman. You can pull a bloke. Why do you need to have Holly? My Holly. Sending her naked pictures of yourself. Yes, I saw them. Staying over." Preparing to deny his accusation, correct him, explain how his comments at the weekend had upset Holly. Preparing, prevented from speaking as he continued, she lowered herself into an armchair.

"You know what. We should close the triangle. Remove the resentment and stabilise the situation." Flummoxed, clueless to his intention, she asked what he meant. "Obviously, I've been shagging Holly for ages, now you're shagging her. Let's close the triangle, you and me, we could get it on." Disbelieving, she engaged his eyes, seeing something she did not like, animation, fury, lust? Certainly, some hint of aggression. Watching his gaze drop, scoping her, aware her skirt had ridden up as she sat, an unconscious gesture he could interpret as an invitation. Standing, belatedly smoothing her skirt, tugging the hem lower, she faced him nervously, her injuries fresh in her mind. Aware she was frightened. Projecting confidence she didn't feel, stepping towards him, then beyond him, she reached into her bag, placing her hand inside to locate her objective, adjusting her position to face him again.

"So? I should just drop my undies, bend over, and let you fuck me. Is that the plan? This is how you plan to win Holly back, by shagging her friend?" Tightening her grip, feeling the tension increase. "Should I take off my top as well, in case you fancy shooting your load on my belly?" Striking a chord, partially regretting the inflammatory comment, expecting his reaction, preparing, ready to defend herself. "Never going to happen."

"You are a cunt, Amy. A fucking horrible cunt." Waiting, letting her absorb his words. "I know your alibi is a crock of shit. I think you could be a killer, as well as a cunt." Taking one step forward. "You might be a fucking psycho," dropping his voice an octave, "but" — hesitating for effect — "I am not afraid of you."

Her hand remained poised at the inner edge of the handbag, the object in her hand remaining obscured from his sight. Fixating on him, her pupils rapidly dilating, she considered their situation. Projecting her maximum assurance, her changing countenance emanating an increasing aggression, she addressed him specifically.

"If you think I am a killer then you are either very brave or incredibly stupid." Detecting confusion in his expression, she went on. "Has it ever occurred to you and your colleagues that maybe people like Jeremy deserve to die?" Continuing her monologue, she expanded. "That they might be abusive to women, that they use their physical advantage to impose themselves, trying to force their sexual proclivities on the fairer sex!" She could hear the increasing passion in her voice. "Sometimes they get what they deserve!" She allowed the veiled self-insinuation to perpetuate between them before changing tack. "Holly and I are friends, only friends. We have never indulged in what you suggested, you sick fucker!" Bringing her hand from the handbag to her side, she continued to confront him.

"Are you confessing to killing Jeremy Campbell-Foulkes?" Uncertainty in his words and his manner.

"That's not what I said." Decisive. Confident.

"You've said enough for me to justify arresting you." Finding his professional confidence, he became more assertive.

"Come on, Terry. Are you going to arrest me or stick your dick in me?" She took a half-step towards him, releasing a confusingly warm smile. "I'm fairly certain you can't do both. What's it going to be?"

Their proximity revealed her existing injuries, imperfections on and around her face. Her earlier concern at his presence had evaporated, her body issuing a challenge as it simultaneously invoked physical attraction. He knew he needed to assume control of this situation, repeating the words he had used earlier. "I am not afraid of you, Amy."

She came closer, reaching her left arm forward to touch his chest, allowing her hand to seductively rest on his torso. Again confused, he endeavoured to rationalise her behaviour. *Was she coming on to him? Did her arm constitute an invitation or was it a barrier, warning him to stay away?* Part of him really wanted her, that reaction was unmistakable, while his brain silently screamed *no* inside his head.

"I know you are not scared of me, Detective, Sergeant, Terry, Holmes." Every word individually accentuated, her facial expression slowly converting from frown to twinkle, eyes suddenly blazing, the skirt sliding further up her thighs as her stance broadened. Her shortening breath causing her to gulp air before she declared, "But you fucking should be!"